SHERRYL WOODS

Stealing Home

mira

If you purchased this book without a cover you should be aware that this book is stolen property. It was reported as "unsold and destroyed" to the publisher, and neither the author nor the publisher has received any payment for this "stripped book."

mira™

Recycling programs for this product may not exist in your area.

ISBN-13: 978-0-7783-1151-5

Stealing Home

First published in 2007. This edition published in 2021.

This edition published by arrangement with Harlequin Books S.A.

For questions and comments about the quality of this book, please contact us at CustomerService@Harlequin.com.

Mira
22 Adelaide St. West, 40th Floor
Toronto, Ontario M5H 4E3, Canada
www.Harlequin.com

Printed in Spain

Praise for the novels of Sherryl Woods

"Sherryl Woods writes emotionally satisfying novels about family, friendship and home. Truly feel-great reads!"

—#1 *New York Times* bestselling author Debbie Macomber

"During the course of this gripping, emotionally wrenching but satisfying tale, Woods deftly and realistically handles such issues as survival guilt, drug abuse as adolescent rebellion, and family dynamics when a vital member is suddenly gone."

—*Booklist* on *Flamingo Diner*

"Woods is a master heartstring puller."

—*Publishers Weekly* on *Seaview Inn*

"Once again, Woods, with such authenticity, weaves a tale of true love and the challenges that can knock up against that love."

—*RT Book Reviews* on *Beach Lane*

"Woods…is noted for appealing character-driven stories that are often infused with the flavor and fragrance of the South."

—*Library Journal*

"A reunion story punctuated by family drama, Woods's first novel in her new Ocean Breeze series is touching, tense and tantalizing."

—*RT Book Reviews* on *Sand Castle Bay*

"A whimsical, sweet scenario…the digressions have their own charm, and Woods never fails to come back to the romantic point."

—*Publishers Weekly* on *Sweet Tea at Sunrise*

Also by #1 New York Times *bestselling author*
Sherryl Woods

The Sweet Magnolias

Stealing Home
A Slice of Heaven
Feels Like Family
Welcome to Serenity
Home in Carolina
Sweet Tea at Sunrise
Honeysuckle Summer
Midnight Promises
Catching Fireflies
Where Azaleas Bloom
Swan Point

Adams Dynasty

A Christmas Blessing
Natural Born Daddy
The Cowboy and His Baby
The Rancher and His Unexpected Daughter
The Littlest Angel
Natural Born Trouble
Unexpected Mommy
The Cowgirl and the Unexpected Wedding
Natural Born Lawman
The Unclaimed Baby
The Cowboy and His Wayward Bride
Suddenly, Annie's Father

Chesapeake Shores

The Inn At Eagle Point
Flowers On Main
Harbor Lights
A Chesapeake Shores Christmas
Driftwood Cottage
Moonlight Cove
Beach Lane
An O'Brien Family Christmas
The Summer Garden
A Seaside Christmas
The Christmas Bouquet
Dogwood Hill
Willow Brook Road
Lilac Lane

Ocean Breeze Trilogy

Sand Castle Bay
Wind Chime Point
Sea Glass Island

Molly DeWitt Mysteries

Tropical Blues
Rough Seas

Nonfiction

A Small Town Love Story: Colonial Beach, Virginia

For a complete list of all titles by Sherryl Woods, visit www.sherrylwoods.com.

Dear Friends,

I'm so delighted to have the very first Sweet Magnolias book available again to coincide with the new *Sweet Magnolias* series on Netflix, starring JoAnna Garcia Swisher, Brooke Elliott and Heather Headley. When I first came up with the idea for a series about three lifelong friends who'd been through thick and thin together, I had no idea how many women would be added to this core group over the years or how readers would come to love that bond and the entire community of Serenity, South Carolina. I hope Netflix viewers will embrace them, too.

As women, I think we've all come to understand that next to family, our friends are the most important people in our lives. And friendships that have stood the test of time, with women who know our history, our mistakes, our dirty little secrets and love us just the same, are the strongest bonds of all. Friends are there to boost our spirits when we're having a simple bad day or a crisis of monumental proportions. They can make us laugh, celebrate with us, cry with us and remind us that even on the worst day life is still worth living.

If you're just meeting Maddie, Dana Sue and Helen for the very first time, I hope you'll love getting to know them. If you're renewing your friendship with them, I hope it brings back a smile or two. Most of all, I hope you have warm, wonderful friends in your life and that you treasure every minute with them.

All best,

Sherryl

Stealing Home

CHAPTER ONE

Maddie focused on the wide expanse of mahogany stretching between her and the man who'd been her husband for twenty years. Half her life. She and William Henry Townsend had been high-school sweethearts in Serenity, South Carolina. They'd married before their senior year in college, not because she was pregnant as some of her hastily married friends had been, but because they hadn't wanted to wait one more second before starting their lives together.

Then, after they'd graduated, there had been the exhausting years of medical school for Bill, when she'd worked as an entry-level bookkeeper, making poor use of her degree in business, just to keep their heads above water financially. And then the joyous arrival of three kids—athletic, outgoing Tyler, now sixteen, their jokester, Kyle, fourteen, and their surprise blessing, Katie, who was just turning six.

They'd had the perfect life in the historic Townsend family home in Serenity's oldest neighborhood, surrounded by family and lifelong friends. The passion they'd once shared might have cooled ever so slightly, but they'd been happy.

Or so she'd thought until the day a few months ago when Bill had looked at her after dinner, his expression as distant as a stranger's, and calmly explained that he was moving out and moving on…with his twenty-four-year-old nurse, who was already pregnant. It was, he'd said, one of those things that just happened. He certainly hadn't planned to fall out of love with Maddie, much less *in* love with someone else.

Maddie's first reaction hadn't been shock or dismay. Nope, she'd laughed, sure that her intelligent, compassionate Bill was incapable of such a pitiful cliché. Only when his distant expression remained firmly in place did she realize he was stone-cold serious. Just when life had settled into a comfortable groove, the man she'd loved with all her heart had traded her in for a newer model.

In a disbelieving daze, she'd sat by his side while he'd explained to the children what he was doing and why. He'd omitted the part about a new little half brother or sister being on the way. Then, still in a daze, she'd watched him move out.

And after he'd gone, she'd been left to deal with Tyler's angry acting out, with Kyle's slow descent into unfamiliar silence and Katie's heartbroken sobs, all while she herself was frozen and empty inside.

She'd been the one to cope with their shock when they found out about the baby, too. She'd had to hide her resentment and anger, all in the name of good parenting, maturity and peace. There were days she'd wanted to curse Dr. Phil and all those cool, reasoned episodes on which he advised parents that the needs of the children came first. When, she'd wondered, did her needs start to count?

The day of being completely on her own as a single parent was coming sooner than she'd anticipated. All that was left was getting the details of the divorce on paper, spelling out in black and white the end of a twenty-year marriage. Nothing on those pieces of paper mentioned the broken dreams. Nothing mentioned the heartache of those left behind. It was all reduced to deciding who lived where, who drove which car, the amount of child support—and the amount of temporary spousal support until she could stand on her own feet financially or until she married again.

Maddie listened to her attorney's impassioned fight against the temporary nature of that last term. Helen Decatur, who'd known both Maddie and Bill practically forever, was a top-notch divorce attorney with a statewide reputation. She was also one of Maddie's best friends. And when Maddie was too tired and too sad to fight for herself, Helen stepped in to do it for her. Helen was a blond barracuda in a power suit, and Maddie had never been more grateful.

"This woman worked to help you through medical school," Helen lashed out at Bill, in her element on her own turf. "She gave up a promising career of her own to raise your children, keep your home, help manage your office and support your rise in the South Carolina medical community. The fact that you have a professional reputation far outside of Serenity is because Maddie worked her butt off to make it happen. And now you expect her to struggle to find her place in the workforce? Do you honestly think in five years or even ten she'll be able to give your children the lifestyle to which they've become accustomed?" She pinned Bill with a look that would have withered anyone else. His demeanor reflected a complete lack of interest in Maddie or her future.

That was when Maddie knew it was well and truly over. All the rest, the casual declaration that he'd been cheating on her, the move, none of that had convinced her that it really was the end of her marriage. Until this moment, until she'd seen the uncaring expression in her husband's once-warm brown eyes, she hadn't accepted that Bill wouldn't suddenly come to his senses and tell her it had all been a horrible mistake.

She'd drifted along until this instant, deep in denial and hurt, but no more. Anger, more powerful than anything she'd ever felt in her life, swept through her with a force that brought her to her feet.

"Wait," she said, her voice trembling with outrage. "I'd like to be heard."

Helen regarded her with surprise, but the stunned expression on Bill's face gave Maddie the courage to go on. He hadn't expected her to fight back. She could see now that all her years of striving to please him, of putting him first, had convinced him that she had no spine at all, that she'd make it easy for him to walk away from their family—from *her*—without a backward glance. He'd probably been gloating from the minute she suggested trying to mediate a settlement, rather than letting some judge set the terms of their divorce.

"You've managed to reduce twenty years of our lives to this," she said, waving the settlement papers at him. "And for what?"

She knew the answer, of course. Like so many other middle-aged men, his head had been turned by a woman barely half his age.

"What happens when you tire of Noreen?" she asked. "Will you trade her in, too?"

"Maddie," he said stiffly. He tugged at the sleeves of his monogrammed shirt, fiddling with the eighteen-carat-gold cuff links she'd given him just six months ago for their twentieth anniversary. "You don't know anything about my relationship with Noreen."

She managed a smile. "Sure I do. It's about a middle-aged man trying to feel young again. I think you're pathetic."

Calmer now that she'd finally expressed her feelings, she turned to Helen. "I can't sit here anymore. Hold out for whatever you think is right. He's the one in a hurry."

Shoulders squared, chin high, Maddie walked out of the lawyer's office and into the rest of her life.

An hour later Maddie had exchanged her prim knit suit and high heels for a tank top, shorts and well-worn sneakers. Oblivious to the early-morning heat, she walked the mile to her much-hated gym, with its smell of sweat pervading the air. Set on a side street just off Main, the gym had once been an old-fashioned dime store. The yellowed linoleum on the floor harked back to that era and the dingy walls hadn't seen a coat of paint since Dexter had bought the place back in the 1970s.

Since the walk downtown had done nothing at all to calm her, Maddie forced herself to climb onto the treadmill, put the dial at the most challenging setting she'd ever attempted and run. She ran until her legs ached, until the perspiration soaked her chin-length, professionally highlighted hair and ran into her eyes, mingling with the tears that, annoyingly, kept welling up.

Suddenly a perfectly manicured hand reached in front of her, slowed the machine, then cut it off.

"We thought we'd find you here," Helen said, still in her power suit and Jimmy Choo stiletto heels. Helen was probably one of the only women in all of Serenity who'd ever owned a pair of the expensive shoes.

Beside her, Dana Sue Sullivan was dressed in comfortable pants, a pristine T-shirt and sneakers. She was the chef and owner of Serenity's fanciest restaurant—meaning it used linen tablecloths and napkins and had a menu that extended beyond fried catfish and collard greens. Sullivan's

New Southern Cuisine, as the dark green and gold-leaf sign out front read, was a decided step up from the diner on the outskirts of town that simply said Good Eatin' on the window and used paper place mats on the Formica tabletops.

Maddie climbed off the treadmill on wobbly legs and wiped her face with the towel Helen handed her. "Why are you two here?"

Both women rolled their eyes.

"Why do you think?" Dana Sue asked in her honeyed drawl. Her thick, chestnut hair was pulled back with a clip, but already the humidity had curls springing free. "We came to see if you want any help in killing that snake-bellied slime who ran out on you."

"Or the mindless pinup he plans to marry," Helen added. "Though I am somewhat hesitant to recommend murder as a solution, being an officer of the court and all."

Dana Sue nudged her in the ribs. "Don't go soft now. You said we'd do *anything,* if it would make Maddie feel better."

Maddie actually managed a faint grin. "Fortunately for both of you, my revenge fantasies don't run to murder."

"What, then?" Dana Sue asked, looking fascinated. "Personally, after I kicked Ronnie's sorry butt out of the house, I wanted to see him run over by a train."

"Murder's too quick," Maddie said. "Besides, there are the children to consider. Scum that he is, Bill is still their father. I have to remind myself of that on an hourly basis just to keep my temper in check."

"Fortunately, Annie was just as mad at her daddy as I was," Dana Sue said. "I suppose that's the good side of having a teenage daughter. She could see right through his shenanigans. I think she knew what was going on even before I did. She stood on the front steps and applauded when I tossed him out."

"Okay, you two," Helen interrupted, "as much fun as it is listening to you compare notes, can we go someplace else to do it? My suit's going to stink to high heaven if we don't get out in the fresh air soon."

"Don't you both need to get to work?" Maddie asked.

"I took the afternoon off," Helen said. "In case you wanted to get drunk or something."

"And I don't have to be at the restaurant for two hours," Dana Sue said, then studied Maddie with a considering look. "How drunk can you get in that amount of time?"

"Given the fact that there's not a single bar open in Serenity at this hour, I think we can forget about me getting drunk," Maddie noted. "Though I do appreciate the sentiment, that's probably for the best."

"I have the makings of margaritas at my place," Helen offered.

"And we all know how loopy I get on one of those," Maddie retorted, shuddering at the memory of their impromptu pity party a few months back when she'd told them about Bill's plan to leave her. "I think I'd better stick to Diet Coke. I have to pick the kids up at school."

"No, you don't," Dana Sue said. "Your mama's going to do it."

Maddie's mouth gaped. Her mother had uttered two words when Tyler was born and repeated them regularly ever since: no babysitting. She'd been adamant about it then, and she'd stuck to it for sixteen years.

"How on earth did you pull that off?" she asked, a note of admiration in her voice.

"I explained the situation," Dana Sue said with a shrug. "Your mother is a perfectly reasonable woman. I don't know why the two of you have all these issues."

Maddie could have explained, but it would take the rest

of the afternoon. More likely, the rest of the week. Besides, Dana Sue had heard most of it a thousand times.

"So, are we going to my place?" Helen asked.

"Yes, but not for the margaritas," Maddie said. "It took me the better part of two days to get over that last batch you made. I need to start looking for a job tomorrow."

"No, you don't," Helen said.

"Oh? Did you finally get Bill to hand over some sort of windfall?"

"That, too," Helen said, her smile smug.

Maddie studied her two friends intently. They were up to something. She'd bet her first alimony check on it. "Tell me," she commanded.

"We'll talk about it when we get to my place," Helen said.

Maddie turned to Dana Sue. "Do you know what's going on?"

"I have some idea," Dana Sue said, barely containing a grin.

"So, the two of you have been plotting something," Maddie concluded, not sure how she felt about that. She loved these two women like sisters, but every time they got some crazy idea, one of them invariably landed in trouble. It had been that way since they were six. She was pretty sure that was why Helen had become a lawyer, because she'd known the three of them were eventually going to need a good one.

"Give me a hint," she pleaded. "I want to decide if I should take off now."

"Not even a tiny hint," Helen said. "You need to be in a more receptive frame of mind."

"There's not enough Diet Coke in the world to accomplish that," Maddie responded.

Helen grinned. "Thus the margaritas."

"I made some killer guacamole," Dana Sue added. "And I got a big ole bag of those tortilla chips you like, too, though all that salt will eventually kill you."

Maddie looked from one to the other and sighed. "With you two scheming behind my back, something tells me I'm doomed anyway."

The tart margarita was strong enough to make Maddie's mouth pucker. They were on the brick patio behind Helen's custom-built home in Serenity's one fancy subdivision, each of them settled onto a comfy chaise longue. The South Carolina humidity was thick even though it was only March, but the faint breeze stirring the towering pine trees was enough to keep it from being too oppressive.

Maddie was tempted to dive straight into Helen's turquoise pool, but instead she leaned her head back and closed her eyes. For the first time in months, she felt her worries slipping away. Beyond her anger, she wasn't trying to hide anything from her kids—not her sorrow, not her fears, but she did struggle to keep them in check. With Helen and Dana Sue, she could just be herself, one very hurt, soon-to-be-divorced woman filled with uncertainty.

"You think she's ready to hear our idea?" Dana Sue murmured beside her.

"Not yet," Helen responded. "She needs to finish that drink."

"I can hear you," Maddie said. "I'm not asleep or unconscious yet."

"Then we'd better wait," Dana Sue said cheerfully. "More guacamole?"

"No, though you outdid yourself," Maddie told her. "That stuff made my eyes water."

Dana Sue looked taken aback. "Too hot? I thought maybe you were just having yourself another little crying jag."

"I am not prone to crying jags," Maddie retorted.

"You think we didn't notice you were crying when we got to the gym?" Helen inquired.

"I was hoping you'd think it was sweat."

"I'm sure that's what everyone else thought, but we knew better," Dana Sue said. "I have to say, I was disappointed you'd shed a single tear over that man."

"So was I," Maddie said.

Dana Sue gave her a hard look, then turned to Helen. "We may as well tell her. I don't think she's going to mellow out any more than she has already."

"Okay," Helen conceded. "Here's the deal. What have all three of us been complaining about for the past twenty years?"

"Men," Maddie suggested dryly.

"Besides that," Helen said impatiently.

"South Carolina's humidity?"

Helen sighed. "Would you try to be serious for one minute? The gym. We've been complaining about that awful gym all our adult lives."

Maddie regarded her with bafflement. "And it hasn't done a lick of good, has it? The last time we pitched a fit about the place, Dexter hired Junior Stevens to mop it out… once. The place smelled of Lysol for a week and that was it."

"Precisely. Which is why Dana Sue and I came up with this idea," Helen said, then paused for effect. "We want to open a brand-new fitness club, one that's clean and welcoming and caters to women."

"We want it to be a place where women can get fit and be pampered and drink a smoothie with their friends after a workout," Dana Sue added. "Maybe even get a facial or a massage."

"And you want to do this in Serenity, with its population of five thousand seven hundred and fourteen people?" Maddie asked, not even trying to hide her skepticism.

"Fifteen," Dana Sue corrected. "Daisy Mitchell had a baby girl yesterday. And believe me, if you've seen Daisy lately, you know she'll be the perfect candidate for one of our postpregnancy classes."

Maddie studied Helen more intently. "You're serious, aren't you?"

"As serious as a heart attack," she confirmed. "What do you think?"

"I suppose it could work," Maddie said thoughtfully. "Goodness knows, that gym is disgusting. It's no wonder half the women in Serenity refuse to exercise. Of course, the other half can't get out of their recliners because of all the fried chicken they've consumed."

"Which is why we'll offer cooking classes, too," Dana Sue said eagerly.

"Let me guess. New Southern Cuisine," Maddie said.

"Southern cooking isn't all about lima beans swimming in butter or green beans cooked with fatback," Dana Sue said. "Haven't I taught you anything?"

"Me, yes, absolutely," Maddie assured her. "But the general population of Serenity still craves their mashed potatoes and fried chicken."

"So do I," Dana Sue said. "But ovenbaked's not half-bad if you do it right."

"We're losing focus," Helen cut in. "There's a building available over on Palmetto Lane that would be just right for what we have in mind. I think we should take a look at it in the morning. Dana Sue and I fell in love with it right away, Maddie, but we want your opinion."

"Why? It's not as if I have anything to compare it to. Besides, I don't even know what your vision is, not entirely anyway."

"You know how to make a place cozy and inviting, don't you?" Helen said. "After all, you took that mausoleum that was the Townsend family home and made it real welcoming."

"Right," Dana Sue said. "And you have all sorts of business savvy from helping Bill get his practice established."

"I put some systems into place for him nearly twenty years ago," Maddie said, downplaying her contribution to setting up the office. "I'm hardly an expert. If you're going to do this, you should hire a consultant, devise a business plan, do cost projections. You can't do something like this on a whim just because you don't like the way Dexter's gym smells."

"Actually, we can," Helen insisted. "I have enough money saved for a down payment on the building, plus capital expenses for equipment and an operating budget for the first year. Let's face it, I can use the tax write-off, though I predict this won't be a losing proposition for long."

"And I'm going to invest some cash, but mostly my time and my expertise in cooking and nutrition to design a little café and offer classes," Dana Sue added.

They both looked at Maddie expectantly.

"What?" she demanded. "I don't have any expertise and I certainly don't have any money to throw at something this speculative."

Helen grinned. "You have a bit more than you think, thanks to your fabulous attorney, but we don't really want your money. We want you to be in charge."

Maddie regarded them incredulously. "Me? I hate to exercise. I only do it because I know I have to." She gestured at the cellulite firmly clinging to her thighs. "And we can see how much good that's doing."

"Then you're perfect for this job, because you'll work really, really hard to make this a place women just like you will want to join," Helen said.

Maddie shook her head. "Forget it. It doesn't feel right."

"Why not?" Dana demanded. "You need work. We need a manager. It's a perfect match."

"It feels like some scheme you devised to keep me from starving to death," Maddie said.

"I already told you that you won't be starving," Helen said. "And you get to keep the house, which is long since paid for. Bill was very reasonable once I laid out a few facts for him."

Maddie studied her friend's face. Not many people tried explaining anything to Bill, since he was convinced he knew it all. A medical degree did that to some men. And what the degree didn't accomplish, adoring nurses like Noreen did.

"Such as?" Maddie asked.

"How the news of his impending fatherhood with his unmarried nurse might impact his practice here in the conservative, family-oriented town of Serenity," Helen said without the slightest hint of remorse. "People might not want to take their darling little kiddies to a pediatrician who has demonstrated a complete lack of scruples."

"You blackmailed him?" Maddie wasn't sure whether she was shocked or awed.

Helen shrugged. "I prefer to think of it as educating him on the value of the right PR spin. So far people in town haven't taken sides, but that could change in a heartbeat."

"I'm surprised his attorney let you get away with that," Maddie said.

"That's because you don't know everything your brilliant attorney knew walking into that room," Helen said.

"Such as?" Maddie asked again.

"Bill's nurse had a little thing going with *his* attorney once upon a time. Tom Patterson had his own reasons for wanting to see Bill screwed to the wall."

"Isn't that unethical?" Maddie asked. "Shouldn't he have refused to take Bill's case or something?"

"He did, but Bill insisted. Tom disclosed his connection to Noreen, but Bill continued to insist. He thought Tom's thing with Noreen would make him more understanding of his eagerness to get on with life with her. Which just proves that when it comes to human nature your soon-to-be ex really doesn't have a clue."

"And you took advantage of all those shenanigans to get Maddie the money she deserves," Dana Sue said admiringly.

"I did," Helen confirmed with satisfaction. "If we'd had to go in front of a judge, it might have gone differently, but Bill was especially anxious for a settlement so he could be a proper daddy to his new baby *before* the ink is dry on the birth certificate. As you reminded him on your way out the door, Maddie, he's the one in a hurry."

Helen regarded Maddie intently. "It's not a fortune, mind you, but you don't have to worry about money for the time being."

"I still think I ought to look for a real job," Maddie said. "However much the settlement is, it won't last forever, and I'm not likely to have a lot of earning power, not right at first, anyway."

"Which is why you should take us up on our offer," Dana Sue said. "This health club could be a gold mine and you'd be a full partner. That's what you'd get in return for your day-in, day-out running of it all—sweat equity."

"I don't see what's in it for the two of you," Maddie said.

"Helen, you're in Charleston all the time. There are some fine gyms over there, if you don't want to go to Dexter's. And Dana Sue, you could offer cooking classes at the restaurant. You don't need a spa to do it."

"We're trying to be community minded," Dana Sue said. "This town needs someone to invest in it."

"I'm not buying it," Maddie said. "This is about me. You both feel sorry for me."

"We most certainly do not," Helen said. "You're going to be just fine."

"Then there's something else, something you're not telling me," Maddie persisted. "You didn't just wake up one day and decide you wanted to open a health club, not even for some kind of tax shelter."

Helen hesitated, then confessed. "Okay, here's the whole truth. I need a place to go to work off the stress of my job. My doctor's been on my case about my blood pressure. I flatly refuse to start taking a bunch of pills at my age, so he said he'd give me three months to see if a better diet and exercise would help. I'm trying to cut back on my cases in Charleston for a while, so I need a spa right here in Serenity."

Maddie stared at her friend in alarm. If Helen was cutting back on work, then the doctor must have made quite a case for the risks to her health. "If your blood pressure is that high, why didn't you say something? Not that I'm surprised given the way you obsess over your job."

"I didn't say anything because you've had enough on your plate," Helen said. "Besides, I intend to take care of it."

"By opening your own gym," Maddie concluded. "Won't getting a new business off the ground just add to the stress?"

"Not if *you're* running it," Helen said. "Besides, I think all of us doing this together will be fun."

Maddie wasn't entirely convinced about the fun factor,

but she turned to Dana Sue. "And you? What's your excuse for wanting to open a new business? Isn't the restaurant enough?"

"It's making plenty of money, sure," Dana Sue said. "But I'm around food all the time. I've gained a few pounds. You know my family history. Just about everybody had diabetes, so I need to get my weight under control. I'm not likely to stop eating, so I need to work out."

"See, we both have our own reasons for wanting to make this happen," Helen said. "Come on, Maddie. At least look at the building tomorrow. You don't have to decide tonight or even tomorrow. There's time for you to mull it over in that cautious brain of yours."

"I am *not* cautious," Maddie protested, offended. Once she'd been the biggest risk-taker among them. All it had taken was the promise of fun and a dare. Had she really lost that? Judging from the expressions on her friends' faces, she had.

"Oh, please, you weigh the pros and cons and calorie content before you order lunch," Dana Sue said. "But we love you just the same."

"Which is why we won't do this without you," Helen said. "Even if it *does* put our health at risk."

Maddie looked from one to the other. "No pressure there," she said dryly.

"Not a bit," Helen said. "I have a career. And the doctor says there are all sorts of pills for controlling blood pressure these days."

"And I have a business," Dana Sue added. "As for my weight, I suppose we can just continue walking together a couple of times a week." She sighed dramatically.

"Despite what y'all have said, I'm not entirely convinced it isn't charity," Maddie repeated. "The timing is awfully suspicious."

"It would only be charity if we didn't expect you to work your butt off to make a success of it," Helen said. "So, are you in or out?"

Maddie gave it some thought. "I'll look at the building," she finally conceded. "But that's all I'm promising."

Helen swung her gaze to Dana Sue. "If we'd waited till she had that second margarita, she would have said yes," Helen claimed, feigning disappointment.

Maddie laughed. "But if I'd had two, you couldn't have held me to anything I said."

"She has a point," Dana Sue agreed. "Let's be grateful we got a maybe."

"Have I told you two how glad I am that you're my friends?" Maddie said, feeling her eyes well up with tears yet again.

"Uh-oh, here she goes again," Dana Sue said, getting to her feet. "I need to get to work before we all start crying."

"I never cry," Helen declared.

Dana Sue groaned. "Don't even start. Maddie will be forced to challenge you, and before you know it, all of Serenity will be flooded and you'll both look like complete wrecks when we meet in the morning. Maddie, do you want me to drop you off at home?"

She shook her head. "I'll walk. It'll give me time to think."

"And to sober up before her mama sees her," Helen taunted.

"That, too," Maddie agreed.

Mostly, though, she wanted time to absorb the fact that on one of the worst days of her life she'd been surrounded by friends who'd given her a glimmer of hope that her future wasn't going to be quite as bleak as she'd imagined.

CHAPTER TWO

It was almost dusk when Maddie walked through the wrought-iron front gate of the monstrosity of a house that had been in the Townsend family for five generations. According to Helen, Bill had reluctantly agreed to let her remain there with the children, since the house would one day be Tyler's. Staring up at the massive brick facade, Maddie almost regretted winning that point. She would have been happier in something cozier with a white picket fence and some roses. The upkeep on this place could bankrupt her, but Helen assured her she'd made provisions for that, too, in the settlement.

As she opened the front door, she braced herself to deal with her mother. But when she walked into the family room at the back of the house, it was Bill she discovered sitting on the sofa with Katie napping in his arms and the boys lounging in front of the TV, their attention riveted on a show she was pretty sure she'd never allowed them to watch. She immediately stiffened at the sight of some sort of extreme-fighting competition.

One thing at a time, she warned herself. Getting rid of her soon-to-be ex was her first priority.

Before she opened her mouth, though, she allowed herself a long hard look at him, something she hadn't dared to do earlier. His blond hair was still thick, but there were a few silver strands she'd never noticed before, and an unhealthy pallor beneath his tan. The lines on his face, which once had lent character to his handsome features, made him look tired now. If it was still her business, she'd have been worried about him.

She reminded herself of how furious she'd been a few hours ago. "What are you doing here?" she demanded, reclaiming her earlier anger. "And where is my mother?"

The boys, used to her neutral tone and careful remarks about their father, regarded her with surprise. Bill merely frowned his disapproval.

"She left when I got here. I said I'd stay till you got home. We need to talk," he said.

"I said all I have to say to you at Helen's office," she retorted, standing her ground. "Do I need to repeat it?"

"Maddie, please, let's not start a scene in front of the kids."

She knew he was less concerned about that than about having to face any more of her justifiable outrage. Even so, he had a point. Tyler was already looking as if he might leap to her defense. He'd felt compelled to do that too many times lately. He'd been stuffing down his own feelings in an attempt to be supportive to her. It was too much of a burden for a sixteen-year-old boy who'd once idolized his dad.

"Fine," she said tightly. "Tyler, Kyle, go upstairs and finish your homework. I'll fix supper as soon as your dad leaves."

"Mine's done," Tyler said, not budging, his expression defiant.

"Mine, too," Kyle said.

She gave them a warning look that had them scrambling to their feet.

"I'll take Katie," Tyler offered, picking up his sleeping sister.

"Goodbye, boys," Bill called after them.

"Bye, Dad," Kyle answered. Tyler said nothing.

Bill stared after them, his expression sad. "Tyler's still furious with me, isn't he?"

"Can you blame him?" she replied, incapable of dealing with Bill's injured feelings.

"Of course not, especially with you feeding his resentment every chance you get," he responded.

"I do not do that," Maddie said heatedly. "As much as it pains me, I've done everything I can to keep them from hating you or seeing how badly you hurt me. Unfortunately, Ty and Kyle are old enough to reach their own conclusions and to see through whatever charade I put on."

Bill immediately backed down. "I'm sorry. I'm sure you've tried. It's just so frustrating. The kids and I used to be so close, but now Katie's the only one who acts as if nothing's changed."

"Katie adores you," Maddie said. "She's six. Even after all these months, she doesn't fully understand that you're never coming back here to live. The boys know exactly what's going on and that their lives will never be the same. Katie just cries herself to sleep every night when you're not here to read her a story and kiss her good night. Not a day goes by when she doesn't ask me what she did wrong and how we can fix it and when you're coming back for good."

She thought she caught a hint of guilt on Bill's face, but then the polite mask she'd gotten used to seeing lately returned. She tried to remember the last time his eyes had lit up at the sight of her, the last time he'd actually met her gaze at all. Sadly, she couldn't. She suspected it was long before he'd announced he was leaving her, most likely in the early days of his affair with Noreen. How had she not noticed such a dramatic change?

"Would you sit down, Maddie?" he said irritably. "I can't get into this with you looming over me."

"Into what? Surely there can't be more bad news. Breaking up our marriage and our family pretty much covered all the bases, didn't it?"

"You know, Madelyn, sarcasm doesn't become you."

"Well, pardon me all to hell!" she snapped, blaming the margaritas for her lack of inhibition. "Sarcasm is pretty much all I have left."

His gaze narrowed. "You never used to swear."

"Until recently, I never had anything to swear about," she told him. "Would you just say whatever's on your mind and leave? As I understand it, this is no longer your home, so I'd appreciate it if you'd call before coming by again."

He gave her a defeated look and for an instant, she almost felt sorry for him. He'd made his choice, he was getting everything he wanted, but he didn't seem all that happy about it. Before she could allow herself to remember the way she'd once loved him, she steeled herself and sat on the edge of a chair opposite him.

"I didn't want things to turn out like this," he said, meeting her gaze for the first time in weeks. "I really didn't."

Maddie sighed. "I know. Things happen."

"If it weren't for the baby…" His voice trailed off.

Maddie's temper stirred. "Don't you dare say that you'd have stayed with me if it weren't for Noreen getting pregnant. That demeans her and me."

He stared at her blankly. "How? I'm just trying to be honest."

"It suggests you're only with her because of the baby and it says you think I'd take you back after you cheated on me if there weren't a baby to consider. You had an affair, Bill. I'm not sure I could have forgiven that."

"Maybe not right away, but we might have fought harder to get back on track, to keep our family intact."

"Okay," she agreed reluctantly. "Maybe we would have, but that ship has pretty much sailed."

"Can you at least promise me you'll do what you can to help me fix things with the kids? I miss them, Maddie. I thought after all these months things would be better, but they're not. I'm running out of ideas."

"What you're running out of is patience," she retorted. "You wanted everything to fall neatly into place the instant you said goodbye to me, but unfortunately kids' emotions can't turn on a dime. They're hurt and angry and confused. You're going to have to work to change that. I can't just wave a magic wand and make it okay. I agreed to let you have as much time with them as you want. What more do you expect?"

"An advocate," he suggested.

"It's one thing for me not to say anything negative about you to the children," she told him. "But I'm not going to be a cheerleader for dear old dad."

"Did you know that Tyler has flatly refused to set foot in my new place as long as Noreen is there? What am I supposed to do, ask her to leave? It's her apartment."

"Ty didn't say anything to me about that," she said, just a little pleased that her son had taken such a stand. She knew, though, that he and his father needed to mend fences. Bill had always been an important part of their oldest son's life. Despite his busy schedule, Bill had never missed a ball game, a school conference or any other activity that meant something to Tyler. Sixteen was the worst possible age to have that kind of supportive relationship disrupted.

"I'll talk to him," she offered, backing off her refusal to become Bill's advocate. She would do it for Ty's sake. "But," she reminded Bill, "he's sixteen and has a mind of his own. I can't force him to do anything. You may have to give it some time, work a little harder to win him back."

"I'd appreciate anything you can do." He stood up. "Well, that's all I really wanted."

"Okay, fine."

"And to say one more time how sorry I am."

She felt the sting of tears in her eyes and blinked hard to keep them from falling. Just in case one escaped, she turned away. "Me, too," she said.

She kept waiting for him to leave, but she wasn't prepared for the quick brush of his lips on her cheek before he strode out of the family room and out of the house.

Now the tears fell unchecked. "Well, damn you all to hell, Bill Townsend," she muttered, hating that the quick, careless kiss had meant anything at all.

"Mom?"

Swiping at her tears, she gazed up at Tyler, who was studying her worriedly. "I'm okay," she assured him.

"No, you're not," he said, then added heatedly, "I hate him for what he's done to you. He's such a lying hypocrite. All that talk he used to give me about how you're supposed to treat someone you care about was just a crock."

"Ty, he's your dad. You don't hate him," she chided. "And what he told you is the way it's supposed to be. People who care about each other should be kind and supportive and faithful. Unfortunately life doesn't always follow the rules."

"You can't make me love him," he said, his tone unyielding. "I heard what he asked you. He wants you to convince me he's not a jerk."

"He loves you. He came over here because he misses spending time with you."

"I'm not the one who left," Tyler said bitterly. "He is. Why should I go out of my way to see him, especially when *she's* around all the time?"

Maddie moved to the sofa and held out her hand. "Come here."

He hesitated, then came closer and awkwardly took her outstretched hand.

"Sit here beside me," she said. When he was seated, she turned and met his gaze. "Ty, you're old enough to understand that things don't always work out with grown-ups just because we want them to. It's not anybody's fault."

"Are you telling me that Dad having an affair and getting Noreen pregnant is as much *your* fault as it is his?"

Her lips curved in a small smile at that. "Well, no, I can't say that, but obviously things weren't good between your dad and me or he wouldn't have turned to her."

"Did you know they weren't good?"

"No," she told him candidly. In hindsight, the signs were there, tiny fissures so small she could be forgiven for missing them, but at the time she'd thought their marriage was as solid as anyone's could be.

"Then it *was* all his fault," Tyler concluded, still being fiercely loyal to her.

As much as she wanted to agree with him, she was determined to be fair. "Spend some time with him, Ty, just the two of you. Listen to his side of things," she encouraged. "You've always been so close. Don't lose that."

"He'll just make a bunch of excuses. I don't want to hear

them." Ty regarded her warily. "Are you going to *make* me spend time with him?"

"I won't force you to, no," she said. "But I will be disappointed in you if you don't at least try to meet him halfway."

"Why?" he asked incredulously. "He walked out on you, Mom. On all of us. Why do we need to be fair?"

"He didn't walk out on you, Kyle and Katie," she said quietly. "He isn't divorcing you. Your dad loves every one of you."

"Man, I don't get you," her son said angrily, yanking his hand away and standing up. "How come I'm the only one in this house who sees Dad for the scumbag he is?"

"Tyler Townsend, don't talk about your father like that!" she said.

His gaze locked with hers, then eventually faltered. "Whatever," he mumbled and stalked out of the room.

Maddie watched him go, her heart aching. "Damn you, Bill Townsend," she said for the second time that night.

The old Victorian house on the corner of Main and Palmetto Lane was at the western fringe of downtown Serenity. Not that there was much of a downtown anymore, Maddie thought as she stood with Helen and Dana Sue. The hardware store had stuck it out, as had the drugstore with its old-fashioned soda fountain, but Willard's Grocery had been empty for a decade, ever since a superstore with discount grocery prices had opened twenty-five miles away on the outskirts of Charleston. It had quickly become evident that residents would rather drive all that way for a bargain than pay a few cents more to keep a local merchant in business.

The white paint on the Victorian was peeling, the shutters were askew and the porch sagged. The lawn hadn't been cut in ages and most of the picket fence was broken. Maddie dimly remembered the place as it had been when old Mrs. Hartley was alive. Yellow roses had tumbled over the white fence, the porch and sidewalk had been swept daily and the shutters had gleamed with dark green paint.

Mrs. Hartley, who must have been in her eighties by then, had sat on the porch every afternoon with a pitcher of iced sweet tea and welcomed anyone who happened to walk by. More than once, Maddie had climbed onto the swing hanging from the porch rafters and eaten sugar cookies while her grandmother had visited with the elderly woman. Nana Vreeland and Mrs. Hartley had been witness to most of the changes in Serenity through the years, and Maddie knew she'd absorbed their love for the small town with its friendly people, old white clapboard churches and acres of green space with a small lake in the middle that was home to a family of swans. Free summer concerts in the bandstand by the lake drew everyone in town on Saturday nights.

Despite Serenity's charm, a lot of people Maddie's age had been eager to leave and never come back, but not Maddie or Bill. They'd never wanted to live anywhere else. Nor had Helen or Dana Sue. The slower pace and sense of community meant something to all of them.

"Boy, this place brings back a lot of memories," Maddie said at last. "What a shame that none of Mrs. Hartley's kids wanted the property or made any effort to take care of it."

"Their loss is our gain," Helen said briskly. "We can get it for a song."

"I'm not surprised," Maddie said. "Are you sure it's safe to go inside? Looks to me as if all sorts of critters might have taken up residence in there."

Dana Sue nudged her in the ribs. "Do you think we've

forgotten about your terror of spiders and snakes? Helen made sure the real-estate agent had it all swept out last week. There's nothing in there but the resident ghost."

"Oh, please," Maddie said. "How can there be a ghost? No one's died here."

"But wouldn't it be fabulous if there were a ghost?" Dana Sue persisted. "Just think of the PR value. There's nothing a Southerner loves quite so much as a good ghost story or bragging rights to having one up in the attic."

"I'm not sure having a ghost would be much of a recommendation for a health club," Helen said. "What if it appears in a mirror one day? It could scare twenty years off someone's life and pretty much destroy the place's reputation as a fitness mecca. I'm not sure even I could win that lawsuit." She met Maddie's gaze. "Ready to go inside?"

"Sure. Why not?" Maddie said, still trying to see what the two of them obviously saw in the run-down house. Even her memories of the way it had once been didn't help her to envision it as a thriving spa.

Not two minutes later, though, once she'd stepped across the threshold and into the sunlight pooling on the old oak floors, her pulse began to race a little faster. The downstairs rooms were huge. The windows were dingy, but even so they let in streaming rays of sun. With pale yellow walls and white woodwork, the spa would be cheerful and welcoming. The floors could be brought back with sanding and a good coat or two of polyurethane.

When she reached the dining room, which faced the back of the property, she realized that the French doors and tall windows opened to a wooded lot with a small stream trickling through it. Treadmills set up to face that way would give the illusion of walking or running outdoors. Wouldn't that afford women a sense of serenity while they exercised?

Dana Sue latched on to her hand and tugged her into the kitchen.

"Can you believe this?" she demanded, gesturing around her. "The appliances are old and the cabinets are a mess, but the room is huge. Just imagine what we could do with it."

"I thought the idea of this place was to make people forget about food, not to feed them," Maddie said.

"No, no, no," Dana Sue chided. "It's supposed to give them a place to make healthy choices. We could set up a counter over here and a few small tables in that area by the door. We could even open it onto the back patio and add a few tables outside."

"Can you cook and serve in the same space?" Maddie asked.

"There won't be any cooking done here, except for whatever classes we offer. I'll cater the salads from the restaurant kitchen. We can get a professional refrigerator or display case for those. And we'll offer smoothies and other drinks. Can't you just imagine what fun it would be to work out with a couple of friends, then sit out there gazing at that stream and eating a chicken Caesar salad and drinking mineral water. You'd leave here feeling a thousand percent better, even if you never lost an ounce. And if we offered a hot tub and massages, oh, my gosh…" She sighed rapturously.

"That sounds great for someone who has all morning or all afternoon, but won't the people who can afford what you're talking about be working?" Maddie asked, continuing to play devil's advocate.

"We've thought of that," Helen said. "We could offer day-long or half-day packages for women who want to be really pampered for a special occasion. But we could also have a half-hour workout and lunch deal for someone who only has an hour-long break from work. And there are so many bedrooms, we could even convert one room to a nursery and hire a day-care worker so moms could exercise in peace."

Maddie regarded them with surprise. It was beginning to seem they had an answer for everything. "You've really given this a lot of thought, haven't you."

Helen shrugged. "What can I say? I hate Dexter's place and I really need to work out. I might as well create someplace I'll enjoy going."

"Me, too," Dana Sue said. "If I own a place like this, though, I'll have to stay in shape. I'll be happy. Doc Marshall will be happy. Even my daughter will stop commenting about the bulge around my middle."

"You do not have a bulge around your middle," Maddie said indignantly. "That's ridiculous!"

"Compared to my daughter, I'm downright obese," Dana Sue insisted. "To tell you the truth, I think Annie's taking the whole dieting thing to extremes, but every time I try to talk to her about it, she freaks out. And I can't get her near a scale to prove my point."

Helen regarded her with alarm. "You don't think she's anorexic, do you? Lots of teenage girls are, you know."

"The idea scares me to death," Dana Sue admitted. "I watch her like a hawk to see what she's putting in her mouth, and she seems to eat okay. Maybe she's just burning it all up. Some people are just plain lucky to have high metabolisms."

Helen exchanged a worried look with Maddie.

"Dana Sue, don't ignore this," Maddie said gently. "It can be really dangerous."

"Don't you think I know that?" Dana Sue snapped in a rare display of temper that proved just how worried she was. "I was there when Megan Hartwell collapsed at the prom, same as you. She nearly died, for goodness' sake."

Maddie backed off. That night had been one none of them would ever forget. It was the first time they'd seen what an eating disorder could do to someone their age. Heck, back then no one had even *acknowledged* there was such a thing as an eating disorder. Before that, Megan Hartwell's dieting obsession had just been a joke among them. If Dana Sue's daughter did have a problem, surely Dana Sue would recognize it and deal with it without Maddie or anyone else nagging her.

"Sorry," she apologized.

Dana Sue gave her a hug. "No, I'm sorry for biting your head off."

"Okay, let's try to focus on this place," Helen said briskly. "Maddie, now that you've seen it, what do you think?"

"I think it's a very ambitious plan," she said cautiously.

"Not for us," Dana Sue said. "We can do anything we set our minds to. We are, after all, the Sweet Magnolias. Everyone at Serenity High knew we were destined to succeed. They said so in our yearbooks."

"They also said we were most likely to raise a ruckus and land in jail," Maddie said.

Helen grinned. "Okay, so it was a toss-up. But we've all stayed on the straight and narrow. And we *have* succeeded."

Dana Sue nodded. "Pretty much."

"Maybe you two can claim success," Maddie said. "Helen not only made it through law school, but she's built an incredible practice all over the state. Dana Sue, you've created a restaurant that's as good as anything in Charleston, and that's saying something. What have I ever done?"

"You put your worthless hubby through med school,

managed a home and raised three great kids. That's nothing to sneeze at," Helen said.

"I just don't know," Maddie said. "This would be a huge time commitment and I really need to pay attention to the kids right now. They need me."

"We know that. We probably understand your priorities better than any other boss would," Dana Sue told her.

Maddie knew that was true, but she still wasn't ready to say yes. There was one significant consideration she couldn't ignore. "I'd be terrified of messing up and costing you a small fortune," she admitted.

"If I'm not worried about that, why should *you* be?" Helen asked.

Despite the reassurance, Maddie couldn't seem to shake the sick feeling in the pit of her stomach that she was getting in way over her head. "How big a hurry are you two in to do this?" she asked.

"I took out an option on the property yesterday for thirty days," Helen said.

"Then give me thirty days to make up my mind," Maddie pleaded.

"What will you know in thirty days that you don't know right this minute?" Dana Sue argued.

"I'll be able to do some cost projections, some market analysis, take a look at what's being offered in other towns in the area," Maddie began.

Helen grinned again. "I told you she'd focus on all that sensible stuff," she said to Dana Sue.

"Well, it's important to know exactly what's involved," Maddie retorted. "And I want to look at the job market while I'm at it. I should see if there's something I'm better suited to do."

"In Serenity?" Helen scoffed.

"I could be qualified for lots of things," Maddie said, though without much conviction.

"You are," Helen concurred, "but not a lot of folks are going to offer you a partnership in your own business based on your résumé."

"I have to look," Maddie said stubbornly. "I have to be sure that this is the right thing for all of us. I'd never forgive myself if I just said yes and you wound up blowing a small fortune because I was incompetent or hadn't done my homework."

"I respect that," Helen said. "I really do."

Maddie met her gaze. "But? I hear a *but* in there."

"*But* you haven't taken a risk in over twenty years, and look where that's gotten you. I say it's high time to just throw caution to the wind and do what your gut tells you to do. You used to trust it."

"So?" Dana Sue prodded. "What's your gut saying, Maddie?"

Maddie gave them a rueful smile. "It's saying yes," she admitted.

"Well, hallelujah!" Dana Sue enthused.

Maddie shook her head. "Don't get too worked up. From what I can see, my gut hasn't been reliable for some time now. Up until a few months ago, I thought I had a good marriage."

"Don't blame your gut for that one," Helen said. "Blame Bill for being an excellent liar."

"Maybe so, but I think this time I'll be more comfortable if I do a little research before taking the plunge. Come on, guys, thirty days. Is that so much to ask?"

Her friends exchanged a look.

"I suppose not," Dana Sue said reluctantly.

"I bet she'll be ready in a week," Helen told Dana Sue.

Maddie frowned. "What makes you so sure?"

"I looked at the want ads in this morning's paper," Helen said. "Trust me, you won't beat our offer." When Maddie started to respond, Helen held up a hand. "It's okay. You need to see for yourself. I understand that."

"Thank you," Maddie said.

"Just in case, though, I think I'll go ahead and start on the partnership paperwork," Helen said.

"Keep on being so smug, and I'll turn you down just to spite you," Maddie threatened.

"No, you won't," Helen said with confidence. "You're way too smart to do that."

Maddie tried to remember the last time anyone had complimented her on her intelligence, rather than her baking or hostessing skills. Maybe working with her two best friends would be good for her. Even if this health-club idea went belly-up, she might walk away with her self-esteem bolstered in a way it hadn't been in years, to say nothing of the fact that they were bound to share a lot more laughter than she'd had in her marriage for a long time now. She ought to say yes for those reasons alone.

Because she was suddenly tempted to do just that, she gave Helen and Dana Sue quick hugs and headed for the door. "I'll call you both," she promised.

And, she vowed, not one minute before her thirty days was up.

CHAPTER THREE

At thirty, Cal Maddox had been coaching high-school baseball for only two years, but he knew the sport as few did. He'd played five seasons in the minors and two years in the majors until an injury had sidelined him. He'd been forced to accept that years in the minor leagues trying to get back what he'd once had would be an exercise in futility.

Sharing his love of the game and his expertise with kids who might still have a shot drew him as nothing else had during those frustrating months of rehab. He owed one man for yanking him out of his initial depression and making him realize that possibilities existed outside of pro ball.

Serenity School Board chairman Hamilton Reynolds, an ardent Atlanta Braves fan during Cal's brief tenure with the team, had sought him out at the rehab center and changed his outlook and his life. He'd convinced Cal to come to Serenity.

In all his years working up to his shot with the big leagues and since, he'd never seen anyone with the raw, natural talent of Tyler Townsend. Ty was every coach's dream, a kid with good grades, an easygoing temperament and a willingness to practice and learn. He'd been all-state his sophomore year and had been headed down that road again this year, at least until a few weeks ago. Now, Cal thought, he was a kid spiraling out of control.

Cal watched Ty's halfhearted pitches to the plate with increasing dismay. The players, who usually had to struggle to make contact with the kid's fastball, were slamming the balls over the fence right and left today. Worst of all, Ty didn't even seem frustrated by his inability to get the batters out.

"Okay, that's it for today," Cal called. "Everybody do a lap around the field, then head for the locker room. Ty, I'd like to see you in my office after you've changed."

Cal headed inside to wait. On some level, he half expected Tyler to blow off the meeting, but twenty minutes later the kid appeared in the doorway, his expression sullen.

"Come on in," Cal said. "Close the door."

"My mom's picking me up in ten minutes," Tyler said, but he sprawled in a chair across from Cal. Though he had the gangly limbs of a lot of boys his age, Ty had none of the awkwardness. His slouching posture now, however, was indicative of his overall bad attitude.

"I think we can cover this in ten minutes," Cal said, hiding his frustration. "How do you think you pitched today?"

"I sucked," Ty responded.

"And that's okay with you?"

Ty shrugged and avoided his gaze.

"Well, it's not okay with me." Cal's words drew no reaction, which meant sterner measures were called for. "Here's the deal. If you expect to pitch our opener in two weeks, you're going to have to show me that you deserve it. Otherwise I'll put Josh in the starting rotation and you'll spend the season on the bench."

Expecting a fight or at least a reaction, Cal was disappointed when Ty merely shrugged.

"Do what you want," Ty said.

Cal frowned at the utter lack of interest. "It is not what I want," he said impatiently. "What I want is for you to get your act together and pitch like we both know you can." He regarded the boy with real concern. "What's going on with you, Ty? Whatever it is, you know you can talk to me, right?"

"I guess."

Cal pressed on, hoping to get some kind of response that would clue him in to what was troubling the boy. "Your other teachers tell me you're not concentrating in class. Your grades are slipping. None of this is like you."

"Well, maybe I've changed," Ty said sourly. "People do, you know. Out of the blue, they just fucking change." He stood up and took off before Cal could react.

Well hell, Cal thought. He'd gotten what he was after—a genuine reaction—but he didn't know anything more than he had before he'd hauled the kid into his office. He wasn't sure which worried him more, the uncharacteristic swearing or the attitude. Cal had heard plenty of foul language in the high-school locker room. But he'd never heard it from Ty before.

Nor had he seen that kind of bitterness and resignation from a boy who could have the whole world of professional baseball at his feet a few years down the road. Normally Ty hung on Cal's every word, determined to soak up every bit of knowledge Cal had to share. His exuberance and commitment to the team had made him a role model for the other kids.

Cal pulled a file and jotted down the Townsends' phone number. Nine times out of ten when a kid lost focus like this, there was something going on at home or he'd gotten mixed up in some kind of substance abuse. Cal flatly refused to believe a kid as smart as Tyler would suddenly start doing drugs; besides, he'd seen no real evidence of that or alcohol abuse so that left some kind of upheaval in the kid's home life.

Cal sighed. There was nothing like calling parents and digging around in their personal issues to make his day. He'd rather take a hard fastball in the gut.

Maddie had been on three job interviews that day. None of them had gone well, pretty much proving Helen's point. Maddie had been out of the workforce too long for her degree or her work experience to count for much. Her résumé of early jobs looked pitiful, especially with the fifteen-year gap since the last one. *She* might think she was executive material, but no one else would so she'd kept her expectations modest.

When each of the human resources people had seen that gaping void, they'd regarded her with dismay. Each had asked some variation of the same question: What have you been doing all this time?

Keeping house, raising kids, resolving squabbles and balancing the checkbook. Not even the unpaid hours she'd put in handling the inevitable billing problems in Bill's medical practice seemed to count for much.

The only thing more discouraging had been her own lack of excitement about any of the jobs. Most of them had been clerical positions, the kind of entry-level work she'd done twenty years ago. It struck her as ironic that all those years of life experience had left her unqualified for even that type of work.

She was still thinking about it—and about the alternative Helen and Dana Sue were offering her—when Ty yanked open the car door and climbed in, his increasingly frequent scowl firmly in place. He'd yanked his T-shirt on inside out, yet more evidence that he wasn't himself. Since he'd discovered an interest in girls, he'd taken more care with his appearance, but today he looked unkempt. Given the streaks of dirt on his arms and his perspiration-matted dark blond hair, it didn't even look as if he'd showered after practice.

"How was practice?" she asked automatically.

"It sucked."

"Having trouble with your fastball?"

"I don't want to talk about it," he said, turning to avoid her startled gaze. "Let's just get the hell out of here. I want to go home."

Keeping her temper in check, she regarded her son with a neutral expression. She would deal with his language later. "Ty, what's going on?" she asked quietly.

Her son's mood had been increasingly dark ever since Bill's last visit. Her attempt to force the issue the other night had apparently fallen on deaf ears. He was still angry and he still wasn't speaking to his dad. When Bill had come by the night before to pick up the kids, Ty had remained locked in his room, refusing to see him.

On some level, she'd counted on the start of baseball season to provide a certain normalcy for him. He loved the game. He excelled at it. He'd claimed there was nothing he wanted more than a shot at being a professional ballplayer. Usually by this time in spring practice, he was quoting Coach Maddox every chance he got. Of course, in the past his father had been there to listen.

When he remained stubbornly silent, she prodded again. "Ty, talk to me. I'm not starting this car until you do. What's going on with you?"

"Why does everybody keep asking me that?" he exploded. "You know what's going on. We've already talked it to death. Dad walked out for some bimbo. What am I *supposed* to do when I find out my dad's a jerk? Can't we just leave it alone? I'm sick of talking about it."

Maddie couldn't really blame him for being sick of the topic, but clearly he needed to discuss it further, if not with her, then with a professional. He needed to deal with his resentment in a more constructive way than lashing out at anyone and everyone around him.

"Sweetie, yes, we've talked about his, and I know you don't understand what your father's done," she said for what must have been the thousandth time. "But that doesn't give you the right to call him names, okay? He's still your father and deserves your respect. I do not want to have to tell you that again, understood?"

He regarded her incredulously. "Come on, Mom. I know you keep painting this rosy picture of things, but even you have to know what a jerk he is."

"What I think of your father isn't the point," she said. "He loves you, Ty. He wants you to be as close as you always were."

"Then why the hell did he leave us for *her?* She's not much older than me."

"She *is* an adult, though," Maddie said. "You, your brother and sister need to give her a chance. If your father loves her, I'm sure she has plenty of good qualities." She managed to get the words out without gagging.

"Yeah, right. I've seen her good *qualities,*" he retorted. "Like a 38-D, I'd say."

"Tyler Townsend!" she protested. "You know better than to make a remark like that. It's rude and inappropriate."

"It's the truth."

Maddie fought to temper her remarks. "Look, change is never easy, but we all have to adapt. I'm trying. You could help me a lot if you'd try, too. You're a role model for Kyle and Katie. They're going to follow your lead when it comes to how they treat your dad and his…" Maddie stumbled. Until the divorce was final and the relationship could be legalized, there was no name for what Bill's new love could be called, at least not in front of her children.

"Special friend," Tyler suggested sarcastically. "That's what Dad calls her. It makes me want to puke."

Maddie would not allow herself to agree with him. That didn't mean it was easy to give him a chiding look. "Careful, Tyler. You're very close to crossing a line."

"And Dad hasn't crossed a line?" he said. "Give me a break."

"Did something happen yesterday that I don't know about?"

"No."

"Are you sure? Did you have words with your father?"

He remained stubbornly silent and kept looking out the window, refusing to meet her gaze.

Obviously she wasn't going to get through to him, not this afternoon. But she had to keep trying. At the very least, she had to rein in his nastier comments.

"Maybe we should table this discussion for now, but in future I want you to speak to your father—and other adults, for that matter—in a respectful manner."

Ty rolled his eyes. Maddie let it pass.

"Let's talk some more about why baseball practice sucked," she suggested, finally putting the car into gear and pulling away from the curb.

"Let's not," he said tersely, then looked directly at her as if seeing her for the first time. "How come you're all dressed up?"

"Job interviews."

"And?"

She resorted to his terminology. "They sucked."

For the first time since he'd climbed into the car, Ty grinned. He looked like her carefree kid again…and so much like his dad had looked at that age, it made her heart ache.

"A chocolate milk shake always makes me feel better when I've had a bad day," he suggested slyly.

Maddie grinned back at him, relieved to see the improvement in his mood. "Me, too," she said, and whipped the car into the left-turn lane to head for Wharton's Pharmacy, which still had an old-fashioned soda fountain.

Ever since her own childhood, that soda fountain had been the place where some of the most important events in her life had played out. She and Bill had shared sodas there during high school. She, Helen and Dana Sue had shared confidences. Bill had even proposed to her in the back booth with the view of Main Street with its flower-filled planters and wide, grassy median. They'd celebrated the arrival of each new baby by making a ceremonious first visit to the soda fountain so Grace and Neville Wharton could gush over the latest Townsend.

Going there today would be bittersweet, but fitting, Maddie thought. Maybe she and her son would be able to start the healing process over chocolate milk shakes. Then again that was asking an awful lot of a shake.

"I was real sorry to hear about you and Bill," Grace Wharton told Maddie in an undertone while Ty was at the counter getting their milk shakes. "I just don't know what men are thinking when they walk away from a fine family to be with a girl who's still wet behind the ears."

Maddie could only nod agreement. As much as she liked

Grace, she knew that anything she said would be reported far and wide by nightfall. Fortunately, Ty came back to their booth before Grace could pry anything more from her.

"I hear you've been looking for a job," Grace said, regarding Maddie with sympathy. "There's mighty slim pickin's here in Serenity. It's a crying shame the way this town has been losing business to those big ole stores outside Charleston. I tell Neville all the time if we didn't do such a good business with the soda fountain, we'd have to shut our doors, too. Goodness knows, the pharmacy's not making money the way it once did. People would rather carry their prescriptions thirty miles than pay a little more for good service right here at home."

"It's affecting you, too?" Maddie asked, surprised. "Don't people realize how wonderful it is to have a pharmacist who knows them and who's willing to bring the prescription right to the door in the middle of the night if need be?"

"Oh, they care enough about that in an emergency, but it's the day-in, day-out prescriptions we're losing and the over-the-counter medicines they can buy cheaper someplace else. Losing that factory over in White Hill hasn't helped, either. Folks there had good jobs with decent pay. Now all those jobs are off in some foreign country." Grace shook her head sorrowfully. "It's a crying shame, that's what it is. Well, I'll leave you two to enjoy your milk shakes. Honey, if you need anything, you just let me know. I'll be happy to look after the kids for you or anything else you need."

"Thanks, Grace," Maddie said sincerely. She knew Grace meant it, too. That was the comfort of a place like Serenity. Neighbors helped each other out.

When she turned to face her son, his expression was troubled.

"Mom, are we short on cash because of Dad leaving? Is that why you're trying to find a job?"

"We're okay for now," she assured him. "But the alimony payments your dad agreed to won't last forever. I'm trying to plan ahead."

"I thought Helen and Dana Sue wanted you to start up a new business with them," he said.

Maddie was astonished. "How on earth do you know about that?"

"Mom, it's Serenity and Dana Sue," he said.

"Are you suggesting this town has a thing for gossip?" she inquired wryly. "And my best friend has a big mouth?"

"I'm not falling into that trap," he sidestepped neatly. "But I do go to school with Dana Sue's daughter."

"And she's been talking about this health-club idea?"

Ty nodded. "I think it sounds cool. I bet it'd be a whole lot more fun than working in some stuffy old office."

"I pretty much think what they want me to do is work in their office," she said.

"But you like them, right? I do. Dana Sue's a riot and Helen gives just about the best Christmas presents ever."

"Ah, yes. Important qualifications for a sound working partnership."

"I'm just saying—"

She gave his hand a quick squeeze. "I know what you're saying and you're right. Working with them would be wonderful."

"Then what's keeping you from saying yes?"

She'd given the offer a lot of thought the past few days and knew exactly why she was hesitating. She'd even explained it to her friends, but it had fallen on deaf ears. "I don't want to let them down," she said honestly. "Right now, I'm just not sure if I can give the job the attention it needs."

"Yeah, I know what you mean," Ty said, startling her.

"You do?"

"I know I'm letting the baseball team down," he admitted. "But I just can't seem to concentrate. That's what Coach was all over me about today at practice. He said if I don't get it together, he'll pull me from the starting rotation."

"Can he do that?" she demanded indignantly.

Tyler shrugged. "He's the coach. It's his call."

"He won't be the coach for long if the team starts losing." Angry on her son's behalf, she said, "Want me to talk to him? It's not fair that he's leaning on you so hard right now. I'm sure if he understood what's going on, he'd cut you some slack."

Ty looked horrified. "No way, Mom. He's right. If I suck, I've got no business being on the field. I just have to work harder, I guess."

"You could call your dad," she suggested. "He's always been able to help you before."

"No!" Ty said fiercely. "I am not calling Dad about anything, okay? I'm not." He pushed his unfinished milk shake aside and left the booth. "I'll wait in the car."

"Ty!"

He didn't even look back.

Maddie stared after him in dismay. What on earth was she supposed to do now? It wasn't as if *she* could start coaching him. She understood quite a lot about baseball thanks to her son's love of the game, but she certainly didn't have any technical expertise. Besides, Coach Maddox had more pitching skill and pro ball experience than anyone in the entire region. If he couldn't get through to Ty, then maybe what her son needed was counseling of some sort to help him deal with the other issues in his life. Maybe it was time to give that possibility serious consideration.

Unfortunately, even suggesting such a thing when Ty was still so angry might make the problem worse. He might think she was losing faith in him. In the past she and Bill would have talked over the situation and made a decision together. Now she'd rather eat dirt than turn to him. She had to handle this on her own.

"Mind a bit of advice?" Neville Wharton asked, slipping into the booth opposite her.

"I'd be grateful," she said.

"If I were you, despite what Tyler says he wants or doesn't want, I'd sit down with the coach and tell him what's going on. Cal's got real good instincts about working with kids if he knows what he's up against."

Maddie tried to imagine spilling her personal humiliation to a man she barely knew. She didn't think she could do it.

Neville smiled. "I know what you're thinking," he said. "That once you tell one person it'll be all over town, but the truth is everyone in Serenity probably already knows what's going on with you and Bill, anyway. And I like the Maddox boy. He's got a good head on his shoulders. The students at school look up to him, especially the boys on the baseball team."

Only someone Neville's age would refer to the baseball coach as a boy, she thought. Cal Maddox had to be thirty at least, given the time he'd spent in the minors and the all-too-brief time he'd been in the Major League before coming to Serenity two years ago to coach.

"I'll give it some thought," Maddie promised. "Thanks, Neville."

"Tyler will be okay," he reassured her. "That boy of yours is just going through a rough patch, that's all. It's tough having his dad walk out. He doesn't know how to handle it. Same as you, I imagine."

He gave her a wink. "And for what it's worth, I think you ought to open that fancy spa with Helen and Dana Sue, too. I imagine even Grace might wander over there for one of those massages, just to see what it's like."

"Is there anyone in this town who hasn't heard about their plan?" Maddie asked, exasperated.

"I doubt it," he said. "I figure those two gals knew you'd be a hard sell and wanted to get folks on their side to help with any convincing that needed to be done."

"Oh, great," she grumbled. "I've half a mind to turn the job down."

He grinned. "You'll get past that," he said with conviction. "A smart gal like you won't walk away from the chance of a lifetime just to be stubborn."

"You realize if we get half the women in Serenity on some sort of health kick, Neville, your soda fountain will suffer," she warned him.

"Nah," he said, showing a complete lack of concern. "I've been in this business more than fifty years. Good intentions can't hold out against hot-fudge sauce for long. And I'll be sure to send my best customers over there to work off the calories. That way we'll both profit."

She studied him with surprise. "Then you really think this health club is a good idea?"

"Are you kidding me?" he asked incredulously. "Have you looked at the magazine racks lately? Fitness and weight loss and all that sort of thing is all anyone writes about these days. That tells me folks must be pretty worked up about it. Women sit at my counter every single day and talk about low-carb this and low-fat that. If it's a craze, you three gals may as well make some money from it. Goodness knows, you won't have any competition from Dexter's."

"No question about that," Maddie agreed. "Thanks, Neville. I'd better get out to the car before Tyler melts. It's hot as blazes out there, even if it is only March."

"I know. Makes you wonder what July will be like, doesn't it?" he said with a shake of his head.

The weather was the least of Maddie's concerns. Even with all of Neville's well-meaning advice, she still didn't know what to do about her one solid job offer…or about her very angry and disillusioned son.

CHAPTER FOUR

When the doorbell rang just after lunch on Saturday, Maddie gladly left it to the kids to answer the door. She had no desire to face Bill after the frustrating week she'd had. These days she didn't want to see him when she was at her best, much less when she was feeling defeated.

She was about to run a hot bath for herself when she heard Tyler's raised voice from the front hall.

"What the hell are *you* doing here? We don't want you in this house!"

Horrified by his language and his attitude, Maddie rushed from her bathroom wrapped in an old terry-cloth robe, her hair piled atop her head in a haphazard knot. "Tyler Walker Townsend, what on earth?" she said, then came to an abrupt stop beside him as she spotted the very pregnant Noreen standing on the doorstep.

Maddie had first met the young nurse when she'd interviewed candidates for the job in Bill's office. She'd been impressed by the woman's résumé and composure. In the weeks after Bill had hired her, Maddie had noticed the woman's efficiency and her warmth with the young patients. She'd had no idea that Noreen's attentiveness had extended to her husband.

On the two occasions when she'd seen Noreen since discovering the woman's involvement with Bill, Maddie had been struck by how self-possessed she seemed, even dressed in her end-of-the-day wilted nurse's uniform. Now, despite her designer maternity outfit, she looked far less sure of herself. There were patches of red on her cheeks from embarrassment and her eyes were shadowed with distress. She looked even younger than her twenty-four years.

"Dad sent *her* to pick us up," Tyler said, his body radiating outrage. "I'm not going anywhere with her. And neither are they." He scowled at Kyle and Katie, who were standing nearby in wide-eyed dismay. Kyle whirled around and ran upstairs. Katie promptly burst into tears and flung herself at Maddie.

"I miss Daddy!" she cried, hiccuping with sobs. "When is Daddy coming home?"

Despite her disapproval of her son's tone, Maddie couldn't help wondering the same thing Tyler had asked: knowing how his kids felt about her, why would Bill send Noreen in his place? Even as she tried to soothe her daughter, she pinned Noreen with an accusing look.

"Where is their father?" she asked.

"Bill was tied up at the hospital," Noreen explained, clearly shaken by Tyler's verbal attack and Maddie's cold reception. "He asked me to pick up the kids. I didn't think it would be a problem."

"Well, you can forget it," Tyler said. "We're not going anywhere with you!"

"Tyler!" Maddie said sharply. She kept her gaze on Noreen's face, trying very hard not to let it stray to her protruding belly. "Obviously, this was a bad idea. Tell Bill he'll have to arrange another time to see the kids."

"But I don't understand," Noreen said. "Saturday afternoon is his time. It says so in the divorce settlement. He went over all the terms with me."

"That's right," Maddie agreed. "It's *his* time, not yours. Now I think you should go. Your presence here is clearly upsetting my children."

"Please," Noreen said. "Can't we talk about this? I'm just giving them a ride, Maddie. Bill will be really upset if he misses his time with them."

"He'll just have to get over it," Maddie said, refusing to back down. "Maybe next time he'll arrange to be here himself."

For an instant, she almost felt sorry for the other woman. Maybe it was of her own doing, but even Maddie could recognize that Noreen was caught in an impossible situation.

Noreen's lower lip trembled. "I just don't get why they hate me so much," she said miserably.

Maddie looked at her son. "Tyler, take Katie in the kitchen and get yourselves a snack, please."

"But, Mom," he began. At a warning glance from her, he sighed and took Katie from her arms.

When Maddie was certain they were out of hearing, she turned back to Noreen. "You're a pediatrics nurse, Noreen. Surely you must have taken some child psychology courses."

Noreen nodded. "Yes, but I still don't get it. Whenever they stopped by the office to see their dad, they were always such great kids. I thought they liked me."

"I'm sure they did when they thought of you as their father's *nurse,*" Maddie said.

When Noreen still looked confused, Maddie added, "I'm

sure Bill will explain it to you. He used to have a functioning brain and at least a tiny bit of sensitivity."

Satisfied that the barb had hit its mark, she quietly closed the door in the woman's face, then went to deal with her kids.

In the kitchen, she pulled Katie onto her lap, then tried to compose herself before facing Ty.

"Young man, if I ever hear you speak to another adult the way you spoke to Noreen just now, you'll be grounded for a month."

Ty looked as if she'd slapped him. "She had no business coming here," he said defensively.

"That's not the point. We've had this conversation before, but you don't seem to have gotten the message. My children are respectful of adults, period."

"Even when they're nothing but—"

"Don't you dare finish that sentence," she told him. "Go upstairs and check on your brother while I try to get Katie calmed down."

A half hour later she was physically and emotionally drained from walking the tightrope between what she knew was right and the vicious words she wanted to utter herself. She needed a break and the kids needed a distraction. Bracing herself for a slew of questions she didn't want to answer, she called her mother. If she'd been willing to babysit once, maybe she could be persuaded to do it again.

"What's wrong?" Paula Vreeland asked the second she heard Maddie's strained voice.

"What makes you think something's wrong?" she said. That was the way her relationship with her mother went. Even the most innocent question had a way of getting her hackles up. Maybe it was because she always sensed some inherent disapproval in her mother's tone, if not her words.

"You sound as if you're on your last nerve," her mother said. "What's Bill done now?"

Since there was little point in denying her husband's role in her mood, Maddie gave her mother an abbreviated version of the scene that had just played out on her doorstep.

"It's plain he wasn't thinking, but women are usually more sensitive to these things. What on earth possessed Noreen to think that she'd be welcome at your house?" her mother demanded.

"I doubt she thought about it at all," Maddie responded. "I imagine she was just doing what Bill told her to do."

"Or she wanted to rub this situation in your face," her mother said heatedly. "Isn't it enough that she destroyed your marriage?"

"Apparently not," Maddie said.

Paula drew in a deep breath. "Okay, there's no point in belaboring the woman's lack of good sense. What can I do to help?"

"The kids could really use a change of scenery," Maddie said. "I hate to ask, but would you mind taking them to your place for a few hours? It won't be the same as going to their dad's, but maybe it'll distract—"

"How about I take them to Charleston instead?" her mother offered. "We'll see a movie, eat hamburgers and greasy fries and I'll bring them home exhausted."

Maddie was surprised. "Are you sure?"

"Believe it or not, I find your children highly entertaining and they don't seem to mind spending time with me. We'll enjoy ourselves."

Maddie decided not to remind her that she'd once vetoed the idea of spending any time babysitting them. At the moment, she didn't really care why that had changed. She was just grateful for it.

"Thank you," she said.

"No thanks necessary," her mother replied. "But one of these days I would like it if we could sit down and talk about why you hate asking for my help not just with the kids, but with anything."

Maddie sighed. How could she tell her mother it was because asking for help—especially from a woman as competent and self-sufficient as Paula Vreeland—always made her feel like a failure?

"Well, you look downright pitiful," Dana Sue observed when Maddie appeared in the doorway to the kitchen at Sullivan's later that afternoon after depositing her surprisingly upbeat kids with her mother. "Come on in here and sit down. I'll fix you a plate of spiced shrimp."

"Save the shrimp. I've already eaten lunch with the kids," Maddie told her, not entirely certain why she'd dropped by. When a leisurely bubble bath had done nothing to soothe her, she'd sought out the one person who could understand what she was feeling. Dana Sue had been through her own nasty divorce from a cheating husband, but at least Ronnie hadn't stuck around Serenity to rub the situation in her face.

Dana Sue set a plate piled high with shrimp in front of her anyway. "Peeling those will keep your hands occupied while you tell me what's going on."

"Are you sure you have time to talk?" Maddie asked, regarding the shrimp without interest but picking one up anyway.

"The lunch crowd has dwindled and it's hours till people start showing up for dinner," Dana Sue said. "But even if I were busier than an ant at a picnic, I'd still have time for you."

"I could chop or dice or something," Maddie offered.

"No offense, but this is my kitchen. Any chopping or dicing will be done by me and my experienced staff. Besides, judging from the expression on your face, I'm not sure you ought to be trusted with sharp objects."

Maddie managed a faint grin. "You have a point."

"What's Bill done now?"

"What makes you think my mood is his fault?" Maddie inquired. Dana Sue was the second person to leap to that conclusion. Obviously her life and her moods were becoming too predictable.

"Because you loved him for more than twenty years. Just because he's turned out to be a low-down skunk doesn't mean he can't still twist you into knots." She looked Maddie in the eye. "What did he do? Do I need to hunt him down?"

"I wish it were that simple. I wish a good swift kick or a smack upside his head would knock some sense into him, but I think he's hopeless. Clueless, anyway." Maddie shrugged. "How could I have been so wrong about him? For twenty years I lived with a man who was smart and reasonably sensitive. Now it's as if he checked his brain somewhere and can't remember where."

"Well, we know he's thinking with another part of his anatomy," Dana Sue offered. "What did he do?"

"He was tied up at the hospital today, so he sent Noreen by to pick up the kids." She twisted the tail off a shrimp with such force that both the shell and the shrimp went flying across the kitchen in opposite directions. She scowled at Dana Sue. "He sent that woman to *my* house to pick up *my* kids."

"I can just imagine how that went," Dana Sue said as she retrieved the scattered remains of the shrimp.

"I doubt it," Maddie told her. "Tyler answered the door and told her to get the hell away from our house. Kyle ran upstairs and locked himself in his room and Katie burst into tears. It took me a half hour to calm her down. It's breaking my heart to see how much she misses her dad."

"And what did Noreen do during all this commotion?"

"Stood there wringing her hands and telling me she just doesn't understand why the kids don't like her anymore. I told her to ask Bill. I should've said that maybe even her little pea brain could come up with an explanation if she really tried."

Dana Sue chuckled. "That would have been a nice shot."

Maddie sighed. "One she deserved, but it hardly solves anything. I'm sure Bill is going to be on a tear once he hears how she was received by me and the kids. I'll have to listen to another of his tirades about how we're not giving Noreen a fair chance, that she's in his life now, that she's having his baby, that I promised to help smooth things over and now they're worse than ever, and on and on and on."

Dana Sue gave Maddie a penetrating look. "Something tells me you're not this upset just because Bill's going to have himself a hissy fit."

"Of course not. I'm upset because my kids' lives have been turned inside out and I can't seem to do a thing to help them. I don't even know where to start."

"Where are they right now?"

"My mother's taken them to Charleston to dinner and a movie."

"Her idea or yours?"

"Mine, if you must know, at least the part about them spending the afternoon with her. I was desperate. I figured they needed a break from me as much as they needed one from Noreen and their dad. All this tension has taken a terrible toll on them."

"And on you," Dana Sue reminded her. "What are you doing for yourself?"

"Running to you," Maddie said.

"If we had our spa, you could soak in the hot tub and have a massage," Dana Sue reminded her.

Maddie frowned. "My thirty days have barely begun. Stop pressuring me. I really don't need that on top of everything else today."

"Just pointing out one of the advantages of going into business with me and Helen," Dana Sue said mildly. "I could list more."

"Not necessary. I think I have a handle on most of them," Maddie admitted.

Dana Sue studied her intently. "Meaning?"

"Nothing," Maddie said. "Ask me a couple of weeks from now."

"You know you're going to agree to this. You're just being stubborn."

"Maybe I'm just enjoying keeping the two of you dangling on the end of my hook," Maddie retorted. "It's rare that I have the upper hand."

She finally popped one of the peeled shrimp into her mouth and savored the burst of spices. "Mmm, these are fantastic!"

Dana Sue chuckled. "I'm glad you like them. For a while there, I thought you were just going to mangle them as some sort of bizarre therapy. How about a glass of wine to go with them?"

"Sure. Wine sounds good," she said as she ate another shrimp, then licked her fingers.

"You know," Dana Sue said, "I think you'd feel a whole lot better about your life if you had something positive to look forward to. You need to remember how capable and smart you are, that marriage to Bill didn't define you. I know launching this place kept me sane when I kicked Ronnie out."

"But you'd been dreaming about opening your own restaurant for years," Maddie countered. "I've never envisioned opening a fitness club."

"Neither did I," Dana Sue admitted. "Not till Helen brought up the idea. Then it just seemed to fit with where we all are right now."

"Just give me some time to catch up," Maddie pleaded. "I'm afraid if I agree to it now, when everything else is so overwhelming, I'll just freak out and ruin it."

"I've seen you in a crisis, Maddie. You don't freak out. You dig in and get the job done. Remember prom when the money we'd been counting on suddenly vanished? You charged out and got donations from every business in town and managed to pull off the best senior prom our school had ever had."

"That was a long time ago," Maddie reminded her.

"But you still have that same drive and ingenuity," Dana Sue insisted. "You just need a new challenge that's more interesting than the annual hospital ball to kick 'em back into gear."

Maddie listened to the conviction in her friend's voice. She wanted desperately to believe her, but after the day she'd had, she didn't have the energy to do much more than eat shrimp and finish the glass of wine Dana Sue had poured for her. When she'd swallowed the last bite and taken the last sip, she stood up and gave Dana Sue a fierce hug.

"Thanks for being here for me."

"Anytime. You were there for me when my marriage broke up. This is the least I can do for you." She studied

Maddie worriedly. "You're not going home to sulk and undo whatever good I've done here today, are you?"

Maddie laughed. "No."

"What, then?"

"I'm going to go home and crunch some numbers and see if all three of us have lost our minds."

A grin spread across Dana Sue's face. "Well, hallelujah!"

"I haven't said yes yet," Maddie warned.

"But you're on the verge of it. I'm calling Helen."

"Don't. She'll just come over and pester me. It'll ruin my concentration."

"Okay, okay. I won't call her tonight, but I'm telling her first thing in the morning. Then you're all coming here after church to celebrate. I'll bring Annie and you bring your kids and your mom. We'll turn it into a party."

"Let's hold off on any celebrating. It might turn out to be a wake, if I decide the numbers don't make sense."

"We can wait but you won't," Dana Sue said confidently. "You seem to have forgotten how you helped me to squeeze every last penny till it squealed when I was opening this place. I'm sure you'll be just as creative with Helen's capital and my contribution."

Maddie shuddered. "*Creative* is not a word I like to hear associated with bookkeeping."

"Whatever," Dana Sue responded with a dismissive wave of her hand. "We're going to open a health club. How wild is that?"

"Pretty wild," Maddie confirmed.

Maybe flat-out insane.

Cal knew Maddie Townsend the same way he knew all the parents of the kids on the team, which was to say better than most teachers knew the parents of their students but far from well. Maddie had always impressed him by never missing a game and being one of those rare adults who didn't torment their kids with unrealistic expectations or him with irrational harassment when their sons were on the field. Her husband was the same way.

Today for the first time when she arrived in his office for their scheduled appointment he noticed deep shadows under Maddie's eyes and a nervous tic in her cheek. Despite the care she'd taken with her appearance, which would have passed inspection at some fancy Junior League function, she seemed uneasy about meeting with him.

"Should we wait for Dr. Townsend?" he asked.

"He's not able to be here," she said tightly.

Cal heard a faint note of bitterness in her voice. "Oh? I've never known him to miss a game or a meeting."

"Actually, I didn't tell him about this one. Tyler asked me not to."

"I see," Cal said, though he wasn't sure he did. "Is there some sort of problem between Ty and his father?"

She regarded him with misery and embarrassment in her eyes. "You may as well know that Dr. Townsend and I are getting a divorce."

Cal knew his mouth must have gaped at that, because she gave him a wry look.

"I know," she said. "I was shocked, too, and I lived with him."

"I'm sorry." The words seemed inadequate, but what else was there to say?

"Not your problem. Could we just focus on Ty, please?"

"Actually, I'm beginning to see what's going on with him," Cal replied. "He's been having a lot of trouble with school lately. I'm sure his other teachers have been in touch with you about that."

She shook her head. "I had no idea. He'd mentioned something about a couple of bad baseball practices, but that's it."

"Well, I'm sure they'll contact you before things reach a crisis stage—or perhaps you should take the initiative, just in case…"

"Just in case what?"

"Kids have been known not to take home notes they don't want their parents to see."

"Surely Tyler wouldn't," she began, then shook her head. "Of course he would. I'll call the other teachers as soon as I get home."

Cal gave her an encouraging smile. She looked as if she could use some moral support. "Hey, he's a good student. A few bad grades don't mean the end of the world. He'll catch up. More troubling to me is his complete lack of interest in his game. He excelled in his classes because he's smart, but he excelled in baseball not just because of talent, but because of his passion for the game. He seems to have lost that."

She sighed. "I thought as much, based on some of his comments to me, but to be honest, I have no idea what to do about it. Baseball was always something he and his dad shared. Bill's not particularly athletic, but he loved the game. He started taking Ty to Atlanta Braves games when he was a toddler. Then he coached him in Little League. I tagged along, but I didn't absorb much about the finer points of the game."

Cal gave some thought to the implications of that. "So, now that his dad's moved out," he suggested slowly, "Ty's rejecting baseball—either deliberately or subconsciously—the way he thinks his father's rejected him?"

She regarded him with surprise. "Why, yes. I think that's

it exactly." She leaned toward him as if he might have other answers to life's mysteries. "What do we do about it?"

Cal hated to admit it with her looking at him so hopefully, but he was as much at a loss as she was. Identifying the problem was a snap compared to solving it, but at least he now knew what he was dealing with. "Let me think about that and get back to you, okay?"

She nodded. "Anything you can suggest will be greatly appreciated. I wish I'd come to you sooner, but the divorce isn't something I've wanted to talk about."

Cal regarded her with sympathy. "No one does, which is probably why kids internalize their feelings."

"You're right again. Believe me, I want to see that old spark back in Ty's eyes when he walks onto a ball field. He needs baseball right now." She studied Cal worriedly. "He mentioned you might pull him from the starting rotation."

"I'll have to if he doesn't get his concentration back, but let's not get ahead of ourselves. Now that I understand what's going on, hopefully I can come up with some way to get him back on track. Maybe this is none of my business, but is the divorce final?"

"The paperwork's done, but we don't have the decree yet."

"Are things settling down some at home, though?"

"Some," she said in a tone that conveyed the opposite.

"They will," he said, feeling a sudden need to reassure her. It was almost as powerful as his desire to get Tyler back in his pitching groove. "I'll be in touch soon, Mrs. Townsend."

"Call me Maddie, please. I'd just as soon not be reminded of anything Townsend right now," she said, giving him a wry smile. "Besides, it makes me feel ancient."

Cal laughed at that. "You're hardly ancient. If I didn't

know you have a sixteen-year-old son, I'd swear you were my age."

Her cheeks turned pink. "Flattery won't get you much more than an extra batch of chocolate-chip cookies next time it's my turn to bake for the team."

"I'll take the cookies, but it wasn't flattery," he told her.

In fact, for the first time since his own divorce from a woman who'd married a baseball celebrity, not a has-been, he was actually feeling a stir of real interest in a woman, and age was the very last thing on his mind. Of course, given the multitude of complications involved, he'd have to be out of his ever-loving mind to do anything about it.

CHAPTER FIVE

The meeting with Cal Maddox had shaken Maddie more than she wanted to admit. Until now, Ty had been a near-perfect kid. He'd never given them any trouble. He'd made good grades and excelled at baseball. Now all of that was at risk. It made her see that building some sort of bridge between Tyler and Bill was more important than ever, but how could she possibly do that without further alienating her son, who claimed to be dead set against his father being in his life?

Maybe she was going to have to swallow her pride and go to Bill and plead with him to take the initiative and make more of an effort to understand his son's point of view. Perhaps if he realized what was at stake, he would keep Noreen out of the picture, at least when he was spending time with Tyler. Right now Bill seemed stubbornly determined to unite them into one big happy family, no matter how his children—especially Ty—resisted the idea. Maybe she could make Bill see how desperately Ty needed some one-on-one time with his dad.

Determined to fix things for her son's sake, she headed for Bill's medical office in a small brick complex he and a business partner had built several years ago. Its professional suites also housed a dentist and an orthopedic surgeon, as well as an outpatient rehab facility for the surgeon's patients.

She used her key and slipped in through the back door. It was the only way to avoid the waiting room and all the curious glances she was bound to receive there. Instead, however, she ran smack into Noreen, who was coming out of Bill's office with her lipstick smudged and her uniform mussed. Maddie had to wonder how the patients would feel if they'd witnessed the same thing.

"Maddie!" Noreen said, looking dismayed as she smoothed the wrinkles in her uniform. "What are you doing here? I had no idea you still had a key."

Maddie bit back an angry retort. The truth was that Noreen had more of a right to be here than she did and that grated.

"I need to see my husband. I gather he's in his office," she said and brushed right past Noreen without further comment.

When she firmly closed the door behind her, Bill looked up from the files on his desk and regarded her with uncertainty. "Maddie, I wasn't expecting you."

"Obviously," she said, noting the fact that his tie was askew and his thick blond hair was messed up. "You know, if you keep this up, your reputation in this town is going to suffer." She leveled a look into his eyes. "But then, Helen has already pointed that out, hasn't she? I'd recommend a few minutes in front of a mirror before you start seeing patients."

His cheeks colored, a sure indication of his embarrassment. "Why are you here?" he asked stiffly. "Just to pass judgment on me?"

"Not my job," she said briskly, fighting the urge to say a whole lot more. She couldn't afford to stir his temper, not when she was on a very specific mission.

"Did you come to apologize about Saturday?" he inquired. "If so, Noreen's the one you really should be talking to."

"Don't push me," she warned. "I'm here about Tyler. I just had a very distressing meeting with Coach Maddox."

Bill flashed her a startled look. "Why wasn't I told about a meeting?" he demanded.

"Because Tyler didn't want you there," she said bluntly. "And that's the heart of the problem. You asked me the other day to help you mend fences with Tyler. I can't do much more than tell him repeatedly that you're still his father and that you love him. Obviously he doesn't believe me. You're going to have to prove to him that your feelings for him haven't changed before he ruins his grades and his chances to become the pro ball player he's dreamed of being."

"What are you talking about?" Bill asked. "Ty's always had excellent grades."

"I haven't spoken to his teachers yet, but Coach Maddox has. Ty's having trouble in everything. I can only do so much. You're going to have to help me fix this."

To her surprise, Bill looked uncertain. "I don't know how," he admitted with rare candor.

"For starters, you could show up to pick up the kids when they're expecting you," she said. "Noreen is not an acceptable replacement, especially not to Tyler."

"He'll just have to get used to—"

Maddie cut him off. "You wanted to know what you can do, right? Then I suggest you listen to me. I'm trying to help before our oldest son spins completely out of control."

He exhaled an exasperated huff. "Fine. Whatever."

"Baseball brought you and Tyler together once," she reminded him. "I think that's the connection that can reunite you now. He's struggling, Bill. The coach says his pitching is off and his place in the starting rotation is at risk."

"That's absurd!" Bill snapped. "He's the best pitcher they have."

"Not right now, he isn't," she told him. "I think you need to come by the house—*alone*—and give him some pointers the way you used to."

"He'll never agree to that," Bill said. "He's not listening to me these days, much less spending time with me. If I show up, he'll just hide in his room."

"Then go to him where he can't hide," she suggested. "Stop by practice this afternoon. You used to do that all the time, just to hang out and see how he was doing. I know he loved that."

Bill's expression turned thoughtful. "I could," he said, then shook his head. "It might make things worse."

"You won't know till you try." She stood up. "I don't think I need to remind you how important this is."

"No, you don't," he agreed. "I'll make the effort, Maddie. I promise."

In the past she would never have questioned one of his promises, but these days she didn't really know this man at all. At least she'd made the overture. Now it was up to him.

"Today?" she said.

He hesitated and her temper stirred, but then he nodded. "Yes, today."

When she turned to leave, he stopped her.

"Maddie…"

"What?"

"Are you okay?"

"I'm fine," she said, forcing a cheery note into her voice. "Way too busy."

"Oh?"

His surprise rankled. Did he think she was sitting around pining for him?

"I guess you haven't heard," she said. "Helen, Dana Sue and I are going into business together."

He stared at her. "What kind of business?"

"We're opening a fitness club for women." She might not have made a firm decision before, but the incredulous expression on Bill's face was enough to solidify her resolve. Not that she was ready to tell Helen and Dana Sue just yet. "You'll have to tell Noreen all about the postpregnancy classes we're going to be offering. Maybe it will help her get her shape back. I noticed just now that she's put on a few pounds that pregnancy alone can't account for. I'm sure she must be aware of your tendency toward a wandering eye."

Before he could say a word to that sarcastic observation, she walked out, pleased that her announcement had left her husband speechless.

Bill stared after Maddie and wondered what had become of the pleasant, accommodating woman he'd married. He didn't know this confident, feisty woman at all.

Then, again, she bore an amazing resemblance to the girl he'd fallen in love with back in high school. It was only their early struggles and Maddie's determination to play the role of supportive wife that had changed her—and the way he'd looked at her—over the years. Her weight had played no part in it, despite what she'd said on her way out the door. He'd always thought she looked damn good, even with the few extra pounds she'd been unable to shed after her pregnancies.

His office door opened and Noreen came in, her expression uncertain.

"She was here because she wants you back, wasn't she?" she asked.

"No, she doesn't want me back," he told Noreen, knowing it was true and in some ways regretting it. "She needed to talk to me about Tyler. Will you look at my schedule this afternoon and make sure I can get out of here no later than four o'clock? If you have to reschedule a couple of patients, do it, or ask J.C. to cover for me."

Thank goodness Maddie had advised him last year to take on a new medical partner. His pediatrics practice had grown too much for him to handle and still have any sort of family life. J. C. Fullerton, who'd just completed his residency, had picked up the slack. J.C. was still single, young and energetic enough to relish the challenges of a demanding small-town practice. There were times when he wondered why Noreen hadn't focused her attention on J.C. rather than him. And truthfully, the fact that she hadn't had flattered him.

"Where are you going?" Noreen asked.

"I need to spend some time with Tyler."

"Want me to come along?"

He knew how sensitive she was about his kids, but he shook his head. "Not this time. I'm just going to stop by baseball practice and see how it's going. You'd be bored."

She rested a hand on her stomach. "I could learn to like it," she said. "After all, one of these days our baby might want to play baseball."

"I think that's a few years down the road, whether we have a boy or a girl," he said. "Now let's get started. Who's waiting for me?"

She looked as if she wanted to say more, but then her innate professionalism kicked in. "Mrs. Nelson is in room one with Jennifer. She says Jennifer's rash still hasn't cleared up. I'm putting Mrs. Davis and Martin in room two. He cut himself on a nail and she wants to be sure his tetanus shot is up to date."

Bill nodded. "See about fixing that schedule while I'm with them, okay?"

"Sure," she said, but she still didn't look happy about it.

He stopped on his way out the door and kissed her. "We're going to be okay, Noreen. It's just going to take some time."

Her blue eyes welled with tears as she looked at him. "I love you. You know that, don't you?"

"That's why I know it will all work out," he said and slipped past her, hopefully before she could tell just how many second thoughts and regrets were whirling around in his head.

Maddie stopped at Wharton's for a hot-fudge sundae on her way home. Learning that her son was in trouble not only on the ball field but in his classes, then giving her soon-to-be ex-husband a wake-up call had drained her. She needed chocolate. Over the years, she'd discovered that there was very little that couldn't be made better by thick, warm, gooey chocolate poured over vanilla ice cream, and no place in town offered a better sundae than Wharton's.

Slipping into a booth by the window, she toed off her high heels and sighed with relief.

"Another job interview?" Grace asked sympathetically.

"Not today," Maddie said. "Just a couple of meetings."

"Looks to me as if they didn't go well," the older woman said. "A hot-fudge sundae kind of day?"

Maddie gave her a weary smile. "Exactly."

"Coming right up."

Maddie closed her eyes as she waited, only to snap them back open when someone slipped into the booth opposite her. She scowled when she saw it was Helen. Normally that would have been a good thing, but right this second she was in no mood for a pep talk.

"You ever think of warning a person instead of sneaking up on them?" she snapped.

"Most smart people are more alert to their surroundings when they're out in public," Helen retorted mildly.

"It's Serenity, for goodness' sakes," Maddie said. "There haven't been a lot of assaults in Wharton's."

"Definitely moody," Helen assessed. "That fits. I was on my way home when I spotted your car. I thought you might want some company."

Maddie regarded her curiously. "Why would you think that just from seeing my car parked on Main Street?"

"It's outside of Wharton's in the middle of the day. That can only mean one thing—a sundae emergency."

Maddie laughed despite herself. "I'm making a vow right this second and you're my witness. I am changing my predictable ways."

"Really? How?"

"I'm not sure. I'll keep you posted." She shrugged. "Or maybe I'll just surprise you."

Grace returned with two hot-fudge sundaes. "Figured you'd be wanting one, too," she said as she set one in front of Helen.

"I was just going to taste some of hers," Helen complained. But she took a huge spoonful, then sighed blissfully.

Grace grinned. "From the looks of her, Maddie's not eating much these days. She needs every one of those calories."

"Hardly," Maddie said. "Since all this mess with Bill started, I've been stuffing my face with everything in sight. I weigh more now than I did right after Katie was born. Maybe opening a new gym *is* a good idea." She savored her first bite of the decadent hot fudge.

"Not a gym, a spa," Helen corrected.

"What's the difference?" Grace inquired, pulling a chair up to the end of the table without waiting for an invitation.

"For one thing, ours won't smell to high heaven like Dexter's," Maddie said.

Helen gave her a sour look. "It's more than that. We'll pamper women. We're going to offer facials and massages and a steam room and sauna."

"Really?" Maddie and Grace said at the same time. Grace sounded intrigued, Maddie skeptical. Saunas and steam rooms were bound to be expensive.

"Was that in the business plan?" Maddie asked.

Helen grinned. "We don't have a business plan," she reminded Maddie. "Unless you've written it. Have you?"

"I've made a few notes," Maddie admitted.

Helen tried unsuccessfully to hide a smile. "Interesting. Then you're on board?"

"Even though you were out of town on a case, I'm sure Dana Sue told you I was crunching numbers, so don't act so shocked," Maddie told her. "And I'm not on board. I'm exploring the situation."

"She's in," Helen said to Grace.

Grace chuckled. "I'd put money on that, too."

"Watch it, Helen," Maddie warned. "I'm not sure I want to go into business with a smug know-it-all. I can still look for another job. The Charleston want ads were fairly extensive in yesterday's paper."

"You'd spend every penny you earned on gas for the commute," Helen countered. "And you'd never have any time for the kids."

"The sacrifice might be worth it just to make sure you don't get your own way yet again," Maddie told her.

Helen held up her hands in a gesture of surrender. "I will await further word on your decision."

"A brilliant grasp of the situation," Maddie said approvingly. "No wonder you excelled in law school."

"Sarcasm doesn't become you," Helen said.

Maddie grinned. "Frankly, I'm rather enjoying this new, say-what-I-think side of me."

There was only one more week of baseball practice before the season opener. Even though he now had some idea of what was going on with his star pitcher, Cal still didn't have a plan for addressing the problem.

If it were entirely up to him, he wouldn't add to Ty's stress by threatening again to take him out of the starting rotation, but the school system, community and parents expected big things from the team this year. That was one reason they'd approved the funding for new bleachers and new sod for the field. A brand-new brick building had been added to house the refreshment stand and restrooms, as well. After all that expenditure, they wouldn't tolerate losses while Tyler tried to regain his emotional equilibrium.

That's what happened when a kid had played as brilliantly as Ty had last year. Expectations were high. Cal had even heard from a couple of Major League scouts who'd noticed media reports about the boy's skill on the mound. Unfortunately, if they saw him right now, they'd wonder what all the hype had been about.

Cal studied Ty's increasingly discouraged expression as his teammates hit pitch after pitch. He was about to join him on the mound for a chat when he spotted Bill Townsend climbing into the bleachers to a row that was shaded from the afternoon sun. Ty noticed his father at the same time. For an instant, based on the expression on Ty's face, Cal thought the boy might toss down his glove and stalk off the field.

Instead, though, Tyler seemed to reach down deep and

tap into all that anger. His next pitch flew across the plate at a burning clip, nicking the outside corner for a perfect strike.

"That was some real heat, Ty. Way to go!" the catcher said, tossing the ball back with a grin.

"I liked it better when I could see the ball coming at me," the batter grumbled, but there was admiration in his voice as well.

More than pleased, Cal wandered over and climbed onto the bleachers next to Ty's dad. "Glad you could stop by," he told him.

Bill gave him an odd look. "I assume you know why I've stayed away."

"Your wife mentioned the divorce," he admitted. "But I think you can see what your presence means to Ty. That's the first decent pitch he's thrown since spring training started."

"At least he's finally putting all that anger he feels toward me to good use," Bill said wryly.

Cal chuckled. "You got that, too?"

"Hard to miss. That ball would have taken my head off if I'd been in its path."

"You sticking around for a while?" Cal asked.

"Is it okay?"

"It's fine with me. I'm going to give the kids a break in a minute. Why don't you ask Ty if it's okay with him."

Cal went down on the field and called everyone on the team in. "You guys are starting to look like a team again," he told them. "Take five and get something to drink. It's important to stay hydrated in this kind of heat. After the break, we'll switch so the rest of you get a chance at bat. Ty, can you stay on the mound for some more batters?"

The boy gave him his once-familiar cocky grin. "You sure you want me to humiliate them like that?"

"You wish," his teammate Luke Dillon said. "I've hit three home runs off you since practice started."

"Pure luck," Ty retorted. "I'm back in the groove today."

"Maybe you shouldn't get too smug," Cal warned him. "A couple of outstanding pitches don't make a season."

"Don't even make a practice, if you ask me," Josh Mason, another teammate, said snidely. "Come opening day, I'll be on the mound. You wait and see."

"No way, sucker," Tyler retorted.

"Okay, enough," Cal told them. "Five minutes, guys. Tyler, why don't you check in with your dad."

Ty scowled at the suggestion, but he grabbed a sports drink and slowly headed for the bleachers. Cal noted that he didn't climb up beside his father but sat down several rows away. It was Bill who finally broke the awkward silence between them. Cal couldn't hear what he said, but Tyler responded with a nod.

At least the two of them were talking, or rather Bill was talking and Ty was listening. Cal wondered how long it had been since that had happened.

He also couldn't help wondering what Maddie had done to bring it about. He doubted it was a mere coincidence that Bill had shown up here today, just hours after Cal's meeting with her. However it had come about, though, he was grateful. Maybe it was a first step in getting his star pitcher back in his groove. Maybe he'd call Maddie tonight and report on the change.

"Idiot," he muttered to himself as he beckoned the players back. He was just looking for an excuse to call Ty's mother and that, as he'd warned himself only a few short hours ago, was a very bad idea.

CHAPTER SIX

"Dad came by practice today," Tyler announced nonchalantly while Maddie was on the patio grilling burgers for dinner that night.

There was a balmy breeze that carried the scent of charcoal through the air. It was one of those scents that always reminded Maddie of summer and childhood and picnics with her friends' families. Her own had never done anything as ordinary as cooking on a barbecue.

She glanced up and studied her son's expression. It was unreadable. "How'd it go?" she asked, careful to keep her tone neutral.

"Okay, I guess," he said. "At least he didn't bring Noreen with him."

"Did the two of you talk?"

"He asked me if it was okay for him to be there," Tyler said, sounding surprised. He met Maddie's gaze. "Do you think he really would have left if I'd asked him to?"

She knew what he was really asking—if she thought his opinion really mattered to his dad. For all his attempted indifference, Ty was desperate to believe that he still counted in Bill's life.

"I imagine that's why he asked," she said. "He wants you to be happy and successful. He isn't out to make your life miserable, Tyler. I think deep down you know that."

"He's done a pretty good job of it, anyway," Ty said with a trace of the familiar bitterness.

"What else did you all talk about?" Maddie asked, anxious to change the subject before Ty started dwelling on all the sins Bill had committed against him and their family, rather than the olive branch he'd extended.

"Nothing much. He gave me a couple of pointers on my fastball."

"Did they help?"

Tyler grinned and for just an instant, he was a self-confident, cocky kid again.

"Yeah, they helped. I threw some heat this afternoon," he exulted. "No one laid a bat on my pitches after that. They said I was awesome, that we're bound to win the state championship if I keep pitching like that. Even Josh Mason said I looked good, and he hates my guts. He wants that starting slot in the worst way."

"And Coach Maddox?"

"He said it was nice to see me remembering at least some of the things I'd been taught."

Maddie bit back a grin at the coach's laid-back response. "I suspect you were hoping for more enthusiasm."

"Naw, he says stuff like that to keep my head from getting all swollen."

She studied her son's happy expression and regretted that she was about to dash some of his excitement, but this was a conversation she couldn't put off. She'd hoped to temper it by fixing one of Ty's favorite meals.

What she'd learned from his other teachers this afternoon had shaken her. There wasn't even a single class in which his marks were above a C. Most were lower and in some he was even in danger of failing. All the teachers had sent home notes to that effect. Maddie had seen none of them. If those grades didn't improve, he wouldn't be playing ball, no matter how fast his pitching was.

"You know, Tyler, not everything's about baseball," she said.

"Everything that matters is," he contradicted, then grinned. "Come on, Mom. Can't you be excited for me?"

"I'm thrilled for you," she said honestly. "It's wonderful to see your enthusiasm for the game coming back, but you do have classes, you know. I spoke to all your teachers today."

His face fell. "How come?"

"Because Coach Maddox mentioned that you'd been having some problems."

"Why'd he do that? I thought he was just gonna talk to you about baseball."

"He assumed I already knew," Maddie said pointedly and watched Ty's face flush. "You need to remember that Coach Maddox is first and foremost a teacher, Tyler. He has to look out for your *whole* performance in school. If you start messing up in your other classes, you could be ineligible to play ball. It won't matter how well you're pitching if that happens. You'll let the team down."

"Oh, come on, Mom, get real," he said with disgust. "I'm not flunking anything. I bet not one single teacher said I was."

"No, you're not failing anything," she admitted. "Not yet, anyway. But they all said you're not working to your potential. For a kid who was getting all A's and B's last year, dropping down to C's and D's is only one step above failing." She leveled a look directly into his eyes. "That's not acceptable, Ty. I expect you to do whatever it takes to bring up those grades, understood? Until I see some improvement, I'm going to be checking every homework assignment and I expect you to show me every test paper."

"No way," he protested.

"That's the rule," she said firmly.

"Or?" The touch of belligerence in his tone set her teeth on edge.

"You don't want to know," she said.

"You gonna ground me?"

"That's one option," she agreed. "Letting the coach bench you is another."

Tyler gaped. "You wouldn't dare!"

"Try me," she said. Before he could escalate the discussion into an argument, she added, "But I don't think it's going to come to that. You're a very smart young man. If you're not doing well in classes, it's because you don't care, not because you don't understand the material. I'm just giving you the motivation to start caring."

"Well, your motivation sucks," he retorted. "I'll tell Dad."

Maddie bristled. "Don't try playing us off against each other, Tyler," she warned. "I think you'll discover that when it comes to what's best for you, Kyle and Katie, your father and I will always be on the same page."

Tyler cast one last incredulous look at her, then turned around and stomped into the house.

"Dinner's in fifteen minutes," she called after him.

"I'm not hungry," he called back.

"Then you'll sit at the table while the rest of us eat," she said.

When he was out of sight, she let out a sigh. Single parenting was turning out to be a whole lot harder than she'd ever imagined it would be. Sure, she knew Bill would back her up, exactly as she'd told Tyler he would, but taking an unpopular stance entirely on her own was something she needed to learn to do. It was something her kids needed to get used to, as well. If she messed up at this, it was her kids who'd pay the price.

But right this second, with Tyler suddenly regarding her as the enemy, she didn't feel even a tiny bit good about it.

Since everyone in Serenity seemed to be aware that Maddie was most likely going into business with her two best friends and opening a fitness club for women, she assumed the real-estate agent, an old high-school friend, wouldn't balk at letting her into the Hartley place so she could get a better idea of what renovations were going to be needed.

It took less than five minutes for her to get a call back from Mary Vaughn Lewis.

"Sugar, I've been expecting to hear from you," Mary Vaughn said. "Helen said I was to let you in whenever you wanted to see the place. I can meet you there in about ten minutes, as soon as Gaynelle finishes blow-drying my hair. Will that work for you?"

Maddie chuckled. "Since I know you'd never be seen in public with a single hair out of place, take fifteen minutes. I'll walk over."

On her way, she admired the bright pink, purple, white and red splashes of azaleas just popping into bloom thanks to the early spring heat wave. People in Serenity spent a lot of time in their gardens, even at the most modest homes. No one hired professionals. Kids earned extra money by cutting grass, weeding and mulching for elderly neighbors. Some of the azalea bushes were so old and so well nourished that they'd virtually overrun the smaller yards.

At the Hartley home, though, only one lone azalea had survived the years of neglect. Its dark pink blossoms provided a sign that there was still some life left in the place.

Maddie opened the front gate and grimaced at the screeching protest of the rusting hinges. She made her way carefully over the weeds growing up through cracks in the sidewalk. Dressed for the place's state of disrepair, she sat down on the front steps to wait for Mary Vaughn. As she waited, she tried to envision the front yard once again being a velvet carpet of green grass, the rosebushes back in bloom and the old wooden fence being upright white pickets. They could put wicker chairs and tables on the porch. She'd seen some cushions with big splashy roses on a dark green background that would be perfect.

She was so lost in her mental planning that she jumped when a shadow fell across the walkway right in front of her.

"About time you got here," she teased, then looked up, expecting to see Mary Vaughn. Instead, Coach Maddox stood there, his lips twitching with barely concealed amusement.

"I had no idea you were waiting for me or I would've been here sooner," he said.

Maddie winced. "Sorry. I thought you were the real-estate agent. She was due here fifteen minutes ago."

"Have you ever known Mary Vaughn to be on time?" he asked.

"Actually she's usually pretty prompt when there's money on the line."

"Unless I've got the rumors all wrong, the money from this sale is all but in the bank. That must be why she stopped me and asked me to tell you it would be another hour before she could get here. She has to show a house to someone who only has an hour to spare this morning." He reached into a pocket and retrieved a key. "Not to worry, though, she sent this along."

Maddie reached for the key, but the coach didn't release it. Somehow her hand wound up entwined with his. Enough electricity zapped between them to light the high-school ball field on a game night. Maddie's gaze locked with his as she grappled with the unexpectedness of her attraction to a man she barely knew. She supposed at some point she'd appreciate that her hormones hadn't died with her marriage, but right this second she wanted to sink through the porch floor. Given the rotted state of the boards, it wasn't entirely wishful thinking.

"Um, Coach, are you going to hand over that key? Or do I need to arm wrestle you for it?"

"That could be interesting, but actually I was hoping to get a look at the place with you," he said, releasing the key. "I've always wondered what this house was like inside."

"Aren't you supposed to be at school?"

"This is my planning hour. I usually try to get out for a walk or a run. It clears the cobwebs out of my brain. I'm not a morning person. If it were up to me, school would start around noon."

Maddie grinned. "Ty would agree with you about that."

"And you? When are you at your best?"

"The crack of dawn," she admitted. "My brain turns to mush later in the day."

He shook his head with a sad expression. "Ah, irreconcilable differences already. That's not good."

Maddie stared at him. "What?"

"Just teasing you, Mrs. Townsend."

"Oh," she said, feeling foolish. "But it's Maddie, remember?"

"Something tells me I ought to keep calling you Mrs. Townsend," he responded, his gaze never leaving hers.

"Why?" she asked, furious at the nervous hitch in her voice.

"To remind myself that you're a parent and I'm a teacher."

Maddie swallowed hard at the realization he was struggling with the same inappropriate attraction she was. "You could be right," she said, then tore her gaze away. "If you have a couple of minutes, come on inside and I'll give you the five-cent tour. I'm afraid it's not worth much more than that now."

"Sure," he said readily, following her into the house. He stopped barely inside the front door. "Man, this place is something."

"A mess?" Maddie asked.

"Not at all. It's got great bones. Tell me what your plans are for each of the rooms."

"Helen could do that better than I can," Maddie told him. "I've only been through the place once. That's why I came back this morning, to check out the validity of my first impression and make some notes on how extensive the renovations would need to be. Why don't you tell me what you see as we walk through. It'll be good for me to hear another perspective."

Cal shrugged. "Sure. I can do that. Should I keep a budget in mind or let myself go crazy?"

"I'm not sure we have the budget for crazy," she admitted. "Stick with practical. If this were going to be your gym, what equipment would you want? What extras would really matter?"

"Remember, I'm a guy and into sports," he said as if there were any doubt about that. "I might not want the same things your clientele is interested in."

"Still, I'm interested in your ideas and impressions."

To her amazement, his perceptions of the uses to which each room could be best put dovetailed nicely with her own. She suspected he'd choose dull, neutral colors for the walls, and he did. He was a guy, after all.

"Did I hear correctly that this place is only going to be for women?" he asked eventually.

Maddie nodded.

"Too bad. Men are pretty much sick of Dexter's gym too."

"Then open your own club," she suggested. "We want someplace special just for women."

"Have you come up with a name?"

She shook her head. "I haven't even agreed to this project yet. I suppose a name is one of the first things we'll have to discuss if we move forward."

"What's keeping you from jumping into this with both feet?" he asked.

"Fear of failure," she said honestly. "I'd especially hate to fail with Helen's money on the line."

"Is she worried about that?"

"No."

"And doesn't she have a reputation for being a good judge of character?"

Maddie nodded.

"Well, then, maybe you should trust yourself at least as much as your friend trusts you." He glanced at his watch. "I need to get back to school. Thanks for showing me around."

"No problem."

He started toward the door, then turned back. "Thanks

for getting your husband to come to practice the other day. It made a world of difference for Ty. A word of caution, though. Don't think everything's back on track just because of one good afternoon."

"Oh?"

"Ty's a teenager. Rebellion's second nature. Add in his issues with his dad and it's only a matter of time before the situation turns volatile again."

Maddie knew he was right, but she wanted to cling to the illusion that things were under control, at least for now. "Will you warn me if you hear anything at school or if he gives you any problems at practice? I'm trying to keep a closer eye on his grades, but Ty's gotten pretty good at keeping important things from me. And maybe especially now, since I told him there'd be severe consequences if he doesn't get his grades up. He might very well keep trying to hide notes or report cards from me."

"So I'll be your early-warning system," he said. "I'll tell you if I notice anything or hear about any problems from the other teachers. This time of year, I pay close attention to the grades of my players. And if you ever have any concerns, just give me a call."

"Thanks for caring so much about my son," Maddie said sincerely. "He looks up to you."

"It's not a one-way street," Cal told her. "Ty's going to be a baseball superstar one of these days. Being a tiny part of making that happen makes me feel as if my life after baseball has some meaning."

Maddie heard an unexpected note of melancholy in his voice and wondered if he even knew it was there. "It must have been tough having your dream end so quickly."

"It was baseball, not life or death," he said cavalierly.

"Smart people don't wallow in self-pity. They find a new dream."

"And yours is coaching high-school baseball?" she asked.

"That's just part of it," he said.

"And the rest?"

He hesitated, then said, "I think we'll save that for another conversation. If I'm late getting back to school and my PE class starts running wild on the playground, my coaching days could be over. See you, Maddie."

"Yeah, see you."

She stood in the doorway and watched as he went down the walk, opened the rusty gate and set off at an easy jog. She watched until he turned the corner and disappeared.

Mary Vaughn strolled up the sidewalk from the opposite direction. "Whoo-ee, that is one incredible specimen of a man," she said. "If my heart didn't belong to Sonny, I would surely take up jogging just so I could run a few laps behind that very fine derriere." She grinned at Maddie. "How about you, sugar? Does he give you any interesting ideas?"

"None I care to share with you," Maddie responded, laughing. In truth, most of her ideas about Coach Maddox were too hot to be shared with anyone, including her best friends. Helen and Dana Sue wouldn't be shocked, but they would be highly motivated to get her what they thought she wanted. There was nothing a Sweet Magnolia enjoyed more than planning a seduction.

Maddie was sitting on the floor up to her eyeballs in calculator tapes and notes when her doorbell rang that night at eight. Only Helen and Dana Sue would risk her wrath by showing up at that hour when the kids were winding down upstairs and Maddie wanted nothing more than to relax with a glass of wine and a long soak in the tub. Before she could even scramble to her feet, the two of them walked in, gloating expressions on their faces.

"I brought Erik's famous chocolate-decadence cake," Dana Sue said, holding it out as if it was a peace offering. Her pastry chef had won the hearts of everyone in town.

"And I brought bubbly," Helen said, displaying a bottle of very expensive champagne.

"Are we celebrating something?" Maddie inquired innocently.

"I told Mary Vaughn to set up the closing on the Hartley place," Helen said. "It'll be ours before the end of the month."

"Isn't that fantastic?" Dana Sue asked. "We're opening our own spa!"

Maddie wanted to share their enthusiasm, but at the moment she was merely annoyed. "Have either of you actually heard me agree to this yet?"

"No, but all the signs were there," Helen said blithely. "Why wait?"

"Because it's common courtesy," Maddie snapped. "You can't snatch a decision this big out of my hands. I have half a mind to walk away right this second, if this is the way things are going to go, with you two bullying me into doing whatever you want."

"Hey, slow down," Dana Sue soothed. "Nobody's bullying anybody. Helen can call and back out of the deal right now if that's what you really want."

Maddie sighed impatiently. "No, that's not what I want. I just want to be asked. I want my opinion to count for something."

Helen sat down on the floor beside her. "Of course your

opinion counts. That's why I acted. I could see it in your eyes the other day. You want to do this but you're scared. I thought maybe it would be easier if the whole decision didn't rest on your shoulders."

Maddie regarded Helen with renewed respect. "You got that?"

"Well, of course I did. How long have we known each other?"

"Long enough," Maddie said. "If I actually count the years, it depresses me. None of us are supposed to be that old."

"We're not old," Dana Sue said vehemently. "We are in the prime of our incredible lives."

Helen laughed. "Indeed we are!" she said, popping the champagne cork. "The Sweet Magnolias are all grown up and about to take this town by storm once again. I think that deserves a drink."

"I'll get the glasses," Maddie offered, but Dana Sue was already on her way to the kitchen. That was the thing about best friends, she supposed. Sometimes they just acted without waiting to be asked. How could she be mad at them for that?

"Do you know how much I appreciate you two?" she asked when Dana Sue returned with three of her best crystal champagne flutes.

"Enough to go into business with us?" Helen pressed.

"Even more," Maddie said with heartfelt sincerity. She lifted her glass. "To the Sweet Magnolias."

"To us," Dana Sue said.

Maddie sipped her champagne and giggled as the bubbles tickled her nose, robbing the moment of its solemnity. "What now?" she asked.

"I think we should name this fancy new place of ours,"

Dana Sue said. "It'll make it seem more real. We can't refer to it as the old Hartley place forever."

"You're right," Helen said. "We need to get some buzz going."

"I don't think buzz will be an issue in Serenity," Maddie said wryly. "Everyone in town already knows what we're up to. Just today Coach Maddox asked why we couldn't let men in, too. And I doubt he's even lived here long enough to be very high up on the town grapevine."

Helen gave her a speculative look. "Coach Maddox, huh? Another meeting to discuss Ty?"

"No, he brought me the key to open up the house. Mary Vaughn was running late."

The other two women exchanged a look.

"Interesting," Dana Sue said.

"Isn't it, though?" Helen said.

Maddie gave them a disgusted look. "Whatever you're thinking, forget it. We need to concentrate on coming up with a name, remember?"

"Cal Maddox is a name," Dana Sue taunted.

"Ha-ha," Maddie replied. "Do we want to call it a gym, a fitness club or a spa?"

"A spa," Helen said at once.

Maddie regarded her doubtfully. "Are you sure that's not too fancy for a place like Serenity? People might think we're too expensive or exclusive or something."

"She has a point," Dana Sue said. "We don't want women thinking we're too uppity for them."

"Then work with me," Helen said. "Put something with it that tones that down, something simple that makes it seem accessible to everyone."

Suddenly Dana Sue's eyes lit up. "I have it!" she said enthusiastically. "Where is this house?"

Maddie tried to grasp her point. "On the corner of Main and Palmetto."

"Exactly," Dana Sue said. "So why not call it The Corner Spa?"

"It sounds cozy," Maddie agreed slowly. "Helen? What do you think?"

"I love it," she said at once. "The Corner Spa it is. Who knows, one of these days there might be one on a corner in every small town in America."

"Maybe we ought to get the doors open on this one and see if anyone comes before we start thinking about expansion," Maddie cautioned.

"It never hurts to dream big," Helen chided. "You used to. You just got out of the habit."

Maddie considered the comment. Maybe Helen was right. Maybe her dreams had spent too many years taking a back seat to Bill's, so many years, in fact, that she'd forgotten all about them.

"That changes tonight," Maddie told them. "From this moment on, I'm going to start dreaming again."

Dana Sue grinned. "I wonder if Coach Maddox is going to figure in any of those dreams?" she asked Helen.

"Is there any doubt?" Helen responded. "I've had a few X-rated dreams about that man myself."

"He's my son's baseball coach!" Maddie said indignantly.

"Meaning I'm not allowed to have wild thoughts about him because your son would be shocked?" Helen teased. "Or are you simply staking ownership?"

"Oh, go suck an egg," Maddie retorted, because she didn't dare answer Helen's question. If she admitted to the jealousy that had streaked through her at Helen's not-so-innocent comment, she'd never hear the end of it.

CHAPTER SEVEN

On opening day of the baseball season, Cal was aware of the precise instant Maddie Townsend showed up with Ty's brother and sister. With his baseball cap pulled low and his sunglasses on, he was able to take a good long look at her tanned legs in a pair of khaki shorts, white sneakers and tennis socks, and the turquoise T-shirt that she'd tucked securely into the waistband of her shorts. It was no more revealing than anything she'd worn to a game before, but now he allowed himself to admire every line and curve of her excellent body.

He was pretty sure he didn't take another breath until he saw Bill Townsend climb into the bleachers and take a seat beside her. Katie immediately crawled into her dad's lap and Kyle traded places to be next to his dad. If Cal hadn't known better, he would never have questioned that they were anything but a typical family.

After watching them a moment longer, Cal exhaled and forced his attention back to the field. He didn't want to observe their interaction and start speculating on whether Bill and Maddie Townsend were making an attempt at reconciliation. To avoid that kind of speculation, he needed to focus on the moment.

In Cal's experience, the opening game of the season had an air of anticipation that couldn't be equaled. It had been true for the first game of spring training when he'd been with the Braves. It had been true for the start of the regular season, as well. In high-school sports, there was the same atmosphere of excitement. In fact, he'd found it even headier in high-school sports, when half the town showed up to cheer on the local team. There was an aroma of hot dogs and popcorn in the air, the sound of the baseball slapping into the catcher's mitt, the exchange of greetings among parents and neighbors. He reveled in all of it, glad he'd discovered this job and this town.

"Okay, guys, this is it," he told the boys gathered around him. "Don't try to do too much out there tonight. Just relax and play your best. Ty, is your arm feeling okay?"

"Never better," Ty said distractedly, his gaze on his mom and dad in the stands as if he, too, wondered what might be happening between them.

"Ty!" Cal said more forcefully than he meant to.

The boy's attention snapped back to him. "Sorry, Coach."

"Baseball's a game of concentration," Cal reminded all of them. "You can't have your mind wandering when you're on the field, okay? That's how balls wind up dropping into the gap and pitch counts get away from you."

"Got it," they chorused dutifully, Ty included.

When his team took the field, Cal watched them with pride. They were a good group of kids. One or two even had some real talent, though none had the potential Ty exhibited. He was their star, and though Cal tried not to play favorites, they all knew it. But if Ty pitched the way he was capable of, the team would win, and that's what most of them cared about.

When the first three batters struck out, Cal let himself

relax. After Luke Dillon hit a home run, the first inning ended with the team up by one. Sometimes, if Ty was in his groove as he appeared to be tonight, that was all they needed.

The second and third innings were more of the same. Ty threw strikes and the opposing team went down in order. The Serenity Eagles added two more insurance runs.

But in the top of the fourth inning, something went wrong. Ty walked the first batter. He threw a lazy, ill-considered pitch to the next hitter and the ball went into center field, scoring one runner and leaving the batter on second base with a solid double.

Cal felt his stomach sink. He waved at the umpire and walked out to the mound, along with the catcher. "What's up, Ty?"

"Nothing," he said tightly.

His catcher, John Calhoun, gave him an incredulous look. "You had nothing on those pitches, Ty," he accused. "You ignored my signals. You gotta get your act together!"

"Is your arm hurting?" Cal asked. "Do you want to come out?"

"No way," Ty replied, scowling at both of them, then looking away.

Cal followed the direction of Ty's gaze and spotted a young, obviously pregnant woman with her arm linked possessively through Bill Townsend's. Katie was now in her mom's lap and Kyle had moved to Maddie's other side.

So, Cal thought, that was the reason for the divorce and the explanation behind Ty's sudden loss of concentration. No wonder the kid was furious with his dad. What kind of man flaunted his new girlfriend—his *pregnant* girlfriend—in front of his wife and kids when his divorce wasn't even final? Until this instant, Cal had always respected Bill

Townsend, but at the moment he wanted to throttle him for his lack of sensitivity—even if it did mean Cal now knew the Townsend marriage was truly over.

"Ty, you have to shake it off," he said quietly. "Nothing that happens off this field matters right now."

"I hate her guts," Ty said bitterly, not even trying to pretend he didn't know what Cal was alluding to. "Why'd she have to show up here? It's embarrassing. It's bad enough that she goes out in public with him, so everyone in town knows he was cheating on my mom. Coming here proves she just wants to be in my mom's face."

Cal glanced at Maddie and saw that her gaze was riveted on the field. When Ty looked her way she gave him a smile and a thumbs-up.

"All your mom cares about right now is you," Cal said.

"But I can't pitch worth a damn with that woman here," Ty said angrily.

"Yes, you can," Cal told him. "Remember what happened when your dad showed up at practice and you pictured him in the middle of the strike zone and threw right at him?"

A slow grin spread across the boy's face. "It brought me right out of my slump," he said, immediately grasping Cal's point.

"Exactly. Use that same technique right now. We're still leading by two runs. It's not too late to save this inning and keep them from scoring again."

Ty nodded, then glanced at his catcher, who'd remained diplomatically silent during the whole exchange about Ty's dad. "You ready for some heat, Calhoun?"

"Bring it on," John said.

"Let's do it, then," Cal told them. He walked back to the bench, but instead of watching the field, he directed a look up at Bill. When he finally caught the man's attention, Cal shifted his gaze to the woman with him and gave a subtle shake of his head. Not five minutes later, he noticed that both of them were gone. He'd counted on Bill to recognize that he was at the root of Ty's lack of concentration and to do what was best for his son. To his credit, he had.

Cal glanced at Maddie and thought he read relief in her expression, too. If he examined his motives closely, he wasn't entirely sure whether he'd forced the issue for her sake or Ty's. Something told him it was a toss-up.

"Mom, Coach Maddox is taking us all out for pizza," Tyler told Maddie after the game. "Can I go?"

"Of course you can," she said at once. "You deserve a celebration."

"I want pizza, too," Katie said with a pout. "Why can't we go?"

"Because it's a team celebration," Maddie told her. "We'll order pizza for you and me and Kyle at home."

"Why don't you come with us," Cal invited. "Once we get to Rosalina's, the boys pretty much ignore me. I could use some adult conversation." He glanced at Ty. "Would it be okay with you if your mom, Kyle and Katie came along?"

Pleased that Cal had been considerate enough to ask Ty's opinion, Maddie studied her son's face. "It's okay to say no, Ty. We don't want to intrude if it would make you uncomfortable."

"Would you guys sit at another table?" he asked, clearly searching for a compromise that wouldn't be an embarrassment for him.

She grinned. "Absolutely. No one will even know we're with you."

"Then it's okay with me," he said with a shrug.

"We'll see you there, then," Maddie told the coach. "Does anyone need a ride?"

He shook his head. "I've arranged for a school bus to drop them all off. The parents will pick them up there in a couple of hours."

"See you in a few minutes, then."

In her car, Maddie barely resisted the urge to check her makeup. This wasn't a date, for goodness' sakes. Cal had asked her to join him and twenty kids. He'd probably just wanted another chaperone.

"I like Coach Maddox," Katie said from the back seat of the car. "He's nice."

"You just like him 'cause he said we could come for pizza," Kyle complained. "Nobody asked *me* if I wanted to go."

Maddie realized with a sudden rush of dismay that he was right. It used to be that Kyle always spoke up and said what he wanted. Since his dad had left, he'd been too quiet. He did what was expected of him but rarely volunteered any of the joking comments they'd all grown used to from him. The silence made it easy to forget that he needed some attention and consideration, too.

"You love pizza and you've always liked hanging out with Tyler and his friends," Maddie said. "I guess I just assumed it would be all right with you. Was I wrong? Would you rather go home?"

"No!" Katie whined. "I don't wanna go home."

"Oh, who asked you, you big baby," Kyle muttered, then added grudgingly, "We may as well go. Katie's going to act like a baby otherwise."

"That's enough!" Maddie said. "If the two of you can't speak nicely to each other, we *will* go home and there won't be any pizza." She glanced in her rearview mirror and saw the two of them scowling at each other. At least she'd succeeded in silencing the argument.

"I expect both of you to be on your best behavior at Rosalina's," she warned. "Otherwise, we're out of there."

Kyle gave her an oddly knowing look. "You're trying to impress Coach Maddox, aren't you?"

"Don't be silly," Maddie said, though she was probably turning a dozen different shades of pink.

"Then how come you looked all weird when he asked us to come with the team?" he persisted.

"Weird how?"

"I dunno. Sorta like the way Patty Gallagher looked when Tyler invited her to the spring dance."

"Your brother asked a girl to a dance?" Maddie asked. It was the first she'd heard about it.

Kyle grinned. "You shoulda heard him. It was really lame, but I guess Patty didn't care 'cause she said yes."

"What about you?" Maddie asked. "Did you invite anyone to the dance?"

"Not me," Kyle said adamantly. "Who wants to get all dressed up and go to some stupid dance?"

"You will when the right girl comes along," Maddie said.

"No way, not after seeing Ty get all tongue-tied and dopey," Kyle insisted. "It was disgusting. At least Coach Maddox wasn't that bad when he asked you out."

Obviously her younger son had developed keen powers of observation. Maddie was going to have to watch herself around him. "Coach Maddox didn't ask me on a date," she reminded Kyle. "He was including all of us in the team's celebration. I thought it was nice, that's all."

"Yeah, right."

Maddie ignored his sarcasm as she turned in to the packed parking lot behind Rosalina's. She finally found a space way back in the last row. Both kids bolted from the car.

"Hurry up, Mom," Katie commanded. "Me and Kyle are starving."

"I'm gonna get us a table," Kyle told her, then took off at a run.

Maddie had a hunch he simply didn't want to be seen walking into the place with his mother and sister on a Friday night. If there was a table in a darkened corner of the room, she'd bet that's the one he'd choose. Fourteen was an incredibly awkward age, too young to drive but already fascinated by girls and thinking about dating—despite claims to the contrary.

Inside, though, she found him standing with Coach Maddox right in the center of the main room. The team was seated around a long stretch of tables that had been pulled together.

"I thought Kyle might want to sit with the team, if that's okay with you," Cal said. "Then you, Katie and I can sit over here where there's at least a slim possibility we'll be able to hear each other."

Maddie glanced at Kyle. There was no mistaking the eager expression on his face. "Just don't bug your brother," she advised him.

"I won't. I promise."

She waved him off to join the team, then gave Cal a look of gratitude. "Thank you for saving him from a fate worse than death."

"Being seen with Mom on Friday night?"

"Exactly."

"I was a teenage boy once, too." He pulled out a chair for her and then did the same for Katie, who seemed completely taken aback at being treated like a grown-up lady.

"I think I owe you for something else you did tonight, too," Maddie told him as she accepted the menu he held out. Now that she was here, breathing in the rich scents of tomato sauce, garlic and the yeasty, thick crust that was Rosalina's specialty, she realized she was as starved as the kids.

"Oh?" Cal asked. "What did I do?"

Maddie lowered her voice so Katie wouldn't overhear. "Bill left and took Noreen with him because of some signal you sent him, didn't he?"

Cal shrugged, looking vaguely embarrassed. "I have no idea."

Maddie regarded him skeptically. "Come on, tell the truth. How'd you manage to get him out of there? Maybe it's a technique I can use when he doesn't have the sense to keep that woman away from us."

"I think he just realized that her presence was upsetting Ty's game," Cal said.

"He's usually too self-absorbed to realize something like that," Maddie persisted, then glanced at her daughter to make sure Katie's attention was elsewhere before adding, "Since you didn't climb into the stands and shake him the way I was tempted to, you must have given him some sort of subtle man-to-man signal."

"It was nothing." Cal glanced deliberately at Katie. "How much pizza can you eat, young lady?"

"Lots and lots!" she said eagerly.

"What kind?"

"Just cheese."

He turned to Maddie. "And you?"

"A couple of slices and a small salad will do it for me." As hungry as she was, she had her limits.

"Just cheese?"

"Unless you'd rather have yours loaded up with extras. I can eat anything."

"Nope. Just cheese works for me." He beckoned to the waitress, the dark-haired, dark-eyed daughter of the owners, "One large cheese pizza, one small salad, one large salad and Cokes all around." He glanced at Maddie. "Is that okay?"

"Perfect," Maddie agreed.

"Put that on the same bill with the team's and I'll take care of it," he told the waitress, who beamed at him with adoration.

"Sure thing, Coach," Kristi Marcella said. "I heard you're off to a great start this season. There are a lot of happy folks in here tonight—I should make great tips. Last season was the best one I've had since my folks made me start waiting tables in here."

"Glad to help," Cal said, chuckling as Kristi left to place their order.

"Must be nice to know you're doing your part for the local economy," Maddie told him. "I wonder what happens when the team loses."

"Tips go down and beer sales go up," he said succinctly. "If we can keep Ty focused and healthy, hopefully that won't happen this season."

Maddie smiled. "I'm sure the waitstaff at Rosalina's would appreciate that. Of course, Kristi's folks might appreciate the beer sales more."

"Mom, can I have some quarters to go play the games?" Katie interrupted. "Danielle's over there with her mom and dad."

"I have plenty of quarters," Cal said, pulling a handful from his pocket. "I always stock up when I'm taking the team out. Treating them to pizza and video games keeps morale up." He handed a few quarters to Katie.

"Thanks," she said.

"If Danielle and her parents leave, you come right back here," Maddie instructed her.

"Okay."

She turned back to Cal. "I probably should know this, but are you originally from a small town? You seem to have fit right in here."

He shook his head. "Cincinnati, actually, but it's a city that loves its baseball. My dad used to talk about the days of the Big Red Machine with Pete Rose and Johnny Bench. He got me hooked on baseball before my sixth birthday. I never wanted to do anything else."

"He must have been very proud when you made the majors," Maddie said.

Cal's expression sobered. "He never got to see me play in them. He died of a heart attack while I was still down in the minors."

"Losing him like that must have been hard."

"Worst time of my life. Maybe that's why I see what's happening with Ty. Divorce isn't the same as death, of course, but when you've shared a dream with someone and they aren't around to see you've fulfilled it, it's tough. At least Ty and his dad have a chance to change that."

"If only my soon-to-be ex wouldn't ruin the fragile peace by bringing his new girlfriend around," Maddie lamented.

"I think maybe he got the message tonight," Cal said. "If not, I'll explain it to him next time I see him." He studied her. "It can't be easy for you, either, him showing up with her on his arm, especially with the divorce not even final and her being, well, so obviously pregnant."

Maddie started to shrug it off, but then changed her mind and opted for honesty. "It sucks, but I'm an adult. I can learn to deal with it for the sake of the kids. And I have my pride, too. Having me pitch a fit or look wounded only makes things hard on the kids, especially Ty. He's old enough to get that his dad didn't just fall for someone else, he cheated on me. The whole baby thing really upsets him."

"I gathered that," Cal said. "What about you?"

"It's a slap in the face, no question about it," she admitted. "Every time I see Noreen, there's no way to pretend that she and my husband weren't sleeping together long before he got around to telling me that our marriage was over."

"I'm sorry."

"It's hardly your fault." She met his sympathetic gaze. "Want to know the real kick in the pants? I'm the one who hired her for his office. Not only was she an experienced nurse, I thought her perky personality meant she'd get along great with his patients. I just never envisioned how well she would get along with my husband."

"Do you blame him or her for what's happened?"

Maddie considered the question. "As much as I'd like to lay it all squarely on her, there's no doubt Bill was equally to blame. And maybe if I'd done more, been a better wife somehow, it would never have happened."

Cal regarded her with dismay. "Wait a second! Surely you're not blaming yourself."

"If my marriage had been a good one, Bill wouldn't have strayed," she insisted. "I bear at least some of the responsibility."

"I don't get that. Did you have any idea your marriage was in trouble?"

"None," she conceded. "And by the way, you sound exactly like Ty. He says the same thing to me."

"Because he's a smart kid. How were you supposed to fix your marriage if you didn't even know it was broken? Don't lay the blame at *your* feet," he said. "I've been around a lot of guys who don't think twice about having a little fling when their team is on the road. Men can always come up with some excuse to get themselves off the hook—the women are too available, too eager, it's lonely on the road, whatever. The bottom line is it's their choice. It's their decision to ignore the vows they took on their wedding day, nobody else's."

Maddie studied him curiously, wondering about the vehemence in his voice. "This sounds like something that really resonates with you. Were you married? Did you ever cheat on your wife?"

"I was married, but I never cheated on her."

Then she got it. "But she cheated on you, didn't she? While you were on the road?"

He shook his head, looking distinctly uncomfortable. "Actually, it was after my injury, when she realized I wasn't going to play ball professionally again. It gave her the perfect excuse to move on to one of my teammates—his face was still going to be showing up in the sports pages. It broke up my marriage and his. Worse, it was a guy who'd stuck by me while I was doing rehab, a man I considered a good friend. I had no idea just how accommodating he was also being with my distraught wife."

"Oh, Cal, I'm so sorry. That must have hurt."

"Let's just say it gave me some real strong feelings about personal accountability between a man and a woman who've vowed to love each other through thick and thin."

He picked up his soda and took a long swallow. When he met her gaze again, his expression was perfectly bland. If she hadn't seen the turmoil in his eyes just a few seconds earlier, she would never have known how deeply the conversation—and the memories—had upset him.

Fortunately, the pizza arrived just then. As if her radar had sensed its arrival, Katie returned and there was no chance for Maddie to ask any of the questions that came to mind. One of these days, though, she thought she might ask Cal Maddox how a person ever got over a betrayal like that. Maybe it would help her figure out how to move on with her life.

Maddie was pacing the floor, her heart in her throat. Ty had asked if he could stay a little longer at Rosalina's and catch a ride home with Luke Dillon and his dad. With Luke by his side assuring her it was no problem, she'd given him permission, but reminded him of his 11:00 p.m. curfew.

Now it was midnight and he still wasn't home. She'd been about to try his cell phone, then saw it lying on the kitchen table. A call to the Dillons only added to her fears. Jane Dillon said Luke had come in with his dad a half hour earlier. After checking, she said Tyler hadn't left Rosalina's with them. Luke had no idea where he might have gone.

"Believe me, I intend to speak with Luke about his role in all this," Jane assured Maddie. "Let me know if there's anything we can do to help you track him down, okay?"

After speaking to Jane, Maddie debated calling Bill, but instead it was Cal Maddox's number that she sought out and dialed. She told herself it was because he'd still been at Rosalina's when she left and might know something. She doubted he would have allowed Ty to leave alone if he'd seen it happening.

"Maddie?" Cal asked groggily. "What's wrong?"

"Ty hasn't come home. I just spoke to Jane Dillon. She says Ty didn't leave with Luke the way he said he was going to. Luke has no idea where he's gone. Did you see him leave? Were they together then?"

"They walked outside together, so I assumed Luke's dad was waiting for them in the parking lot," Cal said. "Don't worry, Maddie, we'll find him. I'll be right there. I'll call some of the other boys on my way."

"You don't need to come over," she said, embarrassed. She'd awakened him out of a sound sleep to deal with her problem.

"I'm on my way," he repeated firmly. "This is my fault. I should have been paying closer attention."

By the time Cal swung his car into the driveway, Maddie was frantic.

"Have you found out anything?" she called before he'd even set foot on the front porch.

"I talked to half a dozen of the guys on the team and they all said Ty left Rosalina's when they did, but none of them was sure how he was getting home or if he planned to go someplace else."

"Dammit. I never should have agreed to let him stay," Maddie whispered. "I should have known—"

"Come on now," Cal soothed, draping an arm around her shoulders and giving her a reassuring squeeze. "He told you he was getting a ride with Luke. Luke even confirmed it. Why would you doubt that?"

"I should have checked with Luke's dad. That's what I usually do, but I was distracted."

Cal gave her an odd look. "By me?"

Now Maddie felt like even more of an idiot. "That's not the point," she said hurriedly. "I have to find him. If Bill finds out Tyler has taken off to who knows where, he'll accuse me of being neglectful. He'll probably be thrilled to have something he can throw in my face."

"I think you should call him, anyway," Cal said.

"If I thought he'd know where Ty is, trust me, I'd call, but he won't. Bill is the last person Ty would turn to."

"Let's go inside and talk about this."

"I won't change my mind," she said stubbornly. Inside, she headed for the kitchen and her third cup of chamomile tea. "Would you like some?" she asked Cal. "Or I could make a pot of coffee."

"How about some bottled water instead?" he asked.

"Sure." She grabbed a bottle out of the fridge. Then she sat down wearily and sipped her already cool tea. When she finally met Cal's gaze, she felt completely at sea. "What do I do now? Tyler's never done anything like this before. He's never blown his curfew, not without calling, anyway. And he's been even more careful lately because he doesn't want to upset me."

"With teenage boys, there's a first time for everything. He probably just had some thinking to do."

Maddie regarded him skeptically. "My son is not known for sitting around pondering life. He's more likely to be somewhere getting into mischief."

Cal nodded slowly. "Okay, then, I have a couple of ideas. How about I go look for him? I'll keep in touch or you can call me on my cell phone if he turns up here."

"I want to go with you," Maddie said at once.

"What about Kyle and Katie? Is there someone who can come and stay with them?"

Maddie hesitated. She could call Helen or Dana Sue. In fact, Dana Sue was probably just closing up the restaurant, so she wouldn't even have to wake her. But she didn't want to involve anyone else in this, at least not until she knew it was a real crisis.

"You go," she said at last. "I'll stay here by the phone in case he calls."

"Maddie, he's going to be fine. You'll see," Cal reassured her. "I'll find him and have him back here before you can heat up another cup of tea."

"Thanks," she said, grateful for the reassurance, even though she wouldn't be entirely happy until her son walked through the front door.

And then she was going to strangle him.

CHAPTER EIGHT

Cal had a pretty good idea where he'd find Tyler. Despite the fact that he'd regained his concentration during the game and the team had won, Ty was a kid who held on to his failures longer than he savored his triumphs. Cal had a hunch he'd find him back at the ball field reliving every minute of that one nearly disastrous inning.

Sure enough, when he drove up, in the faint illumination from the streetlights, he was able to spot a figure hunched over in the bleachers. The boy didn't even move when Cal cut his headlights and engine. Before exiting the car, he made a quick call to reassure Maddie.

"Thank God," she said.

"Give me a few minutes to see if I can find out what's going on with him, then I'll bring him home, okay?"

"Thank you, Cal."

"See you soon." He turned off his cell phone, quietly closed the car door, then walked slowly over to the bleachers. The grass was damp with dew and the air thick with humidity, though the temperature had dropped considerably since game time. There was something oddly unsettling about a ball field draped in shadows and filled with silence. Yet it had been Cal's retreat, as well, whenever he'd had things he wanted to think through.

"Hey, Ty," Cal said.

When the boy looked up, the despair and misery in his eyes was enough to make Cal's heart ache.

"I thought it was my mom who'd found me," he said. "How come you're here?"

"Because your mother's at home worried sick about you. It's past your curfew, Luke Dillon and the other kids had no idea where you'd gone, so your mom called me."

Tyler looked even more surprised. "How come she didn't call my dad?"

"Is that what you were hoping she'd do?"

Ty reacted with defiance. "No, but it's what she usually does."

"I guess she thought tonight I might be more help."

Tyler gave him a knowing look. "Probably because she knew he wouldn't want to crawl out of Noreen's bed at midnight."

Cal bit back a chuckle. He didn't want to encourage the boy's disrespectful attitude toward his dad. "I don't think that entered into it." He sat down beside him. "You want to talk about what's going on with you, or are you ready for me to take you home?"

Ty shrugged. "What's there to talk about? What kind of ball player am I going to be if I freak out every time my dad brings his girlfriend around?" Color flooded his cheeks. "I guess you saw she's gonna have a baby. I mean, how disgusting is that?"

"That innocent baby will be your little brother or sister," Cal reminded him. "How do you feel about that?"

"It sucks," Ty said bitterly. "My mom tries to act like it

doesn't matter to her, but I know better. Why can't my dad see that bringing Noreen around is really mean?"

"You could tell him how much what he's doing bothers you," Cal suggested. "You could tell him how you felt about his girlfriend showing up at the game. It might clear the air between you if you were honest with him."

"Like he'd care about my feelings," Ty said.

"He left tonight, didn't he?"

"Yeah, but probably because Noreen was bored."

"I don't think that was it. I think he saw how upset you were. Talk to him, Tyler. He's your dad, no matter what. He wants the best for you, especially when it comes to baseball. He'll understand."

"But none of that's the point, not really."

"Then what is?"

"I should be able to handle it," Ty said, being way too hard on himself. "What he does shouldn't matter to me, not when I'm on the field." He gave Cal a plaintive look. "You said it yourself. Baseball's all about concentration."

"Sometimes that's easier said than done," Cal observed. "You'll learn how to forget about everything else, Ty. That comes with experience. Or you'll learn how to make it work for you, just like you did tonight and the other day at practice. You applied your feelings to your pitching and threw some of your best pitches ever."

Ty's expression brightened at last. "I did, didn't I? How come I keep forgetting that?"

"Because you're too caught up in what went wrong. Try to remember what went *right* out there."

"Like the fact that nobody got a bat on any of my pitches in the last innings of the game," Ty said, suddenly gloating. "I guess that was pretty awesome."

Cal grinned. "I wouldn't get too cocky if I were you.

You might be the night's superstar, but you still have to go home and apologize to your mom. Something tells me she's not going to let you off the hook as easily as those batters did tonight."

Ty sighed heavily. "Yeah. She's gonna ground me for life."

"Could be," Cal agreed. "Come on, kid. Time to go face the music."

"Will you come in with me?" Ty asked hopefully.

Cal shook his head. "I think you and your mom need to settle some things. I'll just make sure you get safely inside."

Tyler met his gaze. "Thanks for coming to get me. How'd you know where I'd be?"

"I was a kid once, too," Cal told him. "And the ball field was where I felt most at home. It still is."

Ty nodded. "Yeah, for me, too."

Maddie was waiting on the porch when Cal pulled up at the house. She stayed right where she was, giving Ty room to come home like the man he would soon be, rather than the confused kid who'd taken off and worried her. Cal gave her a lot of credit for the wisdom and restraint it must have taken her to do that and not run to her son and drag him into her arms.

Ty turned to Cal. "I'll see you Monday—if I'm allowed out of the house," he said, only partially in jest.

"I'll see you then," Cal told him, responding with more confidence. He trusted Maddie to balance punishment with wisdom. She wouldn't take away baseball, not when it was Ty's only lifeline lately.

He watched as Ty walked slowly toward his mom, then ran the last few steps when she opened her arms. As she held him tight, she gave Cal a wave and mouthed, "Thank you."

He reversed his car to back onto the road, then drove

away, but not before taking one more glance back to see Maddie still clinging to her son. Somewhere deep inside, he wished he was a real part of that scene, wished he'd be going inside with the two of them, meting out punishment to Ty, trying to coax a smile out of Maddie, then spending the night with her wrapped in his arms.

It was the kind of dream he hadn't allowed himself since his marriage crumbled. The kind of dream he shouldn't be having about Maddie Townsend. But something about the woman pulled at him and he had a hunch that sooner or later he was going to do something about it, no matter how much havoc it might cause.

Maddie was still in her bathrobe and the much-needed coffee was still brewing when Helen knocked on the kitchen door Saturday morning. There was only one reason Helen would show up at the crack of dawn. Somehow she'd already heard about Maddie's evening with Cal and she'd come for a firsthand report. Maddie opened the door reluctantly.

"You're certainly out early," she said.

"I came by for coffee and information." Helen regarded the still-brewing coffee with dismay. Then she perked up. "I guess we'll have to start with the information."

"I've got all the figures on the spa in the other room," Maddie said. "I'll go get them."

"Not that kind of information," Helen said.

"Oh?"

"I want to know if the rumors are true."

"That depends on what you heard, now, doesn't it?"

"Don't play coy with me," Helen said. "Did you or did you not have a date with the high-school baseball coach last night?"

"I did not," Maddie said. Under Helen's relentless gaze, she finally sighed. "Okay, I had pizza with him after the game, but it wasn't a date."

How many times was she going to have to have this conversation? Given Serenity's fascination with gossip, most likely quite a few. So she'd better get the story down pat.

"Not even close to a date," she said emphatically. "My kids were there. The entire team was there. I know I'm hopelessly out of practice, but I don't remember dates being like that."

Helen looked disappointed. "No kissing?"

"None."

"No hand-holding?"

"Afraid not."

"Long, smoldering looks?"

Maddie hesitated just long enough for Helen to seize on it.

"I knew it! There *is* something between you and the coach. Way to go, Maddie!"

"Oh, come on. He's a nice guy, but he's at least ten years younger than I am. He's worried about his star player, that's all."

"If he was only worried about Ty, he'd be giving him extra practice time, not huddling over pizza with his mom."

"And Katie," Maddie reminded her.

"Yes, I'm sure your six-year-old was an excellent chaperone," Helen conceded dryly. "Did she ask him what his intentions were toward her mom?"

"Hardly."

"Then you can't say for sure that Cal didn't think of it as a date or at least a pre-date."

"What on earth is a pre-date?"

"An innocent meeting between two people who are seriously considering dating," Helen explained. "To test the waters, so to speak. Will you admit to that much, at least?"

"Obviously last night was a mistake," Maddie muttered.

Helen regarded her incredulously. "Why? You were out with a gorgeous guy who jump-started your hormones. What's so bad about that?"

"I never said he jump-started my hormones," Maddie objected.

"Oh, please, not even twenty years with Bill the Dull could have wiped out all your libido," Helen said, using the nickname she'd pinned on Bill long before she'd begun to think of him as Bill the Scumbag. "And you wouldn't be this uptight about all my questions if there was zero attraction."

Maddie gave in to the chuckle. "Okay, I have noticed that Cal is attractive. It's possible I might have had one or two erotic daydreams about him, but that's it. You've admitted to having a few hot and steamy thoughts about him yourself. I doubt we're alone."

"But he never invited me out for pizza," Helen reminded her. "Or any other woman in town that I'm aware of."

Maddie shook her head. "Forget it, Helen. The situation is impossible."

"Not so impossible," Helen argued. "He asked you out after the game, didn't he?"

"I explained that," Maddie retorted, relieved that apparently no one in the neighborhood had noticed Cal's late-night visit and reported on that, too. It would be a whole lot harder to explain why she'd called him, not Bill or even Helen or Dana Sue, in a crisis.

"Not very effectively," Helen said.

"My point is, if you've heard all about this innocent evening less than twenty-four hours later, then the entire town will know by noon. The last thing I want or need right now is to be the subject of more gossip. Bill's caused more than enough of that."

"Oh, but this is such a nice way to even the score," Helen told her. "I'd like to be a fly on the wall when Bill hears about this."

Maddie was forced to admit—at least to herself—that she wouldn't mind being one, as well. Last night with Cal hadn't been about revenge, but if a couple of hours with a gorgeous man annoyed her soon-to-be ex, so much the better.

Deliberately changing the subject, she said, "As long as you're here, let's make a few plans for the spa. I could use some idea of your budget for the renovations. Were you thinking of applying for a small-business loan? We could qualify. I can pick up the paperwork first thing Monday."

Helen regarded her knowingly, but didn't call her on the abrupt change of topic. "We don't have time to waste applying for a loan. On Monday the three of us can go down to the bank and open an account for the business. I'll put fifty thousand dollars in there to get us started. Then you'll be able to pay the contractors and give yourself a salary."

"Absolutely not," Maddie said, trying not to show her surprise at the figure Helen had tossed out with such nonchalance. Add in the down payment on the building, and she was putting serious money into this project. "I'm not going to take one dime out of the business until it's up and running. It's bad enough that you're providing almost all the financial backing. I don't want you supporting me, too."

"But you're going to be putting in all the hours," Helen argued. "Obviously you should get paid. That way you won't have to touch the alimony and child support Bill will be paying except for emergencies."

"No way. Not until we open our doors," Maddie insisted. "That's a deal breaker for me. I will not be your personal charity case."

Helen looked as if she wanted to continue the debate, but finally, obviously noting the stubborn set of Maddie's chin, she backed down. "Then we'll just have to schedule the opening in two months, instead of six."

Maddie stared at her in shock. "Two? Are you crazy? No contractor around here can work that fast. We haven't even closed on the house yet." She frowned at Helen. "Is there something I'm missing? Do the alimony payments only last a few months?"

"With me as your lawyer?" Helen scoffed. "Don't be ridiculous. That money will roll in for ten years or until you remarry. And it's not a pittance, either. I'm talking about what's fair here. If you do the work, you should be paid. As for the closing on the house, I can hurry that along. And the contractors will do whatever we need them to do, if we pay them enough."

"You'll blow the budget to smithereens," Maddie protested.

"It's only money," Helen said with a shrug. "And as my doctor has been reminding me lately, my obsession with acquiring money is likely to drive me into an early grave. I figure spending some of it might counteract that."

Maddie studied her friend. "Just how bad is your blood pressure?"

"Bad enough," Helen said. "Working out at the spa is going to fix me right up, though, which is another reason for rushing things along."

Maddie frowned at her. "Maybe in the meantime, you should dump out that coffee. Caffeine can't be good for you."

Helen clutched her mug of coffee a little more tightly. "I need the caffeine."

Maddie plucked the mug out of her grasp and poured the coffee down the drain. She did the same with what remained in the pot, just so there'd be no temptation.

"I could really hate you for that," Helen grumbled.

"You'll thank me when you get a good report from Doc Marshall next time you see him. Now, I think we should go for a long walk. I'll go get dressed. You call Dana Sue."

"Fine, whatever," Helen responded. "Just hurry up so we can get out of here before it gets so hot we melt. You know how Dana Sue complains if she sweats."

"Well, she'll just have to get over it. From now on we're all about sweat," Maddie said. "Isn't that the whole point of our spa?"

"I imagine our mamas would insist we merely glow. Southern girls are not meant to sweat," Helen drawled, sounding exactly like her mother, who was now "glowing" at a retirement community in Boca Raton, where she spent her days playing tennis and golf, all thanks to Helen's money.

"We won't get in shape by just glowing," Maddie countered. "I'll be back down here in ten minutes. Tell Dana Sue we'll be by to pick her up in twenty."

"It takes twenty minutes to walk to her house," Helen protested.

Maddie grinned. "Exactly, which is why we're going to jog."

Helen groaned. "My God, we've created a monster."

Bill was sitting in the living room when Maddie got home from her walk with Helen and Dana Sue. She'd left the two of them at Dana Sue's commiserating about her conversion into a drill sergeant.

"I didn't expect to find you here," she told Bill after she'd grabbed a towel out of the guest bathroom and dried her face. "I thought you were going to call before coming by."

"I'm scheduled to pick up the kids," he said. "Do you want me to call for that, too?"

"No, I suppose not. Aren't they ready to go?"

"I told them I needed a few minutes alone with you first," Bill explained.

"Oh?"

"I didn't expect to hear about you cavorting around town with Cal Maddox, Maddie." Bill's tone was scathing. "What on earth were you thinking? He's our son's coach, for God's sake!"

"And your point is?"

"You'll embarrass Ty."

She cut him off. "You really do not want to go there," she said. "If you do, I'll be forced to say some very unpleasant things about Noreen's untimely arrival at the ball field last night." Ty had admitted to her that that had been the reason for his disappearance. He'd gone to the ball field to think things through. She'd promised not to tell his dad, but maybe Bill needed to hear about it.

"I know it was a bad scene," he admitted. "I'm sorry. I had no idea she was going to show up. She's not the least bit interested in baseball."

"But you are," Maddie said. "And she knew I would be there. Do you honestly think she wants the two of us there together without her supervision?"

"Apparently not," he said, running a hand through his hair. "Maddie, I have no idea what to do. I really don't."

"Oh, please, you're not some helpless victim, Bill. Just

tell her to stay away," she suggested. "She's a grown-up. I'm sure she can handle it. Those games are about your son, not about her insecurities. Her presence on his turf upsets him even more than when you insist on trying to throw them together. Surely you saw that for yourself."

"Of course I did," he said. "And if I hadn't, Coach Maddox made it plain enough after he had his chat with Ty on the field." He gave her a weary look. "I heard he pitched great after we left."

"He did. I'm sorry you had to miss it."

"Maybe you and I could alternate going to the games," he suggested.

She stared at him incredulously. "Just so you can take Noreen? I don't think so."

"No, that's not what I meant. It's just that if you're not going to be there, maybe she won't feel so insecure about me going without her."

Maddie hated letting that woman have that much power over them, but after some thought, she was forced to concede that maybe a compromise was in Ty's best interests. "I'll go along with that for now, but only for Ty's sake, not yours and not Noreen's," she said. "That changes at the end of the season if they're playing for the championship. We both need to be there for those games."

"Sure," he said, looking relieved. "Maybe by then the divorce will be final. I think that will help, too. Noreen's still got it in her head that you want me back. I doubt she'll believe otherwise till the ink's dry on the divorce decree."

Maddie gave him a bland look. "Want me to put it in writing for you now? I don't want you back, Bill."

"Because you've suddenly developed the hots for Coach Maddox?"

She held on to her temper by a very fragile thread. "No,

because you're an idiot," she snapped and headed for the stairs. "Get the kids and let yourself out. And leave your key on the table. Don't come by again without calling first, not even for one of your scheduled visits with the kids."

"Maddie..." he called after her.

Ignoring him, she went into the bathroom and turned on the shower so it would drown out whatever excuses he might be making for having suddenly turned into the biggest jerk in all of South Carolina.

Well, that certainly hadn't gone the way he'd expected, Bill thought as he drove away from home. Not home, he corrected. Maddie's house. He had to get used to the idea that he no longer lived there, no longer had the right to come and go as he pleased, even if it was the home that his parents had lived in before them, and his dad's folks before that. Maddie had certainly made it abundantly clear that he was no longer welcome there. Reluctantly, he'd left his key behind, just as she'd asked.

Worse, the kids had refused to go with him. Apparently they'd overheard enough of his argument with Maddie to be more ticked off at him than usual. Maybe not Katie, but she wouldn't go, either, not with Ty and Kyle giving her warning looks.

He debated going back to Noreen's apartment, but the prospect of being shut inside that cramped space all afternoon set his teeth on edge. He'd promised her weeks ago that they'd find someplace bigger before the baby came, but he'd been putting it off. Maybe on some level, he was the one who kept hoping Maddie would decide she wanted him back. Hearing about her date with Cal had pretty much squelched that fantasy.

Helen, who normally got on his last nerve with her smug,

wise-ass mouth, had been right about one thing during that acrimonious settlement meeting. He and he alone was responsible for the mess his life had become. It was up to him to make the best of it.

Hitting speed dial on his cell phone, he called Noreen. For better or worse, she was the woman in his life now. He owed her. And if he thought about it hard enough, he could even recall a time when he'd loved her or at least been infatuated enough to leave his marriage for her.

"Hey, sweetie, where are you?" she asked.

He bit back an impatient retort, telling himself it was entirely possible her question had been nothing more than an innocent inquiry. "I was just driving back home and decided I'm starved. Want to meet me for lunch? The kids aren't with me."

"Really?" she asked.

Bill winced at the pleased surprise in her voice. When had she realized that their relationship no longer meant as much to him as it did to her? He needed to work harder at changing that, for both their sakes.

"Sure. What sounds good to you?" he asked.

"Just about everything," she admitted. "My appetite's gone through the roof."

He laughed. "Yeah, I remember..." His voice trailed off as he realized she wouldn't want to hear about his memories of Maddie's pregnancies. "How about we take a drive over to the coast? We'll find someplace outside to have a burger and fries, maybe take a walk along the beach."

"That sounds wonderful," she said, though her voice had gone flat. She must've known he'd been about to talk about Maddie.

"I'll swing by and pick you up. I should be there in a couple of minutes."

"I'll be ready," she promised. "Love you."

"You, too," he said, regretting he couldn't put more feeling into the words.

God, he'd made such a mess of things, and all because for a very short time Noreen had made him feel young again. Maddie was right. He was an idiot. And now a whole lot of people he cared about were paying the price.

"I never liked him," Maddie's mother declared when Maddie stopped by to pick up the kids from another consolation visit after they'd refused to go anywhere with Bill.

When Maddie had asked them what they wanted to do, all three said they wanted to spend time with their grandmother. Fortunately her mother had readily agreed to take them to lunch and rent a video for them, once again surprising Maddie. She was equally surprised by her mother's claim that she'd never liked Bill.

"You did, too," Maddie said. "You adored Bill."

"Did not," Paula insisted, sitting back on her heels in her garden, her gloved hands covered with dirt and her eyes flashing.

There was no question that this well-tended garden with its bright splashes of snapdragons, delphinium, verbena and exotic flowers Maddie couldn't even name was her mother's milieu. And even streaked with dirt, she looked amazing. Wisps of hair had escaped her straw hat and curled about her cheeks. Her dark blue eyes were the same shade as the delphiniums.

"I said I liked him for your sake, because for some inexplicable reason he seemed to make you happy," her mother told her. "Your father and I always thought you deserved better."

"At the moment, I can't argue that," Maddie said. "But I

loved Bill. For most of the last twenty years he was a great husband and a terrific dad. When I'm not busy being furious, I can admit that a part of me still loves him."

"You'll get over it," her mother said brusquely. "Just think about him cheating on you. That ought to keep your dander up and your sorrow at bay."

Maddie shook her head. "You're not being overly sympathetic, Mom."

"You don't need sympathy. You need a swift kick in the pants. Find a job you love, then go out and find yourself someone new. I always liked what that writer Dorothy Parker had to say."

"Which was?"

"Living well is the best revenge."

"I have a job. I'm surprised you haven't heard."

Her mother met her gaze. "You mean that spa you, Helen and Dana Sue intend to open?"

"Then you *did* hear."

"I had no idea you were serious about that."

"Well, we are," she replied with a touch of defiance.

"It's a great idea," her mother said.

Expecting disapproval, Maddie was about to utter another defiant comment when she realized what her mother had said. "You think so?"

"Well, of course I do. The town can use a place like that." She pulled the gardening gloves off her hands, which were rough and worn from yard work, despite her sporadic attempts to protect them. She held them out for Maddie's inspection. "I would give anything to have someone do a warm-wax treatment on these poor old hands of mine, then give me a proper manicure."

Maddie grinned at her. "Your first one's on the house," she promised.

"You all won't get rich giving things away," her mother chided.

"We will if you go out and tell your friends how fabulous we are," Maddie countered.

Her mother chuckled. "I knew that business degree wasn't a total waste."

"Then you were the only one holding out hope it would come in handy," Maddie said dryly. "At least a few things are coming back to me. I just wish I knew how to handle everything else that's going on."

"Such as?"

"I think Ty's in real trouble," she admitted.

"He's a teenager. It comes with the territory," her mother replied. "Maybe you don't remember your teens that well, but I do."

Maddie shook her head. "No, it's more than that. One minute he's blowing off baseball, acting like he doesn't care about it. The next he's back on track. I never know what to expect."

"Again, he's a teenager. Kids' interests change every twenty minutes at that age."

"Mom, you know better than that. Ty's lived and breathed baseball since he was in Little League. And then there's what happened last night." She gave her mother a brief rundown of Ty's disappearance, leaving out the part about Cal rushing to the rescue.

"His coach is worried about him, too," she summed up.

Her mother's eyes immediately brightened. "Now *there's* a hottie, Madelyn. Maybe you should have yourself a fling with him."

Even though the same thought had crossed her mind, she felt compelled to utter a protest. "Mother! He's ten years younger than I am if he's a day."

"So what?"

She used Bill's objection. "He's Tyler's coach."

Her mother grinned. "Again I ask, so what?"

"It would be…" Words failed her.

"Hot," her mother said. "I think I can guarantee that." She gave her a penetrating look. "And from what I hear, you know it, too. Otherwise you wouldn't be spending time with him. I know all about the two of you huddled together at Rosalina's last night."

"Of course you do," Maddie said, resigned to the fact that there probably wasn't a single human being in Serenity who didn't know about it. "We had pizza after a game, surrounded by a bunch of kids. Does everyone in town have an opinion about that?"

"I'm guessing yes. Cal's a very popular young man. A lot of women in Serenity have their sights set on him. A lot of mothers are gearing up to do some serious matchmaking."

"You included, apparently."

"Well, why not?" her mother demanded. "What's good for the gander is good for the goose. A fling with a man like Cal would undoubtedly put some color back in your cheeks."

Maddie sighed. She'd come over here hoping that for once her mother would act like, well, a mother, rather than a free-spirited woman who lived by her own rules. Growing up with Paula Vreeland, a talented botanical artist and gardener, had been unconventional in many respects. Her mother and father were more likely to take her on an impromptu trip to a gallery opening in New York or a tour of a world-class botanical garden than to an amusement park. Dinner was often leftover caviar and pâté from some party they'd hosted for friends and artists from Charleston, rather than meat and potatoes.

In the quiet, traditional town of Serenity, they'd been regarded with a certain wariness. Only the fact that both had been born and raised right here and had extensive family throughout the state had kept them from being labeled eccentric and treated as outcasts. There had been plenty of times as a kid when Maddie had craved normalcy.

Since Maddie's father's death two years ago, her mother had become even more unpredictable and outrageous. What kind of proper Southern mother recommended that her daughter have an affair with the high-school baseball coach? The entire town would be scandalized.

Giving her mother a strained look, she said, "I honestly don't know what made me think you'd be a help."

Her mother chuckled, clearly not offended by the comment. "Oh, sweetie, I have been. You just don't see it yet."

CHAPTER NINE

After her conversation with her mother, Maddie was reluctant to call Cal to thank him for his help with finding Ty on Friday night, even though she knew she owed him a huge debt of gratitude. Surely by now he, too, was taking heat for the time they'd spent together, or maybe men didn't have friends and relatives who felt a need to meddle in their lives. Anyway, she was probably the last person he wanted to hear from.

Still, despite her parents' other eccentricities, she'd been schooled in proper manners since birth, so Sunday evening she forced herself to pick up the phone and deal with her jittery nerves as she waited for him to answer.

"Maddie," he said at once.

"Since I haven't even said hello, you must have caller ID." Her nerves immediately settled at the warmth she heard in his voice.

"Yes, and I've been forced to screen calls all weekend."

"Let me guess. They've been from the well-meaning and the curious," she said.

"Something like that." His tone was wry. "You, too?"

"You have no idea," she responded. "I guess that pizza

Friday night turned us into hot news for the weekend. I probably should have warned you about that. It was evidently a headline-worthy event on the gossip circuit."

He laughed. "Believe me, I've lived in Serenity long enough to know that a bachelor's life is not private. I've had five calls today alone from mothers and grandmothers offering candidates better suited for me than a mother of three going through a divorce. Although, other than the existence of your children and the impending divorce, you'll be happy to know they all had nice things to say about you."

Maddie groaned. "I'm so sorry."

"Not your fault. The pizza was my idea. And believe me, I enjoyed it."

"Me, too," she admitted. "But what did you get in return? A frantic phone call waking you out of a sound sleep and a late-night hunt for my son, to say nothing of a dose of Serenity's finest meddling."

"Not a problem," he said. "It's all part of the service a coach provides for his team and their families."

Being lumped in with the other team parents dulled any fantasies Maddie might have been harboring. She told herself it was just as well.

"Maybe so," she said, "but that's why I called. I wanted to thank you again for finding Ty. You were a godsend. I have no idea how you knew exactly where to look for him."

"Instinct. I was a lot like him when I was that age and the ball field was my safe haven. I got a lot of thinking done late at night on bleachers just like those. I still go there when there's something on my mind."

"Is that where you decided that playing pro ball was what you wanted to do?"

"Yes, and it was where I finally realized that I needed to go to college first, just in case my career didn't play out the way I envisioned it. Given how things turned out, that was the smartest decision I ever made." He hesitated. "Or maybe the second smartest."

"What replaced it as the smartest?"

"Moving to Serenity," he said at once. "Even with my life around town an open book, I like it here. I enjoy working with the kids. I get a lot of satisfaction out of seeing a young man like Ty really begin to shape up into a fine ballplayer with Major League potential. I owe a real debt of thanks to the man who convinced me my life wasn't over after baseball."

"Sounds as if you'll stick around, then," she said, more relieved that he was content living here than she cared to admit. "I wondered if living in a small town might not be enough for a guy who's had his share of celebrity and traveled to some of the most fascinating cities in the country."

Even as she spoke, she realized how much this conversation meant to her. There was a tiny spark of something between her and this man, and she wanted to see where it led—even as she told herself what a lousy idea it was.

"Celebrity's not all it's cracked up to be," he said. "I learned that the hard way. You can get hooked up with people who never see the real you."

"Your ex-wife, for instance?" Maddie asked.

"Yeah, she'd definitely be on that list. As for big cities, they have their charms, but a visit from time to time is enough for me. Serenity is the kind of place to raise a family. What you describe as meddling, I view as neighbors caring about each other."

She allowed herself a secret smile. "I've always felt that way, too, about the town, though, not about the meddling. I thoroughly enjoy Charleston. I love going to New York for a few days of shopping, seeing some great theater and visiting the galleries. San Francisco is charming and Seattle is gorgeous. But in the end, Serenity is home. I love the way we go all out for the holidays, the summer concerts at the park, the community picnic and fireworks on the Fourth of July. I like going to Wharton's for a sundae just the way I did when I was a kid and knowing that my kids will have that same memory. It's a great place to grow up."

"But it sounds like you've traveled a lot, too," he said.

"My mother's an artist. She's had shows all over the country. Even when I was little I always went with her and my dad."

"Really? Don't tell me your mother is Paula Vreeland!"

"She is," Maddie said, surprised.

"Wow! She's amazingly talented."

"You know her?" she asked.

"I ran into her at a gallery over in Charleston one day. I was buying one of her works and she complimented me on my taste right before the gallery owner introduced us. Her fame is the pride of Serenity, but I hadn't made the connection between the two of you."

"Well, you definitely impressed her," Maddie said, thinking of her mother's description of Cal as a hottie. She'd wondered how her mother happened to know anything at all about the baseball coach. Now, it all made sense.

"I doubt she'd even remember me," he said. "We only chatted for a few minutes."

Maddie wasn't about to tell him her mother hadn't been fascinated by his conversational skills. Nor did she want to mention that Serenity hadn't always been so boastful about her mother.

"I've kept you long enough," she said hurriedly. "It's Sunday night and you must have a million things to do for school tomorrow. I just wanted you to know how much I appreciated your help on Friday night."

"Is Ty doing okay?" he asked, not sounding all that eager to end the call.

"He seems to be. At least he hasn't kicked up a fuss about being grounded. He knew that was coming after the stunt he pulled. School, baseball practice, games and home. That's it for the next two weeks."

"I'll see to it he goes straight home," Cal offered. "I can drop him off after practice if you like."

"Probably not a great idea," she said.

"Are you sure? It's no big deal. Really."

"It would be to some people. Thanks for offering, though. Good night, Cal."

"See you soon."

Even after he'd hung up, she clung to the phone a moment longer, not wanting to break the connection. He was just being nice, she told herself firmly. That was all.

But it had felt a whole lot as if Cal Maddox was turning into a man she could count on. Was that a good thing? she wondered. Or should she be totally focused on learning to stand on her own two feet?

Cal felt as if he were fourteen again and in trouble with the principal. The minute the school secretary called his office Monday morning and told him that Betty Donovan wanted to see him immediately, he guessed it wasn't to praise him for the baseball team's victory on Friday night.

Come on. Just because you have a guilty conscience doesn't mean everyone is bent out of shape because you spent some time with Maddie Townsend, he tried to reassure himself as he headed for the principal's office.

Serenity High School had been built years ago with wide

hallways, linoleum floors that were polished weekly and classrooms with high windows that looked out on a grassy slope in front of the building and on ball fields in the back. He imagined that nothing much had changed beyond a fresh coat of paint since the years when Maddie had attended this same school. The upgrades to the baseball field and the addition of a new cafeteria and gymnasium had come only after long and contentious debate among the local residents who'd had to provide the funding for them.

The principal's office was a cramped space that seemed designed to add to the tension of anyone obliged to enter. Betty Donovan's own preference for stark, unrelieved walls and uncomfortable wooden chairs added to the prisonlike atmosphere.

Cal told himself that was why his nerves worsened when he walked into Betty's office, but the truth was that her troubled expression made him wary. Though she was probably around the same age as Maddie, Betty tended to do everything she could to minimize her attractiveness. She wore severely cut clothes in dark colors, little makeup and kept her hair pulled back in a tight knot. She'd been a principal for a number of years now and he had a hunch she'd chosen her attire and demeanor to impress the older, more experienced teachers with her solemn dedication to duty. And, as a side benefit, she scared the kids to death.

Usually he liked to do whatever he could to coax a smile out of her, but today he was too anxious. Besides, she was clearly in no mood for jokes.

"What's up?" he asked, sitting on the edge of the chair across from her. "You look worried."

"I've been fielding a lot of phone calls this morning."

"About?"

"You and Maddie Townsend."

Even though he'd prepared himself for exactly this, Cal felt his hackles rise. His personal life was none of the school's business. Not that there was anything to tell about him and Maddie. Yet, he amended.

Meeting the principal's gaze evenly and struggling to keep his tone neutral, he merely said, "Oh?"

"Were you two at Rosalina's together on Friday night?" Her tone made it an accusation.

"Yes, along with the entire team and Maddie's other children. Is that some sort of crime?" he asked, anger seeping into his voice. He tried to tell himself Betty was just doing her job as she thought it needed to be done, but her criticism of something that had been totally innocent grated.

She had the good grace to flinch, but then she gathered her composure and pressed on. "Of course not, but this is a small town, Cal. Our teachers are expected to be above reproach."

"What the hell are you suggesting?" he demanded, losing his cool. "Is there something the least bit inappropriate about me having pizza with the parent of one of the team's players, especially when that player has been going through a lot lately and his mother needed some advice?"

Betty regarded him sympathetically. "I'm sure that's all you meant it to be, but people tend to read things into situations."

"They speculate and gossip, you mean."

"I'll say it again—Serenity is a small town."

"Then shouldn't people know Maddie well enough, and me, too, for that matter, not to let their imaginations run wild?"

"I'd hope so, but it's not always the case," she told him. "A word to the wise, Cal. Make sure you keep things on the straight and narrow with Mrs. Townsend. I don't want to spend my days defending you, when there are far more important things I need to accomplish at this school."

"I'll keep that in mind," he said tightly, already determined to do just the opposite, assuming Maddie hadn't had her fill of well-meaning advice and determined that seeing him was more trouble than it was worth.

Betty must have picked up on his belligerence, because she said, "Cal, you're a terrific physical education teacher and a great coach. Please don't do anything you—or I—will come to regret."

He walked out of the office ready to pound something. It was a good thing he had baseball practice in a couple of hours. He'd swing the bat and give the kids some fielding experience. And every time the bat made contact, he'd picture Betty Donovan's self-righteous face on the ball.

Then, once he'd worked off his frustration, perhaps he'd be able to accept that there was a tiny nugget of wisdom in what she'd been telling him.

Helen was waiting with three contractors and Dana Sue when Maddie arrived at the Hartley place on Monday morning at eight. She regarded them with confusion.

"I thought we were just going to make some final notes on what we want done," she told Helen, knowing she was the one behind this unexpected gathering.

"We don't have time to waste," Helen responded briskly. "You said that yourself. You know all these guys, right?"

Of course she did. Mitch Franklin was the best general contractor in the region. He was usually tied up for months. Skeeter Johnson had been doing most of the plumbing in town since Maddie was a kid. He charged an arm and a leg for emergency service and had a waiting list for building jobs. The same was true of Roy Covington, the electrician.

"What kind of bribe did you offer these guys to get them over here on such short notice?" she asked, not entirely in jest.

Mitch grinned. "Hey, I always come when a pretty woman calls."

"Eventually," Maddie said. "And the rest of you?"

Skeeter regarded her with a chagrined expression. "Helen helped me out with a little problem recently. I owe her."

"And I'm a sucker for good coffee," Roy said. "Helen promised me some of Dana Sue's." He held up the take-out cup. "Best in town, for sure."

"Thank you, sugar," Dana Sue said, linking her arm through his. "Now, let's go inside and do some business."

Thankfully Maddie had come with a room-by-room checklist of everything they'd discussed to date. She gave a recitation in each room, Helen and Dana Sue elaborated, and the men's eyes widened as they took notes.

At the end of the tour, Mitch looked a little dazed. "And you want this done when?"

"I'd like to open in June," Helen said.

All three men were shaking their heads before the words were out of her mouth.

"Not enough time," Mitch said firmly.

"That's barely two months," Skeeter said. "No way can we do all that in that amount of time."

"What will it take?" Helen asked, not backing down.

"A miracle," Mitch said.

"Then make us a miracle," Helen said. She glanced at Skeeter. "I got you off on that traffic incident, didn't I? Some would say that was nothing short of a miracle."

Skeeter twisted his cap in his hands and nodded. "But this? I don't know."

"I should be able to get my part done if I bring in some extra help," Roy said. "Come on, Skeeter. Even at your age, you're not too old to enjoy a challenge."

Maddie took pity on him. "Skeeter, we don't want it done halfway. If you can't—"

"Well, of course I can," he said, his pride at stake. "Like Roy said, maybe with some extra help."

"Hire anyone you need to," Helen said, even as Maddie winced. She turned to Mitch. "Well?"

Mitch looked resigned. "If these two old geezers have the stamina for it, I'm not about to be outdone. I'll find the men someplace, even if I have to pull them off some other job."

Helen beamed at him. "I just knew you'd make it work. That's why I called you."

"You called me because you know I owe you for recommending me for about a dozen other building projects in the past ten years," Mitch said dryly. "And because you've always been able to twist me around your finger, ever since I had that crush on you back in third grade. Thank goodness I had the sense not to grow up and marry you. You'd have put me in an early grave."

"As if." Helen stood on tiptoe to plant a kiss on his cheek. "Thank you, Mitch." She turned to Skeeter and Roy. "Gentlemen, it's been a pleasure doing business with you. Get your cost projections to Maddie ASAP."

"Well, I guess we have our marching orders," Skeeter said. "Come on, guys, let's go someplace and figure out how we're going to pull this off."

Mitch winked at Helen. "I suppose some practical ideas will help, since I'm fresh out of miracles."

Once they'd gone, Maddie turned to Helen. "Even though I watched you in action myself in the settlement negotiation, I had no idea the level of your skills when it comes to manipulating men."

"I didn't manipulate anyone," Helen protested. "I just gave them some things to think about. The right men do love a good challenge."

"I can second that," Dana Sue said. "But it was surely a privilege to watch a master at work."

Maddie grinned at them. "Ladies, I actually believe we're about to be in business."

"Was there ever any doubt?" Helen asked immodestly. "I told you we'd pull it off."

"I'll remind you of that on May fifteenth, when the place is still in chaos," Maddie said.

"Bite your tongue," Dana Sue said. "Given the money this is going to cost, we'd better be finished on time. I'd say you need to go home and come up with a staffing proposal and a first-class marketing plan so this place is packed from day one."

"Amen to that," Helen agreed. She gave Maddie a hug. "I'll leave this in your capable hands from here on out. Keep me posted if there are any glitches. Oh, and closing is tomorrow. Since Dana Sue's restaurant is closed on Tuesday, I think we should have dinner tomorrow night to celebrate. My place, seven o'clock. We'll make it an early evening, Maddie, so Ty and Kyle should be able to hold down the fort at home."

"Hold it!" Maddie hollered as Helen breezed out the door. The woman didn't even slow down.

She turned to Dana Sue. "She didn't mean that, did she? This whole thing isn't on my shoulders now, is it?"

Dana Sue grinned. "I believe it is. Welcome to the world of partnership, sweetie. There's not a thing I can do to help till we're ready to finish up in the café part of things."

"You're abandoning me, too?"

"Organization and follow-up are two of your best skills," Dana Sue told her. "You'll be fine. And if you need either one of us, you know we'll be there in a heartbeat, though frankly, I'm still a little miffed that you didn't call me when Ty went missing the other night."

Maddie stared at her. "How on earth do you know about that?"

"The Dillons were in for dinner on Saturday. Jane mentioned how frantic you were when she spoke to you. Why didn't you call me?" She gave her a knowing look. "Was it because you wanted to give Cal a chance to ride to the rescue?"

Maddie moaned. "Are there no secrets in this town?"

"I live a few blocks from you. I saw his car in the driveway on my way home. When Jane told me about Tyler, I added up two and two."

"And came up with a hundred and twelve, if you ask me," Maddie grumbled.

"Am I wrong?"

Maddie hesitated, then admitted, "Not entirely. I just thought he might have a better idea about what Ty was thinking after I left them at Rosalina's."

"Of course you did," Dana Sue said, smirking.

"Well, I did."

"And it had nothing to do with wanting to lean on those big, broad shoulders."

Maddie frowned at her. "You are a very annoying woman." And perceptive, but she didn't say that.

"I know you like the back of my hand, sweetie. The man gets to you. Admit it."

"A little," Maddie said eventually. At Dana Sue's chiding look, she added, "Okay, a lot. But it begins and ends there."

"Why?"

"The list goes on and on."

"And how many of the things on that list really matter?" Dana Sue asked. "Something tells me most of them are just excuses for not putting your heart at risk."

"Could be," Maddie allowed. "Then again, maybe I just don't want to turn into a laughingstock when people figure out I'm attracted to my son's *much younger* baseball coach."

"Since when have you ever given two figs about what anyone in this town thinks? Remember when you organized that protest at the school over the impending dress code? Every teacher, every parent and most of the school board thought you ought to be locked in your room for impertinence, but you stood your ground. Thanks to you, we weren't all dressed in little navy blue uniforms with patent-leather shoes."

"There are days when I see what kids are wearing to school now that I regret that," Maddie said. "And the tattoos and piercings—I don't even like to think about them."

"I've had a few disagreements with Annie about those," Dana Sue said. "She will not be piercing or tattooing anything until she's grown up and out from under my roof."

"Famous last words," Maddie said.

"Don't say that. It makes me want to run over to the school now to check on her."

"I was just teasing," Maddie assured her. "Annie's a good kid. Too thin, maybe, but a good kid. I think Tyler will do something nuts long before Annie does."

"That's not all that encouraging. Isn't he the boy who ran off and stayed out past curfew just this past weekend?"

Maddie sighed. "I see your point." She regarded Dana Sue wistfully. "I never thought I'd be facing my kids' teenage years all alone."

"You're not alone," Dana Sue said fiercely. "You have me and Helen and even Bill, if you want him." She grinned. "And something tells me it wouldn't take much to have Cal involved if you want him to be."

"Dana Sue!"

"I'm just saying he probably understands more about teenagers than the rest of us combined."

Maddie thought of his understanding of Ty and nodded slowly. "I think you're right about that."

"Then think of him as a resource," Dana Sue said. "Any little tingles you get in the process are just a bonus."

She hugged Maddie. "Gotta run."

Maddie sank down on the front steps of their soon-to-be spa. Her life certainly was taking some unexpectedly fascinating twists lately. She could only pray they would all turn out to be for the better.

"Where's Kyle?" Maddie asked when she'd put dinner on the table that night. From the moment she'd had a home of her own and kids, Maddie had insisted on family meals with traditional fare. There would be no catch-as-catch-can suppers of caviar or cold hors d'oeuvres or, in the case of her lean, jam-packed early years with Bill, fast-food burgers eaten on the run.

"Beats me," Ty said, sitting down and reaching for the bowl of mashed potatoes.

"Katie, have you seen your brother?"

"In his room," she said. "I told him to come down, but he said he wasn't hungry."

"Okay, you two go ahead and eat. I'll get him," Maddie said, then glanced around to make sure everything they'd need was on the table. Katie loved to help, but she hadn't totally mastered place settings and things like salt and pepper shakers yet. Maddie's quick, automatic survey stopped her in midstep. Once again Katie had set a place for her father.

Maddie bit back a sigh. Obviously they needed to have another talk. Katie simply refused to believe that her dad wasn't coming home again. Not even visiting him at Noreen's had helped her to grasp the permanence of the change.

Upstairs Maddie found Kyle lying on his bed staring at the ceiling. She noticed that his hair, closer to her dark blond than to Bill's or his brother's golden shade, was too long and his jeans were an inch too short. He needed a trip to the barber and the mall. He'd rather eat dirt than do either, which was probably why he hadn't mentioned that he was outgrowing his clothes and couldn't see past the hair in his eyes.

"Hey, kiddo, dinner's on the table," she said.

"Not hungry."

"Doesn't matter. You know the rule around here. We all sit down to eat together." She recalled that only a few months ago Kyle had always been the first one at the table, anxious to try out his new jokes, ready to tease his little sister and to bug his big brother. His dad had been his best audience, laughing at his material, no matter how silly it was.

Maddie sat down beside him. "It still feels weird, doesn't it, without Dad here?"

He avoided her gaze and remained silent.

"It feels weird to me, too," she said. "But we'll get used to it and things will be like they were before."

"How can they be if Dad's not there?" he scoffed. "Come on, Mom, admit it. The whole family thing is lame."

"Family is not lame," she said emphatically. She'd spent the first twenty years of her life craving exactly what she'd worked so hard to create for her kids—a traditional family life. "It's the most important thing in the world. These are the people who will love you unconditionally, no matter what you do."

Kyle rolled his eyes. "Like I believe that. Dad's gone, isn't he?"

"Well, no matter where your dad is, he loves you. Katie idolizes you and Ty has always looked out for you. I think you're the funniest kid in the whole wide world. Even your terrible jokes are better than anything on TV."

She got a faint smile in return for that.

"No way," he protested.

"Yes," she insisted. "And your dad took one look at you on the day you were born and fell in love with you. He would do anything in the world for you."

"Except stay," Kyle said softly. He met her gaze, his eyes swimming in tears, then looked away and mumbled, "I asked him to."

Maddie felt tears sting her own eyes. "You did?"

He nodded. "I cut school and went to his office the day after he moved out and talked to him. He said no. He said his life was with Noreen and this new baby now, but that it didn't mean he wasn't still our dad."

Maddie ignored the news that Kyle had cut school without her knowing about it. "Didn't you believe him?"

He shrugged. "I guess." He finally lifted his gaze to meet hers, his eyes filled with misery. "How can I hate a little baby who's not even born yet?" he asked in a small voice.

"Oh, Kyle, you don't hate the baby," she said. "You might be jealous and angry and even blame the baby for having what you wish you had, but you don't hate the baby. In fact, I predict that when that baby gets here, you're going to fall in love with it the same way you did when Katie was born." She forced a grin. "As I recall, you weren't too happy about her impending arrival, either. Now I'll bet you can't imagine your life without her."

"I guess."

"Come on. You know it's true. You might think she's a pest, but you love being the big brother for a change."

A grin slowly spread across his face. "I'm holding out for when she gets old enough to date. I am going to give her such a rough time…"

Maddie nudged him with an elbow. "See, you're looking toward something positive in the future already. Now, come on down and eat dinner. I made meat loaf and mashed potatoes."

His eyes lit up. "My favorites. How come you did that? Nobody else likes meat loaf."

"Just you and me," she said with a wink. "I figured we deserved it."

He regarded her with sudden understanding. "That's why you made spaghetti last night, 'cause it's Katie's favorite, right?"

Maddie nodded.

"I'll bet tomorrow night's pork chops," he said, "'cause that's Ty's favorite."

"Yep."

He gave her a sly look. "And Dad hated all of them, huh?"

She chuckled. "Yes, he did, but it's a whole new world around here now, so watch out."

"You know what Dad hated worse than meat loaf, pork chops and spaghetti?" he asked.

"What?"

"Pizza with sausage and pepperoni," he said, regarding her hopefully.

Ruffling his hair, she stood up. "If you don't have pizza

after Ty's game on Friday, I'll put that on the menu for Saturday."

"All right!" He hesitated, his mood suddenly deflating. "Why wouldn't we have pizza after Ty's game like we did last week?"

Maddie debated the wisdom of telling him about the deal she'd made with his dad to attend alternate games. Truthfully, though, she didn't have a choice. Better she tell him now than have him caught off guard on Friday.

"Because I won't be at the game this week," she said. "Your dad's going instead."

"And that means we can't go?" he asked incredulously.

"No, of course not," she assured him. "You and Katie will go with your dad."

"This is because Noreen showed up last week and ruined it for everybody, isn't it? She gets all weird if you're around Dad, right?" he demanded, radiating indignation.

"Your dad and I reached a compromise we felt was in everyone's best interests," she said, determined to be fair.

"Well, it sucks," he said heatedly. "And I'm gonna tell Dad that."

With a sigh, Maddie watched him dash out of the room and take the stairs two at a time. Not five minutes before, she'd almost believed that the way to cheering up her kids was as simple as feeding them their favorite foods. Now she knew better. It would never be that easy. They all had a long way to go and there was a potential minefield around every bend.

CHAPTER TEN

The din was unbelievable. Maddie closed the door to the kitchen, where she'd set up a temporary office space for herself now that the Hartley place was officially theirs. Thanks to more of Helen's wizardry, the phone had been installed by nine this morning and all the contractors were on the job doing demolition work. Why she'd thought she would get anything done in the chaos was beyond her. The sound of sledgehammers was giving her a headache.

"You got a minute?" Mitch asked, opening the door cautiously.

"Sure. Come on in. How do you stand the noise?" she asked him, rubbing her temples.

He grinned. "I'm usually making some of it myself, so I hardly notice. For you, I'd recommend earplugs, or working at home till we get the rest of the demolition done."

"When will that be?"

"Next week. Then we'll be sawing and hammering all day."

"You're not wasting any time, are you?"

"According to Helen, we don't have any to waste." He eyed her hopefully. "Just how firm is that deadline? Any wiggle room?"

She grinned. "If you're expecting me to give you a reprieve, think again. I report to Helen, too, and believe me, once her mind's set on something, that's the way it's going to be."

He laughed. "I figured as much. I guess it was just wishful thinking."

Maddie sobered. "Even so, we don't want you cutting any corners on quality just to meet the deadline, Mitch."

He gave her a wounded look. "I don't cut corners, not ever. What would that do to my reputation? We'll do whatever it takes to get the job done and get it done right. My wife will kill me if I don't. She wants to sign up the minute you're ready to start taking memberships."

"Tell her she can come by next week," Maddie said eagerly. "The sooner we can let people in here so they can start the buzz on what's happening, the better."

Mitch held up his hands. "Whoa! Not a good idea. This is still a construction zone, Maddie."

"Which is why I'm going to direct people around the outside of the house to that door right there," she soothed. "I noticed you're stacking your materials on the other side. They'll never step into the area where you're working or get near the stockpile of materials. I won't even let them peek into the main part of the house unless you give me an okay."

He was still frowning, but he finally nodded. "I suppose that would be all right. I just don't want any accidents on this site, especially not involving people who don't need to be here."

Maddie nodded. "I understand, but I'm on that same timetable you're on. Not only does the construction have to be completed by June, but I have to hire employees and sign people up for memberships. Otherwise all we'll have is a beautiful, empty and very costly building."

"Fair enough," he agreed, then grinned at her. "You

know, Maddie, you all think Helen is the tough one, but you're not half-bad at negotiating yourself."

"Thank you," she said, allowing herself to bask in the unexpected praise for a skill she'd forgotten she possessed. "Now I'd better get back to this pile of catalogs on fitness equipment and spa treatments. I am in way over my head."

"You know, you could ask Dexter. That gym may be a run-down disgrace, but the equipment's first-rate."

"Yes, I'm sure Dexter would be pleased as punch to help out the competition," Maddie replied. "He's already scowling at me every time I go in to use the treadmill. I'm surprised he hasn't banned me from the premises. I'll be glad to get at least one piece of equipment up and running in here so I don't have to face him first thing in the morning."

"Are you still paying your dues over there?" Mitch inquired wryly.

Maddie nodded.

"Then you have nothing to worry about." He rose and headed for the door, then turned back with a wink. "And as long as you're there, don't ask Dexter anything, just jot down the manufacturer of the equipment."

"You have a very sneaky mind, Mitch. I like that."

After he'd gone, she regarded the stack of catalogs with renewed dismay and came to a quick decision. She wasn't quite ready to risk Dexter's wrath by taking notes in his gym, but there were some fancy spas over in Charleston she could visit. Maybe Dana Sue could take a break and go with her.

Unfortunately, Dana Sue wasn't at the restaurant and she wasn't picking up on her cell phone. Helen was undoubtedly in court. Which left who? Surely there was someone who wouldn't mind going to a couple of spas on the pretense of looking into a membership. The only person who came to mind was her mother. She'd been full of surprises lately, so maybe she'd accept Maddie's impromptu invitation. Before Maddie could change her mind, she picked up the phone and dialed.

"What?" her mother said abruptly, a sure sign she was caught up with a new painting.

"Mom, it's me," Maddie said, her enthusiasm waning. Her mother hated being interrupted when she was working. Maddie could remember a hundred times as a child when she'd been scolded for daring to intrude. The sting of it had stayed with her.

"Oh, Maddie, hello. How are you? And what on earth is that awful noise?"

Maddie debated for an instant, then decided she might as well ask, since she'd already dragged her mother away from her painting. "We're in the throes of demolition at the spa, which is exactly why I'm calling you. I need an excuse to get out of here. I'm going to run over to Charleston. I thought you might want to come along."

"Really?" her mother said, sounding shocked and perhaps even a little pleased by the invitation.

"If you're too busy with your painting, I understand," Maddie told her, ready to be rebuffed.

"Frankly, I can use a break," her mother said, surprising her. "The fine details are getting harder and harder on my eyes. What's on the agenda in Charleston?"

"I want to check out the competition, see what the spas offer over there."

"Sounds like fun," her mother said. "Why don't I call Chez Bella and see if they can fit us in for facials. My treat."

Maddie shook her head. "Mother, you are a constant source of amazement to me."

"Because I offered to treat you to a facial?"

"No, because you've heard of Chez Bella. It's the most exclusive spa in Charleston. I've read about it in magazines, but I've never even set foot inside and until the other day I thought you thought places like spas were a waste of money."

"True enough but whose paintings do you think hang in the lobby?" her mother said with a hint of pride. "Bella says they provide just the right note of local color and serenity."

Maddie knew that there were businesses and private homes all over the world in which her mother's paintings hung. She'd long since lost track of all of them.

"You're kidding me," she said. "That's wonderful. I can hardly wait to see them. I'll pick you up in fifteen minutes."

"Make it a half hour. I've been working, remember? I have to get the paint off and change into something presentable, if I'm walking into Bella's. I do have an image to maintain."

Maddie laughed. "Yes, I know how much you care about your avant-garde image. Try not to choose anything too outrageous."

As she hung up, she tried to recall the last time she and her mother had done anything together just for the fun of it. She couldn't. Well, maybe it was time to start.

Chez Bella was everything Maddie knew she didn't want The Corner Spa to be. It was too pretentious, too elegant, too exclusive. She knew it the moment she stepped into the lobby with its pink-marble floors, flocked wallpaper and expensive antique furnishings. Her mother's paintings, a collection of botanical prints, all signed and numbered, were some that Maddie herself owned. Here, however, they had been framed in ostentatious gold-leaf frames that overpowered the delicacy of her mother's work. She bit back a groan when she saw them, then glanced at her mother, who looked a little shell-shocked as well. Obviously she'd never seen them on display, either.

"I wasn't expecting this," her mother muttered. "Framed like that they could be hung in a brothel."

Maddie had to bite back a laugh as they were joined by a perfectly dressed, perfectly made-up, perfectly coiffed woman who beamed at her mother.

"I am so honored that you have finally taken me up on my invitation," Bella Jansen said. "And what do you think of your artwork? It is perfect for this room, is it not? Our clients comment on the beauty of the paintings all the time. I send them straight over to the gallery that handles your work."

Maddie noticed her mother's hesitation and wondered if she would thank her or cut the woman to ribbons for her tastelessness.

"I'm always pleased to see my works being enjoyed, and if that translates into sales, all the better," Paula said at last. "Bella, I'd like you to meet my daughter, Madelyn."

"Ah, Madelyn, I see the resemblance. You have your mother's flawless skin. I promise it will glow when you leave here today."

"Thank you for fitting us in," Maddie said politely, though she could hardly wait to get out of the place.

Bella hurried them into the back of the spa, which was just as tasteless as the lobby, though crowded with women willing to pay its very high prices. Still, as they were whisked into treatment rooms that smelled faintly of lavender, gowned in soft pink robes that bore the spa's insignia, she sensed that she was about to be pampered in an extraordinary way.

The beauty technician who gently massaged and exfoliated and creamed her face was a magician. Maddie nearly fell asleep under her ministrations, though she desperately wanted to make mental notes on everything from the products to the techniques.

“Tell me about these products,” she asked.

“They are the top of the line,” Jeanette assured her in a soft South Carolina drawl. Her dark hair was cut pixie short, which emphasized her creamy complexion and huge brown eyes. “I studied for a few months in Paris and worked in other places, and I’ve never found any better. Bella insists on quality. That’s the only reason I came here.”

Maddie thought she heard a faint hint of dissatisfaction in the woman’s voice and wondered if she would be even remotely interested in making a change. Poaching employees at Bella’s spa while getting a facial struck her as especially bad manners, though.

“Do you have a card, Jeanette?”

“Of course.”

“Would you mind putting your home number on it? I’d like to discuss something with you, but I’m afraid now’s not the time.”

The young woman gave her a puzzled look, but shrugged and jotted down the number.

“I’ll be in touch,” Maddie promised, giving her a generous tip, even though her mother was paying the bill. She wanted Jeanette to remember her when she called.

Back in the lobby, her mother signed the credit-card receipt for an exorbitant amount of money, then gave Bella a dutiful peck on the cheek.

“Thank you so much,” she told her. “It was very gracious of you to take us at the last minute.”

“I hope you’ll come again,” Bella said. “I would love to brag that the incredible Paula Vreeland is one of my regulars.”

"I'm sure I'll be back," Paula replied, then tucked her arm through Maddie's and hurried her outside.

As soon as they reached the sidewalk, Paula shuddered. "I certainly hope you girls have better taste than that woman. Do you have any idea how badly I wanted to rip my paintings off the wall and walk out with them?"

Maddie grinned. "I'm actually a little surprised that you didn't."

"I didn't want to embarrass you, or Bella, for that matter. She's a nice woman, just a little misguided in the taste department."

"She docs seem to have a very loyal clientele, though. The place was bustling."

"Did you discover anything that might be helpful?"

"How not to decorate," Maddie said at once. "And an excellent technician who might be interested in making a change. I have her card in my purse."

Her mother grinned. "You impress me."

Maddie basked in her approval. "You're the second person today to say something like that to me."

"You sound surprised."

"I guess I am. I've spent so long being a wife and mother, I wasn't sure I'd ever had any real business sense. I'm discovering that I do remember a few things from that expensive education you and Dad paid for."

"Didn't I tell you that one of these days you'd start seeing all the good things to come out of this divorce?" her mother said, regarding her with delight. "You're finding yourself again, Maddie. I couldn't be more proud."

Maddie thought about that, then asked, "You never lost yourself when you were married to Dad, did you?"

"Never. He wouldn't have allowed it." A nostalgic smile curved her lips. "Then, again, neither would I."

Maddie wished she'd been that wise during her own marriage, or perhaps that Bill had been a different man. Maybe it wasn't too late to make up for that.

Cal picked up the phone to call Maddie Townsend, then hesitated. For several days now he'd been telling himself he needed to speak to her again about Ty, but a part of him knew that his desire to see her was about something else entirely. He put the phone back in its cradle and nervously drummed his fingers on his desk.

There were plenty of women out there who weren't mothers of teenage kids. There were more than enough females his own age who came without baggage or complications. And probably even in Serenity, there were a handful that wouldn't get his principal's knickers twisted into a knot. But not one of them made him hunt for an excuse to see them again.

He rolled his eyes at his uncharacteristic loss of confidence. He *had* an excuse to see Maddie again. The perfect excuse, one so innocent that no one would see through it, least of all Maddie herself. He was a coach worried about a member of his team. She was the kid's mother. That gave them plenty to talk about. And he already had plenty of indications that she valued his viewpoint when it came to Ty.

So what if she was miles out of his league financially or older than him by ten years or so? It wasn't as if he planned to ask her to marry him. It wasn't even a real date. He was going to suggest coffee. He was planning to talk about Ty, compare notes on how he was getting along. What could be more innocent and uncompromising than that? He was friendly with other parents, had even had dinner in some of their homes.

It all made perfect sense, he thought wryly, until he considered the way his pulse raced at the thought of seeing Maddie again. The last time he'd felt that particular mix of anticipation and nerves, he'd been about to steal home plate in a critical game. He'd never again experienced that kind of emotional high. If he felt that way now, it was not about some perfectly normal parent-teacher conference.

"Oh, get over yourself," he muttered. Maddie Townsend would jump through hoops for her son. She would certainly agree to have coffee with him to talk about the kid. They'd spend an hour together, two at the most. What was the big deal?

He dialed her number and cursed when the answering machine picked up. He left a terse message asking her to call him, then resigned himself to waiting.

When she hadn't returned his call by the next day, it threw him—until he caught Ty regarding him with an unmistakably guilty expression.

He strolled over to confront the boy. "Hey, Ty," he said, keeping his tone casual. "I left a message for your mother yesterday. I really need to speak to her."

"About what?" Ty asked suspiciously.

"Does that really matter?"

"It does if it's about me."

Cal didn't want to discuss his reason for calling Maddie. "Right this second, the subject isn't the point," he told the boy. "You didn't by any chance intercept the message, did you?"

Ty gave him a belligerent look. "So what if I did? What if I don't want the two of you talking about me behind my back?"

"Then you did erase the message?" Cal pressed, wanting to be absolutely sure.

Ty's expression remained unyielding, but the color in his cheeks deepened.

"We're both worried about you," Cal told him. "Would you like it better if I set up a meeting with you present?"

"Oh, just do whatever you want," Ty retorted, his tone filled with disgust. "That's what adults do, anyway."

"We don't have to ask your permission, that's true," Cal told him, keeping his own voice quiet and reasonable. "But what you think does matter to us."

"You must not have met my dad," Ty said. "*Nothing* matters to him."

Before Cal could respond, Ty picked up a baseball and headed for the mound. Oddly, despite the heated exchange, he managed to get his concentration under control and pitched the best fastballs and curves he'd thrown in weeks. Once again, Cal couldn't help but be impressed by Ty's ability to grasp the lesson about using his emotions to help, not harm, his game. His raw, natural talent was maturing nicely. He just prayed the kid wouldn't squander it.

"Nice job," Cal told him when he came off the field.

Ty merely shrugged. "Whatever."

Cal sighed. He didn't envy any parent of a teenage boy with their raging hormones and erratic mood swings. Add in the divorce factor and it must be hell. If he could offer any insights that might be helpful to Maddie, he owed it to her to try.

He gave a self-deprecating laugh at his supposedly noble intentions. They were exactly the kind that paved the way straight to hell.

That night when Cal called Maddie again, she answered the phone, but she sounded completely frazzled.

"Maddie, it's Cal. Is this a bad time?" he asked.

"It's not if you can fix a leaking pipe before my kitchen floods. I called Skeeter, but he's not available."

He laughed. "Well, I'm not Skeeter, but I do have tools and a working knowledge of plumbing basics. I'll be right there. Oh, and try cutting off the water before I get there."

"Don't you think I've tried that?" she said, clearly exasperated. "The knob's frozen or I'm not strong enough to turn it."

"Where's Ty?"

"In his room doing his homework," she answered. "But he's in a funk."

"And Kyle?"

"He's studying at a friend's house."

"In that case, I'll hurry."

When Cal got there, he walked in the open front door and headed for the kitchen, pausing only to holler upstairs. "Ty, could you come down here? I could use your help."

In the kitchen, Maddie regarded him with a look of such relief that he couldn't seem to stop himself from dropping a quick kiss on her forehead. He had to work hard to ignore the drenching her T-shirt had taken and the way it clung to her breasts.

"Help has arrived," he said and dropped onto the soaking-wet floor to reach for the cut-off valve. One hard twist did the job and the leak slowed to a drip.

"Thank goodness," Maddie said. "I was running out of towels."

Ty walked into the kitchen just then and the look plastered on his face was anything but friendly. "What are you doing here?" he demanded.

"A little plumbing job for your mother, something you could have done," he said.

Ty flushed as he looked around the soaked kitchen and

the mound of wet towels. "I didn't know it was this bad," he muttered defensively. "Sorry, Mom."

"Well, it's not too late to redeem yourself," Cal told him.

"I don't know anything about pipes and stuff," Ty said. He cast a judgmental look at his mother. "Dad always called Skeeter."

"Well, Skeeter's not available," Maddie said.

"Which is why it's good to know how to fix something like this yourself," Cal said. "Ty, you can hand me my tools, okay? I'll tell you what I'm doing so you'll know what to do next time."

"Okay," Ty said grudgingly, but he listened and did everything Cal asked of him.

Cal noticed that Maddie hung on his every word, as well, clearly determined not to feel helpless the next time a plumbing catastrophe struck.

Twenty minutes later, the washer in the drain had been replaced, the seal was tight and the water was back on.

"You made that look easy," Ty said, regarding Cal with a mix of astonishment and respect.

"It's all in knowing what to do. Think you could do it yourself?"

"Sure." He glanced from Cal to his mother. "Are you two gonna talk about me now?"

Cal laughed at his dismayed expression. "No, I think we'll save that for another time. Go on back to your homework. Thanks for the help."

After he'd gone upstairs, Maddie regarded Cal curiously. "Why did he think we were going to talk about him?"

Cal explained about the intercepted message.

Maddie's gaze followed the direction in which her son had gone. "I can't believe he'd do something like that, not after the lecture I gave him about hiding the notes his teachers sent home for me."

"Come on, Maddie. You were a kid once," Cal reminded her. "Can you really blame him? He's probably had his fill of adults doing things and making decisions behind his back."

"You have a point," Maddie acknowledged. "Can I get you something? Coffee? A beer? Bottled water? I made a cake earlier. It's chocolate with fudge icing. We could take a slice and eat it outside. There's a wonderful breeze tonight."

"Now you're talking my language," Cal enthused. "I can't recall the last time I had homemade cake."

"You're kidding. I would have thought every available female in town would be showing up on your doorstep with baked goods."

"I must be putting out the wrong vibes. The ones who show up on my doorstep tend to offer themselves."

Maddie chuckled as she cut the cake. "That must be awkward," she commented, then studied him. "Or do you like it?"

"No, it's awkward," he said. "I haven't done a lot of dating since my divorce, but I do prefer to do the asking myself."

"Just an old-fashioned guy, huh?"

"Apparently so." He accepted the plate from Maddie, along with hers. "Or else once burned, twice shy. Laurie pursued me till she convinced me to marry her. I was flattered by the attention till I realized I was just the first ballplayer she managed to suck in, not the first she'd pursued. Or the last."

"You want some milk with that?" she asked, holding up a carton.

"Perfect."

They took the snack outside and settled into comfortable wicker chairs side by side. Cal was relieved that Maddie hadn't jumped all over his comment about his ex-wife. He wasn't even sure why he'd mentioned Laurie. Usually he avoided the topic of his marriage like the plague. To be sure they didn't go down that path, he directed the conversation elsewhere.

"I missed you at Ty's game Friday night," he said, hoping his tone was casual and gave away nothing of the disappointment he'd felt at not seeing her.

"I wanted to be there," she admitted. "But Bill and I made a deal. We're going to alternate going to the games."

"You think that will keep his girlfriend away?"

"Something like that. I assume it worked since Ty didn't come home all worked up."

"She wasn't there," Cal said, impressed by her thoughtfulness but worried about the toll the gesture must take on her. "But do you really want to miss seeing your son play?"

"Of course not, but I think this is best for now."

Cal barely managed to contain his skepticism. It was Maddie's decision, after all. Eventually, he released a sigh and let himself relax. "This is nice," he said as a ceiling fan stirred the air, which had cooled slightly with the setting of the sun. "You must enjoy sitting out here and watching the world go by."

"Usually I do. It's nice to have neighbors stop to chat, but it can have its drawbacks."

"Such as?"

She met his gaze. "At least half a dozen cars have driven past and slowed down since we've been out here. By tomorrow morning word of this will be all over town. I'm sorry," she said. "I wasn't thinking when I suggested we come out here. We should have gone out back or stayed in the kitchen."

"My car's in the driveway. We're probably better off out in plain view. If we were anywhere else, people would just wind up speculating about what we're doing," Cal said realistically.

"You don't sound especially worried either way," she noted.

"Should I be?" He studied her, more concerned by her reaction than any impact the gossip might have on him. "Is this a problem for you, Maddie?"

She hesitated just a moment too long. It was enough to tell him she was uncomfortable with all the talk about the two of them.

Cal immediately put his plate aside and stood up. "I should go."

"No, don't," she said at once. "Please, Cal. I don't know why I let it bother me that people in this town talk about everybody's business. I should be used to it."

"Everyone craves a little privacy from time to time, but we're not doing anything wrong, Maddie. I'd like to see anyone make something out of us sitting on your front porch on a lovely spring evening."

But even as he made that reassuring statement, he knew it was wishful thinking. It was bound to come back to haunt them both. And despite Maddie's evident discomfort, after the pointed warning he'd had from his principal, he was pretty sure who'd feel the backlash first. What he didn't know was why it didn't really seem to matter.

CHAPTER ELEVEN

"This has been a day from hell," Helen announced as she poured margaritas for herself, Maddie and Dana Sue at what had become their Tuesday-night ritual for catching up on their lives and on the progress at their new fitness club. It was nearly the middle of April and they were all beginning to feel the pressure of that self-imposed June opening date.

"Bad day in court?" Maddie asked sympathetically. "Did opposing counsel make you look bad?"

"No, my client had a sudden series of insights into things he'd never mentioned to me before. Naturally all of these insights were designed to impress upon the court just how innocent he was."

"Which had exactly the opposite effect," Dana Sue guessed.

"And made me look like an idiot besides," Helen confirmed. "I honestly don't know what people are thinking sometimes."

"They're not thinking. They're desperate," Maddie suggested. "They're grasping at straws."

"Why can't they just trust me? I know what I'm doing." Helen took a quick gulp of her strong drink, then sighed.

"Oh, well, I suppose I should be used to it by now. Nobody trusts a lawyer, not even the people who need them."

Dana Sue exchanged a look with Maggie and grinned. "Oh, goody, a pity party. And for once it's not about you or me."

Helen frowned. "I'm not always the strong one," she said. "I have my moments of insecurity and vulnerability."

"We know that, sweetie." Dana Sue held out a batch of her extra-hot guacamole. "Have some of this. It'll blow all those nagging doubts right out of your head. You'll be back to your old, confident self in a minute."

"Worked on me," Maddie said as Helen scooped the guacamole onto a chip. "Ever since Dana Sue made that stuff on the day you tried to convince me to partner up with you to open this spa, I've developed a whole new outlook on my capabilities."

"Is the guacamole responsible for that?" Helen asked archly. "Or is it the attention of the hunky baseball coach?"

"Cal is not on the agenda tonight," Maddie told them firmly.

"Ah, that must mean there's something you don't want us to know," Helen deduced.

"I know," Dana Sue said, grinning like a woman just itching to share a secret.

Helen beamed. "Do tell."

Oblivious to Maddie's frown, Dana Sue said, "Cal paid another visit to the house the other night. Those two were all cozy on the front porch with milk and cake. I'm betting it was Maddie's famous chocolate cake with fudge frosting." She turned to Maddie with a worried expression. "Should you even be baking things like that these days? I don't even let myself go into the kitchen at Sullivan's when Erik's baking the dessert specials. I'm afraid the calories will grab on to my hips if I even walk into the room."

Maddie scowled fiercely at the pair of them, though she doubted it would have any effect. For the moment she focused on the cake, since the subject of Cal was obviously going to be tricky.

"I didn't bake that cake for myself," she said piously. "The kids love it. I happened to have some left when Cal stopped by. Offering it to him was a good way to keep from eating the entire leftover cake myself."

"But you were eating something totally decadent right out there where anyone could see," Dana Sue teased. "I'm pretty sure that's counterproductive to the image we're trying to promote about being three health-conscious women."

"Who are currently drinking margaritas and eating guacamole," Maddie retorted. "I'd say the pot's calling the kettle black about now."

Helen held up a hand. "Hold it! I don't give two figs about what Maddie was eating or our current indulgence in an alcoholic beverage. I want to know what Cal was doing over there."

"He came to fix a leak under the kitchen sink," Maddie said. "Satisfied? It was hardly a seductive scene."

"A leak under the sink," Helen said, amusement in her voice. "And Skeeter, who's underfoot at the spa all day long, couldn't have been persuaded to stop by to fix that leak? I know it's not the same as having the work done by someone who looks like Cal, but Skeeter is a professional plumber."

"Don't you think I thought of calling Skeeter first? Thanks to all the work he's doing for us during the day, he's handling a lot of his other calls in the evening. I couldn't track him down and Cal happened to be available."

"Oh, really? He happened to be available?" Helen said

skeptically. "How did that come about? Was he just wandering down the street? Driving by?"

"He called, if you must know," Maddie muttered.

"Does he do that often?" Helen asked.

Maddie scowled at her. "Look, just because you had a tough day in court, you don't get to come home and try out your interrogation techniques on me."

Helen laughed. "But you are so much more fun than most of my clients, and your social life has become downright fascinating."

"I don't have a social life," Maddie maintained.

"You just have the sexiest man in Serenity under your kitchen sink," Dana Sue said. "That's an image that would make my day."

"Mine, too," Helen agreed. She fanned herself dramatically with a cloth napkin. There were no paper products on Helen's table, not even on her outside patio.

"Then perhaps this image will perk you up even more," Maddie said, whipping out some papers and handing them over.

"What are these?" Helen asked.

"Has your drink blurred your vision?" Maddie inquired tartly. "Those are the membership rosters as of today at five o'clock and the new employee hires, respectively."

Dana Sue stared at her. "We have members? We have employees?"

"What do you think I've been doing over there?" Maddie didn't even try to hide her exasperation. "You two had an idea. I'm making it happen. That's what you asked me to do, remember? You wanted me to take care of all those pesky details you don't want to bother with—hiring, marketing, construction oversight, actually getting the doors on this business open."

"Well, bless your heart," Dana Sue said.

"My God, this is impressive," Helen murmured as she flipped through the pages. "You actually stole a technician away from Chez Bella? How did you manage that? She'll never make the tips here that she made over there."

"No, but she'll be in charge of the spa operation at an increase in her base salary," Maddie said. "I know it's stretching the budget a bit, but it's worth it. She's really, really good. You're going to love her. She's experienced and energetic and as excited as we are about starting something new from the ground up. I thought I'd ask her to join us next Tuesday, if it's okay with you."

"I can't wait to meet her," Helen said. "And look at the number of women who've already signed up to join. I was sure we'd have the whole place to ourselves for the first couple of months."

"One of the joys of living in Serenity is that it doesn't take much to get some buzz going," Maddie told them. "Once I put out the word that folks could stop by to check the place out, every woman in town wanted to be the first to take a peek inside. And believe me, a peek is all they get. Mitch was very clear about that. I thought that would be a disadvantage, but it's turning out to be terrific. It's just whetting their appetites for more."

She grinned at them. "Ready for more?"

"Bring it on," Helen commanded.

Maddie offered them a folded brochure on pastel-pink paper. "Based on our last discussion and my conversations with Jeanette about a few limited spa services, I made a quick-and-dirty little flyer about what we'd be offering, our introductory price list and a little bit about the three of us and why good health for women is so important. Since I started handing them out, I haven't had one person walk away without signing up for something." She gave them a satisfied grin. "Just wait till we announce our cooking classes. Dana Sue, maybe you could start working on a couple of ideas for those. I could get out a press release and that would widen the buzz around the region."

"You designed this?" Helen asked incredulously, studying the brochure front and back.

"It's just something I did in a hurry on the computer at home," Maddie said defensively. "I know we'll want to refine it and have it done professionally once we've fine-tuned everything. Jeanette has some great ideas for expanding the spa services, but we didn't want to get too far ahead of ourselves."

"No, no, I think it's fabulous," Helen said. "I had no idea you could do this kind of graphics work."

"I took a few marketing and design classes at college," Maddie said. "My program's not terribly sophisticated and I'm rusty, but some of it came back to me."

"Looks to me as if a lot of it came back to you. Next time I want something printed for my law practice, I'm coming to you," Helen declared.

"And I want you to create new summer menus for the restaurant," Dana Sue said eagerly. "This is really good, Maddie."

Maddie felt tears stinging her eyes at their praise. "Come on, you guys, the flyer's nothing special."

"Don't you dare say that," Helen chided. "You've got a real knack for this stuff, Maddie. You're turning out to be our secret weapon." She held up her glass with its last few drops of margarita. "Ladies, I think we're going to have a success on our hands."

"Hear, hear," Dana Sue added.

Maddie sipped her margarita right along with them and

basked in this triumph. She really was making a contribution to their partnership, after all. A few weeks ago she would never have believed it possible. When the time came, maybe she'd be able to accept her paycheck without feeling as if she hadn't earned it.

All Maddie's high spirits were dashed when she turned in to the driveway at home just as Bill was bringing the kids back from their evening together. Ty was out of the car practically before his father cut the engine and Kyle was right on his heels. When Bill removed Katie from her booster seat in the back, she sobbed and clung to his neck.

"Don't go, Daddy. Please don't go," she begged. "You live here."

Bill cast a helpless look in Maddie's direction. As heartsick as she was about Katie's pain, Maddie wasn't going to help him out this time. She shrugged to indicate he needed to handle his daughter's heartbreak on his own, since he was the cause of it.

Inside, she found Ty in the kitchen rummaging in the refrigerator.

"I thought your dad took you out for dinner," she said. Not that her son wasn't a bottomless pit, but it usually took more than an hour for a meal to wear off.

"I wasn't hungry then," Ty said.

"He brought Noreen again," Kyle said, joining them. He grabbed a jar of peanut butter, some jelly and a loaf of bread.

Maddie sighed. Ty's hatred of Noreen was wearing off on his younger brother. It had to stop. "Boys, can't you at least give her a chance?" she pleaded. "For your dad's sake and for your own, for that matter."

Kyle shrugged. "She's okay, I guess, but she acts all weird around us."

"She's a big phony," Tyler added bitterly. "She pretends to be all interested in what we're doing. She asks a whole bunch of questions and stuff."

"Maybe she *is* interested," Maddie suggested.

"No way," Ty said. "She's just doing it to impress Dad. She looks at him, not us. I know a snow job when I see one. And Dad just eats it all up. He gets mad at us for not buying it."

Maddie hated being put in the position of advocate for Bill's girlfriend, but she had no choice. "Guys, maybe she's trying the best way she knows how," she told her sons. "This is an awkward situation for her, too. Cut her some slack. Answer her questions as if you think she's really interested. Maybe all of you can get to know each other and find some common ground."

"I don't want to get to know her," Ty said heatedly. "I want her to disappear."

Just then Bill walked into the kitchen with Katie. "Well, you can forget that," he said harshly. "Noreen is part of my life now, which means she's part of yours."

"Like hell!" Ty said, storming past his father. "As far as I'm concerned, you can both disappear."

Maddie was horrified. "Tyler Townsend, you get back here right this instant," Maddie ordered in a tone that stopped him in his tracks. She waited till he took a cautious step back in her direction. "That is no way to speak to your father. I want you to apologize now."

Ty stared her down and remained stubbornly silent.

"Fine, then. We'll just add another week to your grounding."

There was a flash of hurt in his eyes right before he took off, pounding up the stairs. Kyle gave Maddie a disappointed look, as well, a look that told her he'd expected her to understand their side better than she had.

And she did. She really did. She turned slowly to Bill. "I think it's best if you go."

"Can't we talk?"

"Not tonight," she said. "Frankly, I don't have the stomach for it."

"I'll take Katie up to bed and then I'll go."

"No, I'll take her," Maddie said firmly.

"But—"

"I think you've done enough to upset their lives tonight. Just go and let me pick up the pieces."

Bill regarded her with dismay. "Nothing I do anymore is right, is it?"

Maddie met his gaze evenly. "You're your own worst enemy."

She scooped Katie out of his arms. "Let yourself out."

"Maddie," he said when she was halfway out of the room.

She hesitated but didn't turn back.

"Have lunch with me tomorrow," he said. "Help me figure this out. Please."

Bill had never asked for her help before, not like this. And with her kids involved, how could she deny it?

"I'll meet you at Sullivan's at twelve-thirty," she said grudgingly.

"Does it have to be there?" he asked.

She knew why he objected, because Dana Sue would be on the premises watching the two of them like a hawk, but she refused to back down. "Yes, it has to be there. And try to be on time. I have a busy day tomorrow."

He looked taken aback by that, but before he could comment, she left the room and took her exhausted daughter upstairs.

* * *

Bill hated the thought of having any kind of personal conversation with Maddie in a restaurant owned by one of her best friends. He knew Dana Sue would be hovering around them like a mother hen at the first sign he was upsetting Maddie.

He'd never paid that much attention to friendships in his own life. He had a few golf buddies and a lot of professional associates, but no one to whom he would consider baring his soul. After seeing the way Dana Sue and Helen had rallied around Maddie when her marriage had broken up, he'd wondered what it would be like to have people like that in his corner.

For years the only person he'd needed was Maddie. And now she was no longer available. He was just starting to realize how much he missed their talks, how much he'd relied on her insights, how much he'd counted on her backup with the kids.

And how unfair he was probably being asking her to help him fix a disaster of his own making.

He stood up when she walked across the restaurant, impressed with how much she'd changed recently. It wasn't her outfit. She'd always dressed in a way that made him proud. It was her demeanor. There was a new confidence radiating from her. He'd been noticing that more and more lately.

He brushed her cheek with an impulsive kiss as he would have a few months ago, and winced when she regarded him with dismay.

"Sorry," he muttered. "Old habit."

"I only have an hour, so tell me what's on your mind," she said briskly.

"The kids, of course," he said irritably. "And I've already ordered for us to save time."

"Fine," she said. "Bill, surely you're not surprised that they're still upset by all the changes they've gone through."

"Maddie, it's been months now. I really thought they'd get over it once they got to know Noreen, but they hate her. At least Ty does and Kyle's starting to act the same way. They're not willing to give her a chance. How do I make that right?"

"Maybe by warning them when you intend to include her," she suggested mildly. "I gather they were caught off guard last night. They were expecting to have dinner out alone with their dad. They need to spend time with you, Bill. They need to know that you're still their dad, first and foremost."

"I can't tell Noreen she has to stay home," he said, as a waitress brought their salads.

"Why not?" Maddie demanded, after the waitress had left. "If she upsets your children, why can't you simply explain that there are going to be times when you need to see them on your own to make this transition easier. I don't think she's an evil person or even insensitive. If you explain it to her, she ought to be able to handle it and not think you're trying to cut her out of their lives or yours. But if she really is that insecure, you're going to find being married to her a pretty rocky road."

"Okay, I see your point, but if the kids don't spend any time with her, how will they ever get to know her?"

Maddie gave him an impatient look. "It's a balancing act, okay? You set aside time just for them. You include Noreen on other occasions. It's not that complicated."

"But—"

"Look, you asked for my advice and I'm trying to give it to you. You don't have to take it. Ignore it and watch things continue to deteriorate until you have no relationship with your children at all. It's up to you." She rose to her feet.

"Where are you going?"

"This was a bad idea. I'm going back to work."

"But we're not finished," he said, desperate for her to stay. "You haven't even touched your food."

"You're wrong, Bill. We are most certainly finished. That was your choice, too."

She was gone before he could think of a single legitimate reason to keep her there. And now he felt as if all the life had been sucked right out of him.

"Can I get you anything else?" Dana Sue inquired.

Bill looked up at her, expecting to see her gloating over his dismay, but instead her gaze was sympathetic. That was harder to take than Maddie's departure.

"No," he said stiffly. He pulled a couple of twenties from his wallet and left the money on the table.

"But you never ate," she said, trying to hand it back.

"No, but I took up a table at the busiest time of the day. Give the money to the waitress."

He left, knowing that he'd managed to surprise one person today, aside from himself. All those sudden insights about just how much he'd lost when he'd walked away from his marriage were going to weigh on him for a long time to come.

It was after six when Maddie glanced up from all the papers and catalogs she'd been working on and spotted Cal standing in the doorway of her makeshift office, his expression troubled.

"This is a surprise," she said, regarding him warily and regretting that she couldn't take even a minute to appreciate the very masculine way his jeans hugged his thighs and the dark blue T-shirt emphasized his muscular shoulders. "I can't sign you up for a membership, you know. You're unmistakably the wrong gender."

"Bet I could talk you into it," he said, a faint grin crossing his lips. "But that isn't why I'm here."

She stared at him and waited.

"Ty didn't show up for baseball practice today," he announced, pulling out a chair opposite her. "Any idea why?"

Maddie felt her stomach plummet. "Did you call the house by any chance?"

"No answer," he said tersely. "And I drove by before coming here, but no one answered when I rang the bell."

"Dammit," she muttered. "I am going to kill my soon-to-be ex-husband."

"What does he have to do with this?"

She met his concerned gaze evenly. "I really shouldn't be dumping my problems on you, Cal. It's not fair."

"When it affects someone as important to my team as Ty is, then I'm more than willing to listen and do whatever I can to help. I mean that, Maddie."

She heard the sincerity in his tone and fought the temptation to spill everything—Bill's insensitivity to his children's feelings, her own frustrations, Ty's anger, the changes in Kyle's previously upbeat personality, Katie's wrenching sorrow. But despite what he said, these weren't Cal's problems to solve.

"It's nothing new. Ty's still having difficulty adjusting to the new woman in his dad's life."

Cal nodded. "But what happened yesterday or today that would make him skip practice? He's a responsible kid, Maddie. Even when he wasn't playing his best, at least he showed up."

She finally described the awkward dinner the kids had

had with their father and Noreen the night before and the argument that had ensued at the house. "Ty and Kyle think I don't understand what they're going through. I think they're both feeling very alone right now." She gave him a helpless look. "I keep trying to find some middle ground, some way to help them make peace with their dad's decision, but obviously I'm not succeeding."

"Any idea where Ty might be now?"

"If he's not at the ball field, no," she said, reaching for her purse. "Which means I need to start looking."

"I'll drive you," Cal said.

"You don't need to."

"It'll be easier for you to make some calls to his friends, while I drive," he said.

She nodded, unable to argue with that. "Thank you."

As she passed by, he gave her shoulder a light squeeze. "You're a good mom, Maddie. Don't doubt yourself on that score."

"Then why is my sixteen-year-old son so terribly unhappy?"

"Because he's filled with all sorts of conflicting emotions that he has no idea how to handle," Cal said.

"Conflicting emotions?"

"I imagine a part of him does want to make peace with his dad, to reconnect with him. It's baseball season and you told me yourself that it's something they always shared. Now it's a source of conflict because you and his dad don't even come to the same games. If he's glad to see his dad, even a little bit, he feels disloyal to you. And here you are pushing him toward his dad and this new woman. It's bound to be confusing."

Maddie stared at him in wonder. "How'd you get to be so smart?"

"Not smart. I just spend a lot of time with teenagers, and more than I'd like to see are going through this or something similar. And I was a teenage boy once, too. I remember the highs and lows. There never seems to be much middle ground."

She forced herself to ask the question that had been tormenting her for some time now. "Do you think Ty needs professional help?"

He met her gaze. "Do you?"

"I don't want to believe he does. I'm his mom. I ought to be able to fix this, but I don't want to let my ego get in the way and wind up hurting him even more. He can't keep running away. One of these days he's going to wind up in real trouble. He needs to find some other way to deal with his anger."

"Then talk to him and keep on talking, even when you think he's not listening. You're tuned in, Maddie. I don't think this is going to spiral out of control without you noticing. And you've got a second pair of eyes in me. Believe me, I intend to explain that skipping practice hurts the team and it won't be tolerated."

"I will never be able to thank you enough for caring about my son," she said.

He gave her a look she couldn't quite interpret, but it sent a little shiver down her spine and made her wonder—not for the first time—if Ty wasn't the only one Cal cared about. But that issue was way too complicated for this afternoon. Right now, all that mattered was finding her son.

CHAPTER TWELVE

There were at least a dozen different moments while he and Maddie searched for Ty that Cal wanted to reach out and pull her into his arms to comfort her. But though her lower lip quivered and tears welled up in her eyes as every place they checked turned up empty, she didn't lose it. Not once.

"I better call Bill," Maddie finally said, sounding resigned. "He needs to know what's going on. Maybe he's even heard from Ty, though given the way things are between them, I doubt it."

"Still, it's hard to tell what Ty might do. He might even have gone to have it out with his dad," Cal said. He glanced over and caught the reluctance in Maddie's expression. He came up with a brief reprieve. "Would you prefer to go by the house first, see if Ty's turned up there? Maybe check on Kyle and Katie? I know you're worried about them being there by themselves, even though Kyle's babysat before. Once you've checked on them, you can call Bill with the latest information we have."

"Yes, let's do that," she said gratefully. "Maybe Ty's called the house since the last time I checked with Kyle."

She'd spoken to Kyle less than five minutes earlier, but

for now she needed to cling to whatever hope she could. Cal wouldn't take that from her.

When they arrived at Maddie's, Cal pulled in to the driveway right behind another car that was just cutting its engine.

"Who's that?" he asked.

"My mother," Maddie said, shoving her door open and climbing out just as the passenger door in the other car opened and Ty emerged. When he spotted his mother and Cal, he hung his head, the picture of guilt.

"I'll be inside," he muttered and headed for the house.

Paula Vreeland got out from behind the wheel and smiled wearily at Maddie. "I've been trying to reach you, but I don't have your cell-phone number and you weren't answering at home or at the spa. The last time I called here, I spoke to Kyle and he said you were calling in, so I decided to just come on over."

"Where did you find Ty?" Maddie asked.

"He found me," Mrs. Vreeland said, a note of amazement in her voice. "He turned up at the house this afternoon. He admitted he'd skipped baseball practice and that you didn't know where he was. I insisted he call you." She shrugged. "He refused, so I tried."

"I'm glad he came to you," Maddie said. "But why?"

"We've been closer lately," her mother replied. "He thinks he can talk to me."

"He can talk to *me,*" Maddie protested, looking wounded.

"You and I know that," her mother soothed, "but it's Ty's perception that matters." She studied Maddie worriedly, then said, "He asked if he could move in with me for a while."

Maddie's mouth dropped open and her eyes filled with tears. Cal put a steadying hand on her shoulder. He could only imagine what a shock her mother's announcement must be.

"Why?" she asked her mother, sounding completely bewildered. "Did he tell you?"

"Why don't you two go inside and discuss this," Cal suggested. "Now that we know Ty's okay, I'll take off."

"Stay," both Maddie and her mother said at once.

It was Maddie's imploring look that got to him. "Of course, if you think I can help."

Inside, there was no sign of Ty. He'd obviously retreated to his room. "How about I go upstairs and try to talk to him?" Cal suggested. "Maybe I can get another perspective on what's going on with him. I can also explain the rules and consequences for missing practice, while you two have some time alone to figure out how you're going to handle this."

Mrs. Vreeland gave him a grateful look. "I think that's an excellent idea, Cal. Come, Maddie. I'll help you fix dinner. I'm sure the children are starved."

Maddie gave her an incredulous look. "You cook?"

Mrs. Vreeland chuckled, which broke the somber mood. "I realize you didn't have a traditional childhood, darling, but there were occasional meals on the table. How did you think they got there?"

"Dad? The housekeeper of the month?"

"Usually," her mother replied breezily. "But there were a few occasions on which I recalled all those lessons my mother gave me in the kitchen in her mostly wasted attempt to turn me into a proper Southern belle. Let's see if I can't whip up one of her tuna casseroles right now. That's good old-fashioned comfort food." She winked at Cal. "You'll stay, of course."

"Let's see how it goes," Cal said.

But despite his cautious reply, he knew in his gut there was no way he was walking away from this family as long as they showed any sign of needing him. Staying by Maddie's side felt right, and after getting it so wrong with Laurie, this felt damn good.

"Are you sleeping with him yet?" Maddie's mother inquired as she rooted through the cupboards for the ingredients for a tuna casserole.

"Mother!" Maddie exclaimed indignantly. "Don't you think there are more important things we should be discussing?"

Her mother grinned unrepentantly. "I suppose that depends on your point of view. Falling for a man runs pretty close to the top of most women's priority lists."

"Not when they have a son in crisis," Maddie retorted. "Besides, who said I was falling for Cal?"

"It's in your eyes when you look at him," her mother said, stirring the tuna and cream of mushroom soup together as the noodles simmered on the stove. "And in case you were wondering, it's in his eyes, too."

"I wasn't wondering," Maddie mumbled, but her cheeks were burning. "Mom, what on earth possessed Ty to come to you and ask to move in?"

"I think that's obvious. He's feeling torn between you and his dad. I'm neutral ground."

It was similar to something Cal had said, and it still cut Maddie's heart in two. "But I've done everything I can think of to make him not feel that way," she protested. "I've bent over backward to keep my feelings hidden, to try to broker some kind of relationship we can all live with."

"But don't you see, in some ways that just makes it worse," her mother explained. "He's furious on your behalf and you don't let him see that you are, too. I don't expect you to bad-mouth Bill, even though he deserves every vicious thing you might say, but you can own your own feelings. How's Ty supposed to interpret it when you act as if everything's just hunky-dory? Do you want him to think you're a doormat? What will that tell him to expect from the women in his life when the time comes for him to have a serious relationship?"

Stunned by the idea, Maddie could almost feel the color draining out of her face. "That's the last thing I want."

"Then sit him down and tell him how you really feel," her mother advised. "Let him know it's okay to be angry and hurt, but that it doesn't mean he can't still love his dad and you both. He needs to see you standing up for yourself, Maddie, not being some kind of martyr for the sake of the children."

Maddie had never thought of her actions in that way, but she could see her mother's point.

"Would it be best for Ty to stay with you, at least for the time being?" she asked, hating the idea but willing to consider it.

"Absolutely not," her mother said at once. "Not that I don't want him there. If it turns out that it's the best place for him to be, I'd welcome him. But I think he belongs here with you. He just needs to feel as if you're all on the same team, trying to get through this together. Include him, Maddie. Don't isolate him. Kyle, either. They're both old enough to be told the truth, to help you define how this new family is going to work."

Maddie buried her face in her hands. "This is so hard. How does anyone ever get it right?"

Her mother gave her a sad smile. "I doubt anyone ever gets it entirely right. People just muddle through and try not to do too much damage along the way." She glanced toward the ceiling. "Something tells me that having Cal in your corner won't hurt, either. Ty idolizes him and Cal seems to have a good head on his shoulders, in addition to having very good taste in women."

"Mother!"

"I'm just saying—"

Maddie frowned at her. "I know what you're saying, but I do not want you endorsing my love life, assuming I ever get around to having one again."

"It would be a crying shame if you didn't, that's all I'm saying." After one last stir of the ingredients, her mother tucked the casserole into the oven. "And now I think my job here is done. Tell Ty to stop by or call me anytime he wants. Maybe I can do a better job as a grandma than I ever did as a mother."

"You were a good mother," Maddie protested.

Her mother gave her a chiding look. "Don't rewrite history, darling. I loved you with all my heart, but I was obsessed with my work. I'd like to think I've finally found a better balance in my life. I just wish I'd had that epiphany in time to be a better mother to you."

She pressed a kiss to Maddie's forehead, then gave her a breezy wave as she exited.

"Mom, how are you going to get out of the driveway?" Maddie called after her. "Cal's parked behind you."

"Not to worry. That's why they invented power steering. I've gotten out of plenty of tight places in my life." She grinned. "And you have a big lawn."

Maddie was still chuckling when she looked up and spotted Cal.

"Is your mother leaving?"

She nodded.

"But I'm parked behind her."

She grinned at him. "She doesn't seem to think that will be a problem."

"Good God," he murmured and headed outside.

When he returned, there was a look of wonder on his face. "She's a little crazy, but she pulled it off. Not a scratch on either of our cars. I'm not sure I can say the same about your rosebush."

Maddie shrugged. "I've always hated that rosebush. Bill planted it. He thought it would save him from having to buy me roses for our anniversary every year. How'd things go with Ty?"

"He'll be down in a minute. You can ask him yourself. I think I'll take off."

A part of her knew he was right to go and give her much-needed time with her son, but another part of her wanted him to stay right there and provide backup when she was at a loss about what to say.

She gave him a rueful look. "I won't deny that I'd like it better if you'd stay. But you're right. Ty and I need to talk."

"I'll call you later to find out how it went," he promised.

Maddie nodded, already looking forward to the call more than she probably should. "Thanks for everything, Cal."

"Anytime." He hesitated, then met her gaze. "It's your turn to come to Friday's game, right? You weren't there for the one we played yesterday."

She nodded.

"Pizza after?"

It was her turn to hesitate, but then she nodded, granting herself that one small pleasure in a sea of uncertainty. "Sure. It sounds good."

Besides, what was one more complication in her life? At least this one gave her something to look forward to.

* * *

Maddie was just pulling the tuna casserole out of the oven when Katie appeared in the kitchen doorway, her thumb stuck in her mouth. Maddie regarded her with dismay. She'd thought the thumb-sucking was a habit broken long ago.

"How's my girl?" she asked, trying not to show how worried she was by the regression.

"Okay," Katie said, but her sad eyes told another story. "Is Daddy coming home for dinner?"

"No, sweetie, we've talked about that," Maddie said gently. She pulled out a chair and sat down, then beckoned to her daughter. "Come sit with Mommy."

Katie scrambled eagerly into her lap, then leaned against her chest, thumb still firmly in her mouth.

"Your dad doesn't live here anymore," Maddie told her, brushing a wayward curl from Katie's silky cheek. "You've been to his new house. Except when he goes out for dinner with you, Kyle and Tyler, that's where he eats now."

Katie heaved a resigned sigh. "With Noreen."

"That's right."

"How come?"

Maddie bit back her own sigh. It was a question she'd asked herself a million times over the past few months. She still didn't have a clear answer, at least not one suitable for a six-year-old who still idolized her dad.

"Because that's where your dad wants to be now," she explained carefully. "But he still loves you and your brothers very much and he wants you to be part of his new life with Noreen. That will never change. He will always be your dad." How many times was she going to have to repeat these same words to her children? Until they truly believed them, she supposed.

Katie certainly didn't look convinced, just sad. "Ty says he 'bandoned us."

"He moved out, that's true," Maddie conceded. "But he did not abandon you. He loves you."

Katie regarded her with solemn blue eyes. "Does he still love you?"

"No, baby. I'm afraid not."

"Are you sad?"

"A little bit, because your dad and I had you and Kyle and Tyler and I thought we'd be a family always, but sometimes life doesn't work out the way we expect. When it doesn't, we just have to accept it and make the best of things."

Tears welled up and spilled down Katie's cheeks. "I miss Daddy," she whispered. "Ty doesn't. He hates him. He's glad he's gone."

"I don't believe that," Maddie said. "He's just hurt and confused right now, but deep down, Tyler loves your dad just as much as you do."

She glanced up and saw Ty just outside the kitchen door. He looked as if he wanted to contradict her, but at her warning look, he remained silent.

Maddie brushed the tears from Katie's cheeks. "Why don't you go upstairs and tell Kyle that dinner's ready, okay, sweetie?"

Katie gave her another fierce hug, then climbed down and took off past her older brother.

"Why'd you tell her I love Dad?" Ty demanded angrily. "She's right. I hate him."

"Even if you do, which I don't believe, it's not something your six-year-old sister needs to hear. She needs to know it's okay to love her dad, even if she's sad and disappointed. Don't take that away from her, Tyler. This is hard enough as it is." She met his gaze. "Can you at least watch what you say around her?"

He flushed guiltily. "I guess."

"Thank you."

"Are you gonna let me move in with Grandma?"

"No," she said flatly.

He stared at her incredulously. "How come? I thought you'd be glad to get me out of the house, especially since you think I'm such a bad influence on Katie and Kyle."

"We're a family," she reminded him. "We stick together."

"I guess Dad didn't get that message," he said sarcastically.

"Apparently you missed it, as well," she retorted. "And for the record, one thing we do in this family is let each other know where we are at all times. I'm going to let today's incident pass, since you're already grounded, but add it to the list of things you think about while you're confined to the house."

"I went to Grandma's," he said. "What's the big deal?"

"The big deal is that you skipped baseball practice, where you were supposed to be. You let your coach and team down. You scared me to death. You've always been more thoughtful than that, Ty. I don't expect that kind of inconsiderate behavior from you and I won't tolerate it. In addition, you worried Coach Maddox, who's been nothing but good to you. And he and I spent more than an hour riding all over town trying to find you. None of that is acceptable. Frankly, if I were your coach, I'd bench you for missing practice."

Ty's eyes widened at that. "Did he tell you he was going to do that? He didn't say it to me. I mean, he talked about rules and consequences and stuff, but he didn't bench me."

"I'm just saying what I'd do in his place."

"I guess it's a good thing you're not the coach," Ty muttered.

"For your sake, yes, it is," she agreed. "But I am your mother and I expect your respect and consideration. Another incident like this and I'll have to reevaluate whether baseball means as much to you as you claim it does. It might turn out that it will no longer be the exception that gets you out of this house."

He swallowed hard and for the first time looked as if he finally understood the seriousness of what he'd done. "I'm sorry, Mom. I didn't do it to be mean or anything. I just wanted to talk to someone who'd be on my side."

Maddie felt a new ache in her heart. "Ty, I am *always* on your side. Please believe that."

He regarded her with a guilty expression. "I know, Mom. It won't happen again, I promise."

Maddie suspected it would, at least in some form or another, but for now she was satisfied that she'd gotten through to him.

She set the tuna casserole on the table, then pulled a salad from the fridge.

"Who made the casserole?" Ty asked, regarding it warily. "It doesn't look like yours."

Maddie grinned. "Your grandmother made it. She was proving a point."

"That she ought to stick to art?"

"Don't let her hear you say that." Maddie smiled. "I watched what went into it. It should be okay."

"Meaning it'll taste good or that we won't die?" Ty asked skeptically.

Maddie studied the bubbling concoction with her own share of skepticism, then shrugged. "Both, I hope."

* * *

On Friday afternoon Bill started thinking about that night's game against the high school's biggest rival. Everyone in town turned out for this game. The rivalry had gone on for at least fifty years. Decorated cars traveled in a caravan marked by pom-poms and banners whether the game was played in Serenity or in the neighboring town.

Bill had never missed it, not in all the years he'd attended high school, not since Ty had started pitching for the team. It was Maddie's turn to attend the game but he couldn't help wondering if she would mind switching with him just this once. Or maybe they could both go. Perhaps Noreen wouldn't even have to find out about it. Where baseball was concerned, anyway, since he and Maddie had worked out their new arrangement, she seemed to be less insecure. Lately there'd been no reason for Noreen to check up on him, so she'd kept her distance from the ball field. He had to admit, everyone seemed happier.

As soon as he'd seen his last patient, he grabbed his briefcase and jacket and headed out the door. Unfortunately Noreen caught up with him.

"Where are you going?" she asked.

Bill bristled, though her tone was merely curious rather than possessive. "I have to run an errand," he said mildly. "I should be home for dinner in a couple of hours. Anything you need?"

He was surprised by how easily the lies tripped off his tongue. Maybe he'd perfected the skill when he'd been cheating on Maddie.

"Nothing," she said, but continued to study him quizzically. "Does Ty have a ball game tonight?"

He nodded.

"Didn't you go to the one earlier in the week?"

Again, he nodded, knowing that she'd figured out just what so-called errand he intended to run. He might as well admit it. "I thought I'd drop by the field just for an inning or two, not the whole game."

"Maddie's going to be there, isn't she?"

"I imagine she will be," he conceded. "But I won't sit with her. I won't even go into the stands. I can watch from the car. It's a big game. I'd like to see at least a little of it."

"I could ride along with you," she suggested. "If it's important to Ty, I'd like to be there, too. It'll give us something to talk about next time we're all out together." She met his gaze, her expression sad. "I know he doesn't want me there, Bill, but if I stay in the car, he won't even have to know I'm there. He's your son. I just want to find some common ground, maybe make things better for all of us."

Bill sighed and pulled her into his arms. "I know you do. And I know I'm asking a lot when I ask you to stay away from his games, but it's the way it has to be for now. Baseball's the most important thing he has in his life right now. He doesn't need any distractions."

"And that's all I am to him, right? A distraction," she said bitterly, jerking away from him. "I don't expect him to ever think of me as his mother, but couldn't he at least try to see me as a friend?"

"In time," Bill said. "I know he will in time. He's a teenager, Noreen. You can remember what that was like. It's confusing enough without having your family split apart."

She studied him for a long time, then sighed. "Maybe you should have remembered that before you got involved with me," she said wearily. "I'll see you at home."

Bill watched her square her shoulders and lift her chin as she walked away, but he knew there were tears spilling down her cheeks. Despite her role as the other woman in this situation, she was a good, decent person. Otherwise he didn't think he would have allowed her to come between him and Maddie.

"Noreen, wait," he called after her. "Let's go to Rosalina's for pizza."

She turned back, swiping at the tears glistening on her cheeks. "Really?" she asked, her expression brightening as if he'd offered her the moon.

He grinned. "Sure. Why not? We can hang out till the team comes in. The local radio station broadcasts the games, so they'll have it on at Rosalina's and we can listen to it together."

"How's Ty going to feel if we're there when he comes in?" she asked.

"We won't stay," Bill said, warming to the idea. "We'll just say hello, congratulate him on his pitching if they win and then take off. I'm sure it will be okay as long as we don't stick around."

Noreen looked doubtful. "He's embarrassed about me, especially in front of his friends," she reminded him.

"Then we'll go before he gets there," Bill said, knowing she was right. "But you and I will be able to share the game and you'll have something to talk to him about the next time we get together."

"Perfect," she said, beaming at him. She stood on tiptoe and kissed him. "Thank you."

"Don't thank me," he said gruffly.

After all, if he had a decent bone left in his body, he'd try to remember that this was the woman he'd chosen over his family. She didn't deserve to spend one single moment thinking she was second best.

The truth was, as young as she was, Noreen had borne up amazingly well under the judgmental scrutiny of Serenity's nosiest residents, especially once she'd been unable to hide her pregnancy. She'd known that most of the town had taken sides and that Maddie had won the contest. But not once had she expressed a single ounce of self-pity. In fact, she'd done everything she could think of to stand tall and fit in, especially when it came to his children. It was the circumstances, not Noreen, that had made that impossible.

Bill looked at her glowing face, saw the eagerness shining in her eyes and impulsively leaned down to kiss her. "Have I told you lately how beautiful you are?"

She gave him a tremulous smile. "Not really."

"Well, it's true. I don't know how I got so lucky."

Unfortunately, he also had no idea why his good fortune wasn't making him happy.

CHAPTER THIRTEEN

Nearly a dozen pieces of top-of-the-line exercise equipment had arrived at the club Friday morning. Most were still in their boxes and had been shoved to one side in what would be the main workout room, but Maddie had persuaded Mitch to unpack and hook up one treadmill just so she could give it a try. He'd positioned it in front of the wide expanse of windows facing the woods, just as she'd envisioned it.

Now, at the end of a long and tedious day, she had maybe ten minutes before she needed to leave to pick up Katie and Kyle and get to the field for Ty's game. She climbed onto the machine, checked the settings and started it up. As she settled into an easy stride, she gazed out at the tranquil setting and felt her cares slip away. If it could do that for her in under a minute, just imagine what it would do—

"My turn," Helen said.

Maddie was so startled she nearly stumbled off the platform. "Where'd you come from? Don't sneak up on a person that way!" She climbed off and let Helen take her place.

"I saw Mitch earlier and he mentioned that the equipment had arrived. I was anxious to get a peek. Is that the rest of it over there?" She nodded toward the assortment of boxes across the room.

"Yep. If all of it is as great as this, our members will be ecstatic," Maddie said.

"Why didn't you have Mitch's crew unpack it?"

"There's still too much work to be done in here. It would be in the way and get filthy besides." Maddie grinned. "I couldn't resist trying one machine, though." She ran her fingers over the elaborate control panel. "Isn't it fabulous?"

"Not just the treadmill, but this view," Helen said, already looking more relaxed. "Honestly, I could swear I feel better already."

"I know," Maddie said excitedly. "I did, too. I'm really starting to believe this place is going to be a wonderful addition to the town."

Helen regarded her with an odd expression. "You didn't believe that going in?"

"Not really. I was too focused on what it would mean for me to have a project I could sink my teeth into," Maddie admitted. "And of course, there were the health benefits for the three of us."

Helen gave her a wry look. "I could have bought us all memberships in Chez Bella a lot cheaper."

"I know, but you wouldn't have *owned* it," Maddie said with a laugh. "You do have control issues, you know."

Helen shrugged, not denying it. "You going to the game?"

Maddie glanced at her watch and realized she was now running late. "Yes, and I need to pick up the kids. You want to come along?"

"Not tonight. I have to be in court on Monday and it's going to take me all weekend to get my ducks in a row."

Maddie studied her worriedly. Helen spent way too much

time getting her ducks lined up. "Come over for Sunday dinner," she suggested. "You'll need a break by then. It's been a while since you've spent any time with the kids."

Helen gave her a sly look. "I will if you'll promise to tell me everything about your date with Cal."

"I don't have a date with Cal."

"What would you call it? He invited you to have pizza after the game again, didn't he?"

"With the team," Maddie said. "And my kids."

"Even better than a date," Helen said.

"How do you figure that?"

"He's blending right into your life," Helen explained. "The steamy sex will come along in due time."

Maddie rolled her eyes, but she couldn't seem to stop the little buzz of anticipation that Helen's words triggered.

"I'll see you Sunday," she told Helen. "Don't stay on that treadmill too long. You don't want to wear it out before we get the doors open."

Helen merely waved, then set the machine's speed up another notch and began to jog. Compulsive, type A, Maddie thought as she observed her silently. She couldn't help wondering if exercise would be as good for Helen as the doctor believed or if it would just be one more thing Helen obsessed over.

The team was jubilant. Ty had only pitched five innings before Cal had taken him out for a reliever, but their lead had been protected. They'd walked away with a shutout over the toughest team in their division and their biggest rival in the entire region. Emotions always ran high at these games and tonight had been no exception. Cal couldn't have been more proud of the way they'd all pulled together.

When he walked with the team into Rosalina's, he immediately looked for Maddie, who'd left the ball field ahead of him. He spotted her sitting all alone at a table in a darkened corner, far away from the cluster of tables that had been set up for the team. Kyle was by himself at the team table, looking angry. Another glance around the crowded room revealed why. On the opposite side of the restaurant sat Bill Townsend with his very pregnant girlfriend. Some of Cal's excitement died as he realized the amount of tension their presence was bound to cause.

Though he was tempted to walk over and say something, Cal knew it wasn't his place. At the ball field, Ty's father might tolerate Cal's interference in his personal life because of its effect on Ty, but here, he'd probably resent the hell out of it. And he'd be justified.

As soon as the team was settled, Cal crossed to Maddie's table and pulled out a chair. "Where's Katie?" he asked, leaving the topic of Bill up to her.

"Playing the games with Danielle and Danielle's folks," she said. "Thank heavens she didn't spot her dad in here."

"I gather you weren't expecting him, either."

"No."

"At least he's keeping his distance from Ty," Cal said, observing the couple across the room. "After the incredible game Ty pitched, it would be a shame to have Bill's presence spoil the evening for him."

Even as Cal spoke, he watched Ty leave his teammates, a mutinous expression on his face, and walk over to his dad. Whatever he said had Bill rising to his feet and Noreen looking embarrassed.

"Think I should go over there and run interference?" Cal asked.

Maddie shook her head, even though her eyes were dark

with worry. "Let Ty handle this. He needs to be able to deal with his dad."

Cal noticed that Bill's fists were clenched, but there was no shouting. Eventually he and Ty appeared to relax. Ty accepted his dad's outstretched hand, then went back to his seat.

"Thank God," Maddie murmured.

A moment later Bill and Noreen headed for the door. Right before they left, Bill detoured toward Cal and Maddie, leaving Noreen waiting.

"I know you probably think I shouldn't have come here tonight, especially not with Noreen," he told Maddie. "We really had planned to be gone before the team got here, but when the bus pulled up outside, I decided to wait for Ty and take a minute to congratulate him. I didn't intend to make him uncomfortable."

Cal watched Maddie's struggle to keep her emotions in check.

"Did your conversation with Ty go okay?" she asked eventually, her tone perfectly neutral.

Bill regarded her with unmistakable relief. "As a matter of fact, it did. He was even civil to Noreen when she congratulated him."

"I'm glad."

He looked from her to Cal, acknowledging him for the first time. "Congratulations on the win, Coach."

"Thanks."

"I didn't expect to see you two here together again," Bill said, his disapproving gaze shifting back to Maddie. "You know how people in this town love to talk. Next thing you know, they'll be turning the two of you into an item. Are you sure that's a good idea?"

Before Cal could respond, Maddie frowned and countered, "I wasn't the first one in our family to stir up gossip, and I doubt I'll be the last. If you were all that worried about talk, you might have done a few things differently yourself."

Bill looked as if he'd bitten into a very sour lemon. With a terse "Good night," he turned and stalked away, his back rigid.

"I am so sorry," Maddie apologized.

"For what?"

"Anything he might have said that made you uncomfortable. He was being more of a jerk than usual tonight."

"He's jealous," Cal told her.

"Jealous?" Maddie echoed. "No way."

Cal grinned. "Some men might think I'm worthy of jealousy, especially when I'm out with the mother of their children."

Maddie blushed. "I didn't mean you aren't worth being jealous over, just that there's nothing between us to stir anyone's jealousy."

Cal's expression sobered as he met her gaze and held it. "Are you sure about that, Maddie?" he asked quietly.

"I—" her blush deepened "—I don't know what you mean."

"Yes, you do," he said. "But I'm not going to push you, not tonight anyway. One of these days, though, maybe we ought to talk about what's going on here."

"We're friends," she said, sounding a little desperate to pin a label on it right now.

"We are," he agreed.

But if he had his way, it was going to turn into something more. And maybe it was only his ego talking, but he was pretty sure she wasn't going to fight him when the time came.

Maddie was relieved when an entire week went by and she barely saw Cal. There were no crises with Ty. She went to the Wednesday afternoon game, then slipped away before it was over. It was Bill's turn to attend the Friday night game. She could use every second she was away from Cal to regain her equilibrium. He confused her. He seemed to be hinting at a future she didn't want to allow herself to consider.

Okay, she wanted to consider it, but it wasn't sensible or practical with her kids already so confused about Noreen. A relationship with Cal would be the stuff of fantasies, a man ten years her junior actually thinking she was hot enough for an affair. And that's all it could be. Surely he wasn't thinking beyond that, not with all the baggage she carried. And Cal had baggage, too, for that matter. Trust issues.

Still, in a moment of extreme weakness, she imagined crawling into bed with that hard, muscular body, making love to him, letting herself come apart in the safety of his arms. Because that's what she knew above all—she would be safe with Cal. He'd shown time and time again that he was willing to put her needs first, that he cared for who she was as a woman and a mother, not just as a potential lover.

Oh, God, she thought, moaning at the ridiculousness of her fantasy. It would never happen. She couldn't allow it to happen. Bill had been right about one thing—Serenity was a small town where reputations could be made or broken in a heartbeat. Maybe her ex could get away with his indiscretion simply because everyone accepted that men were weak, even idiotic from time to time, especially as they approached middle age. Women, down here in the world of Southern belles, were expected to live by a higher standard. Men slapped them up on pedestals and expected them to stay put.

"My, my, that's a lovely blush on your cheeks," Dana Sue noted, breezing into Maddie's office with a file folder. "Thinking about Cal, I assume."

"What's in the folder?" Maddie asked, refusing to get drawn into that discussion, especially right now when her defenses were low and her mind was dodging X-rated fantasies.

"You can't avoid this conversation forever," Dana Sue said.

"Oh, but I can, especially since we've already had it way too many times," Maddie corrected. "Come on—what's in the folder?"

Her friend regarded her with disappointment, but eventually relented. "A schedule for cooking classes," she said, handing it over. "See what you think."

Just then Jeanette wandered in, wearing a sample of the new smock they were considering for their spa clients. "Good. You're both here," she said, tugging at a hemline that barely reached her thighs. "This'll save us a couple of bucks, maybe, but I think it's too short. We don't want people to have to wear their street clothes while they're getting treatments. We want them to feel pampered."

"True," Dana Sue said.

Jeanette went on. "A good smock or robe will make them feel as if they're being wrapped in luxury. If we buy good quality, the smocks will last forever, even with constant washing. I think it's a good investment, but it's not my money."

"Do you have a sample of the one you prefer?" Maddie asked.

Jeanette grinned and brought her hand out from behind her back. "I was hoping you'd ask." She held out a satin-textured, polyester robe in pale peach that tied around the waist. "We could have our logo embroidered on this in white. It would only cost a little extra and it would be so classy."

"Classy is what we're going for," Dana Sue said. "And

Helen is all about classy. I vote yes. Want me to call her and run it by her, Maddie?"

Maddie winced. Did she have to run all the financial decisions past Helen? Helen hadn't asked her to. She said she trusted Maddie's judgment.

"What's this going to do to your budget?" she asked Jeanette. They'd gone over the figures the week before and she'd discovered that Jeanette had mastered them and had a terrific grasp of which corners could be cut and which would compromise their image.

"It would double it," Jeanette admitted. "But I could order a little less skin-care product initially to balance it out, though frankly, as soon as people have one of our treatments, the products we use are going to fly off the shelves."

"Then it doesn't sound as if that's a smart option," Maddie told her.

Jeanette's expression turned thoughtful. "How far ahead have you projected a budget for supplies?"

"Not that far," Maddie admitted. "Three months ahead now and I was going to do a six-month projection after we get the doors open. Why?"

"I was wondering if you'd figured in replacement costs for the smocks. If you had, we could make up the difference there. These are excellent quality, so we wouldn't have to replace them nearly as often."

She and Dana Sue looked at Maddie expectantly.

"Do it," Maddie said at last. "But please, please find a way to cut some other corners till we can get this place up and running."

"The grand opening is less than a month away," Dana Sue reminded her. "And you've said yourself that memberships are way ahead of projections."

"And I've already started booking treatment appointments," Jeanette said. "In fact, we're booked solid for the first two weeks, both facials and massages. I've had a lot of requests for manicures and pedicures, too, so we need to get a manicurist on board as soon as we can so I'll be able to start booking those appointments."

Maddie brightened. "Really?"

Jeanette grinned. "I told you I know how to organize this kind of stuff. And once we do that friends-and-family special the week before we open, I think we're going to be booked through summer," she said. "I might have to hire additional help beyond what we've talked about, especially if we want to add herbal body wraps."

"There's no money in the budget for even one more person yet," Maddie warned. "Besides, it'll do people good to know that we're booked so far in advance. That just adds to the aura that we're the hottest new spot in town."

"Which we will be," Dana Sue said. "Now, let's talk food. Look at the class schedule, please."

Maddie handed a copy to Jeanette and looked over her own sheet.

"Oh, my God, sign me up," Jeanette murmured eventually. "I may not want to know how to cook these things, but I sure want to be around when you're serving them up."

Dana Sue laughed. "Which one sounds the best?"

"Desserts, of course," Jeanette said. "Can you really do a bread pudding that won't send me to carbohydrate hell?"

"I think Erik has the recipe just about down pat," Dana Sue said. "Maybe I'll have him make it for next Tuesday when we get together, and you can tell me what you think."

"Count me in," Jeanette said. "I haven't touched bread pudding since I left home, but even the thought of it makes my mouth water."

"If you can't make it till next Tuesday, we do serve it at

the restaurant," Dana Sue told her. "Of course, for now it's still the old-fashioned, full-calorie version complete with a scoop of homemade cinnamon ice cream on top."

Jeanette stared at her with openmouthed awe. "I am so there." She turned to Maddie. "Will you come with me? Just for dessert. My treat. You'll still be at home in time for dinner with the kids, if you can eat another bite after all that decadence."

Maddie started to decline, then decided that a half-hour indulgence was well deserved after the long weekdays she'd been putting in. She could take some home to the kids, too. Bread pudding was one of Katie's favorites, and Erik's version of it had earned her daughter's devotion. She begged for the treat whenever they went to the restaurant.

Dana Sue grinned at her. "I'll make up a to-go carton for Katie," she said, as if she'd read Maddie's mind. "I'll even put it in a cooler so the ice cream won't melt."

"Then let's get out of here," Maddie said. "There's nothing on this desk that can't wait till tomorrow."

And her quandary over Cal could wait another day, too.

Maddie and Jeanette were just finishing up their bowls of bread pudding when Betty Donovan left her own meal, crossed to their table and pulled out a chair without waiting to be asked.

"Excuse me for interrupting," the high-school principal said with a brief glance at Jeanette, "but I really need to speak to Maddie."

Jeanette gave Maddie a questioning look, then stood up. "I need to be going anyway. Thanks for coming with me, Maddie. I'll settle up with Dana Sue on my way out."

"See you in the morning," Maddie told her, then drew in a deep breath as she turned to face the principal. "What's this about? I assume it's nothing pleasant. Otherwise, you wouldn't have been so rude to my friend."

Maddie had known Betty for years. The woman was as uptight now as she'd always been, but she'd never been flat out rude before. Betty blanched at Maddie's comment.

"I'm sorry. You're right. I could have handled that better," she admitted. "I had a lousy day at school and I assumed you wouldn't want someone else hearing what I have to say, so I chose to be direct."

"Then by all means, continue being direct," Maddie said tightly. "Is this about Tyler?"

"No, from everything I hear from his teachers, your son's doing better in school these days. I assume your husband laid down the law."

"You assume wrong. Bill's not much help in the discipline department these days. Come on, Betty, whatever's on your mind, just spit it out."

"Okay, then. It's about you and Coach Maddox."

Maddie immediately tensed. "What about us? Not that there is an *us*."

"Oh, please, you can hardly deny that there's something going on between you," Betty said.

"I most certainly can—and do—deny it," Maddie retorted. "He's Ty's coach and my friend. That's it."

"That's not the way it looks to the other parents. They're convinced that Ty is getting preferential treatment from the coach because you and Cal are so cozy. I field a dozen calls after every game you attend. It's as if you're rubbing the relationship in people's faces."

Maddie held on to her temper by a very fragile thread. "I shouldn't even dignify that with a response, but I will. My son is the best pitcher on our team. Any preferential treatment he might get—and frankly I doubt it's any—is because of that and nothing else. To suggest otherwise demeans not only my son but Coach Maddox. The coach can stand up for himself, but I will stand up for my son, so you need to tell those busybodies reporting to you to get a life and stay the hell out of mine."

She stood up and tossed her napkin on the table, hoping the other woman didn't see that she was trembling. "Now, if you'll excuse me, I have to pick something up in the kitchen and get home to my kids."

Betty stood up, too. "I'm just trying to give you fair warning," she said, not backing down. "I'm sure you don't want this to get ugly."

"It can only get ugly if you let rumors and innuendo become more important than facts." Again, she started to walk away, then turned back. "You have a lot of influence with the parents, Betty. You're in a position to put a stop to this. Show some backbone and do it."

It was probably the right thing to say, but it was a mistake. Maddie knew it the instant she saw the flash of fire in Betty's eyes. They might never have been friends, but now Betty would definitely consider her an enemy. Not that Maddie cared, but she didn't want it having repercussions at school for her kids.

Before Maddie could offer a more tempered remark, Betty said, "I've warned Cal about this, too." Her expression was triumphant when she saw she'd taken Maddie by surprise.

"When did you speak to him?" Maddie asked.

"A few weeks ago. He wasn't inclined to take me seriously, either. I thought, having lived here all your life, you might be more sensible. Obviously I was mistaken."

"What is it you think we need to do?" Maddie asked. "Put up a banner at the games denying we're involved?"

"Simply staying away from the games might be a start," the principal suggested.

Maddie regarded her incredulously. "My son is the star pitcher. I won't be banished from his games because people choose to gossip."

"Up to you," Betty said with a shrug. "At the very least, I would suggest you avoid any more cozy little get-togethers with the coach at Rosalina's."

"Where an entire town is apparently watching everything we do," Maddie responded. "What could possibly be more out in the open than that? We're not snuggled up in the corner. We're not all over each other. We're not sneaking around behind anyone's back. My relationship with Cal is completely aboveboard. We haven't done a thing I would be ashamed for my children or anyone else to see."

"How many times has Cal ridden to your rescue lately when it comes to Ty?" Betty asked.

"Is that a crime, too?" Maddie was bewildered. "I'd think you'd be thrilled to have a teacher who genuinely cares about his students."

"Cal's concern for Ty is admirable," Betty admitted grudgingly. "It's the depth of his relationship with *you* that I question." She leveled a look into Maddie's eyes and there was a faint trace of sympathy in her expression. "I know you're going through a tough time, Maddie. Bill has behaved abominably. I really do understand that, but think about the harm you could be doing to Cal if you come to rely on him too much."

"What kind of harm?" Maddie asked slowly, though she already knew.

"If enough parents get stirred up, whether their attitudes are justified or not, the school board will have no choice but to examine whether Cal belongs in this school system."

Maddie's mouth fell open. She hadn't expected that. A censure of some sort, perhaps, a stern warning from the school board chairman even, but firing him? It was absurd.

"You'd fire him?" she demanded, making no attempt to hide her incredulity. "Over a couple of pizzas with a parent? That's insane."

"It could come to that," Betty declared grimly. "It's not the pizzas. It's the appearance that there's much more between you. As I said earlier, there's a standard in Serenity that we expect our teachers to adhere to."

And as Maddie knew all too well, in a town like Serenity, appearances were sometimes all that mattered.

"Let me ask you something," Maddie said. "Are you this interested in the social lives of all your teachers?"

Betty flinched. "I've warned other teachers from time to time when their behavior caused talk," she said stiffly. "We expect the staff at the high school especially to set an example, and Coach Maddox should be an exemplary role model."

"Did you mention to him before you hired him that you expected him to remain celibate and preferably alone for the duration of his teaching days in Serenity? Is there some morals clause that specifies that?"

"Don't be ridiculous. I never mentioned any such thing. But if parents lose confidence in a teacher or a coach, I have no choice—"

Maddie cut her off. "You always have a choice. If it's not about some morals clause that's probably not enforceable even if it does exist, then it's the fact that he's seeing *me* that's the real problem." The color that bloomed in Betty's cheeks proved she was right.

"This is personal, isn't it?" Maddie went on. "You've

never gotten over the fact that Bill chose me over you, have you? Well, now that you've seen how that turned out, perhaps you should thank your lucky stars." She leveled a look into the other woman's eyes. "I know you and everyone else in this town has gotten used to me being the dutiful wife who's easily cowed, but trust me, you do not want to make an issue out of this. I've lived in this town even longer than you have and I know about *all* the scandals, including a few I'm sure you'd like to see remain buried."

She whirled away to the sound of Betty's sharply drawn breath. She made it into the kitchen before the trembling in her limbs nearly felled her. Clutching the stainless-steel countertop, she bit back the urge to scream.

Dana Sue rushed over and put an arm around her. "What on earth? Are you okay?"

"I will be," Maddie said grimly. "But I'd get Betty Donovan out of here if I were you."

"Why?" Dana Sue shook her head. "Never mind. I'm on it. Do you need anything before I get back?"

"Nothing, though you might want to lock up the knives."

Dana Sue cast such a frantic glance toward her sharply honed carving knives that Maddie smiled, despite her outrage.

"Just teasing, I swear," she assured her friend. "But not about getting that woman out of here. If I see her again before I leave here, I won't be responsible for the scene I cause."

"Give me five minutes," Dana Sue said. "Kicking her to the curb will be my pleasure. I never did trust her. She was always a Goody Two-shoes."

The immediate display of loyalty bolstered Maddie. Her warning to Betty to back off had been pure bravado, but now, with Dana Sue's unquestioning support, she knew she could fight Betty, the school system or anyone else she had to.

She just prayed it wouldn't come to that.

CHAPTER FOURTEEN

Maddie was calmer by the time Dana Sue returned to the kitchen.

"She's gone," Dana Sue said. "Now, would you mind telling me what the hell she said to get you this upset? You haven't let Betty Donovan get under your skin like this since she announced she was better wife material for Bill than you were way back in tenth grade."

Maddie didn't think she could repeat Betty's accusations and warnings right now, not without getting all stirred up again just when she was finally getting a grip on herself.

"Could we talk about this another time?" she pleaded. "I need to get home to the kids and make dinner. I'm already running late."

She could tell from Dana Sue's determined expression that she wasn't going to get off that easily, but just then the restaurant's sous chef shouted that the orders were starting to back up.

"I need some help in here!" he said in a commanding way that immediately captured Dana Sue's attention.

Judging from her expression, he'd also stirred her ire. Maddie didn't know the man Dana Sue had hired just a month ago to help in the kitchen, but she had a hunch he wouldn't be around long. This kitchen was Dana Sue's domain. Her new pastry chef was an easygoing man who'd fit in perfectly, but this guy clearly had some control issues that guaranteed he and Dana Sue would be butting heads in no time.

Casting another scowl in the man's direction when he repeated his demand for help, Dana Sue muttered, "Okay, okay," as she moved back to the food preparation area. Even as she began to work, her gaze strayed back to Maddie. "I'm not forgetting about this," she told her. "I will see you first thing in the morning."

Needing the reprieve, Maddie would have agreed to just about anything. "Fine," she said.

"Your cooler's by the door," Dana Sue called after her.

Maddie stared at her blankly. "Cooler?"

"With the bread pudding and ice cream for Katie," Dana Sue reminded her with exaggerated patience.

"Of course," Maddie said. "Thank goodness one of us has a functioning brain."

She picked up the cooler and fled, knowing she was only postponing the inevitable.

Unfortunately, while she escaped Dana Sue's inquisition, she ran right smack into another potential minefield. Cal was waiting for her at the house.

"Is there a problem?" she asked as she exited the car trying to ignore the little *zing* that zipped through her at the sight of him. He was wearing faded jeans that hugged his thighs and hips, a navy blue T-shirt that made his eyes bluer than ever, and his hair was damp as if he'd just taken a shower. He looked so thoroughly male and she was feeling so rebellious, she was tempted to grab him and head for the nearest motel.

She knew she wouldn't, of course, but she had a hunch that *zing* was going to be even more difficult to resist now that she knew he was essentially forbidden.

"Nope, no problem," he said, sliding his hands into his pockets, an innocent enough gesture that had the electrifying effect of stretching denim taut over a very intriguing bulge. "I just gave Ty a ride home from practice and decided to stick around till you got here."

"Any particular reason?" she asked, dragging her gaze away.

"It's been a while since I've seen you."

"Not long enough," she muttered.

He regarded her with a puzzled expression. "What?"

"Nothing. You may as well come on in," she said ungraciously, then winced at her tone. She tried to counter it with a smile. "You can talk to me while I get dinner on the table."

He followed her into the house and immediately began to set the table. She glowered at him.

"Did I ask for your help?"

"No, but I was brought up to pitch in," he said, his tone even.

"So were my kids, but you don't see them rushing in here," she grumbled. She didn't need more evidence of his thoughtfulness, not when she was trying to remember he was off limits.

He paused and stared at her. "Is something wrong, Maddie? You seem a little tense and out of sorts."

"I'm fine," she insisted, her back to him so he wouldn't be able to read her expression. She was a crummy liar. Everyone said so.

He walked up behind her, not really crowding her, but making her all too aware of his presence. Her whole body hummed. Her response had to be the aftereffect of her conversation with Betty. It just had to be. She could not want this man this much.

"Maddie?" he said softly, then waited until she released a sigh and turned to face him. "What's going on?"

She barely resisted the urge to throw herself into his arms. Since doing such a thing would inevitably wind up leading down a path that was already stirring up more trouble than either of them could handle, she stood there rigidly, carefully avoiding his gaze.

"I'm waiting," he said, then tucked a finger under her chin and forced her gaze to meet his. "Talk to me."

"I don't want to," she said, aware that she sounded as petulant as Katie.

Cal chuckled. "Do it, anyway. You'll feel better. I promise."

"No, I won't. Once this can of worms is opened, neither one of us is going to feel better."

He looked taken aback. "What can of worms is that?"

"You and me and the Serenity Board of Education," she said succinctly.

"Excuse me?"

Since it was obvious he wasn't going to be satisfied until she explained completely, she decided to get it over with. "I had a little run-in with Betty Donovan earlier. She wants to make a mountain out of this molehill," she said, gesturing from him to her.

"Us," he said flatly. "Dammit, I thought I'd told her to get her nose out of my business."

"I'm sure you did," Maddie said. "But stopping Betty when she's on a self-righteous mission is like trying to slow a runaway freight train by waving a flag at it."

"What did she say to you?"

"In a nutshell? That we're behaving inappropriately and setting a bad example for the children of this community."

"That's hogwash!"

"Well, of course it is," Maddie said. "But that doesn't mean she can't make trouble for you, Cal. A lot of trouble." She met his gaze. "Which means you can't just show up here anymore. And I can't have pizza with you after the games. I'll turn to somebody else if I need help with Ty or leaky pipes or anything else. I will not let you jeopardize your career."

"You let me worry about my career," he said fiercely, then hesitated. "Or is there more at stake, Maddie? Has she threatened you, too?"

"No, only with the harm that I might be bringing down on you," she admitted. "There's nothing else she can hold over my head, except for the threat of a little embarrassment. I think I neutralized that."

He gave her an odd look. "Meaning?"

"Let's just say there are a few things in Betty's past she would prefer never came to light."

His lips twitched. "Do tell."

"Not a chance. I'm saving those big guns for when and if we need them."

"You surprise me," he said.

"You didn't think me capable of blackmail?"

"Something like that."

"I like to think even some of us baseball moms are capable of hidden depths," she told him.

He cupped her face in his hands and studied her with a look she couldn't quite interpret.

"Amazing," he murmured right before he lowered his mouth to hers.

Even though she'd fantasized about such a kiss, even though she'd been anticipating it for some time now, Maddie was pretty sure her heart stopped. When it started again, it thundered in her ears. And all the while Cal's mouth moved over hers, tasting, savoring, lingering sweetly in a way that produced astonishing heat. Her hips swayed into his, fitting snugly against an impressive arousal. The shock of that had her stumbling back and thinking of what would happen if the kids wandered in.

"We can't," she said, turning away, her cheeks burning.

He laughed. "Oh, darlin', I think we've just proved we can."

"You know what I mean," she said impatiently. "Didn't you listen to a word I've been saying?"

"Every one," he said dutifully, though the corners of his mouth were twitching up.

"Well, then?"

"I'm not letting anyone dictate what I do in my private life," he told her.

"Is this some kind of weird challenge now?" she demanded. "I've been declared off limits, so now you want me?" She told herself it was irrelevant that she'd had a similar thought about him only a few minutes earlier.

Cal's lips curved again. "Hardly."

"You don't want me?" she asked, furious at the sudden self-doubt that stirred in her.

He reached for her hand and deliberately placed it over the zipper of his jeans. The denim was straining to contain the evidence of just how much he wanted her.

Again, thinking that her kids could walk in, she jerked her hand away. "Stop, Cal. The kids are here."

"Okay, you're right, but look at me," he commanded.

Maddie forced her gaze to his.

"I couldn't fake that if I wanted to," he said, his expression serious. "And so you know, I've wanted you that badly since the first day I set eyes on you. I even remember what you were wearing when you climbed up into the stands at Ty's first game. A pink blouse that should have looked all prim and proper, but you'd tied it at the waist and there was a tiny little bit of flesh showing. I couldn't take my eyes off that."

Maddie swallowed hard. "I see."

His gaze burned into her. "Do you? Do you understand that I won't walk away from this—from us—without a fight?"

What on earth was she supposed to say to that? she wondered.

Bring it on?

Cal left Maddie's before the kids came down to dinner. He didn't want to have to hide his fury over Betty Donovan's open declaration of warfare from them. Nor did he want to have to disguise the way he was feeling about their mother. Things were confusing enough for all of them right now. He totally got why Maddie would worry about that, as well as Betty's threats.

What he wanted to do was barge into the principal's home and give the woman a piece of his mind, but that wasn't smart, either. He'd been around Serenity long enough to understand that there were certain politics at work here. He needed to handle this just right or he could lose everything—his job and a woman with whom he was falling in love.

Just thinking about the L word should have stopped him in his tracks, but it didn't. He actually smiled. That's when he realized that he wasn't just falling in love with Maddie. He was already head over heels in love with her. He didn't know how or why that had happened, but he wasn't going to fight it. No, he was going to fight *for* it.

Still pondering that amazing truth, he drove aimlessly for a while down two-lane country roads that wound through pine trees and palmetto groves, the last red glow of the setting sun filtering through them. For most of the drive, the green landscape was broken only by the occasional field with a farmhouse or double-wide trailer sitting on the property, but to his dismay there seemed to be an increasing number of clear-cut acres obviously about to be turned into housing developments or strip malls.

Eventually he found himself back in Serenity and in front of Paula Vreeland's house. Every light was blazing, which told him she was home. Since there weren't a dozen cars in the driveway, he also assumed she was alone. He'd instinctively felt a certain connection with her the first time they'd met. Now that he knew she was Maddie's mother, the connection felt even stronger. Maybe she could offer a fresh perspective on all this.

His knock on the front door went unanswered. He wandered around to the back and spotted what had to be her studio. There, too, lights were blazing.

Crossing to it, he tried to make as much noise as possible so his unexpected arrival wouldn't alarm her. She was waiting for him at the door of the studio, her expression amused.

"I suggest you never try out for a job that requires sneaking up on people," she said. "You'd be a terrible covert operative."

"I didn't want to take you by surprise," he said.

"You didn't, though I am a little surprised that you're here at all."

"Do you mind?"

"A visit from a handsome man? Never," she said at once. "Come on in and have a seat. I'll clean the paint off me and we can have some tea." She took a closer look at him. "Or a drink."

"Tea will be fine," he assured her. "Mind if I look around?"

"Be my guest. You displayed great insight when you bought one of my paintings a while back. I'd like to hear what you think of these."

Cal wandered from canvas to canvas, surprised by her switch to oils and a far splashier palette than he'd seen in her prior work. "You're trying something new," he said carefully as he stood back to try to get the full effect. "Why?"

She came up beside him. "You don't like them?"

"I didn't say that. I was just wondering why you'd make such a dramatic shift in style."

"Boredom," she suggested. "Maybe I wanted to see if I have something different in me."

"Are you happy with the results?"

She linked her arm through his and studied the canvases along with him. "Artistically I think they're just fine," she said, then grinned up at him. "But I have to say they leave me cold. Sometimes people should just stick to what they know."

"And sometimes it takes a change to make them see that."

She gave him a knowing look. "But you didn't come over here to see what I was up to in my studio, did you? Is this about Maddie?"

He nodded.

"Then shouldn't you be talking to her about whatever's on your mind?"

"I have," he said. "And I will again. I thought maybe you could offer another perspective."

"I try to stay out of my daughter's business," she said,

then grinned again. "But if you want to talk about *your* business, I'm all ears. Let's get that tea. I might even have a couple of slices of pecan pie left. Interested?"

"Did you bake it?"

"Heavens, no! I know my limitations," she said with a laugh. "This came from the bake sale at church. It's excellent."

Once they were seated at the kitchen table, Cal looked around the basically sterile, purely functional room and couldn't help comparing it to the cozy warmth of Maddie's kitchen.

"Quite a contrast, isn't it?" Paula said. "Maddie set out to make her home everything ours wasn't. She knew instinctively what it took to make a home, even out of that Townsend mausoleum."

Before he could reply, she gave him a penetrating look. "Are the two of you having problems?"

"I'm not sure there's going to be a two of us," Cal said candidly. "There seems to be a lot of opposition piling up."

"From whom?"

He told her about his run-in with his principal, and then Maddie's.

"And you think that's going to scare Maddie off?" she concluded.

"I'm almost a hundred percent certain it will. She'll walk away to protect me, whether I want her protection or not."

"Let me ask you something," Paula said slowly. "And I'm not asking as some sort of overprotective mother. I'm asking because I think you need to know the answer. I *know* Maddie will need to know it."

"And the question is?"

"Is this just a game to you?"

"Maddie asked me something very similar tonight," he said.

"And?"

"I'll tell you what I told her—that there's something important going on between the two of us, and I will not walk away from it because a bunch of busybodies object."

"No matter the consequences?"

He looked her squarely in the eye. "No matter the consequences," he said firmly. "At least for me. If I think Maddie's going to be hurt, I might have to rethink that."

She smiled at him then. "I like you, Cal Maddox."

"The feeling is mutual."

"Maddie will not make this easy, not only because some gauntlet has been thrown down, but because she's been badly burned by Bill's stupidity. You'll need to give her time. Maybe a lot of it."

He grinned at that. "Hey, haven't you heard? I'm young. I have lots of time."

"I wouldn't go around reminding people of the age thing," she advised lightly. "It's bound to make a few folks uncomfortable."

"Are you one of them?"

She laughed. "Hardly. I envy my daughter. If I were a few years younger or you were a few older, I might even give her a run for her money."

He stood up and winked at her. "I'll keep that in mind if things don't work out so well with Maddie."

Paula's expression sobered. "Make them work, Cal. I think you're going to be good for her."

He dropped an impulsive kiss on her cheek. "I promise to try," he said.

And all the way home, he pondered just what he needed

to do to give Maddie everything she deserved and not more chaos that she didn't need.

Noreen was fluttering around their cramped apartment as if she were about to entertain the governor of South Carolina. It was driving Bill nuts.

"Sweetheart, will you please calm down?" he pleaded. "It's dinner, not a gala for two thousand."

"But it's the first time all three of your kids will be having dinner in our home," she said. "I want everything to be perfect."

He saw the mixture of hope and panic in her expression and immediately took her in his arms. "Wanting 'perfect' is almost a guarantee that something will go wrong," he chided her. "Relax. However it turns out, we'll be fine."

She lifted her gaze to his, every insecurity in her eyes. "I want to believe that. I really do," she declared. "But I know how much your children matter to you and I've gotten in the middle of that. I want to make things right."

"You can't do it by trying too hard," he told her. "Tonight's just one more step on a long road, nothing more. Don't put so much pressure on yourself, or on them."

He was still surprised that all three kids had agreed to this dinner. He detected Maddie's hand in it. She must have called on all her coaxing skills to pull it off.

"Are you sure fried chicken will be okay?" Noreen asked him. "I mean, I know most kids love fried chicken, but maybe burgers would have been better. Or pizza. We could still order pizza."

He rested a finger against her lips. "Hush. Dinner will be fine. You make incredible fried chicken. They'll love it."

The doorbell rang and Noreen jumped.

"Oh, God, I'm going to throw up," she said and ran from the room.

Bill stared after her, wondering if it was her pregnancy or nerves behind the nausea. Probably some combination of the two.

He opened the door and Katie threw herself at him.

"Daddy, Daddy, I missed you so much," she said, clinging to him.

Bill hoisted her up, then held out his hand to his sons, determined to act casual. "Kyle, Ty, glad you could make it."

"We can't stay long," Ty said at once, brushing past him. "It's a school night."

"I know. Dinner's almost ready. It's fried chicken. I told Noreen that's one of your favorites."

"I *love* fried chicken," Katie announced.

"Me, too," Kyle said, shooting his brother a look that dared Ty to contradict him.

"Well, come on in and have a seat. Noreen will be out in a minute. Would you like to take a look around the apartment? Last time you were here, you didn't really stay long enough to get a good look at the place."

"What's to see?" Ty asked. "It would fit in our living room."

So, Bill thought, resigned, Tyler was here, but he was intent on making things difficult.

"It may be a little small," Bill agreed, refusing to rise to the bait. "But Noreen's got a real knack for decorating. Once we move, I think she'll have a chance to prove that."

Kyle studied him with a stricken expression. "You're going to move?"

Katie seemed to sense the sudden tension. "No, Daddy. You can't move. Not again." She wrapped her arms around his neck and clung with all her might.

"Shh, baby," he soothed. "Not far away. I just meant that when the baby comes, we'll need someplace bigger, but it will be right here in Serenity, I promise. You'll still see me all the time."

Katie studied him with watery eyes. "Promise?"

"Promise," he said.

"And we all know what your promises are worth," Ty muttered.

Bill frowned at him. "That's enough," he said sharply. He wanted tonight to go smoothly for all their sakes, but he'd just about reached his limit with Ty's attitude.

Noreen breezed into the room just then, her cheeks flushed, her eyes overbright. "Hello, everyone. I'm so glad you could come tonight." She focused on Ty. "Maybe you could help me get dinner on the table."

Bill watched his son struggle between the sharp retort on the tip of his tongue and the good manners he'd been taught. For the moment, the manners triumphed. He followed Noreen into the kitchen. Bill watched them go with a mix of admiration for Noreen's gumption and fear over the potential for fireworks.

Instead, the only sound coming from the kitchen was murmured conversation until Noreen called out that dinner was on the table.

To Bill's amazement and relief, she managed to keep the conversation flowing smoothly throughout the meal. Even Ty was drawn in, albeit with obvious reluctance. The fried chicken was a hit, as were Noreen's potato salad, coleslaw and the apple pie she'd baked for dessert.

"Mom's going to be outside in five minutes," Ty said eventually. "We need to go."

"First there's something we wanted to discuss with you,"

Bill said, locking gazes with his oldest son, silently commanding him to remain where he was.

Three pairs of eyes stared at him expectantly. Bill knew what he was about to say wouldn't really come as a shock, but that didn't mean it wasn't likely to stir up a hornet's nest. He almost regretted his promise to Noreen to get into this tonight, especially after everything else had gone so smoothly.

Finally he drew in a deep breath and just blurted it out. "Noreen and I want to ask all of you to be a part of our wedding."

Ty stood up from the table so quickly his chair tumbled over backward. He left it there.

"No way!" he said furiously.

Bill gave him an imploring look. "I really would like it if you and Kyle would stand up for me, be co-best men."

"You've got to be kidding," Ty said, regarding him with disgust. "Do you really think putting us in tuxedos and parading us in front of a bunch of people like we're all happy about you getting married will make them forget what you did to Mom?"

"It's not about that," Bill said. He knew it was up to him to make this work, but he cast a helpless look toward Noreen. Maybe she could think of something to say to smooth things over. Instead, she remained stoically silent.

Bill struggled to find the words that would reach his son. "A wedding is about new beginnings," he told him. "We want you guys to be a part of ours. And it won't be a big wedding, just a few friends and you guys." He smiled at Katie. "We'd like you to be our flower girl. Noreen's even picked out a gorgeous dress for you."

Katie looked from him to her brother, clearly torn. "I want to be a flower girl," she said wistfully.

"Then do it," Ty exploded. "Do whatever the hell you want, but leave me out of it."

He slammed out of the apartment.

"I'd better go after him," Bill said, casting an apologetic look at Noreen.

"Forget it, Dad. I'll go," Kyle said. "He won't listen to you right now. Besides, Mom's probably waiting."

Bill sighed heavily. "Will you talk to him?"

"I can try," Kyle said. "But I think you'd better count us out, except for Katie."

Bill stared at him, trying not to let his disappointment show. "You, too?"

Kyle shrugged. "Sorry." He held out his hand. "Come on, Katie. We need to go."

"Now?"

"Yes, short stuff, now."

"Can I still be in the wedding?" she asked plaintively.

Bill gave her a weary smile. "We're counting on it," he said quietly.

As she and Kyle left the apartment, he felt as if his heart had just been splintered in two.

Noreen came around the table and wrapped her arms around him, then rested her head atop his. "I'm sorry," she whispered.

"Me, too."

"Maybe they'll change their minds," she said hopefully. "The wedding's still a month away."

But when he felt a tear splash against his cheek, he knew she didn't believe that any more than he did.

CHAPTER FIFTEEN

Ty was grimly silent when he climbed into the car after leaving his dad's. The slam of the car door said a lot, but Maddie knew better than to press him for details about his mood right away. He'd tell her what had happened in his own good time. Or one of the other kids would.

"Are Kyle and Katie on their way down?" she asked.

"I guess."

"How was dinner?" she asked, figuring that was safe enough.

He slouched even lower in the back seat. "Fine."

"Your dad's okay?"

"I don't want to talk about Dad. I want to go home."

"I can't drive off and leave your brother and sister here," she reminded him, meaning it as a joke.

"Don't you think I know that?" he snapped, clearly not seeing the humor.

Maddie drummed her fingers on the steering wheel, trying to figure out what might have set Ty off yet again and what was taking the other two kids so long. It wasn't as if sitting on the street outside Bill's apartment was her idea of a fun way to spend the evening after a twelve-hour day at work. Maybe Ty had caused another scene and Kyle and Katie were trying to smooth things over with their dad.

"Mom?" Ty said, sounding surprisingly hesitant and very young.

"Yes."

"Is the divorce final?" he asked. "I know you and Dad did all the paperwork and stuff, but you'll tell us when it's final, right?"

"Yes, of course," she said. "Why? Did that subject come up tonight?"

"Not exactly."

He fell silent, and Maddie waited for what seemed like an eternity.

"It's just that Dad said he and Noreen are getting married," he finally explained.

Ah, she thought, so that was it. Astonishingly, she felt no punch-in-the-gut sensation at the news. Her only concern was for Ty.

"You knew that was going to happen sooner or later," she said gently.

"But it can't happen before the divorce is final," he said. "So that means it's going to be final soon. I mean, they didn't give us a specific date or anything, but they wouldn't be planning a wedding if the divorce wasn't going to be final for months, right?"

"I have no idea what their timetable is, though I'm sure your dad would like to marry Noreen before the baby comes," she admitted. "As for the divorce, I haven't been keeping track. Helen would probably know."

"Don't you even care?"

She met his troubled gaze in the rearview mirror. "Ty, once the decision was made, I had to accept that the marriage was over and that your dad was moving on," she said, careful to keep her tone neutral. "I'm sure seeing the final decree will be upsetting, but I've tried to make peace with what's happened."

Despite what her mother had advised, Maddie still didn't want her kids to know how distraught she'd been in the first couple of months after she'd learned about Bill's betrayal. What good would it do? Those feelings were mostly in the past now, anyway. If she dredged them up, the kids would only feel more compelled to choose sides. Ty had already done that and it was clearly tearing him up. And now the sad truth was, she honestly didn't care anymore about what Bill did with the rest of his life, except where it concerned their children.

She caught a glimpse of the frown on Ty's face and knew he'd been expecting more of a reaction.

"But shouldn't it be a big deal or something?" he asked. "You guys act like it doesn't even matter, like it's just a bunch of details and paperwork. You always taught us that getting married was, like, this huge commitment."

"And it is," she assured him. She struggled to find the right words. "My marriage to your dad will always matter. I loved him with all my heart for a very long time, and because of that, I have you, Kyle and Katie. Nothing matters more to me than our family. And I am very sad that your dad will no longer be a part of my life in the same way, but part of growing up is learning to accept change, whether we like it or not."

"Change sucks," Ty declared.

She smiled at that. "Yes, sometimes it does," she agreed. "But we have to accept it, nonetheless."

"I don't think I can accept this one," Ty said, sounding miserable. "I can't stand up for Dad while he marries her."

Now Maddie felt as if she'd been punched in the gut. "Your dad wants you to be his best man?"

"Me and Kyle," he said. "And he wants Katie to be the flower girl."

"I'm sure it would mean a lot to him," she said, fighting the sting of tears. Dammit, she didn't want her kids to be a part of that travesty of a wedding ceremony, but saying so would be wrong. She wouldn't allow herself to do anything that would widen the divide between the children and their dad. To do so would smack of petty revenge and she wanted desperately to rise above that.

"I won't do it," Ty said fiercely. "It would be like saying I think it's okay for him to be with Noreen."

"He's going to be with her, whether you approve or not," she reminded him. "Wouldn't it be better to deal with that, instead of waging a losing battle?"

"Do I have to?" he asked, sounding the way he had at five when he'd been told to apologize for not sharing a toy.

"I can't make you," she conceded. "But the only person you're hurting is yourself."

"And Dad," he said with a touch of defiance.

"Oh, sweetie, what's the good of that?"

"I want him to hurt the way we do," he said.

"But in the end, it won't change anything," she said. "It'll just make a lot of people miserable on what should be a happy occasion."

"Are you going to go to the wedding?"

"No," she said flatly. Not that there was any chance Bill—or more specifically Noreen—would want her there.

"Then why do I have to?" Ty asked.

"Because you're very important to your dad and he wants you there. Sometimes you have to be mature enough to do things just because they're important to someone you love."

"Growing up sucks," he grumbled.

Maddie chuckled. "Yep, sometimes it does." And tonight was definitely one of those times.

That conversation was still fresh in Maddie's mind when Cal showed up at the spa a few days later. She'd checked with Helen, and Ty's assumption had been right. She would soon be a free woman. Would that make any difference at all in her relationship with Cal? Would she allow herself to look at him differently? Would he panic and take off the instant he knew she was truly available? Would the talk about them around town die down if Bill had remarried and she was single? Maybe part of the simmering attraction they both felt was that for right now their relationship was wrong. Until she had those divorce papers in her hand, she was still married, even if reality said otherwise.

She met his gaze and felt that fluttering in her stomach that told her the attraction wasn't dying anytime soon.

"I thought you'd be here," Cal said, holding out a bag filled with still-warm pastries from the bakery and two cups of very strong coffee. "And since you've been getting over here at the crack of dawn, according to Ty, I figured you hadn't had breakfast."

"Shouldn't you be at school?" she asked, accepting the coffee and trying to ignore the tempting, sugary scent of the pastries. Even if she'd skipped breakfast for a week, she shouldn't touch those.

"The kids are tied up with standardized testing all day," he said. "I'm supposed to be making lists of all the equipment and checking it out for next year, but I decided to take a break and sneak over here to see how things are progressing."

Maddie seized on the neutral topic. "Did you look around? What do you think?" she asked, eager for his impression. She thought the place was amazing, but she welcomed an outside viewpoint.

"The place looks incredible," he told her. "I can't believe what you've accomplished in such a short time. I haven't peeked at the locker area or treatment rooms, but the workout area is topnotch. That's first-rate equipment in there. Mitch says you're still on track for opening in two weeks."

Maddie shuddered at the reminder. "He might be on track, but I feel as if I'm on a runaway freight train. I have checklists of my checklists and not nearly enough things are getting crossed off on any of them."

"Anything I can do to help?"

"Not unless you want to unpack and fold several dozen towels," she said. "Or figure out a way to display a few dozen cases of lotions and creams."

"I could do that," he said.

She regarded him with astonishment. "You really would, wouldn't you?"

He shrugged. "Why not, if it would help?"

She wanted to tell him that Bill would never have deigned to put himself out like that. Instead, she merely said, "Thanks anyway, but I'd better leave that to Jeanette. She seems to have her own ideas about where everything in the treatment area belongs. Besides, she likes to ooh and aah over all the creams and oils. She doesn't want anyone else to touch them."

He grinned at the faint testy note in her voice. "Ah, she's challenging your control, is she?"

Maddie winced at his perceptiveness. "Something like that."

"You hired her because she has certain skills, right?"

"Yes."

"Then let her do her job and check those things that she can do off your list."

"Did you really come over here just to bring me coffee and ply me with sage advice?"

"No, I came to ask you if you're coming to tomorrow night's game. It's a big one."

"Ty mentioned it, but it's Bill's turn."

He frowned. "I think it would mean a lot to Ty if you were both there. It would mean a lot to *me* if you were there."

She studied him curiously. "Any particular reason?"

He leveled her a look that could have seared a steak. "Do you really need to ask?"

She felt herself flush. "In that case, are you sure my presence wouldn't be a distraction?"

"Probably, but it would definitely be worth it." His gaze locked with hers. "Come to the game, Maddie."

"I'll think about it."

"If you do, I'll spend all day Saturday over here being your personal slave. You can assign me to all the last-minute, dirty little chores that need to get done."

She grinned at him. "An intriguing offer," she admitted. "What do you get out of any of this?"

"Time with you," he said candidly. He stood up and leaned across her desk until his mouth was scarcely an inch from hers. "And if I'm very, very lucky maybe I'll even be able to lure you into that hot tub I hear you had installed upstairs."

He brushed a quick kiss across her lips, then backed away. "Think about it," he said, and then he left.

Maddie stared after him, her lips on fire. The man really was dangerous. *Think about it,* he'd said so damn innocently. As if that image of the two of them sharing the hot tub weren't indelibly burned into her brain. She couldn't recall the last time temptation had been so irresistible.

Cal was surprised when Maddie actually showed up at the game on Friday night. He hadn't been sure if she'd rise to his challenge. The fact that she had gave him hope.

Maddie had shown up in a pair of conservative khaki shorts, a prim little blouse tucked into the waistband and a pair of sneakers. He wondered if she'd chosen that outfit to remind him of what he'd said about what she'd been wearing the first night he'd seen her. There were plenty of women in the stands wearing less, but Maddie was the only one who kicked his hormones into overdrive.

Because of that, he kept his gaze deliberately focused elsewhere, at least until he spotted Bill Townsend climbing into the stands to sit beside her. Then he could hardly manage to drag his gaze away. He hadn't counted on the streak of jealousy that seeing those two together would set off.

He kept stealing glances, wondering if she and Bill were merely being civil or if there was still something between them. He couldn't imagine being married to a woman like Maddie for twenty years and having three kids, then walking away as if none of it mattered.

"Coach?"

Cal dragged his attention away from the bleachers to Luke Dillon. "What?"

"The umpire wants to see you at home plate."

"Sure," Cal said. He glanced around at the players. "You guys ready to play some ball?"

The question was met with a loud cheer that made him smile. "I thought so."

He met with the umpire and the opposing coach, then sent his players onto the field. From the moment Ty threw his first pitch, Cal knew he was seeing something special. Nobody was going to hit that fastball. And his curves were catching the corners of the plate. This time when Cal glanced into the stands, his gaze sought out not Maddie but a scout from his old team. Patrick O'Malley gave him a wide grin and a thumbs-up, confirming every instinct Cal had ever had about Ty's talent.

At the end of the game, Patrick was waiting for him.

"Are you sure that boy's only sixteen?" the scout said wistfully. "I'd sign him tonight if I could."

"Sorry. He's still got two more years of high school left, but come with me and I'll introduce you to his parents. It won't hurt for you to get to know them now. If he's as talented as we both think he is, you're going to want to establish a relationship with his folks."

He led Patrick over to Maddie and Bill, who were congratulating Ty. Because he didn't want the boy to hear their conversation, he sent him off to join his teammates, then turned to Maddie and her soon-to-be ex-husband.

"Bill, Maddie, I'd like you to meet Patrick O'Malley. He's a scout for the Braves. I invited him tonight to see Ty pitch."

Maddie regarded him with surprise. "Is that why you were so insistent I be here tonight?"

He nodded. "I knew Patrick would want to meet you. He's as impressed by Ty as I thought he would be."

"But Ty's still in high school," she protested.

"It's never too early for me to start keeping an eye on a player," Patrick told her. "Your son has what it takes to go pro, right out of high school if that's what he wants."

Maddie's expression froze. "You mean he'd skip college?"

"Maybe delay it," Patrick said. "We'd have to see where things stand in a couple of years."

Maddie turned to Bill, her gaze narrowed. "Did you know this was a possibility?"

"Any kid dreaming of going pro wants to believe it's possible," Bill said. "But it doesn't happen that often."

"And not with my son!" Maddie said fiercely. She frowned at Cal. "From the day Ty was born we've planned and saved for him to go to college. That is *not* going to change. How could you do this without even discussing it with me?"

"I thought you'd be pleased," Cal said honestly, taken aback by the genuine outrage in her voice.

"Do I look pleased?" she demanded. "My son will go to college and that's that. Once he's graduated, *that's* the time to have this conversation." Her gaze locked with his. "We'll discuss this another time. I'm out of here."

Cal would have gone after her, but Patrick held him back. "Let her go. You know that's how a lot of parents react at first. Heck, you were smart enough to turn down the chance to go pro straight out of high school yourself. Don't blame her for feeling that way about her son."

"I'll talk to her," Bill promised. "She'll come around if it's what's best for Ty."

Cal wondered about that. He'd seen something in her eyes he'd never expected. Maddie looked as if he'd betrayed her when all he'd wanted was to give her son the opportunity of a lifetime. He'd been thinking like a coach, not a parent. Since Patrick was right about his having made a different decision for himself, his lack of foresight when it came to Ty made him question whether he was the right man for a woman with three kids, after all.

"I have never been so furious with someone in my entire life," Maddie declared to Helen and Dana Sue the next morning. Cal's presumption had kept her awake all night. Somehow Ty had found out who Patrick O'Malley was and why he'd been at the game. Because of Cal her son's hopes had soared, then come crashing back down when Maddie had to tell him that what Cal was promising wouldn't happen.

Now her son was furious with her and she was wondering why she'd ever believed that Cal truly had her family's best interests at heart.

"I imagine he thought you'd be excited for Ty," Dana Sue suggested.

"Well, of course I am," she huffed. "It's amazing that a professional scout thinks he's that good."

"Then why is what Cal did so wrong?" Dana Sue asked.

"He went behind my back," she said. "I'm Ty's mother. He should have consulted me."

"Maybe he didn't trust his own objectivity," Helen suggested. "Maybe he didn't want to say anything till he knew how the scout would react."

"Why are you two defending him? Do you honestly think my son should skip college to play baseball?"

Helen took her shoulders in a firm grip and steered her to a chair. "Sit. Now listen to me. No one is saying that Ty has to skip college. No one knows what will happen over the next two years. He could decide he wants to be an astronaut or something."

Maddie rolled her eyes. “Not likely.”

Helen frowned. “I’m just saying that it’s pretty amazing to know he might have an opportunity that a lot of young athletes can only dream about. Maybe you should be grateful to Cal for making that happen instead of jumping all over him.”

Dana Sue nodded. “Come on, sweetie. A professional baseball scout thinks your son is capable of going pro! How cool is that?”

Maddie sighed. “Very cool,” she admitted eventually. “I guess the prospect just caught me off guard. It forced me to face the fact that Ty will only be mine for a couple more years, then he’ll be off on his own, whether it’s playing ball or going to college. I’m not ready for that. And the reality is, if baseball is what he wants, once he turns eighteen, I won’t have that much say about it, anyway.”

“Letting go won’t be easy,” Dana Sue agreed. “Sometimes I worry myself sick wondering what kind of choices Annie will make once she’s on her own. I’m not convinced she’s making very good ones now.”

Maddie was instantly alert to the worried note in Dana Sue’s voice. “Such as?”

“It’s the eating thing. She seems to be putting food in her mouth, but she keeps losing weight. Something’s wrong, I just know it. If it keeps up, I’m terrified she’ll end up in the hospital.”

“Has she been to see Bill?” Maddie asked.

Dana Sue made a sound of exasperation. “She says she’s too old to see a pediatrician and that he’s a jerk for what he’s done to you.”

“I can’t argue with that,” Maddie said. “But what about Doc Marshall?”

“To be honest, I’m afraid to push it,” Dana Sue said. “I’m

afraid it'll just make things worse between us. We've always been so close, but now she thinks anything that comes out of my mouth is automatically suspect."

Maddie grinned. "She's a teenager. She's only a little bit younger than Ty, and look at the grief *he's* been giving me. What did you expect?"

Dana Sue's expression turned wistful. "*Gilmore Girls,* I guess."

"It's a TV show," Helen reminded her. "Maybe I could take Annie to Charleston for a girls' day out. We haven't done that for a long time. We could shop, go to lunch. If she's got an eating disorder, maybe I can pick up on it."

Dana Sue's expression brightened. "Would you do that? She loves going places with you. I'll pay for whatever shopping she does."

"No, it's my treat," Helen said. "I love spoiling Annie, Maddie's kids, too. They're all I've got."

"You'll have your own one of these days," Maddie assured her.

"How?" Helen asked. "With my social life, it would take a miracle. And since I'm the same age as you guys, time is running out. Things start getting pretty dicey after forty."

"Then we'll make you a miracle," Dana Sue said. "You'd be a great mom."

"I'm a self-absorbed workaholic," Helen countered. "That is not good mom material."

Maddie gestured around them. "But this place is going to change that. We're going to fix your health and your priorities."

Helen looked doubtful.

"We are," Dana Sue promised. "You wait and see." She turned back to Maddie. "And you're going to work things out with Cal."

"I don't know why you're so sure of that," Maddie said. "After the way I treated him last night, I doubt he'll even speak to me."

"You're wrong about that," Helen said, her lips curving into a grin. "Gotta go."

"Me, too," Dana Sue said, hurrying off after her.

Maddie turned slowly to see what had sent them fleeing and spotted Cal standing in the doorway.

"Safe to come in?" he inquired.

Relief spilled through her. "Sure, though I have no idea why you'd want to after last night," she told him. "I overreacted."

"Not really. I caught you off guard and I'm sorry. I was trying to do a good thing."

"I know that," she said. "But in the future…"

"In the future, I'll run anything having to do with your kids by you first," he promised.

"Thank you." She studied him curiously. "Is that the only reason you came by?"

He shook his head. "I told you I'd help out around here today. Just tell me what you need me to do."

She recalled the reward he'd claimed to want—some time alone for the two of them in the hot tub. "And the hot tub?"

His gaze held hers. "I'm counting on it."

Her heart skipped several beats as she looked into his eyes. "Cal," she began, her voice oddly choked.

"Yes, Maddie," he said, amusement lacing his voice.

"I, um, have a really long list of chores around here today. The kids are spending the day with their dad, but they'll be home right after dinner."

"Then we'd better hurry," he said, still not looking away.

Oh, sweet heaven, she thought, her heart thundering.

It took every ounce of self-restraint she possessed not to toss her stupid list in the trash and haul the man straight upstairs.

In the end, Maddie did what she always did—the responsible thing. And by the time she and Cal finally made it upstairs, put on their swimsuits and crawled into the beckoning hot tub, they were both so beat, they were content merely to sit silently side by side and let the water soak away their aches and pains. As electrifying as the occasional brush of his thigh against hers was, as amazing as it felt to have him link his fingers through hers, neither of them had the energy to do more.

In a way it made their few stolen moments alone even more tantalizing. There was so much promise in the fleeting touches, such tenderness and consideration in the way Cal took his cues from her, demanding nothing, but hinting at so much more.

Finally she looked into his eyes. "You envisioned a different outcome, didn't you?"

His slow smile warmed her.

"I'm with you," he said. "That's enough."

"It's too soon for anything more," she said with regret. "And there's no time, anyway. The kids will be home soon. I need to be there."

His gaze held hers. "We'll go then, as long as you promise me a rain check when the time is right."

"You have it," she said without hesitation, then stood up.

Cal rose from the water, as well, and caught her hand before she could step out of the tub. "One more thing," he said.

She held her breath at the heat in his eyes. "Yes?"

He cupped a hand behind her neck and touched his lips to hers. The simmering awareness that had been there all day flared into a full-fledged inferno. The water in the hot tub felt ice-cold by comparison.

When he released her, he ran a thumb along her cheek. "Just that," he said.

That kiss kept her floating all the way home. It sizzled in her memory, overshadowing the far more chaste kiss he gave her at her front door.

"Good night, Maddie."

She knew his leaving was for the best, but she wasn't ready for him to go. She settled for inviting him to dinner the following Tuesday.

"Are you sure?" he asked.

"Of course, why?"

"How do you think the kids will react?"

"They'll be thrilled," she said confidently.

Cal still looked doubtful. "If it turns out you're wrong about that, let me know."

"I'm not wrong," she assured him, but after he'd gone, she began to have her own doubts. Maybe it was too much to expect them to embrace yet another change in their lives, no matter how innocently she presented it.

Determined to deal with the subject head-on, she mentioned the invitation as she, Ty and Kyle sat at the kitchen table having milk and cookies after Katie had gone up to bed.

Ty looked at her as if she'd announced plans to race around the streets of Serenity stark naked. "You what?" he asked.

"I asked Coach Maddox to join us for dinner this Tuesday," she repeated.

"You can't be serious," he said, obviously dismayed. "Why would you do that?"

"I thought you liked Coach Maddox," she said, perplexed by his reaction. "He's been over here before."

"As my coach!" he shouted. "Not with you! This is like a date or something."

"Not really," she denied, hating that they were reacting exactly as she'd feared they might. "It's dinner. We're friends. It's not the big deal you're making it out to be." Okay, okay, maybe she wanted or even expected things to be different, but friends were what they were right now. Period.

Hot-tub fantasies aside, she amended.

Ty clearly wasn't appeased.

"Sure," he said sarcastically. "Dad has his *special friend* and now you have yours. Way to go, Mom!" He tore out of the room and thundered up the stairs, then slammed the door of his room to emphasize his displeasure.

Maddie stared after him, then turned around to see Kyle regarding her warily. "Not you, too," she said.

"It is a little weird, Mom. He's Ty's coach. And he's way younger than you."

"I invited him to dinner," she said defensively. "Not to move in."

Kyle gave her a look that was wise beyond his years. "Don't you think that's how it started with Dad and Noreen, too?"

CHAPTER SIXTEEN

Maddie spent most of Sunday afternoon at home working on designing the invitations for the spa's grand opening. To stay within her self-imposed printing budget, she'd found samples of elegant but less costly paper and was going to print the invitations on her computer, assuming she could design something classy enough to suit her partners. She had half a dozen alternatives for Helen, Dana Sue and Jeanette to decide among when they all came by for Sunday supper. And one or two of those were pretty impressive, if she did say so herself.

She was just finishing up and tucking everything into a file folder when everyone showed up.

"Where are the kids?" Helen asked as they all followed Maddie into the kitchen.

"Eating pizza upstairs," Maddie admitted.

"Banished to their rooms?" Dana Sue asked. "What did they do?"

"To be honest, both of the boys are furious with me, so I figured having them at the table would spoil our appetites."

"What brought that on?" Jeanette asked. "Anything you want to talk about?"

Maddie hesitated, not sure she wanted to tell them about their reaction to her inviting Cal for dinner until she'd had more time to think about it and decide what she ought to do. She knew Helen and Dana Sue, at least, would have strong opinions. Jeanette might be more circumspect, but she was learning to hold her own with the rest of them, so even she might not be counted on to keep silent.

She delayed answering by handing each of them bowls and plates to sit on the dining-room table. She'd baked a chicken, made a pear-walnut-and-blue-cheese salad and grilled some vegetables. It was probably the healthiest meal she'd ever set before them. The kids would have hated it.

"Ty's figured out that there's something going on between you and Cal, hasn't he?" Helen guessed as they all sat down to eat. "And he's comparing it to what his dad did."

Maddie stared at her, startled by her intuition. "How did you come to that conclusion?"

Helen shrugged. "It was bound to happen."

"Why? Cal and I haven't really done anything," she said, tired of making the same denial over and over. "We've never even gone on a date. I just asked him to come to dinner on Tuesday. I figured I owed him for everything he's done for me and Ty."

"No, you wanted to spend an evening with him at your table to see if he fits in," Helen corrected. "At least be honest with yourself about your motives."

Maddie started to argue, then sighed. "Okay, maybe." She regarded her friends with dismay. "I wasn't expecting such strong reactions from the boys. They were appalled. Should I cancel?"

"Absolutely not," Dana Sue said vehemently. "If you do, the kids will know that all they have to do to chase off any man is pitch a fit. I've had exactly five dates since I kicked

Ronnie to the curb and Annie has hated each and every one of them on sight. Not that her opinion doesn't matter, but we're talking about my life here. It's hard enough getting to know someone new and giving them a fair chance without having your kids chime in. Any dates I have from now on will not involve meeting my daughter until I know if they have staying power."

"And we already know that Cal has staying power," Helen said. "Dinner can only be a good thing. He knows the kids already. He'll overlook it if they start out resenting his presence. I imagine he's been in trickier situations. He deals with teenagers all the time."

"I suppose," Maddie said doubtfully. She picked at her food.

"Okay, what else is wrong?" Helen demanded. "It's not just about the kids' reaction, is it?"

"Maybe I'm being foolish," Maddie admitted. "I mean, what kind of relationship can I have with a man who's so much younger than I am? I'm not cut out for a fling."

"Come on, Maddie, get serious," Helen scoffed. "Is that all you think Cal is interested in?"

"I don't know," Maddie said candidly.

"I don't think you're giving him enough credit," Helen told her. "Stop worrying. Don't pin a label on what's happening or anticipate problems that might not arise."

"I already know it will be a problem with the school system," Maddie said glumly. "Betty Donovan will make sure of that."

"Cal knows she's on the warpath, right?" Helen asked.

Maddie nodded.

"Is he worried?" Dana Sue asked.

"Apparently not."

"Then you shouldn't worry, either," Dana Sue advised.

Maddie turned to Helen. "Will he have a legal leg to stand on if they do try to fire him?"

Helen grinned. "He will if he hires me," she said. "Stop borrowing trouble. Don't make excuses to stop this before it even gets started. I predict Cal Maddox will be the best thing that ever happened to you."

Jeanette, who'd been quiet for some time, nodded. "If he'd ever looked in my direction, I surely wouldn't turn him down. Face it, Maddie, every female in town is bound to be a little jealous if you two go public. Just smile and let them wonder what they're missing."

Maddie chuckled despite her concern. "You are very bad."

Jeanette grinned. "So the man in my life likes to remind me."

"Is this mysterious guy of yours coming to the opening?" Dana Sue asked her. "We're dying to meet him."

"Oh, he'll be there," Jeanette said with what sounded a lot like grim determination. "In fact, I'm hoping once he sees Serenity, he'll want to move here. The commute from his place in Charleston is getting really old."

"And if he doesn't?"

Jeanette's expression sobered. "Then I might have to rethink some things."

"You wouldn't leave us, would you?" Maddie asked, not trying to hide her alarm.

"No way," Jeanette said. "I love what we're doing here. If I leave anything, it would be Don. I don't think I can stay with a man who doesn't totally support what I want to do."

"And you think he doesn't support you in this?" Maddie asked.

Jeanette shrugged. "He's been ticked off about the amount of time I've been spending at the spa. He says it's cutting into our time together, which it is, but that won't be forever. I'm beginning to think he's basically a pretty selfish man."

"Or maybe he just doesn't do well with change," Maddie suggested, hating the idea that they'd come between Jeanette and someone who was important to her. "Give him some time to adjust."

"I am, which is why I haven't dumped him already," Jeanette told them. "Opening day is his chance to come through for me." She shrugged, her expression wistful. "We'll see."

"Men *are* a complication, aren't they?" Dana Sue said with a sigh, then grinned. "But when they're good, they're worth it."

"Amen," Helen and Jeanette said.

Maddie wasn't so sure. She thought of the turmoil her kids were in between Bill's behavior and the new role Cal might be playing in her life. Maybe things would be a whole lot easier for all of them if she kept all men at arm's length and just resolved to be the best single mom in Serenity.

Then, again, how much fun could a cranky, discontented single mom possibly be?

Bill arrived at his office on Monday morning after stopping by the hospital to check on a patient who'd had an emergency appendectomy on Sunday evening. Noreen was waiting for him with an oddly expectant expression on her face.

"What's going on?" he asked as he slipped out of his jacket and put a white lab coat over his shirt. Some days he didn't bother with the lab coat, but this morning there hadn't been one decently ironed shirt in his closet. Noreen didn't have Maddie's knack with an iron. He supposed he was going to have to start taking his shirts to the dry cleaners if he expected them to be starched and pressed the way he liked them. It was just one more change in his life he was going to have to accept.

Noreen closed the door to his office. "I heard something this morning that I thought you ought to know," she said as if she could barely contain herself.

He frowned at her eagerness to share some nonsense she'd picked up around town. "Gossip?" he asked disdainfully. "Noreen, you know how I feel about that." For one thing he figured people in their position had no business talking about anyone else.

"I know, I know," she said. "But I really think you should make an exception for this. I stopped by the drugstore for breakfast since we didn't have any eggs in the house. The whole place was buzzing."

Bill resigned himself to hearing what had everyone in town stirred up. It didn't take much, especially not with Grace Wharton willing to stir the pot.

"Maddie's having an affair with Cal Maddox!" Noreen announced, her expression gleeful. "See, I told you you'd want to know."

"That's absurd," he said emphatically, but the story resonated a little too much. His knees suddenly felt weak. He sat down hard, then considered the possibility that there could be some element of truth behind the gossip. He'd seen the two of them together more than once himself. He'd even sensed some kind of spark there. Still, he felt the need to deny the rumor. "She has to be a decade older than he is. What could he possibly see in her?"

Noreen gave him a pitying look. "No wonder your marriage was on the rocks when we met if you couldn't even see how gorgeous and desirable your wife is."

"Believe me, I know how attractive Maddie is," he said tightly. He'd felt more than a few sparks himself lately, quite possibly because he knew she was now out of reach.

He focused on Noreen. "Come on, think about it. You know Maddie would never do something that would make her the object of ridicule, not after what you and I did to her. Sure, she's spent a little time with Coach Maddox, but an affair? That's nuts. People in town just like to talk."

"Maddie and Cal were over at that spa till all hours on Saturday night," Noreen said, a triumphant gleam in her eyes. "Grace saw them leaving together. Then Cal told someone yesterday that the place has an awesome hot tub, that he'd tried it out himself on Saturday. Now, you tell me if that doesn't sound as if there's something going on."

Bill felt his stomach plummet. He knew better than to listen to even half of the rumors that flew around Serenity, but if there was even a tiny chance that this one was true, he had to take it seriously.

"Go tell my first patient I'll be right with them," he said curtly. "I have a call to make."

Noreen frowned. "You're calling Maddie?"

"Well, of course I'm calling Maddie," he said impatiently. "Did you think I'd let this pass?"

He could tell from her expression that she'd had another mission in mind. No doubt she'd wanted him to accept that Maddie had moved on. She hadn't intended to make him jealous.

Which, of course, she hadn't, he told himself. He was not jealous of anything Maddie might choose to do with her life. He just didn't want to see the mother of his children make a fool of herself.

Yeah, right. That didn't exactly explain the dismay that was eating at him when he picked up the phone.

* * *

Maddie was in the midst of one crisis and had two more on hold when her cell phone rang. She fumbled in her purse trying to retrieve it while she finished up with Skeeter on the other phone. She punched the talk button, told whoever it was to hang on, then finished up with the cantankerous plumber.

"Friday," she told Skeeter. "That's absolutely the final deadline. The grand-opening party is a week from Friday and we open for business on the following Monday. I've got the inspector scheduled for 9:00 a.m. this Friday, so everything has to be in working order. We cannot afford not to pass inspection."

"I promised you everything would be ready, didn't I?" Skeeter grumbled. "I've been passing plumbing inspections in this town since you were in diapers."

"You also promised me that the toilets would be installed last week," Maddie retorted. "They're still sitting in boxes."

"Today," he assured her. "I'll be there in an hour. I just have to get Mitzi Gleason's drain unclogged before she pitches another hissy fit."

"One hour," Maddie agreed. "Otherwise, I'll hunt you down at Mitzi's and it won't be pretty."

Skeeter laughed.

"I am not kidding," she assured him and hung up, then put the cell phone up to her ear. "Sorry to keep you waiting."

"What the hell is going on over there?" Bill demanded. "I don't have all day to sit around and wait for you."

"You could have hung up," she suggested mildly. "That's what you usually do."

"This is too important. I need to see you," Bill announced in that commanding tone she knew all too well. "I have a half hour at noon."

"Well, I don't. I'm at work. I'm no longer at your beck and call," she snapped, in no mood to indulge his imperious demands.

"Then I'll come there," he said. "It won't leave much time, but we have to deal with this."

"Deal with what?"

"You and Coach Maddox, that's what," he said. "Are you out of your mind, Maddie?"

It was one thing for her teenage sons to have issues with her inviting Cal over to dinner. It was another thing entirely for her ex-husband to think he had any say whatsoever in the matter.

"May I remind you yet again that your chance to control my behavior ended when you decided to walk out the door."

"The man is ten years younger than you are," Bill said.

"Noreen is sixteen years younger than *you* are," she returned.

He ignored that. "I warned you before about this," he said self-righteously. "You're making a fool of yourself, Maddie. And you're embarrassing your children. I can only imagine what Ty must think. People all over town are talking about you and his coach cavorting around in some hot tub. Noreen heard about your affair when she was at Wharton's this morning."

"Noreen is now reporting to you when she hears gossip about me? How lovely! I wish someone had been kind enough to share the news of your affair with me. I might have been more prepared when you announced you wanted a divorce."

"That's not the point, dammit!"

"Then what *is* the point?"

"You're having an affair with your son's baseball coach," he all but shouted. "Do you know how disgusting that is?"

"Disgusting?" She tried to calm down, to no avail. She wanted to tear across town and scratch his eyes out. Maybe Noreen's, too, while she was at it.

"Do you have a better word for it?" he asked.

"First, let's get our facts straight," she suggested. "There is no affair."

"People are saying—"

"People say all sorts of things in Serenity," she reminded him. "Only a quarter of what they say is true, if that. You're usually the first one to remind me of that."

"You're not sleeping with him?"

Maddie thought she detected a hint of relief in his voice. "No," she said firmly. "But let's discuss why you thought it would be any of your business if I were."

"Because I still care about you," he said fiercely. "I don't want you to make a public spectacle of yourself."

"Let's back up a minute," she said slowly, her temper still seething. "If I spend a little time chatting with a man ten years younger than I am, I'm a fool and an embarrassment. When you get a woman who's sixteen years younger than you pregnant before you even ask for a divorce from your wife, you're what? Some paragon of reason and virtue? I don't think so, pal."

"Maddie, you need to be reasonable. Think about the kids," he said, still oblivious to his adherence to a double standard.

Unable to take his attitude a second longer, she slammed the phone down without hitting the Off button first. She hoped it hurt his eardrums. Nothing was likely to hurt his oversize ego.

When lunchtime rolled around, Maddie was still seething about being the subject of gossip over at Wharton's

Pharmacy. She decided the best way to defuse it was to march into the place with her head held high. As long as she was right there in plain view, no one was likely to say a word about her. And maybe she could set Grace straight about a few things while she was at it. The truth might not be half as much fun for Grace to spread, but she would no doubt repeat whatever Maddie told her.

Unfortunately, though, Maddie wasn't quite brave enough to face down everyone alone. She picked up the phone and called her mother, who, thanks to her fame and her eccentricities, had had her own share of experiences with the town rumor mill.

"Do you have lunch plans?" she asked without bothering with any pleasantries.

"No. Why?" her mother asked.

"Apparently Cal and I are the hottest item on the menu today at Wharton's. I'd like to go over there and put a stop to it, but I could use backup."

"Count me in. Grace Wharton is a wonderful, kind woman who'd give anyone the shirt off her back—but not before she fills them in on the latest gossip."

"I'll swing by and pick you up," Maddie said. "Ten minutes?"

"I'll be ready," her mother said. "Want me to bring along the shotgun I'm rumored to have in the hall closet?"

Maddie chuckled, knowing her mother's hatred of guns and also how that particular rumor got started. When some neighborhood kids had targeted her mother for a few pranks, Paula Vreeland had gone to the gun range and made a tape recording of weapons being discharged. She'd played it at top volume just when the kids were sneaking around her house and pretty much put the fear of God into them.

The next day there wasn't a soul in Serenity who wasn't

talking about the wacky artist who'd pulled a shotgun on a bunch of kids. Even the police had come by to see if her weapon was registered, only to discover that the only gun on the premises was on a tape recording. But they'd kept her secret, the pranks had stopped, and the rumors had never died.

"I think we can handle this without weapons," Maddie said.

Twenty minutes later, when they walked into the drugstore and everyone in the place fell silent, Maddie almost regretted her decision to confront the situation head-on. She and her mother slipped into the one available booth. Maddie grabbed a menu and hid behind it. Her mother tugged it out of her hands.

"Look them straight in the eye," Paula advised. "You have nothing to hide, remember?"

"Would you tell me why I'm suddenly some kind of tramp or something when no one said a single word about what Bill and Noreen did."

Her mother regarded her with astonishment. "Of course they did. They said plenty, just not in front of you. People respect you too much to want to embarrass you."

"Not anymore, apparently."

"Sweetheart, this is today's news. Tomorrow it will be someone else. All you have to do is hold your head up. In fact, I have an idea."

Maddie regarded her nervously. Her mother's ideas tended to border on the outrageous. "What?"

"Come on," Paula said, stepping out of the booth. "Come with me."

"We're leaving?" Maddie asked eagerly and slid from the booth.

"Of course not. We're going to say hello to a few people. Let's start with the mayor."

She latched on to Maddie's hand and dragged her straight to the booth where the mayor held court every day at noon.

"Good afternoon, Howie," Paula said, using the familiar form that only those who'd known the man since grade school could get away with. "How've you been?"

Howard Lewis's complexion paled. "Fine, just fine," he blustered. "How about you? And you, Maddie? How's that little club of yours coming along?"

"We're almost ready for our grand opening," Maddie said. "I hope to see you and Mrs. Lewis there."

"Wouldn't miss it," he said. "Always like to support new businesses in town."

"And the rest of you?" Maddie inquired, turning to his companions—the town's primary insurance agent, a real-estate broker and a retired marine. "Will you be coming with your wives? I know you were on the invitation list."

"Imagine so," Realtor Harmon Jackson said without much enthusiasm. "Delia hates missing anything that's going on in town. She always wants to be first to know what's happening."

"I imagine Coach Maddox will be there," Wilson McDermott said, then gasped in pain. He scowled at the mayor, who'd apparently stomped on his foot under the table. "What'd you do that for?"

Maddie drew in a deep breath. This was her chance and she knew it. "I imagine he didn't want me to get the idea that y'all had been talking about the coach and me just before I walked over here," she said cheerfully, then beamed at the mayor. "Isn't that right?"

Since the mayor seemed speechless, she shrugged. "Not that there's anything to say about the two of us, of course. Coach Maddox has been real good to my son, since Ty's his star pitcher," she told them. "The whole family is grateful to him. He even had a Major League scout here last week to take a look at Ty. Maybe you could tell folks that if the subject comes up." She turned back to her mother. "I'm starved. Maybe we should order."

"Good idea," Paula said, barely containing a grin. As they walked away, she murmured, "Maybe they won't even be able to choke down their lunch after all that crow they've had to eat."

Back in their booth, Maddie took a long swallow of the chocolate milk shake that Grace had automatically brought for her. Then she met her mother's gaze. "That was almost fun."

"Indeed it was," her mother agreed, then sighed. "It won't be the end of it, you know."

"No, but maybe the talk will die down at least for the rest of the day."

"You can always dream," Paula said. "But frankly, I wouldn't waste my dreams on the likes of them. I'd stick to Cal. That's the kind of fantasy that can keep you warm at night."

"It's also the one that's making me the talk of the town."

"What do you care, if he's with you at the end of the day?"

"But he's not," Maddie said emphatically.

Her mother patted her hand. "Give it time. He will be."

Maddie, puzzled, studied her mother. "And that's okay with you?"

"Of course. Why wouldn't it be?"

"You don't think it makes me look foolish or pathetic?"

"Sweetheart, if a man like Cal falls for you, there is nothing foolish or pathetic about you. The only people who say otherwise are jealous. It's that simple. Follow your heart, Maddie. It won't steer you wrong."

Maddie wished she shared her mother's confidence in that.

CHAPTER SEVENTEEN

Cal was in his office a half hour before baseball practice when Ty walked in without bothering to knock. Looking as if he was spoiling for a fight, he slammed the door behind him.

Cal met his stormy gaze with a steady look. "You seem upset."

"Gee, you think?" Ty retorted, dropping his backpack on the floor.

Cal frowned at him. "Okay, cut the attitude and sit down. Do you have a pass to be out of class?"

"No," Ty said belligerently.

"Then this must be important," Cal said, trying to remain calm. He'd done everything he could to cut the kid some slack, but Ty was about to cross a line in a way Cal wouldn't tolerate. He wanted to be sure Ty understood that. "I'll make sure you have a note this time, but don't expect me to do it again. There are procedures you need to follow. Understood?"

Ty's hard stare challenged him, but it was the boy who blinked first. "Yeah, I guess," he said finally.

"Okay, then. Which class did you cut?"

"It doesn't matter," Ty said sullenly. "I can deal with it."

Cal barely contained a sigh. "It matters if the teacher decides to throw you into detention for cutting. That means you'd miss our last practice before our first playoff game. Let's try not to let it go that far."

"Okay, okay. It's just history. I'm acing it. Mrs. Reed doesn't care what I do."

"Trust me, she cares," Cal said, jotting down a note to the history teacher and signing it. "You can give her this when you leave here."

"It's last period," Ty said. "I may as well cut the whole class. I'll take the note in tomorrow."

"No, you'll take it today," Cal stressed. "Even if the last bell has rung."

"But then I'll be late for practice," Ty protested.

"And you know the consequences for that," Cal said.

Ty regarded him with dismay. "You'd make me run laps?"

"If you're late, yes, so let's get this conversation over with so you can get to your history class before school lets out. And when you see Mrs. Reed, you might want to add an apology of your own."

"Whatever," Ty said, stuffing the note into his backpack.

Cal leaned back in his chair and studied his star pitcher. "So? Let's hear it."

Ty leveled a defiant look straight into Cal's eyes. "Are you and my mom getting it on?" he asked bluntly.

Cal stared at him, stunned by his audacity. "Excuse me?"

"You know what I mean," Ty said. "I want to know if you and my mom are—"

Cal cut him off before he could use the crude word Cal was pretty sure was on the tip of the boy's tongue. "I know what you meant. I just wonder why you think you have a right to ask such a thing."

"She's my mom," Ty said heatedly. "That gives me a right."

Cal could see the turmoil in Ty's eyes and felt for him. It must be hell to have one parent go off and start a new relationship and then discover that the other parent might be getting involved with someone new as well. He wondered how Maddie would want him to handle this. Unfortunately, she wasn't here and Ty was. And Cal only knew one way to deal with kids—be honest. Still, he wasn't entirely ready to be discussing his sex life—or his much-anticipated sex life—with one of his students.

"Would it really bother you if I were seeing your mother?" he asked carefully.

"Is that some polite way of asking if it's okay for you to, you know…"

"Actually, no. I was only referring to dating," Cal said. "Are you worried about all this because your mom invited me to dinner tomorrow night?"

Ty nodded. "It's kinda creepy."

Cal had anticipated the dinner might be more of a problem than Maddie had thought. Teenagers generally didn't like the idea of their parents having a sex life, whether it was with each other or someone else. That was at the core of Ty's animosity toward Noreen, he sensed.

Wanting to be sure he understood exactly what bothered Ty the most, he asked, "Creepy how?"

"I don't like to think about my parents…you know." He flushed as he confirmed Cal's guess. "I mean, I know my dad and Noreen must have, 'cause she's gonna have a baby, but you and my mom? No way." He regarded Cal earnestly. "I mean, you're my coach and even kinda my friend. She's way older than you, too. I don't want the guys on the team making all sorts of comments about you and my mom."

"You think they'd talk about us?" Cal asked, already knowing the answer. Of course they would.

"Sure," Ty said. "Everybody else in town's going to talk, too. They do about my dad. Even though they try to shut up when they know I'm around, I've heard plenty of stuff and none of it's very nice. I don't want 'em talking about my mom like that."

"You shouldn't let what other people say bother you or control what you do," Cal told him, though he knew that was tough to do when you were a kid and all you wanted was to fit in. He and Maddie were having a tough enough time grappling with it at their ages.

"My dad says that, too," Ty said. "I figure it's a crock. Nobody wants their private business spread all over town."

"True enough, but let's leave the gossip factor aside for the moment," Cal suggested. "You realize that your mom shouldn't be—and probably won't be—by herself forever. She deserves to meet someone and fall in love again."

Ty's eyes widened. "She's in love with you?"

Cal held up his hand. "No, I'm not saying that. Right now your mother and I are good friends. We enjoy spending time together. I'd like to keep on seeing her and get to know you, your brother and sister better, too. Could you, maybe, allow us that? If you make it too big a deal, she might decide to stop seeing me."

"Maybe that would be best," Ty said.

"Even if I can make her happy?" Cal asked.

Ty frowned at the question. "What makes you think you can make her happy?"

"To be honest, that's why people date, to see if they can make each other happy," Cal explained. "Look, give it some thought. I'll make you a promise. If things do get serious between your mom and me, I'll talk it over with you first. See how you feel about it then." He shrugged. "Maybe you'll even like having me around a little more."

Ty studied him intently. "You'd really care what I think?"

"Of course. I know how important you, Kyle and Katie are to your mom, so you're part of the package. I certainly don't want to replace your dad in your lives, but I would want us to get along. You're a great kid, Ty. I know what you can do on a ball field and I know how smart you are, but I'd like the chance to discover what else there is about you that makes you unique. The same with Kyle and Katie."

Cal gave Ty a moment to digest this before he said, "Okay? You feel better now?"

"I guess," Ty said, then added grudgingly, "And I guess it would be okay if you come to dinner tomorrow." His gaze challenged Cal. "As long as there's no funny stuff going on, if you know what I mean."

Cal bit back a grin. "No funny stuff. Got it. Now, take that note back to class so you don't wind up in detention and miss practice."

Ty took off, dragging his backpack behind him. Cal stared after him. What on earth was he getting himself into? Knowing he was ready for a relationship with Maddie was one thing. Knowing he'd have to form strong relationships with her two teenage boys and their little sister was quite another. Maybe he was in way over his head.

Oddly enough, though, he no longer felt even the slightest inclination to bail.

After the episode at Wharton's, Maddie buried herself in work. She'd made arrangements with her mother to pick up the kids after school and take them out for dinner so she could work into the evening. Maybe if she dealt with all the last-minute crises at the spa, she wouldn't have to deal with the far more complicated crisis that Cal represented.

So far, though, it wasn't working. She still had plenty of time to wonder if she was doing the right thing by having him over for dinner tomorrow night despite Ty's emphatic objections and Bill's ridiculous determination to interfere in her life.

Since she wasn't accomplishing much anyway, she opened the screened, sliding glass door to let in a breeze, climbed onto one of the treadmills and set it into motion. The sun was setting outside the window, splashing orange and pink light over the last of the azaleas and the dark green forest of trees just beyond the creek. The breeze brought with it the scent of rain, and she saw darker clouds start to roll across the horizon from the west. A crack of lightning split the sky and the last rays of the sunset disappeared behind the clouds. She took a deep breath and ran a little faster, as if trying to outrun the storm.

She was just working up a good sweat when Cal suddenly appeared on the other side of the screen. Startled, she stumbled and nearly rolled off the back of the machine.

"Sorry," Cal said, sprinting inside to catch her and shut down the machine at the same time.

She poked him in the chest. "Dammit, Cal, you scared me!"

"Sorry," he said. "The front door was locked, but I saw your car out front and the lights on around here."

"You're wet," she said, still trembling, either from the fright, from her workout or perhaps just from being held in his arms. Most likely the last. God, he felt good. Smelled good, too. She breathed in the musky masculine scent.

"The rain caught me just as I came around the corner of the building," he told her.

He started to release her, but she kept him still by resting her hand against his cheek. "No, don't let go," she whispered, her gaze locked with his. "I was just thinking about you."

"Were you?"

She gave him a rueful look. "We're the talk of the town."

He winced. "Sorry again."

"Not your fault," she said. "I gather we were spotted leaving here Saturday night and then you mentioned something about the hot tub to someone." She grinned. "You can imagine how it went after that."

"How'd you find out? I'm sure someone was only to eager to tell you," he said.

"Bill called."

"That must have been awkward," he said, searching her face.

"That's one word for it." For some reason, standing here with Cal's arms around her, instead of feeling guilty or angry, she felt good. Very good, in fact.

Cal brushed a strand of hair from her face. "We could really give them all something to talk about," he suggested, a glint in his eyes.

Maddie laughed. "Believe me, I've considered that."

"And?"

Since he was so close and felt so wonderful, she rubbed a thumb across his lower lip, then traced her fingers over the faint and oh-so-masculine stubble on his cheek. "Probably a bad idea," she confessed eventually. "Not that I'm not tempted."

"Me, too," he said. "But I trust your judgment. Besides, I had a visit from your son this afternoon. He cut his history class to have a little heart-to-heart with me."

Maddie groaned. "Oh no, what did he say?"

"He wanted to know just how far things had gone between us. Those weren't exactly the words he used, though."

This time she did back up a step and covered her face with her hands. "I am so sorry. I knew he was upset about me asking you to dinner, but I had no idea he'd confront you."

"I think it's good that he did," Cal said. "Now it's all out in the open."

She studied him. "What's out in the open?"

"The fact that I would like to spend more time with you."

Her heart stilled, then pounded. "You told him that?"

"Yes, and I told him that if things got serious between us, I would talk it over with him and his brother and sister."

Maddie felt as if she were still on the treadmill and it was running away with her. She couldn't keep up.

"I can't do this," she whispered, suddenly panicked by how quickly things seemed to be moving.

He regarded her with confusion. "Do what?"

"You, me, any of this. It's too complicated. We have to call it off. Not that there's anything to call off. I mean, we haven't done anything to apologize for, not really." She couldn't even look him in the eye as she rambled on, embarrassed by her son's behavior, her assumptions, pretty much everything, including her own steamy fantasies.

"But after we talked, Ty said he's okay with me coming to dinner tomorrow," Cal protested.

"It's more than that," she insisted. "Could you just go, please? I can't think with you here."

He didn't budge. "Maybe you shouldn't be thinking. It's been my experience that too much thinking keeps people from being in touch with their real feelings."

"We don't have real feelings for each other," she said,

wishing it were true. "We're infatuated, maybe in lust. That's it."

"Speak for yourself," he told her.

"I am. Please go," she begged, failing to keep the note of desperation from her voice.

"Not until we talk this through," he said stubbornly.

"There's nothing to talk through, Cal. It has to stop now." Before she fell head over heels in love with him.

She glanced up and caught the frown on his face.

"Okay, let's deal with this one thing at a time. Are you canceling my invitation to dinner? That seems to be what triggered all of these doubts."

She sighed heavily, but managed to keep her tone firm. "Yes, I am definitely canceling dinner. I had no idea a simple invitation would get so complicated."

"Why did you ask me in the first place?"

"I wanted to thank you for being such a good friend to all of us," she said. When he regarded her with skepticism, she shrugged. "Okay, I wanted to spend a normal evening with you and my kids."

"What's changed?"

"I explained that. The boys got all worked up. Bill's in a frenzy. The whole town's talking about us. I'm not sure it's worth adding any more fuel to the fire. It'll just create problems."

"For whom?"

Now, *that* was the sixty-four-thousand-dollar question. "Mostly for you, I think."

"I'm not worried," he said.

"Only because you don't understand how small-minded people in small towns can be once they get a whiff of scandal."

He regarded her with amusement. “Me coming to dinner will create a scandal?”

She knew it sounded ridiculous, but he obviously didn’t truly grasp how badly things could get blown out of proportion. “Not by itself, no, but along with everything else—the parents thinking you’re giving preferential treatment to Ty because of me, the whole hot-tub story, the get-togethers at Rosalina’s—yes, that can be twisted into something ugly.”

He looked disappointed in her. “So you’re going to let people with nothing better to do than gossip dictate what you do? I thought you were stronger than that.”

“Strong? Me? You must have me confused with someone who’s not going through a divorce and dealing with three kids who are a mess because of it.” She regarded him intently. “I have to think about the boys. It’s been confusing enough for them lately. And then there’s Katie. She’s heartsick that her dad’s not home. Besides, it’s not as if you and I are…” Her voice trailed off.

He grinned. “As if we aren’t what? Dating? An item? Lovers?” His gaze held hers. “Serious?”

She gasped.

“The town gossips aren’t the only ones who’ve made that leap, Maddie. It’s crossed my mind, too. Not five minutes ago, as a matter of fact. Hasn’t it crossed yours?”

When she didn’t answer him, he let the silence drag on.

“Okay, yes,” she admitted eventually. “It’s crossed my mind.”

“But?”

“It would be complicated,” she repeated. “Very complicated.”

He studied her with a frown. “You’re not just talking logistics, are you?”

“No. I think the reactions we’ve gotten to this dinner

invitation pale by comparison to the commotion that going any further with the relationship would cause."

"And that matters because…?"

"Your job, for one thing. We already know that your principal is eager to make an issue out of us seeing each other."

"If I'm not worried about that, why should you be?"

"Maybe you *should* be worried," she told him. "I don't think you realize how far Betty might go."

"Oh, I realize that," he replied. "But in the end, she'll lose. And even if she doesn't, I've learned one thing by walking away from baseball—there are always other opportunities in life."

"But you're a good teacher and a great coach," she protested. "I don't want the kids to lose you."

"Frankly, neither do I," he admitted. "But we're talking about my personal life, not some crime I've committed. I can handle a little heat, if it comes to that." He tucked a finger under her chin and held her gaze. "Come on, Maddie, you're going to have to come up with a better excuse than that to break things off."

"Okay, then, my kids," she said. "I can't put them through any more turmoil."

"I get that," Cal said quietly, his gaze steady. "I really do. And believe me, I am not suggesting we turn their worlds upside down by doing something drastic. But don't you think if we did a few things together—dinner, a picnic, a ball game, whatever—they might get used to me being around? Something tells me your ex wasn't that considerate. He didn't let them get used to much of anything before he announced he was marrying Noreen, did he?"

"No. I think that's what hurt most of all," she conceded. "It was just dumped in our laps. One day we were a family and the next day we weren't. And to top it off, Bill had a whole new family waiting on the sidelines. He still can't understand why the kids are so resentful."

"Well, I do understand that," Cal said. "And I'm willing to do whatever it takes to get them used to the idea of you and me together."

Amazement and a faint hint of longing spread through her. "You almost sound as if you're thinking long-term," she said, wonder in her voice.

"I am," he admitted. "I have been from the minute I thought I had a chance with you. I respect you, Maddie. You're all about family. It would be wrong to offer you anything less."

"I don't know what to say to that," she whispered, shaken and more than a little intrigued. She hadn't even allowed herself to fantasize about a serious relationship with Cal.

"Does knowing what I want scare you?" he asked.

She lifted her gaze to his, then answered from her heart. "Not half as much as it probably ought to."

He smiled. "Then how about I walk home with you and say hello to the kids. Nothing else, just hello."

"That's it?"

"That's it." He winked at her. "Of course, if it goes well, I'll be over for dinner tomorrow night."

"You're one of those 'give the man an inch and he'll take a mile' guys, aren't you."

"Apparently so." He studied her. "Is it a deal?"

"Maybe you should kiss me again," she suggested.

"To seal the deal?"

"To remind me of why I'm suddenly willing to throw caution to the wind for you."

He laughed. "I can do that," he said and covered her mouth with his.

The kiss stole breath and thought and apparently common sense, because in that moment, with his lips on hers and his heart beating strong and sure beneath her hand where it rested against his chest, just about anything seemed possible.

A reporter from the Serenity weekly newspaper was sitting in Maddie's makeshift office, her tape recorder running as she interviewed Maddie, Dana Sue and Helen about why they'd decided to open a fitness club in Serenity.

"I suppose each of us had her own reasons," Helen said. "But the one thing we all agreed on was that the women of Serenity need a place they can go to get healthy, a place where they feel pampered and maybe even make new friends."

"It's definitely about more than getting a good workout in pleasant surroundings," Dana Sue said. "It's going to be a gathering place for women, someplace where they'll feel totally comfortable letting their hair down."

"No men allowed, then?" Peggy Martin asked.

"Not after our grand opening," Maddie confirmed.

Peggy turned to her. "Does that mean there will be no more late-night visits by Coach Maddox?" she inquired, her saccharine tone belying the glint of malice in her eyes. "I understand he's been a regular here lately."

Before Maddie could gather her composure and answer, Helen stood up. "I believe you have everything you need," she told Peggy. "I'm due back in court in an hour."

"But she didn't answer my question," Peggy said, even as Helen snapped off the tape recorder.

"No, she didn't," Dana Sue replied. "Because she knows you asked it because you've got a burr up your butt because Cal never gave you a second glance."

Peggy looked as if she had a whole lot more she wanted to say, but Helen latched on to her elbow and guided her to the door.

"Thank you so much for coming by," Helen said through clenched teeth. "I'll be speaking to your boss later about our advertising plans in the *Serenity Times.*" She gave Peggy a hard look. "Or not."

Maddie winced at the less-than-subtle threat. When Helen had escorted the reporter out the door, Maddie turned to Dana Sue. "She shouldn't have done that," she murmured. "Now we have an enemy."

Dana Sue shrugged. "We were bound to have one or two."

"But it might be better if they didn't work for the local paper," Maddic said wryly.

"Oh, I imagine Walt Flanigan will keep Peggy's worst instincts in check," Dana Sue said. "He's more concerned about advertising revenue at the *Times* than he is about Peggy's right to target a local business in her newspaper column. She was out of line. This was an interview for a feature story about The Corner Spa, Maddie, not about your personal life. If she wants to stir up real trouble, she ought to dig around for some corruption at city hall. I hear Mayor Lewis had dinner with the woman whose company is bidding on the town's office-supply contract."

Maddie chuckled despite herself. "That's his wife, and you know it. And she only wins that contract after competitive bidding. Howard's a stickler for that. He even recuses himself from the vote."

Dana Sue grinned. "But with the right spin, anything can be made to seem a little shady. Let Peggy focus her mudslinging tendencies somewhere else."

"But she was right," Maddie said. "Cal was here a couple of nights."

"So what?"

"The Corner Spa is for women," Maddie reminded her. "We're building our reputation on that."

"Oh, for goodness' sakes," Dana Sue said impatiently. "Skeeter and Roy and Mitch have been crawling all over this place, along with all their workers. What's one more man on the premises before we get the doors open?"

"We both know Cal wasn't working when he was here," Maddie said.

Dana Sue grinned. "I'd be disappointed if he had been."

Maddie rolled her eyes at Dana Sue's unrepentant expression. "Well, I'll make sure he understands that he can't be coming around here after the opening," she vowed.

"Maddie, don't let anything Peggy Martin said get under your skin and ruin what's happening with you and Cal."

"If she were the only one with something to say, I could handle it," Maddie said. "But she's just the tip of a very large iceberg."

"Sweetie, this is Serenity, South Carolina. Just how long do you think an iceberg stands a chance in the heat down here?"

Maddie chuckled again, her dark mood finally lifting. "You have a point."

"Well, of course I do. Now I'm going to hightail it over to the restaurant and try to get some food prepared before the lunch crowd starts complaining that all we've got on the menu is a house salad and dessert."

"So, what's on the menu today?" Maddie asked. "Maybe I'll stop by."

"Great idea," Dana Sue said. "Showing your face in public is one way to quiet all the talk. And, along with baked pork chops served with mashed sweet potatoes, I'm making a new chicken salad with a lime-cilantro dressing. You can tell me what you think."

"Sounds more Southwestern than Southern," Maddie commented.

"Don't tell anyone or they'll want the chicken in it fried, not baked, and they'll demand I dump ranch dressing all over it," Dana Sue said with disgust. "I'm trying to broaden tastes around here."

"Well, the menu sounds fantastic to me. Count me in." Maddie stood up and gave Dana Sue a fierce hug. "I am so glad you're my friend."

"Right back at you."

But once she was alone, Maddie couldn't help wondering whether Peggy Martin's unanswered question and the way she'd been unceremoniously escorted from the premises were going to come back to haunt them.

CHAPTER EIGHTEEN

It seemed as if everyone in town had shown up for the grand opening of The Corner Spa on Friday night. With no baseball game scheduled, the place was so crowded Maddie could hardly breathe. Dana Sue's hors d'oeuvres were being devoured at an alarming rate. People were raving about the luxurious atmosphere in the treatment rooms with their subdued lighting and lavender scent, the spotlessly clean locker room and showers, the café with its comfortable tables and chairs and its glass-fronted showcase that would eventually hold a variety of healthy salads, fruit and yogurt parfaits, fat-free muffins and other tempting treats.

They'd picked up a dozen new memberships in the first half hour. Jeanette was manning the information-and-membership desk for the moment and she was swamped, but she gave Maddie a thumbs-up.

Maddie retreated outside to try to catch her breath. Within minutes Helen and Dana Sue found her. Helen was carrying three glasses of champagne. She handed one to each of them.

"Ladies, I think we're a success!" she said, grinning and clinking her glass to theirs.

"It's a party," Maddie cautioned, unable to let herself relax and enjoy the moment. Too much was riding on this for all of them. "Let's not get ahead of ourselves. Let's see if we continue to stay ahead of projections once the doors are officially opened on Monday."

"Oh, stop being so gloomy," Dana Sue scolded. "Have you listened to those women inside? They're crazy about the place."

"And their husbands are green with jealousy," Helen said. "I even overheard a couple of them vowing to get on Dexter's case to clean up that gym of his."

Just then, Jeanette slipped outside to join them. Her cheeks were flushed with excitement, but her eyes were vaguely troubled. "Here you are. I was looking all over for you."

Maddie took one look at her agitated expression and felt her stomach sink. Jeanette was the calmest person she knew. She claimed that practicing yoga and meditation kept her that way, and it was essential for making clients feel soothed and pampered during and after a facial.

"What's wrong?" Maddie asked.

"Nothing major," Jeanette said.

Maddie grimaced at the attempt to placate her. Because Jeanette had been on-site every day, she knew better than any of them that Maddie's nerves were stretched to the limit.

"Just tell us, okay?" Maddie said. "And who's on the desk? You didn't just go off and leave it empty, did you?"

"Of course not. I left your mom holding down the fort and promised I'd be right back," Jeanette assured her. "As for the rest, like I said, it's nothing major. At least, I don't think it's major, but you know this town better than I do."

Helen frowned. "Jeanette!"

"Okay, okay. I overheard this woman talking to a group of women," Jeanette reported. "She said she hoped we enjoyed tonight, because once tomorrow's edition of the paper hits the streets, we might not have much to gloat about." She looked at each of them. "Any idea who she is or what she meant?"

"Peggy," the three of them responded in unison.

Maddie groaned. "I knew it. She's going to rip this place to shreds in her column, or at least me."

Jeanette looked confused. "Why would she do that? And why would she show her face tonight if she intends to print some negative article in tomorrow's paper?"

"She wants to be sure word gets around so the paper sells out the second it hits the stands," Helen guessed. "A sellout will convince her boss that her brand of reporting is just what he needs to boost circulation."

"But why attack this place?" Jeanette asked, still looking bewildered. "I'd think everyone in Serenity would want a new business to succeed."

"Most people do feel that way," Maddie responded.

"Peggy's upset because she came over here the other day with her own agenda to embarrass Maddie and I kicked her out," Helen said. "This is payback." She gave Maddie's hand a squeeze. "Don't panic. I'll deal with this."

"How?"

"I didn't go to Walt Flanigan the other day, but it's not too late to explain a few facts of life to Peggy's boss now," Helen said, her expression grimly determined.

"It's too late if the paper's already gone to press," Maddie told her. "Besides, you could make it worse. If it hasn't gone to press, there would still be time for Walt to insert something about you trying to blackmail him to keep something negative out of Peggy's column. He'd manage to come off sounding indignant and we'd look desperate. Any way you slice it, this is very bad PR."

"Come on, you guys," Dana Sue said. "Nobody pays any attention to what Peggy writes in that rag. Forget about it. How much harm can she do, really? Most of the town is here tonight. They know what this place is like. And they know us. They're going to realize that anything bad she writes is just sour grapes."

Maddie wasn't so sure about that, but she couldn't think of a single strategy they could use to deflect the damage. "I suppose we'll just have to wait and see what she wrote, then figure out how to counteract it."

"A strategy meeting first thing in the morning, then?" Helen suggested.

"I'll be here at eight," Maddie said.

"I'll bring the coffee and some apple-cranberry muffins," Dana Sue offered. "Jeanette, can you get back over here by eight?"

"Not a problem," she said. "I'm staying at the Windsor Motel right now."

"Here in town?" Maddie asked, studying her worriedly. "What happened?"

Jeanette shrugged as if it were no big deal, but the sorrow in her eyes gave her away. "I left Don. He said he wouldn't drive all the way over here for some stupid party, so I told him I wouldn't drive back and forth from here to be with him. I packed up and moved my stuff on Wednesday. I'll start looking for someplace to rent permanently after things here settle down. It's been too busy this week to even think about that."

"Oh, sweetie, I am so sorry," Dana Sue said, giving her a hug. "The guy's a jerk."

"I know," Jeanette said. "That made it easier to walk away."

"Are you really okay with that?" Maddie asked.

"Not yet," Jeanette admitted, then added with a touch of defiance, "But I will be. Right now, all I care about is making this place wildly successful."

"Come on, then," Helen said. "Let's put on our happy faces and go back inside and make this party rock."

Maddie had barely stepped into the kitchen, when Cal appeared beside her.

"Everything okay?" he asked.

"Everything's fine," she said, forcing a smile. "But you probably shouldn't be in here."

He gave her an odd look. "Because?"

"Because..." Her voice trailed off. She was tired of making excuses for liking this man, for being with him. "Because it's probably a mistake," she said, then met his gaze. "But you know what? I don't give a damn." She stood on tiptoe and pressed her mouth to his, then grinned at the look of surprise on his face. "It's a new day," she declared. "Get used to it."

He grinned back at her. "Not a problem, darlin'. Definitely not a problem."

Of course, she thought, he was wrong. Something told her the problems were about to get much, much worse.

Bill watched Maddie emerge from the kitchen with Cal Maddox beside her. He noted the color in her cheeks and the smile on her lips and knew with absolute certainty that the rumors were true. There was definitely something going on between the two of them. He was shocked by how empty and alone that made him feel, even with Noreen right here beside him. He was also stunned by a primitive desire to punch Cal in the face and tell him to stay the hell away from his woman. Unfortunately, he'd lost that right.

He'd almost told Noreen that they couldn't come tonight, but he'd seen the anticipation in her eyes and known he couldn't disappoint her. For months they'd hidden their relationship from everyone. Now that his divorce from Maddie would be final in a few more days and there was no reason to live in the shadows, he owed it to Noreen to show the world that they were together. He certainly couldn't treat the woman he intended to marry as if she were some dirty little secret.

He turned and met her knowing gaze.

"You wish you weren't here, don't you?" she asked with rare insight.

"It's uncomfortable being around Maddie these days," he admitted.

"Because you still feel guilty or because she's moved on to someone new?" Noreen asked, watching his face closely.

"Maybe a little of both." Because Noreen suddenly looked so stricken, he lifted her hand to his lips and brushed a kiss across her knuckles. She merely sighed.

"I wish things were different," she said wistfully. "I thought they would be."

Before he could respond, his former mother-in-law stepped up beside them. She cast a pitying look at Noreen, before turning to Bill. "I'm surprised to see you here, but I suppose I shouldn't be. You never did have a single shred of decency or sensitivity, despite that blue blood of yours."

"Maddie sent us an invitation," he said stiffly. "I assumed she wouldn't have done that if she didn't want us to come."

"Oh, please, you can't be that stupid, Bill. Maddie's a

smart businesswoman. She would never deliberately exclude a prominent local doctor, not even her cheating husband."

"Let's go," Noreen said, tugging on his arm. "She's right. I don't know what I was thinking. We don't belong here. This is Maddie's night."

Bill glanced across the room and spotted Maddie with her arm tucked through Cal's. They were laughing with the mayor and his wife. How many times had she done exactly that with him? In the early years, as she worked to help him build his practice, invitations to their dinner parties had been much sought after. He wondered how many of those same people, if forced to choose sides, would pick him and Noreen over Maddie and whoever was in her life? Probably far fewer than he cared to imagine. Maddie was the one with the gift for making people feel welcome, the talent for knowing exactly the right thing to say.

He forced a smile for his mother-in-law. "Lovely to see you as always," he muttered.

Though her dark eyes were blazing, Paula's smile was more genuine. "Wish I could say the same."

"Is she always such a bitch?" Noreen asked as Paula walked away in a swirl of brightly colored silk.

"No," he said. "She reserves it for me. I was never her first choice for her daughter. She thought I wasn't good enough." He shrugged. "As it turns out, she was probably right."

Even as Noreen uttered an emphatic and loyal denial, Bill couldn't shut off the cascade of regrets tumbling through his mind. He had a beautiful young woman who adored him on his arm. She was carrying his child.

And all he could think about was the woman he'd left behind.

* * *

"I can't believe Walt Flanigan let Peggy get away with this," Dana Sue declared the next morning at the spa office, throwing the local weekly onto the desk. "It's slanderous or libelous or whatever it is when you print something that's blatantly untrue."

"Libelous," Helen muttered, her expression dark. She turned to Maddie. "I'll have a lawsuit on his desk Monday morning, if you say the word."

Peggy had taken the slew of rumors about Maddie and Cal that were swirling around Serenity and twisted them into some sort of dark tale of wickedness and sin, with The Corner Spa as their private hideaway.

Maddie balled the newspaper up and threw it in the trash. "You can't do anything," she told Helen. "She's managed to toss just enough truth in there to keep it legal. Besides, taking her to court would only give her another chance to spew all this garbage in print. I picked up the last copy in the newsstand on Main Street outside of Wharton's, so Walt's going to be ecstatic at the bump in circulation. Everyone who wants to read about Cal's and my supposed sins has already done it. What's the point of giving Peggy more ammunition for another attack and Walt a chance to sell even more papers?"

She met their worried gazes. "I am so sorry. I knew I was playing with fire. I should have been more careful."

"Don't be ridiculous," Helen said heatedly. "You and Cal haven't done anything wrong. He's single. You're about to be single."

"But the divorce isn't final yet," Maddie reminded her. "I'm sure that will matter to some people."

"Even if you point out that your ex-husband is already living with his pregnant girlfriend?" Jeanette asked incredulously. She was on her third cup of coffee, keeping pace with Helen. Both looked as if they wanted to hit something on Maddie's behalf.

"Double standard," Dana Sue said bitterly. "It's alive and well here in Serenity. Don't you know our belles must be above reproach?"

"That's nuts," Jeanette said.

"No, it's real life," Maddie told her. "And I knew it. Goodness knows, I had enough warning signs. Betty Donovan…" she began, then faltered. "Oh, my God—Cal. He needs to know about this. The you-know-what is going to hit the fan at the school. You know it will."

"Call him," Helen advised. "Go on into the other room and call him while we talk about what to do."

Maddie left the three of them talking about their options, went outside and punched in Cal's number on her cell phone.

"Hey, beautiful," he said. "Basking in your success?"

He sounded so cheerful Maddie knew he hadn't yet seen the local paper. "Not exactly," she told him.

"Okay," he said, his tone sobering. "What's wrong?"

"You need to pick up the *Serenity Times*, assuming you can still find a copy," she said. "Peggy Martin has a tell-all column about the two of us in there."

"What is there to tell?" he asked.

Maddie almost smiled at his bewilderment. "Quite a lot if you take the few things you do know and spin them. Apparently we're having quite a torrid affair at the club."

"You're kidding! She printed that?"

"And more," Maddie told him. "You need to buy the paper and then figure out what you're going to tell Betty Donovan and the school board. I suspect you'll be hearing from them first thing Monday morning, if not before."

She tried to force a lighter note into her voice. "They'll probably try to come after me for contributing to the delinquency of a minor."

"Not even a tiny bit amusing," Cal said. "Stop worrying about this, Maddie. I'll handle Betty. What about you? Are you okay?"

"Actually I'm mad as hell, but I don't think going over to the paper and ripping Peggy's bleached-blond hair out by the handful would be an appropriate response. A picture of that would probably make the wire services."

"Might be worth it," he commented. "I know I'd like to see that."

"You have weird taste in entertainment," she responded, but she was smiling. "I need to go. Helen, Dana Sue and Jeanette and I are planning our strategy for dealing with the situation. I just thought I ought to fill you in, so you'd know what to expect if you set foot out your door today."

"One thing before you go," he said. "Do the kids know?"

"No, I haven't been home since I saw the paper. We don't have it delivered, so they won't see it."

"Don't you imagine there might be some calls at the house? Their friends might be only too happy to spread the word," Cal said. "Want me to go over and field any calls?"

Maddie considered the offer for about two seconds, then sighed. "Bad idea," she told him. "I think my house is the very last place you ought to be today, but you're right that someone needs to be there until I can get back. I'll get my mother to go over."

"Will I see you later?"

As much as she wanted to see him and draw on his strength, Maddie knew there was no way to do that without adding fuel to the fire. Nosy neighbors were probably already staking out her house and his.

"I don't think so," she said. "We need to keep our distance till this dies down."

"You honestly believe it'll die down?"

"Eventually."

"Well, don't expect me to wait forever, Maddie. I'm not going to let a little gossip ruin what we have."

"Sweetie, this isn't a little gossip," she told him glumly. "It's a killer hurricane. The winds are just now kicking up. You wait and see."

She'd seen it before. Once this kind of thing took off, there was no stopping it till it destroyed everything in its path.

Maddie and the kids were in a pew near the back of the church on Sunday morning when Cal slid in beside her. As he nodded to Ty and Kyle, she regarded him with dismay.

"You didn't say anything about coming to church this morning," she murmured as the congregation stood for the processional.

"Last-minute decision," he said, holding a hymnal where they could both see it. "After our conversation about what Peggy wrote in yesterday's paper, I figured you'd disapprove."

"I have to admit I don't think it's the smartest decision you've made lately." She nodded toward the church members who were sneaking looks in their direction. "Are you trying to deliberately set tongues wagging?"

"Actually I was hoping that people who come to church might be more open-minded and tolerant, especially if they see we're not trying to sneak around behind anyone's back."

Maddie bit back a sigh. "You are such a dreamer."

Cal grinned. "That's me, the eternal optimist. Now sing,

darlin', before tongues start wagging that we're here on a date, rather than participating in the service."

Though she had a whole lot more she wanted to say, she found her place in the hymn and dutifully sang. She was surprised when Cal's voice blended with hers. This time when the folks closest to them turned and looked their way, there were at least one or two nods of approval and encouragement.

At the end of the service, when Reverend Beale reminded everyone of the fellowship gathering in the church hall, Cal glanced her way.

"I don't think so," she said tightly, knowing that he wanted to continue this ill-advised public declaration.

"The best way to silence gossip is to confront it," he told her as the congregation began to file out. "We don't have anything to hide, Maddie. Scurrying out of here will make it look as if we do."

"Staying will make it look as if we're flaunting an affair right under their noses," she countered.

He grinned. "But we're not having an affair."

"Yet," she muttered.

Cal's grin spread. "That's the most promising thing I've heard in ages. Come on, sweetheart, I feel like some cake and coffee." He raised his voice to draw Ty and Kyle's attention. "I'll bet the kids would like something to eat, too, right, guys? And Katie will probably go to the social hour after Sunday school, right?"

"Yes, but there's plenty of food at home," Maddie said before they could answer. "We're having Sunday dinner at two."

"But it's lots more fun to have dessert first," Cal taunted. "Be wild, Maddie."

She wanted to be, she really did, but she knew this town

and these people. If she and Cal walked into the social hall together, it would be open season on the two of them. It was as good as admitting that Peggy was right, that they were an item and they didn't care what anyone thought. Cal was obviously ready to make such a public announcement. She wasn't sure she was, not when she understood the potential consequences more clearly than he did.

Just then Helen walked up and linked her arm through Maddie's. "Cal's right. Katie's waiting inside. Now's not the time to chicken out," she whispered, then beamed up at Cal and tucked her other arm through his. "Let's go stir things up."

"Okay, okay," Maddie said. "But I want to go on record as saying that this is a really bad idea. We're not taking into account the impact this will have on the kids."

"It's okay, Mom," Ty said. "Kyle and me can handle it. What Peggy wrote in the paper was mean and it was nothing but a bunch of lies."

Maddie flinched. "You saw the paper?"

Ty rolled his eyes. "Are you kidding? At least ten kids from school called us before Grandma even got to the house. The first one read it to us. After that I hung up on everyone else."

Cal regarded him with approval. "Good for you."

Maddie didn't even know what to say. "I had no idea," she said eventually. "I'm sorry."

Kyle shrugged. "It's no big deal, Mom. Dad pretty much got us used to hearing all sorts of bad stuff."

Maddie frowned. "All the more reason for me not to put you through any more of that. There's no way I'm going to drag you into that social hour now."

Helen gave her a chiding look. "If you don't fight for what you want, who will?" she said. "Today's the day to take a stand and let folks know that your private life is your business and no one else's."

"Amen to that," Cal said.

Maddie frowned at Helen. "You're just hoping this will erupt into some sort of harassment lawsuit or something so you can charge into court and defend us."

Helen feigned dismay. "The thought never crossed my mind," she insisted, then winked. "But you do have my number if either of you need it. It would make my day to haul Betty Donovan into court by the seat of her starched knickers."

Maddie chuckled despite herself. "That is an intriguing image, all right."

Cal gave Maddie a lingering look. "Okay, the boys and I are up for this. How about you? Tell the truth, Maddie. Don't let us pressure you into doing something you're going to regret."

"Hey, I'm as eager to put a few people in their places as you are," she said with grim determination. "I just hope we don't all live to regret it."

Cal, Maddie and Helen had debated the wisdom of joining the fellowship hour for so long that Ty and Kyle had tired of it and gone on ahead, clearly anticipating the outcome of all the talk. When Cal and Maddie finally did walk in, the entire crowd fell silent. Even on a ball field when thousands were waiting for him to make a play or get a hit, Cal had never felt more the center of attention. He'd rather be standing flat-footed, taking a called third strike, than facing the animosity he felt in this room where people were expected to put on at least an appearance of warm-spirited generosity and friendliness.

Leaving Maddie and Helen just inside the door, he spotted Kyle and Ty by a table laden with baked goods. They looked a little shell-shocked.

"Coach," several men murmured with a nod as he passed, but not one engaged him in conversation, probably due to the sharp-elbowed digs their wives had given them.

At the table, Ty and Kyle were already setting down their empty plates.

"This sucks," Ty said. "I guess Mom was right. It was a mistake to come. I'll go find Katie."

"Yeah," Kyle agreed. "Why's everyone mad at us? Gossiping is bad enough, but it's like they're blaming us for you liking Mom."

"No one's mad at you," Cal said.

"Okay, but they're acting all crazy because of you and Mom," Ty said. "They think you're sleeping together."

Cal gave him a hard look. "What do you think?"

Ty shrugged. "Mom's not that dumb."

Cal winced at the assessment. "I thought we had this conversation. You told me you wouldn't be upset if your mom and I were dating."

"But everybody thinks there's more going on," Ty said. "Me and Kyle have heard them talking. They're joking about why Mom would want to be with a guy as young as you. They figure you're some hot stud or something. I told you it was going to be weird."

Cal clung to his patience. He didn't want to have to defend himself or Maddie to her children, but thanks to that damn newspaper column, combined with human nature, it was evident he was going to have to.

"Age doesn't have to be an issue in a relationship," he explained. "Life experience is what counts."

"Yeah, well, Mom's got a *lot* more life experience than you," Ty said. "Why would you want to date her?"

Cal decided it would be wildly inappropriate for him to point out that their mom was hot. Instead, he said, "Because she's funny and smart and caring. Those are the qualities that really matter in a woman. Those are the qualities that'll last."

Ty gave him a knowing look. "I guess it doesn't hurt that she looks good in shorts, though, does it?"

Cal tried not to grin. "Nope, it doesn't hurt," he admitted. He met Ty's gaze man-to-man. "I made you a promise the other day. I intend to keep it."

"What promise?" Kyle demanded, clearly not trusting a lot of promises made by grown-ups these days.

"That I will do my best never to hurt your mom, and she and I will do our best never to hurt you," he told them. "So, despite what anyone else might think, is it okay with you if we spend some time together?"

"It's not up to us," Kyle said, sounding resigned. "Adults do what they want to do."

"In the end, everyone should always make their own choices, yes," Cal agreed. "But what you think does matter to us and it will always be an important consideration in whatever we do."

Ty regarded him with a perplexed expression. "Can I ask you something?"

"Anything," Cal said.

"How come all these people in here are making such a big deal about you and Mom in the first place? It's not like you're cheating on anyone the way Dad did."

"Double standard," Cal admitted. "Men think they can do things women can't. And before you ask, no, it's not fair."

Just then they heard a commotion from across the room.

Cal turned to see Helen backing Betty Donovan into a corner.

"Oh, brother," he muttered and headed over there, Ty and Kyle right on his heels.

Cal arrived just as Reverend Beale interceded, spreading inane platitudes far and wide, all the while casting a disapproving look in Maddie's direction.

"Time to go," Cal said, swooping in just as Maddie looked as if she wanted to join in the fray. "Ty, find your sister."

"Go ahead," Helen encouraged, then turned a frown on the principal. "I have a few more things I want to clear up here."

Taking his cue from Maddie's panicked expression, Cal grasped Helen's arm and guided her out of the hall before she could make matters worse.

Outside, he looked from one pair of tumultuous eyes to another. "What the heck happened in there?"

"Hell froze over," Maddie said tersely.

Cal stared at her. "I beg your pardon."

Helen chuckled, her tense expression relaxing. "Maddie told Betty it would be a cold day in hell before she let an uptight prig like her dictate who she could and couldn't see."

"Uh-huh," Cal said, still waiting for the punch line.

Maddie shrugged. "She told me to get out my winter coat because she was about to prove me wrong."

Before he had any idea just how furious Maddie was or what she intended, she grabbed a fistful of his shirt and dragged him close, then pressed her mouth to his. Heat shot through him, but he had enough reasoning power left not to let himself get too carried away right there on the steps of the church.

"Not that I'm complaining, but what was that for?" he

asked, struggling to catch his breath when she finally released him.

"I am so tired of letting other people control my life," she said, her cheeks flushed. "That was my declaration of war."

"An interesting approach," he said, then draped an arm over her shoulders. "But maybe we ought to go home before you get any other ideas."

She shot him a defiant look. "I will not be bullied."

"Good for you," he declared, fighting a smile.

"Yeah, Mom, way to go," Ty added, back and holding Katie's hand. He grinned at Cal. "Is it okay if I deck anybody who brings up this subject at school?"

"No," Cal and Maddie said in unison.

"Too bad," Ty said, and walked on ahead to join his brother.

Once they'd walked the half mile to her house, Maddie seemed a little less sure of herself. Inside, she lifted her gaze to his. "I just made things worse, didn't I?"

"I suppose we'll have to wait and see," he told her, then touched a finger to her lips. "Just so you know, though, it was definitely worth it."

"Really?"

"Oh, yeah."

The corners of her mouth curved upward. "Good to know."

CHAPTER NINETEEN

Five women quit the spa on Monday morning. Not one of them would meet Maddie's eyes when she announced her intention.

Fighting a rising tide of panic and already debating what to do about the PR disaster, Maddie wasn't prepared for the arrival of Helen and Dana Sue at midday. Judging from their dire expressions, they'd heard about the defections and concluded, as Maddie had, that she was a liability for The Corner Spa.

"You heard," she said grimly. "You don't have to say it. Having me involved with this place is going to be the kiss of death. I'll quit."

"You most certainly will not," Helen said fiercely.

"We're here to close ranks," Dana Sue explained. "Now change into your workout clothes and let's get in there and work up some sweat. We'll all feel better."

The last thing Maddie felt like doing was working up a sweat, especially when it also meant being the object of more speculative stares. She wanted to hide out in her office instead. "I don't know—"

"This is no time to run off with your tail between your

legs," Helen said, essentially repeating the advice she'd given Maddie on Sunday. "You've done absolutely nothing wrong. You're spending time with an available man. If that were a sin, every woman in this town would've sinned at some time or another, including the very proper Agatha Nixon."

Maddie rolled her eyes. "I think we all know that she's probably never done anything more with a man than bake chocolate-chip cookies for him."

Dana Sue grinned. "Are you saying you and Cal have gone beyond the cookie-baking stage?"

Helen immediately frowned at her. "Not the point," she said. "Whatever heat these two generate is their business. I don't care if they blow up the damn oven."

"Well, of course," Dana Sue said, looking miffed. "I was just teasing."

"Not the time for it. We need an immediate show of solidarity." Helen studied Maddie. "You do want this man in your life, don't you?"

"Yes," Maddie said, then heaved a sigh. "But not if it's going to cause all this trouble."

"That must make Cal feel all warm and fuzzy," Helen said with disgust. "If you want him, we'll figure this out. If you're just in temporary lust, then get over it and we'll all go back to work."

Now it was Dana Sue's turn to frown. "Geez, Helen, could you be any less understanding?"

"I'm on a tight schedule," Helen retorted. "If you want understanding, send an email to Dr. Phil."

Maddie held up her hands. "Okay, you two, that's enough. I will not have you fighting because of me. I have no idea how all this got so out of hand."

Dana Sue chuckled. "I can explain it. There are at least

twenty women in this town who had their eyes set on Cal, either for themselves, their daughters or their granddaughters. You dashed their hopes—that's how it got out of hand. Pure, spiteful jealousy, all wrapped up in a pious need to protect our innocent children."

Maddie hadn't wanted to believe that about women she'd known most of her life, but she couldn't deny that Dana Sue had it exactly right. "Well, be that as it may," she said, "the fact remains that as long as I'm going to be pilloried by the residents of Serenity, my connection to this place is a bad idea."

"You're not quitting and that's that," Helen declared. "Now, get into your workout clothes and let's get into the gym. I called Elliott Cruz on my way over here and told him we need him here early today to design a workout regimen for us that will take our minds off our problems. He has an hour before his first appointment."

Dana Sue grinned at the mention of the personal trainer they'd hired. "Just looking at Elliott's abs will take my mind off my problems," she said. "Frankly, I think once women get a look at him, our memberships will go through the roof and all this nonsense will be a thing of the past."

"And when folks see how you've trimmed up, Maddie," Helen added, "they'll know exactly why Cal's attracted to you. You'll be a walking advertisement for this place."

"People are *canceling!*" Maddie cried.

Helen waved dismissively. "And a dozen more will join just to see what all the fuss is about," she said confidently.

"If you're so sure of that, why did you rush over here?" Maddie asked.

"Because I knew *you* wouldn't be sure of that," Helen told her.

Maddie's eyes stung with tears. "I will walk away if it

turns out you're wrong," she told them. "I won't become a liability to you guys."

Dana Sue grinned. "Have you ever known Helen to be wrong?"

"Once in ninety-four," Helen conceded. "Paul Colson was not wearing a bad toupee at the annual pink-and-blue ball in Charleston. That actually was his hair, poor man."

Maddie recalled the incident vividly. On a bet, Helen had tried to snatch Paul's hair from his head. For her antics she'd suffered several embarrassing moments and the threat of a lawsuit.

"Do you have any idea how much I love you guys?" Maddie told them, sniffing. She reflected how often her friends gave her occasion to say this. Very often.

"Well, of course you do," Helen said briskly. "Treadmill in five minutes. I mean it. I'm paying Elliott for a private session."

Maddie was there in four, braving the curious or downright antagonistic looks of the other women working out. When Elliott joined them, his muscular body taut and trim, his coal-black hair almost shoulder length, he immediately drew their attention away from Maddie.

As the workout progressed, with Elliott issuing commands and demonstrating various machines in a way that showed off his bulging muscles, Dana Sue made an effort to draw a few of the other women into a conversation about their high-school days. The antics of the Sweet Magnolias seemed to be the highlight. Even women from neighboring towns had heard their share of tales about Helen, Dana Sue and Maddie at their most outrageous young selves.

"Not bad," Elliott said eventually. He winked at Helen. "I expect to see more progress the next time we work out."

"If I progress any further, I'll probably collapse," Dana Sue said.

"Hey, no defeatist attitudes allowed in here," Elliott chided. "Now I see that my next client has arrived, so I'll see you ladies later."

After he'd crossed the gym, drawing admiring gazes as he went, Helen regarded the dozen or so gaping women with a satisfied expression, then winked at Maddie. "I think our work here is done."

"Thank you," Maddie said, giving her a hug.

"We didn't do anything except get in our workout a few hours early and offer a little eye candy to the paying customers," Helen said. "Call us if you need us back over here, okay? Moral support is part of our deal."

Cal spent most of Monday enduring speculative looks from his fellow teachers and some serious ribbing from a bunch of teenage boys who clearly had no idea just how serious the situation was. All of it was getting on his nerves, along with the deafening silence from Betty Donovan's office.

School was out in fifteen minutes and he had yet to be summoned into her presence for another stern lecture. He wanted to believe she'd thought better of her stance, but a reality check told him she was just mustering her forces.

Twenty minutes later, as he waited on the ball field for his players to show up for practice, school board chairman Hamilton Reynolds walked over to the bench and sat down beside him. He looked as if he'd just been pulled off a golf course and wasn't all that happy about it.

"You've gotten yourself into a real pickle," the seventy-year-old retired banker said, though without the kind of rancor Cal had been expecting from the man who'd put his own reputation on the line to bring Cal to Serenity.

"I've been spending some time with a woman," Cal conceded. "I'm not sure why that's such a big deal." He met the older man's gaze. Ham Reynolds had become a friend, one of the few Cal counted on for total honesty. "Or why it's anyone else's business."

"I like you, Cal. You know that. I think Serenity is lucky to have you," Ham said with sincerity. "So I'm going to explain a few facts of life to you. This isn't New York City or Hollywood, where anything goes. We care about who influences our children in this town."

Cal barely resisted the urge to remind him that Bill Townsend was a damn *pediatrician,* which put him in a position to influence as many impressionable kids as Cal could. But nobody was raising a ruckus about his illicit affair with his very young nurse.

Ham gave him a knowing look. "I know you're just itching to throw Bill Townsend's relationship back into my face, and you'd have a point. Want to know the difference?"

"I'd love to hear it," Cal admitted.

"You're a Major League ballplayer. Bill Townsend gives them *shots,* for Pete's sake. How many kids do you think like or respect him for that?"

"I'm a *former* Major League ballplayer," Cal corrected.

"My point is that your past sets you up on a pedestal for a lot of these kids. Not only that, you're coaching a winning baseball team and that gets you a lot of attention in this town and around the region. You need to think before you engage in some kind of hanky-panky with the mother of one of your players."

Cal met his gaze. "Would it help if I told you that I did think before I started spending time with Maddie? I thought about what an incredible mother she is, what a charming, intelligent woman, and what a raw deal she got from her husband. I thought about how her kids needed someone steady in their lives, not to take the place of their dad, but just to be there for them. I started out by wanting to be her friend, maybe a mentor for the kids, and somewhere along the way, I fell in love with her." He held Ham's gaze. "I will not apologize for that, not to you, not to the school board."

Ham looked visibly shaken by his declaration. "You saying you intend to marry Maddie?"

"We haven't discussed it," Cal said. "Despite what you've read in the paper and heard around town, we're still finding our way with each other. There is no affair, Ham. I give you my word on that. What there is, is a strong friendship I don't intend to lose, and maybe a whole lot more."

"Then you'd ignore me if I advised you that the smart thing would be to stop seeing her?" Ham said.

"Yes."

Ham's gaze remained steady. "She's that important to you? You'd give up your job, if it came to that?"

"Without a single hesitation," Cal told him.

For the first time since he'd sat down beside Cal, Ham's expression softened. "Well, I'll be damned."

"Is it going to come to that?" Cal asked him. "Are you going to fire me?"

"I don't have that power," Ham said. "It's up to the school board."

Cal gave him a wry look. "I may not have been in Serenity all that long, but even I know that they follow wherever you lead."

"You're giving me more credit than I deserve, especially in a situation like this," Ham said. "Some parents are riled up. I'd say the next school board meeting could get ugly.

And there are at least some on the board who don't like to go against public opinion. They don't need to have the law on their side. They'll just act and worry about any legal consequences later."

"Come on, Ham. Lay it on the line. Which way is this going to go?"

"I can't say for sure," the older man insisted. "But you come into that meeting and tell them what you told me, and I'll fight to keep you on staff." He shrugged. "Have to say you're right about one thing."

"What's that?"

Ham grinned. "I don't lose many battles I set out to win."

"Thank you."

"Don't thank me yet," Ham cautioned. "Thanks to all this commotion, a special meeting's been called for tomorrow night at eight. If I were you I'd come in there prepared for a fight. Think of it as game seven of the World Series, ninth inning, with everything on the line."

"Not that there's any pressure," Cal said, laughing.

"You can handle it, son. I've seen you in plenty of tough spots."

Cal thought back to the day Hamilton Reynolds had walked into the rehab center where he'd been hiding out as much as recovering from his injury. The old man hadn't shown him an ounce of pity, just said he'd heard that Cal had his teaching credentials and they could use a man like him back in Serenity to coach their high-school team. He'd thrown Cal a lifeline and it appeared he was doing it again.

"No matter how it goes, I want you to know I appreciate everything you've done for me," Cal told him.

Ham clamped a firm hand on his shoulder and gave it a reassuring squeeze. "You've never let this team or this town down. I intend to see that folks remember that. There's not going to be some ridiculous witch hunt on my watch." He stood up and glanced toward the field, where Ty was throwing one strike after another. "That boy as good as I think he is?"

Cal grinned. "Even better."

"Wouldn't be, if you hadn't been here to guide him. Remember that, you hear me?"

Cal watched the old man go, then turned around to face the team, all of whom were pretending they hadn't noticed the visit from the chairman of the school board.

Ty left the mound and walked over to him. "Was that about you and my mom?"

"Don't worry about it," Cal said.

Ty looked disappointed. "You promised you'd be straight with me."

"You're right," Cal said. "Okay, there's going to be a special meeting of the school board tomorrow night to discuss all the talk that's been stirred up."

Ty's expression turned worried. "Are you in trouble? Are they gonna fire you?"

"I'm sure it won't come to that," Cal said, praying that he wasn't placing too much confidence in Ham Reynolds's powers of persuasion.

"Does Mom know?"

"Not yet," Cal admitted. "And I'm thinking maybe she doesn't need to know. It will only upset her."

Ty gave him a knowing look. "Do you really want to be around when she finds out later?"

Cal chuckled. "You're a very smart kid. I'll talk to her after practice."

He'd just have to find some way to make sure she didn't hold herself responsible for putting his career in jeopardy, not when the truth was that he'd gone after her with his eyes wide open.

* * *

Maddie spent Monday afternoon in her office processing the handful of new memberships that had come in. Helen had been right. The curiosity seekers had started arriving in midafternoon and had almost made up for the women who'd canceled their memberships first thing in the morning.

Even so, Maddie was still in a foul mood when the door to her office flew open.

"I hope you're satisfied!" Peggy Martin declared. "Thanks to you, Cal's going to be fired."

Maddie's heart stopped, then raced. "What are you talking about?"

"There's going to be a special school board meeting tomorrow night to consider whether or not to fire him. They'll probably ride him out of town on a rail just because you had to get even with Bill for dumping you."

There were so many things wrong with that statement Maddie didn't know where to begin.

"I don't suppose you stopped to consider your role in this," she said finally.

Peggy stared at her blankly. "Me? What did I do?"

"You were so desperate to get even with me, you just had to twist every little rumor you'd heard into something ugly, then put it in the paper," Maddie accused. "If anyone's to blame for this mess, it's you."

Peggy stared at her with pure venom. "Don't you dare try to turn this around on me. All I did was report the facts."

"Oh, please, you spun a bunch of gossip into something tawdry."

"There wouldn't have been any gossip if you'd stayed away from him," Peggy snapped.

"And let you have him?"

"At least I'm not ten years older than he is and the mother of one of his players," Peggy said. "I know this was about Bill. It killed you that he left you for a younger woman, so you set out to get even in the most public way possible."

Maddie knew that denying the accusation would be a waste of time. "What time is the meeting tomorrow?"

"You're not planning to be there, are you?" Peggy demanded incredulously. "That would pretty much seal Cal's fate."

"What time is the meeting?" she repeated.

"Eight," Peggy said finally. "But if you care even a little bit about Cal, you'll stay away."

She whirled around and left, nearly running into Cal as she did so. She scowled at him, then kept on going.

Cal heaved a sigh. "Messenger of doom, no doubt."

"Something like that."

"I'm sorry. I wanted to let you know about the meeting before someone else did."

"I wish you had. Maybe I could have thought of a quick comeback when Peggy started accusing me of ruining your life."

He sat on a corner of her desk, his thigh pressed against hers. "You're not ruining my life," he assured her. "You're the best thing in it."

"You still going to feel that way if the board fires you?"

"I'm not worried about it," he said, and a hard look in his eyes suggested he wasn't lying. "Neither should you."

She stared at him with amazement. "How can you be so calm?"

"I'm putting my faith in the system and in Hamilton Reynolds."

Maddie sat back. "You've talked to Ham?"

"At length."

"And he's on your side?"

Cal nodded. "It's going to be okay, Maddie. This is all much ado about nothing. The board has to at least listen to the parents. That's their obligation, but saner minds will prevail. I believe that."

"Ham has a lot of influence in this town, that's true," she conceded. "But it won't hurt to have a few more people there in your corner."

"You going to be one of them?"

She studied him intently. "Unless you think me being there will make things worse."

"I told you, I'm not worried," he said. "And I want you there. I have a couple of things I intend to say that you need to hear."

"Such as?"

He shook his head. "I've already run it by Ham. He thinks I'll be persuasive."

"You don't care about my opinion?" she asked, miffed.

"Of course I do, but this is one time I want to call the shots. Just let me do this my way, Maddie."

"But I've lived in Serenity my whole life," she protested. "I know how these people think."

"Remember what I told you about thinking too much? Sometimes it's better to go with your gut. I want the people of this town to listen with their hearts, not their minds." He smiled. "And that's all I intend to say on the subject for now."

"But—"

He leaned down. "Hush, Maddie."

Apparently not content to see if she'd keep silent on her own, he covered her mouth with his. He had a very persuasive mouth. In no time at all she couldn't have formed a coherent thought if she'd wanted to.

He pulled her up and into the V between his legs, surrounding her with heat and filling her with longing. She rested her hands on the hard muscles of his thighs and let him have his way with her mouth, his tongue tangling with hers. Every part of her turned into molten liquid, so hot and needy that she would have dragged him down to the floor in another instant, but he ended the kiss on a ragged sigh.

"This is the kind of thing that got us into this fix in the first place," he murmured, his hands still cupping her face, his eyes still filled with heat.

Dazed, Maddie reached for him. "Don't care," she whispered as she managed to steal another kiss.

She felt his lips curve into a smile against hers.

"Told you thinking was highly overrated," he said.

Maddie was the one who pulled back slightly this time. "Okay, buster, now that you've proved your point, what are you going to do about it?"

Cal laughed. "Is that a challenge?"

She gazed into his eyes and, to her astonishment, saw love shining back at her. It made her knees weak, but also steadied her resolve. "Yes," she said without hesitation. "Yes, it is."

"Then I think we've got places to go and things to do," he said, latching on to her hand.

"Go where?"

"My place," he said at once.

"What's wrong with here?" she demanded impatiently.

"Nothing if you don't care about the photographers I saw lurking in the bushes when I came in."

Snapped back to reality, Maddie groaned. "Why didn't you tell me?"

"And spoil all this fun? Besides, there are no windows

in this room and the doors are locked. I made sure of that. Come on, darlin', let's get out of here."

"We can't leave together," she told him. "And we can't go to your place. They'll just follow us. I'm sure at least one of them reports to Peggy, and she's determined to turn this into the scandal of the year."

Cal sighed. "Rain check, then?"

"You've got it," Maddie said.

It seemed that somewhere along the way, he'd also gotten her heart.

CHAPTER TWENTY

The high-school auditorium was packed. Built years ago, the stage had oak floors polished to a shine and heavy velvet curtains with gold fringe. Long tables sat center stage with nameplates in front of the places for each of the five school board members, most of whom were standing to the side in a small cluster, whispering among themselves. They waved off anyone else who approached, perhaps in an attempt to demonstrate that they were going into this meeting with their objectivity intact.

It was evident to Maddie, though, that everyone else in town had already taken sides. The tension in the room was palpable with neighbor pitted against neighbor. While most of the hastily made, hand-lettered signs in the room supported Cal with a Save Our Coach slogan, there were more than a dozen individuals vocally demanding he be fired. They could be heard lobbying Cal's supporters.

Though the air-conditioning was on, it labored to fight the heat in the packed room. Maddie could feel a trickle of perspiration running down her back as she faced down Cal's detractors with her chin held high.

"I still think you should let me represent you," Helen told Cal.

"I don't need representation," he said. "I'm going to tell them how I feel about Maddie. If they want to fire me for that, so be it."

"They don't even have a right to ask questions about your personal life," Helen said. "At least not the kind of questions some of them are going to ask. You haven't broken any laws. You haven't even broken that ridiculous morals clause in your contract, which by the way, I will negotiate out of there before you ever sign another contract with this school district."

"They're just trying to protect the kids," he said.

"From what?" Dana Sue demanded. "Seeing two people together who genuinely care about each other?" Her gaze narrowed. "You do care about Maddie, right?"

Cal exchanged a glance with Maddie that reminded her of the heat between them the night before.

"I care," he said quietly.

Helen continued to regard him with dismay. "I still think it's risky for you to stand up there without an attorney. If they're going to attack with lies and innuendos, you'll need me to object strenuously for the record. That's the best way to keep them in line."

"I appreciate your concern," he told her. "I really do. If you think I'm about to leap off a bridge and land in a legal quagmire, feel free to jump in and stop me. Anything short of that, leave this in my hands."

Helen nodded, but she didn't look happy.

The grim-looking board members took their places. The school board secretary, who doubled as Betty's secretary at the high school, sat down to record the meeting. Hamilton Reynolds called the special meeting to order. "Now, then," he began, "I guess we all know why we're here tonight. I wish even half you folks would show up when the education of your children is on the agenda."

Maddie heard Cal's sigh and saw him relax. She turned to him. "You're right. He's definitely on your side. He's only that cranky when he's out of patience with folks who are wasting his time."

Cal nodded. "I know. He told me he was, but a part of me wondered if the pressure might not change that by tonight."

"If there's one thing I know about Ham, it's that he's a man of his word," Maddie said, feeling marginally better herself.

"I suppose the first thing we need to do is hear from Betty Donovan, since it's one of her teachers we're discussing," Ham said. "Betty, you want to summarize the issues as you see them?"

Betty walked stiffly to the microphone down front. Even though Cal and Maddie were right in the front row, she was careful not to glance their way.

"This is a disciplinary action against Cal Maddox," she began. "One of the most important things that any teacher in this system does is to set an example for our students." She waved a copy of Saturday's paper. "Right here is the proof that Coach Maddox is not setting the right kind of example. He's been a good teacher and an outstanding coach, but that's not enough, at least here in Serenity where we live by a high moral code. I recommend that he be fired, with cause, for carrying on with the mother of one of our students."

She was about to walk away when Ham held up his hand.

"Hold on a minute, Betty. That paper you're waving around down there is the *Serenity Times,* am I right?"

"Well, of course it is."

"You didn't write that article yourself, did you?"

She stared at him. "Don't be ridiculous. I'm not moonlighting as a reporter."

"Of course you're not," Ham agreed. "Which brings me to my point. Did you see any of these alleged misdeeds yourself?"

"No, but they're right here in black and white."

"So are the comics, but that doesn't make 'em fact," Ham said, drawing chuckles, though mostly from Cal's supporters.

"Well, I saw enough with my own two eyes," Betty huffed. "I saw the two of them all cozy over at Rosalina's on two different occasions."

"Following baseball games, am I right?" Ham asked.

"Yes."

"And the entire team and a few other parents were there?"

"Well, yes."

"Did they do anything inappropriate? Any kissing, for instance? Holding hands, for that matter?"

"No," she admitted with a pained expression.

"Thank you, Betty. That will be all."

"But—"

"That's enough," Ham said. "Anybody else want to speak? And before you say yes and walk up to that microphone, I want you to consider whether you've ever actually witnessed any of this so-called inappropriate behavior everyone's all worked up over. If all you have is hearsay, then I request that you keep your opinion to yourselves. We don't condemn people in this town based on gossip, at least not as long as I have anything to say about it."

There was a lot of grumbling among those clustered on the right side of the auditorium, but no one stood up, not even Peggy Martin, who was so red-faced over Ham's implied criticism of her reporting she looked as if her head might explode.

"Okay, then," Ham said, looking satisfied with himself. "I'd vote on this right now, but we need to balance things out before we do. Anyone here feel inclined to speak on Coach Maddox's behalf?"

Cal was about to stand up, when Ty leaped from his seat and headed for the microphone.

"I just have one thing to say," he said. "That newspaper story is a bunch of lies. I know my mom and I know Coach, probably better than almost anybody in this room does. They're great influences on me and my brother and sister and on every other kid they know. Anybody who says otherwise doesn't know what they're talking about."

The entire baseball team rose to their feet and erupted into cheers as Ty returned to his seat.

Maddie glanced at Cal and saw that his eyes were damp with tears. She'd never felt prouder of her son. Whatever his own misgivings about Maddie's relationship with Cal, he'd come through for them when it counted.

"He's something, isn't he?" she said, wiping at a few tears of her own.

"He should be," Cal said. "You raised him. Now let me get up there and say my piece."

The cheers that had started with the team escalated when Cal stood up. A lot of folks in town cared as much about his leadership on the ball field as they did about whatever example he set. And his team was going to play for the state championship on Friday night. A lot of parents wanted him to know they appreciated the hard work that had made that happen. In fact, he had to turn around and silence them before he could speak. Maddie saw the look of wonder in his eyes as he faced the solid show of support.

"Frankly, I wasn't expecting this," he told the board. "Mrs. Donovan is right about one thing. Teachers do have to set an example for the children in their care. I've tried to do that, both in what I teach them and in how I live. I came to Serenity because Hamilton Reynolds convinced me I could find a home here, and I have. In fact, I've found more than that. I've found a woman who is everything I've always wanted."

He glanced at Maddie, his heart in his eyes, then turned back to the board. "So, at least some of what you've heard and seen in the paper is true. I have spent time with Maddie Townsend and hope to spend even more with her in the future. A lot of you have known her all her life. You know it's true when I say that she's someone who's worthy of respect and deserving of love." He faced her again and looked deep into her eyes as if there weren't another soul in the room, then said quietly, "She has both of those things from me."

When he finally turned back to the board, he said simply, "If you want to fire me because of that, so be it, but I'd say Maddie's integrity and my feelings for her set an example a lot of folks in this town want for their kids."

He returned to his seat, picked up Maddie's hand and kissed her knuckles, then cast a defiant look up at the board members. "There you go," he said. "I kissed her right here in plain sight."

Ham shook his head, but he was clearly fighting a smile. "Anybody on the board have anything to say?"

"I've heard enough," Roger Tate grumbled. "Let's just vote and put an end to this. I'm about to miss my favorite TV show."

"Can't vote," Ham said. "There's no motion on the table. Any of you want to make one?"

"What happens if we don't?" George Neville inquired. "Does the whole thing just die, the way it should?"

"It would," Ham said. "But I think we owe the coach more than that for putting him and Maddie through this. I think we owe him a vote of confidence."

"So moved," George said at once.

"Second," Roger said.

The five members of the board voted unanimously in support of Cal and the job he was doing. Ham glanced over at Betty Donovan after the vote. "You have any problem with that?"

Though her cheeks flamed, she gave him a curt shake of her head. "None."

"Good, then this matter is settled," Ham declared. "Coach, we expect you to win that state championship for us, you hear?"

Cal met his gaze. "We certainly intend to do our best."

Ham winked at him. "Can't ask anyone to do more than that."

Maddie studied the exchange. Once she and Cal had made their way through the throng of well-wishers and emerged on the sidewalk outside the school, she looked into his eyes. "Just how well do you know Ham Reynolds?"

"He recruited me for the job," Cal said. "I thought everyone in town knew that."

"But there's more to it, isn't there?"

Cal met her gaze. "He saved me," he said simply. "I was at the lowest point in my life and he walked into my rehab room and yanked me back from despair. I owe him for that and for tonight."

"Not for tonight," she told him. "You earned that vote in there. Don't you ever think otherwise."

Bill had chosen a seat in a back corner of the auditorium and watched Maddie stand solidly behind Cal Maddox during a hearing that would have humiliated a lot of women. A lot of men, for that matter. He wasn't sure he could have withstood it if anyone had called him on the carpet for his behavior with Noreen, and he had a whole lot more to apologize for than Maddie or Cal did.

Not for the first time he wondered how he'd let his life spin so wildly out of control. Blaming it on a midlife crisis was too easy, too simplistic. He'd been restless, that was true enough. And he'd been open to the adoration of a beautiful young woman. It had been a balm to his ego after life at home had become so hectic that he and Maddie rarely found time for each other.

But what part of him had been so jaded and selfish that he hadn't recognized and valued the woman who'd borne his children and helped him attain professional success? How could he possibly have thought that hot sex was more important than everything he and Maddie had achieved together?

"They got off easy," Noreen commented beside him, dragging his attention back to here and now.

"I don't think we're in any position to cast stones," Bill told her.

She looked rattled for a moment, then sighed. "No. You're right about that. Can I ask you something?"

"Of course."

"Do you regret where we are now? I mean, together and on the verge of getting married, with a baby already on the way?"

Bill didn't want to have this conversation, not now and certainly not here, but she deserved some kind of answer. He chose his words carefully, hoping to avoid an argument. "It's way too late for regrets, don't you think?"

Noreen's expression turned sad. "In other words, you do have regrets. You're just burying them under obligation."

"I didn't say that," Bill said irritably.

"You didn't have to," she said, squeezing past him to leave. "I'll wait for you in the car."

"Noreen," he protested, but she was already gone, moving with surprising speed for a woman who was eight months pregnant.

He stared after her, overwhelmed by more regrets. It wasn't just his own life he'd messed up, he realized with sudden insight, or his family's. Noreen was paying a price as well. Friends had deserted her when they'd learned of the affair. Even in the office, his other staff members treated her coolly. If she clung to him a little more tightly than he might have liked, it was understandable.

What the hell was he supposed to do? he wondered. Was there any way to make any of this right?

He thought of Cal's very public declaration of his feelings for Maddie, and of Ty's defense of both of them. Even if there was some way to make things right for Noreen without marrying her, it was probably too late to change anything with Maddie. She'd obviously moved on, and who could blame her?

In some deep dark corner of his soul, he wondered if he'd come here tonight hoping for a different outcome, one that would have sent Cal away from Serenity. Probably so. But that was only vindictive, wishful thinking. Reality was that Cal was here and was becoming a part of the family Bill had walked away from. He wondered if he'd ever find a way to make peace with that.

"Hey, Mom, do you think we could stop by Wharton's for a milk shake?" Ty asked, walking beside her and Cal on their way home from the meeting, Dana Sue and Helen bringing up the rear.

"I vote yes," Dana Sue said.

"Count me in," Helen said.

Cal grinned at Maddie. "If I get a vote, it's yes, too."

Maddie regarded them all with unease. "Don't you think that might be a little too in-your-face for tonight? Some people are still unhappy about Cal and me."

"Absolutely not," Helen said emphatically. "I think a celebration is called for, and Wharton's is where we've always held celebrations."

Maddie knew when she'd been overruled. "Okay, then. Wharton's it is. I think I'll call Mom and tell her to bring Katie and Kyle and meet us there. They should be part of this, too."

She drew her cell phone out of her purse and called her mother.

"The meeting's over?" Paula asked.

"A few minutes ago," Maddie confirmed.

"And?"

"The board gave Cal a vote of confidence," Maddie reported. "We're all heading to Wharton's to celebrate. Can you bring Katie and Kyle and join us?"

"Katie's already asleep," her mother said. "But Kyle could walk over and meet you there. It's only a few blocks and it's still light out."

"Perfect. Thanks, Mom."

"Anytime. I'll be glad to see him out of here. He's beaten me at five straight games of hearts. He tells those corny jokes of his and gets me to laughing so hard I can't concentrate."

Maddie stopped in midstride. "Kyle's been telling you jokes?" she asked.

"Sure. Why are you so surprised?"

"Because for the longest time after Bill left, he stopped telling them. Maybe he's finally getting back to normal."

"Or just figuring out what the new normal is," her mother suggested. "I'll tell him about Cal. He's been worried. He'll meet you at Wharton's. I'll call you back on your cell when he leaves the house so you can be watching for him."

When she'd tucked the phone back in her pocket, Cal regarded her with curiosity. "Everything okay?"

"Better than okay. Kyle's been telling Mom some of his jokes. It's the first time he's done that since Bill left. For the longest time, he'd pretty much stopped laughing."

Ty overheard her and groaned. "You really think that's a good thing? Kyle's jokes are dumb."

"They are not," Maddie insisted. "I predict we'll see him on *Saturday Night Live* someday." She tousled Ty's hair, even though he tried to duck out of reach. "It'll be on right after you play in game one of the World Series."

Ty grinned at that. "When you dream, Mom, you dream big."

Maddie glanced up at Cal and thought about a few of the dreams she'd been having about him lately. "Yeah, I do," she said.

Cal winked at her. "Nothing wrong with that. People with big dreams work harder to make them come true."

When they walked into Wharton's, Grace hurried over to greet them. "I heard what happened at the meeting tonight, Cal. I couldn't be happier for you."

Maddie was tempted to point out her role in spreading at least some of the gossip that had necessitated the meeting in the first place, but what would be the point? Grace loved to talk. It was as much a part of who she was and why Wharton's had endured all these years as the friendly service her husband gave in the pharmacy.

Grace helped them pull two big tables together and saw them settled. "Chocolate milk shakes all around, I imagine."

"Yes, ma'am," Cal said. "Anybody want anything else? This is on me."

Ty grinned at him. "In that case, I could use a burger. Making a speech is hard work."

"Come to think of it, I'd like a burger, too," Cal said. "I was too nervous to eat before the meeting."

Ty regarded him with surprise. "You were nervous, too?"

"Sure. Give me a ball and bat and I know what to do. Standing up and talking to folks, especially when it really matters like tonight, well, I'd rather choke down a bucketful of worms."

"Hey, maybe we should go on one of those TV reality shows," Ty suggested. "You know, the kind where they make you eat gross stuff."

"If you do, you're on your own," Maddie declared with a shudder just as her phone rang. It was her mom telling her Kyle had left the house.

"Amen to that," Dana Sue added. "I wonder what's keeping Annie. I called her, and she said she'd walk over and meet us here, too."

"Don't bother ordering a milk shake for her," Ty said, immediately drawing a worried look from Dana Sue.

"Why do you say that?" she demanded.

"Because she never drinks them," Ty responded innocently. "She just stirs the straw all around until the shake melts, then finds someplace to dump it out."

Dana Sue exchanged a worried look with Helen and Maddie.

"I didn't know that," she said.

Ty suddenly looked guilty. "Maybe I shouldn't have said anything. I just figured she didn't really like 'em but ordered one just to fit in. It's no big deal."

"It's okay, Ty," Maddie soothed. "Dana Sue, try not to

make too much out of it. I'm sure Ty's right, that she orders them because everyone else does, then changes her mind about wanting it after taking a sip or two."

"Do you honestly think my penny-pinching daughter who saves all her money for clothes would waste money that way?" Dana Sue said heatedly. "I'm telling you, she's—" She broke off when Annie came through the door, Kyle right on her heels. They'd apparently met along the way.

Maddie studied the girl intently and saw why Dana Sue was so worried. Annie was about the same height as her mother, five-five or so, and couldn't weigh more than a hundred pounds if that. Her clothes hid the fact that she was too thin, but there was no disguising that her face was beginning to look gaunt.

Still, when she smiled, her face lit up and it was almost possible to think that Dana Sue was imagining that Annie had an eating disorder.

"Hey, Coach, I heard the good news," Annie said. "Congratulations! The whole thing was bogus in the first place."

"Thanks," Cal said.

Annie gave Maddie a kiss on the cheek. "Bet you're relieved, too."

"I am," Maddie confirmed.

"Was Uncle Bill at the meeting?" she asked, still using the honorary title she'd given him, just as she called Maddie and Helen her honorary aunts.

"I didn't see him," Maddie said. "Why?"

Annie grinned wickedly. "I just figured he was probably eating his heart out, knowing you're with somebody as cool as the coach now."

"Annie!" Dana Sue protested, then chuckled herself. "He *was* there. I saw him and Noreen in the back."

Ty frowned. "Dad was there with Noreen?"

Dana Sue nodded. "Don't make a big deal out of it, Ty. I'm sure your dad was there to lend his support to Cal. And I'm also sure he was very proud of the way you spoke up."

Annie gave Ty a look that Maddie recognized as hero worship. She was barely a year younger than Ty, and there was no mistaking her feelings for him—and the fact that he was oblivious to them. Maddie hoped he wouldn't inadvertently hurt Annie's tender heart one of these days.

"You got up in front of everybody and made a speech?" Annie asked him with awe.

"It was no big deal," Ty said.

"It was a big deal to me," Cal corrected. "And I think it impressed the board, too."

Grace returned then with their milk shakes and the burgers for Cal and Ty, then looked at Kyle. "Burger and shake for you, I imagine."

"You bet," Kyle said eagerly.

Then Grace turned to Annie. "What about you, young lady? You want a milk shake, too?"

Maddie watched Dana Sue observe her daughter with bated breath as she waited for Annie's answer.

"No, it's late," Annie said eventually. "I'll just have some water with lemon."

"Come on, Annie," Dana Sue encouraged. "It's a celebration. Have something more than that."

Annie scowled at her mother. "I don't want anything else," she said forcefully. "Maybe you can eat this late but I can't."

"That's okay," Helen said, stepping in before the battle of wills could escalate. "Annie's right. I'll probably be up half the night if I finish this entire milk shake." She deliberately pushed it away, though she'd taken only a few sips.

Dana Sue sighed, but she let the subject drop.

Maddie's gaze kept drifting toward Annie as they sat there. She barely touched her water, but her conversation was animated. In most ways, she seemed like a perfectly healthy teenager, but Maddie wasn't convinced that Dana Sue wasn't right to worry about her. Something wasn't entirely right.

Cal leaned closer. "Stop worrying," he whispered in her ear.

She regarded him with surprise. "What makes you think I'm worrying?"

"I can see the way you're watching Annie and I can practically hear those wheels in your head grinding away," he told her. "Dana Sue's on top of this."

"You think so?"

He nodded. "And she has all of you for backup if she needs it."

"Then you think there's a problem, too?" she said, meeting his gaze.

Cal didn't deny it. Instead, he merely said, "It's nothing that's going to be solved tonight, okay?"

Maddie nodded. But first chance she had, she was going to do some research on eating disorders and pass it along to Dana Sue. Maybe they were all wrong, but she would hate herself if they did nothing and something bad happened to that beautiful child.

CHAPTER TWENTY-ONE

It was midafternoon the next day before Maddie had a chance to take a break from work. They'd been overwhelmed with new members in the morning. Apparently word of Cal's exoneration had spread, and now everyone, including a couple of those who'd walked out on Monday, wanted to join The Corner Spa. Helen had cynically suggested that they were hoping to achieve the same results Maddie had, since she'd so obviously toned up lately and managed to snag herself a hunk like Cal.

"I don't think Cal is after me for my amazing body," Maddie had replied. "If he is, he's in for a major disappointment. Some things simply can't be fixed at this late date."

"I watched him last night," Helen assured her. "I doubt there's anything about you that could disappoint that man. He's yours for the taking. If a man ever said about me what Cal said to the school board about you, I'd have the ink dry on our marriage license before the end of the day."

Maddie had merely rolled her eyes. "You are so far ahead of yourself on that. I'm not even sure you can call what Cal and I do dating, much less courting. We've never been to a movie or a play or even out to dinner, unless you count pizza after the games. Marriage seems pretty far down the road. Besides, my divorce isn't even final yet."

"But with a chassis like Cal's, I imagine you could get to the end of that road in record time," Helen said with a wicked grin, then added, "And the divorce will be final in a couple of days."

Maddie sucked in a deep breath. "What do you mean the divorce will be final in a couple of days?" she asked, taken aback by how quickly a twenty-year marriage could be ended. "Based on what you said the last time I asked, I thought it wouldn't be for a few more weeks, at least."

"That was the timeline," Helen confirmed. "But Bill's lawyer's been hurrying it along, and I saw no reason to put up any roadblocks," Helen said. "Gotta run. I'm due in court."

Throughout the busy day, Maddie hadn't allowed herself to ponder Helen's comments about Cal or the news about her divorce. Thankfully she'd had too much to do. And in the few minutes of downtime she had managed to find, she'd done some research on eating disorders. Reading through it in the late afternoon, she was more alarmed than ever about the possibility that Dana Sue's daughter was anorexic or bulimic.

"Jeanette, can you keep an eye on things around here for a while?" she asked. "I need to take some papers over to Dana Sue."

"Not a problem," Jeanette said, as eager as always to do whatever was asked of her. "I have some clients coming in for treatments, but I can use the room down here and listen for the phone."

"Thanks," Maddie said, grateful for Jeanette's calm, willing demeanor that acted as a balm to Maddie during the sometimes frantic days she had juggling the spa's increasing demands. "If anyone calls for me, I should be back in an hour at the most."

"Take your time."

Maddie walked the few blocks to Sullivan's New Southern Cuisine at a brisk pace. It really was amazing just how fast and how far she could go these days without needing to stop and catch her breath. The workouts she'd been snatching at the gym were paying off. Her body might not be as taut and firm as a twenty-year-old's, but she was in darn good shape for forty. Maybe if she took Elliott Cruz up on his repeated offer to give her free personal-training sessions, she could even fix up those few remaining problem areas.

At Sullivan's, she found Dana Sue in her cramped office, a large bowl of bread pudding in front of her.

"Uh-oh, you caught me," Dana Sue said, looking guilty. "I needed comfort food."

"You need to remember that carbs are bad for you," Maddie corrected, regarding her with concern. "Have you tested your blood sugar today?"

"No," Dana Sue admitted.

"What is wrong with you?" Maddie snapped impatiently. "Are you as determined as your daughter to kill yourself?"

Dana Sue immediately dropped the spoon and burst into tears.

"Oh, God, I am so sorry," Maddie whispered, stepping over a box of aprons and kneeling down to wrap Dana Sue in her arms. "I don't know what I was thinking. That was cruel."

"No, you're right," Dana Sue said between sobs. "I'm setting a terrible example for Annie." She grabbed a wad of tissues from the box on her desk and mopped her eyes. "I was praying that I'd gotten it all wrong about Annie, but last night I could see in your eyes and in Helen's that I wasn't wrong. You're both as worried as I am."

"Yes, but it's not too late to fix this, sweetie. I did some research. That's why I came over, to bring it to you." She gestured toward the folder she'd dropped on the floor. "We can talk about it if you want to."

Dana Sue shook her head. "And before you say it, I'm not in denial. It's just that I've spent hours and hours on the computer myself. I've probably read whatever you have in there. I've even tried talking to Annie, but she blows me off. I'm at my wit's end." She pointed to the half-eaten bowl of bread pudding. "Thus the need for comfort food. If we'd had macaroni and cheese on the menu today, I'd have had that with a side of mashed potatoes."

Maddie snatched up the half-empty bowl. "I'll be right back."

"Where are you going?"

"To dump this out and bring you back something that might actually do you some good. Do you have the makings for a grilled-cheese sandwich in that fancy restaurant kitchen of yours?"

Dana Sue regarded her with horror. "You are not cooking in my kitchen."

"I can make a grilled-cheese sandwich, for goodness' sakes," Maddie protested. "Or if you don't trust me with that, how about a chicken Caesar salad?"

Dana Sue stood up and brushed past her. "Not in *my* kitchen," she repeated. "I'll make the sandwich. You want one, too?"

"Sure," Maddie said, following her across the deserted restaurant.

She had to admit as she watched Dana Sue work that there was a huge difference in the end product. She would have slapped a slice of cheese between two slices of bread and grilled it in a pan. Dana Sue's sandwich was in a whole different category. She used freshly baked sourdough bread, added some grilled peppers and jalapeños, then layered it all with Monterey Jack cheese and tucked it into the oven.

She worked with a kind of nervous efficiency that told Maddie she was still upset. And when the sandwiches were in the oven, she picked up a sponge and began cleaning everything in sight.

"Dana Sue, the kitchen is spotless."

"You never know when the health department might show up," Dana Sue countered. "They're never going to find a crumb much less a single trace of grease in here, not even when we're at peak volume in the dining room."

"I doubt they could find anything they'd disapprove of with a magnifying glass," Maddie commented. "Now sit down and talk to me. There's no point trying to avoid this."

Dana Sue sat with reluctance, then cast a look filled with misery at Maddie. "What am I going to do about Annie?"

"Let's worry about you for a minute first," Maddie said. "Do your blood test."

"I will, after I eat."

"Now, Dana Sue."

"Oh, for pity's sake," Dana Sue grumbled. "The kit's in my office. I'll be right back."

When she came back a few minutes later, her face was pale. "It was high," she admitted. "Who knows what it would have been if you hadn't stopped me from binging on that bread pudding."

"I know you hate this, but you have to think about what you're eating," Maddie told her. "Not just for your sake, but for Annie's. The problems may be very different, but they both involve food. Have you told her about the diabetes?"

"I don't have full-blown diabetes, not yet anyway," Dana Sue said. "I'm borderline. I can still control it with diet and exercise."

"Then all the more reason to get this under control before you do need insulin," Maddie replied calmly. "Have you told Annie?" she repeated.

"No," she admitted.

"Maybe you should. Maybe you could work together to tackle the issues both of you are facing."

"Annie won't even admit she has a problem," Dana Sue reminded her. "Until she does, I don't know how to help her."

"Yes, you do," Maddie corrected. "We've talked about this before. If she won't go to Bill because she's mad at him or because she thinks she's too old for a pediatrician, take her to Doc Marshall. Let him give her some cold hard facts about the damage anorexia or bulimia can do to her body."

"You're right," Dana Sue said. "That's what I need to do. It's just that she gets so upset every time I say anything, it makes me wonder if I'm all wrong. What if I take her and there's nothing wrong? What if she's just going through some sort of growth spurt and her weight will catch up one of these days?"

"Then you'll find that out. The more important question is, what if you're right and she's in serious trouble?"

Dana Sue glanced toward the clock on the wall. It was after five. "I'll call Doc in the morning."

"Call him at home now," Maddie insisted. "I have his number." She pulled her address book from her purse and gave Dana Sue the number, then waited as she dialed.

"No answer," Dana Sue said, then hung up.

Maddie frowned at her. "Why didn't you leave a message?"

Dana Sue flushed guiltily. "I'll call him later. I promise."

"You have to, sweetie."

"I know." Dana Sue retrieved their sandwiches from the oven and looked at hers with distaste. "I don't think I can eat this now."

Maddie picked it up and handed it to her. "Yes, you can. In a few minutes this kitchen is going to be chaotic. You don't want to pass out midway through the dinner rush, do you, especially now that you've gotten rid of your sous chef? If you can't keep up with the orders, it'll definitely be bad for business."

Dana Sue gave her a wobbly smile. "You really are bossy, you know that?"

"Just part of my charm," Maddie told her. "Now, I need to get back to the club. I left Jeanette holding down the fort by herself."

"She's become a real asset, hasn't she?" Dana Sue said. "It feels almost as if she could be an honorary Sweet Magnolia, she fits in so well with us."

"I don't know what I'd do without her," Maddie admitted. "She's taken on a lot more responsibility than she signed on for, especially now that she's not driving back and forth to Charleston. I still feel awful that her relationship fell apart over this job."

"She doesn't seem that broken up about it," Dana Sue said. "In fact, I've seen her in here having dinner with Elliott. I think there's something going on there."

Maddie regarded her with surprise. "Really? You think so? I haven't noticed anything between them at the spa. In fact, they barely speak. I thought maybe they didn't like each other much."

Dana Sue grinned. "Your relationship radar is not as fine-tuned as mine, and besides, maybe they're being discreet at work. How would it look to the members if the hunkiest man at the spa is obviously smitten with someone else? It would destroy the fantasies that get them through the crunches and weight machines."

"Obviously I need to get my radar tuned up," Maddie said. "I'll be more observant when I get back there." She glanced at her watch. "And I'd better hurry, too."

"I appreciate your coming over here," Dana Sue said. "I needed to hear all that stuff." She studied Maddie intently. "Now, would you mind if I gave you some advice?"

"Can I stop you?"

"Not likely," Dana Sue replied. "Don't let what a few narrow-minded people in this town have said keep you from throwing caution to the wind with Cal. He's a good guy, Maddie. A really good guy."

"I don't need you to tell me that."

"No, but you may need your friends to tell you that you'd be a fool to let him get away."

"What makes you think I'd do that?"

"I saw Bill last night, remember? He didn't look happy."

There was something in Dana Sue's tone that rattled her. "Meaning what?" Maddie asked.

"It wouldn't surprise me if he decides one of these days that he wants you back."

Maddie stared at her incredulously. "Don't be ridiculous. He's about to marry his pregnant girlfriend. They've been together for almost a year, so it must be the real thing, especially if he was willing to tear his family apart over her."

Dana Sue didn't look impressed by her argument. "Your marriage didn't break up until seven or eight months ago when he told you Noreen was pregnant. Before that, he thought he could have his family and his girlfriend, too. Have you heard anything about them setting a date?"

"Not a date," Maddie said. "I'm sure he's waiting till he knows exactly when the divorce will be final, but he did ask Kyle and Ty to be his best men."

"Don't hold your breath," Dana Sue murmured, her skepticism plain.

"Come on," Maddie protested. "Do you really think he's not going to go through with it? How would it look if he walked away from Noreen now? In Bill's world, men can make all kinds of mistakes as long as they do the right thing in the end."

"Maybe so," Dana Sue agreed. "But like I said, he didn't look happy."

"There are bound to be some rough patches," Maddie said. "That doesn't mean he's about to bolt on Noreen. And it certainly doesn't mean he wants to come back to me."

"I'm just saying, if he does, don't be in a big hurry to dump a man like Cal to go running back to Bill. There's no comparison between those two."

Maddie honestly didn't believe the issue would ever come up. Even so, on her way back to the spa, she couldn't help wondering how she would feel if it did. A few months ago she might have seized the opportunity to save her marriage, to rekindle things with the father of her children, but now?

And if she were being totally honest, she knew her ambivalence wasn't all about Cal, either. She'd changed, mostly for the better. She doubted Bill would be comfortable with any of those changes. In fact, given some of his comments about the spa and her general change in attitude, she was sure he disapproved of the new, more self-assertive Maddie.

But what if he *could* handle the newly self-confident businesswoman she'd become? a nagging voice persisted. Maddie sighed. It simply wasn't something she'd allow herself to consider.

* * *

Even when he wasn't going to one of Ty's games, Noreen beat Bill home most evenings by a couple of hours. He expected to walk in and find dinner on the table, maybe even some music and candlelight. She'd always tried to create a romantic ambience for their meals.

But instead of walking in to the aroma of food cooking or a table set for two, he found Noreen sitting on the sofa, her face puffy from crying and a stack of luggage sitting beside the door.

"What's all this?" he asked, crossing the room to sit beside her. When he reached for her hand, she pulled away. "Why the tears? Did something happen?"

"Something's been happening for some time now," she said, sniffing.

An odd knot formed in his gut. "Tell me."

"You've fallen out of love with me," she said sadly.

He was about to protest, but she waved him off. "Don't even try to deny it, Bill. I knew it was a long shot, you and me, but I thought we had a chance, especially when I found out about the baby. Instead, the baby only complicates things."

He felt completely at a loss. "So…what? You're kicking me out?"

She shook her head. "I'm leaving. I'm moving back home to Tennessee. My folks will help with the baby. I'll be able to find another job without a problem. Nurses are in big demand everywhere."

Bill couldn't seem to catch his breath. He wasn't sure whether the tightness in his chest was panic or overwhelming relief. "But what about me? That baby will be my son or daughter. I don't want him or her to grow up not knowing me."

"Do you really want another child?" she asked wearily. "Tell the truth. From the beginning you've thought of this baby as a burden. I think you blame it and me for ruining your life."

"No, I don't," he said emphatically, then sighed. "At least not entirely. Mostly, I've blamed myself. I'm the one who was married and had three kids at home. I should have used better judgment from the beginning, instead of taking advantage of you just because my ego needed a boost."

"But it was great for a while, wasn't it?" she asked wistfully.

"It was," he said without hesitation. "I fell in love with you. You're an amazing, vibrant woman. And you were exactly what I needed in my life when you came to work for me."

Her smile wobbled. "I wish that were true. I think you wanted to believe you were in love with me, especially after we found out about the baby, but face it, you love Maddie. With me gone, you'll be free to go back to her."

Bill thought of the way Maddie had looked at Cal after the meeting earlier in the week. "I think that ship has sailed," he told Noreen. "Maddie's with Cal Maddox now."

"They're not married," Noreen reminded him. "It's not too late to fight for her, if that's what you want." She touched his cheek, then let her hand drop away. "If you don't fight for her, I'll be really furious with you. I'd hate to think I'm walking away for no good reason."

"If the only reason you're leaving is to give me another chance with Maddie, then you should stay," he said. "I know things have been tough the last few months since everyone found out about us, and my kids haven't made it any easier, but we can make it work, Noreen. Besides, as far along as you are with this pregnancy, you shouldn't even consider moving. Your doctor is here."

"I visited my old doctor when I went to see my parents a month ago," she told him. "He has my case file and he'll take over now."

Bill stared at her with dismay. "Then you've been thinking about this for a while now," he said, his tone flat.

"I had to," she said. "I could tell our relationship was all wrong, even if you didn't want to admit it. And just so you know, I'm not leaving for you or Maddie. I'm leaving for *me.* You do love me, I believe that, Bill. But you're not *in* love with me, not the way I want the man I marry to be."

He studied her intently and saw a surprisingly mature and steady resolve behind the sorrow in her eyes. "This is really what you want?"

"Not what I want, no, but what I know is best," she told him, then stood up. "I'd better go. It's a long drive and I'd like to get in a couple of hours before it gets dark."

"Why don't you wait till morning? Or fly?"

"The airline would never let me on the plane," she said, her hand on her belly. "Besides, I'll need my car in Tennessee."

"Let me take you."

"No. I don't want to say goodbye all over again, not in front of my parents. I want to say it right here. Besides, I don't think I could stand spending hours in the car with you rehashing all this."

"What can I do, then?"

"Be happy," she said quietly. "I'll be in touch to make arrangements about getting the rest of my things."

"Do you want me there when the baby comes?" he asked.

"That's up to you," she said, her expression wistful. "If you want to come, I won't stop you. If you want to be a part of the baby's life, as difficult as that would be for me,

I won't prevent that, either. How could I possibly deny my child the chance to know a dad as great as you?"

"Great? Hardly. I've failed my kids."

"No," she said fiercely. "All three of them are proof of what a terrific dad you are. And with me gone, you'll be able to work out your differences."

She reached for her luggage, but Bill grabbed it first. "You can't be carrying anything this heavy. I'll take it down."

She backed off. "Fine."

He studied her, surprised that she really was going to leave. He'd half expected her to back down. "There was never any chance I could talk you out of this, was there?"

A tear leaked out and tracked down her cheek. "Yeah, there was, but you blew it the second you didn't deny that you were still in love with Maddie."

Bill felt an ache in his heart, knowing just how badly he'd failed this beautiful young woman. But Noreen was strong, stronger than he'd realized. She'd do okay, and his son or daughter would be lucky to have her. And he'd do his part, as well. He'd pay child support, visit when he could, make sure that the child never paid for the mistakes made by its parents.

He loaded Noreen's bags into the trunk of her car, kissed her one more time, then stood on the curb as she drove away. He felt completely and utterly alone, even more so than when he'd walked away from his family or seen Maddie with Cal Maddox. At least then he'd had Noreen in his life, a woman who'd deserved better than he'd ever had to give.

And now? Now he had to figure out if going back to Maddie was what he really wanted. And if it was, how the hell was he going to convince Maddie to let him?

* * *

For a couple of weeks now, ever since Cal had declared his feelings for her at the school board meeting, Maddie had been struggling to sort out her own feelings. She knew that sooner or later Cal was going to leap right over a courtship period and ask for more. He might be eager to drag her off to bed and she might be just as anxious for him to do it, but she knew now the kind of man he was. Respect and tradition were too important to him. He wasn't going to subject her to more gossip in a town that had already proved just how deep it'd dig for a scandal.

Looking for answers, she dropped by her mother's. She found Paula gardening in the backyard, pulling weeds from around her pink, purple and yellow snapdragons. She seemed oblivious to the dirt streaked on her face and clothes and just as oblivious to the hummingbirds darting in and out among the hollyhocks, which were just starting to break into bloom.

Maddie automatically picked up a pair of pruning shears and went to work on a rosebush. She didn't have her mother's flair for gardening and she'd made only a few distracted snips when Paula snatched the shears from her hand.

"Give me those. You're going to kill it." She gave Maddie a penetrating look. "What's wrong?"

"I think it might be getting serious between me and Cal," she said.

"Well, hallelujah! That's a man with backbone, to say nothing of a great rear end."

Maddie chuckled despite herself. "You *would* notice that."

"Well, of course. I'm not dead. What about you? Have you noticed?"

Maddie blushed. "Oh, yes."

"Then what's the problem?"

"The kids, Bill, everyone."

"The kids have always liked Cal. They're just struggling with the idea of him in a new role in their lives. As for Bill, he doesn't get any say in this. And that mess with the school board is in the past. What's really stopping you? Why are you overthinking something that ought to be totally instinctive? You love the man or you don't."

"Not that simple," Maddie said.

"Yes, it is," her mother said just as firmly.

She thought of the accusation Peggy Martin had made. It had been eating at her for a few weeks now. "What if I've talked myself into having feelings for him just to get even with Bill? What if I'm only trying to prove that I'm able to attract a younger man?"

Her mother gave her a penetrating look. "Is that what you're doing?"

"I don't think so, but how do I know that for sure?"

"You imagine your life without him," her mother said simply. "If Cal's not that important or just passing through, you'll know it."

"That doesn't make sense," Maddie said. "I loved Bill for years. I couldn't imagine my life without him. But now that he's been gone for nearly eight months, I've managed. The world didn't come to an end."

"Maybe he wasn't your soul mate," her mother said quietly.

"The way Dad was yours," Maddie said with sudden understanding. Her mother, for all her carefree, irrepressible ways and outlandish comments about other men, had never had eyes for anyone but Maddie's father.

Paula's smile was tinged with sadness. "Exactly."

"And you think Cal could be my soul mate in a way that

Bill never was? We've only been seeing each other a few months. How can that be?"

"All it takes is a split second if it's the right person. Did I ever tell you about the night I met your father? It was at a dinner party. He was there with someone else. So was I. On the surface, you'd think we wouldn't have a thing in common. I was an unpredictable artist. He was a staid economist. But I looked across the table at him that night and I knew he was the one. He was everything I needed. We complemented each other."

Maddie smiled. "Sometimes I envied that, the way you didn't need anyone else. I felt…extraneous."

"We never meant for you to," her mother said, giving her a fierce hug. "We both adored you. Neither of us could quite get over the fact that we'd created something so incredible. Your father would have been so proud of the way you've handled all the changes you've had to face this year, Maddie, he really would."

Maddie couldn't seem to keep herself from asking, "What would he have thought of Cal?"

"He'd've liked him, but it doesn't really matter what he'd think or what I think. Do you think Cal's the one?"

Like a film playing out in Maddie's mind, the years ahead flickered past, scene after scene with Cal at the heart of them, just as he'd already become the core of so many family occasions. He'd fit in easily and without rancor, despite the uneasy initial welcome he'd received from her kids. He'd never demand more of any of them than what they'd had to give, but he'd give unconditional love back to them, as much as they needed, more than they sometimes deserved.

Since the first time she'd met with him to discuss Ty, she'd felt stronger with him beside her, more herself than she had in years. She wasn't playing a role, as she often had with Bill. She was simply being the best she could be, aware that it was enough for this man. More than enough.

She stood up suddenly. "I have to go."

"You going to say yes, then?"

Maddie grinned. "He hasn't asked a question yet."

Her mother smiled in a way that suggested she knew something Maddie didn't. "He will," she said confidently.

"Have the two of you talked?"

"All the time," her mother said. "But about him asking you to marry him? No, we haven't talked about that."

"Then what makes you so sure he's going to ask?"

"The way he looks at you. It's the way your dad looked at me."

"And Bill never looked at me like that?"

Her mother shook her head. "Not even on your wedding day. He looked as if he'd just acquired a brand-new Mercedes—happy and proud of himself."

"And how does Cal look at me?"

"As if he can't believe his luck and would do anything on earth to make you happy." She grasped Maddie's shoulders and looked her in the eye. "And that, my darling girl, has nothing to do with age, so forget about that once and for all. Age is a non-issue."

Maddie hugged her mother. "I love you."

"I know," Paula said.

She spoke with the same infuriatingly calm smugness that usually drove Maddie nuts. Today, it made her laugh.

CHAPTER TWENTY-TWO

When Cal arrived at Maddie's, he was relieved to find her gone. He needed to sit the three kids down and have a heart-to-heart with them. He'd promised Ty if his relationship with Maddie got serious, he'd let them know and ask their opinion. He and Maddie had been seeing each other more regularly lately and he'd decided tonight was the night. He was more nervous about it than he'd been during his first at-bat in the Major League.

When he had all three of them settled on the living-room sofa, he sat on a chair across from them, then stood up and began to pace, trying to come up with the right words.

"Coach, are you okay? You're acting really weird," Ty observed.

Cal forced himself to sit back down. "I'm here to ask you guys something, but I'm not sure if it's a good idea. I mean, maybe I should talk to your mom about this first. If I tell you and then she's not interested, well, it could be awkward."

Katie left the sofa and crawled into his lap. "Did you want to help us plan our party? I love parties. Mom does, too."

Cal stared at her blankly. "A party?"

"It's Mom's birthday tomorrow," Kyle explained. "We've been trying to figure out what to do to celebrate. Before, we always had a big party, 'cause Mom says birthdays should be really special, but maybe she's not in the mood for it this year. You know, because…"

"Because?" Cal prodded.

Kyle squirmed, clearly uncomfortable with the question. "Dad's gone, for one thing."

"I see," Cal said, wondering just how big a role Bill had played in the family celebrations. Would his absence cast a damper on everything from here on out? Would every holiday or celebration bring back a thousand memories of the way things used to be?

Ty gave him a pointed look. "Or maybe she doesn't want a party because she doesn't want you to know how old she is."

Cal chuckled, despite Ty's somber expression. "I think you can stop worrying about that one. I know how old your mother is. I just didn't know her birthday was this week."

"Really?" Ty asked skeptically.

"Really."

"Isn't she lots older than you?" Kyle said, frowning. "Isn't that one reason everybody's been so weird about you two?"

"Let's not make her sound ancient," Cal advised, ignoring the part about what other people thought. As far as he was concerned, that was no longer an issue, and he was pretty sure Maddie was finally on the same page. He looked from Ty's face to Kyle's. "Come on, guys. It's ten years. That's not so much. It's the same difference there is between Ty and Katie. You two get along okay, don't you?"

Ty gave him a scathing look. "She's my *baby* sister. It's not the same thing at all."

"I am not a baby!" Katie protested.

Cal didn't even try to hide his amusement at the sibling bickering. "And compared to your mom, I'm hardly a baby, either."

"Then you really don't care?" Ty persisted. "Dad left her because he wanted someone lots younger. Are you gonna do the same thing?"

"Never," Cal assured him. "I want to marry her. Does that sound like I care about how old she is?"

Cal hadn't meant to blurt it out like that. He knew he'd blown it when he saw shock register on all three faces.

"I'm sorry, I didn't mean for it to come out like that," he said hurriedly. "I came over here to ask you guys how you would feel about it if I did that, asked her to marry me, I mean. So, what do you think? Would it freak you out?"

The question was greeted by a deafening silence. Cal felt his stomach twist into knots as he considered the very real possibility that he hadn't won them over, after all. He knew Maddie well enough to know that she would never consider marrying anyone if her children disapproved.

"Come on, kids, say something," he pleaded. "I'm dying here."

"You'd move in here and be our dad?" Katie asked, looking perplexed.

"Your stepdad, actually," he said, determined not to blur that line. "You *have* a dad and he will always be a big part of your lives." He turned to Ty, knowing that his reaction was the most critical. "Well? Do you hate the idea? I know you weren't that happy about us dating and we haven't really been on that many dates. But I know what I want and I think your mom wants the same thing."

"You think she wants to marry you?" Ty asked, frowning.

Cal nodded. "Look, I know you're still furious with your

dad for leaving you all to be with Noreen, so it's important to me that you're happy about me and your mom. Could you accept me being with your mom and here with all of you?"

Ty seemed to struggle for words, but at least he hadn't outright rejected the idea. Cal held out hope.

"The whole dating thing was really weird for me when I figured out you and Mom were more than just friends, especially when everyone in town was talking about you guys," Ty said finally, his face scrunched up in a deeper frown. Then he met Cal's gaze. "But it's been okay, you being around more. Having you here all the time, like a real part of the family, might be kinda cool." His expression brightened. "I could get baseball tips anytime I want."

Cal chuckled. "You get that now, without me getting to tell you to take out the garbage."

"You'd ask me to do that?"

"I might."

"And you'd make me keep up my grades?"

"You bet."

Tyler actually smiled.

Kyle leaned forward. "What about me? What would you make me do?"

"That's easy," Cal said, grinning. "I'd make you tell me a new joke every night. Maybe one at breakfast, too." He paused thoughtfully. "And you'd have to mow the lawn and help with the dishes."

Kyle sat back. "Cool."

"I don't want chores," Katie announced.

"'Cause you're a little princess," Kyle teased.

Cal grinned at her. "I'm afraid you'll have to come down out of your tower with me around, Princess Katie. I might insist that you bake me cupcakes."

Katie giggled. "I love cupcakes. I could bake you a million."

Cal looked around at these three kids who'd become so precious to him. They'd slipped into his heart as if they were always meant to be there. "Then we're agreed? It's okay if I ask your mom to marry me?"

Ty appeared thoughtful. "Maybe you should let us ask," he suggested.

"Why?" Cal asked.

"Since Dad left, she pretty much says yes to anything we want."

Cal smothered a laugh. "That's definitely one way to go," he agreed. "But I think I'd better handle this one. I could ask her during her birthday party tomorrow, then you'd all be here." If he was setting himself up for humiliation, so be it. They all had a stake in Maddie's response. Besides, as a last resort, he might need to call on their powers of persuasion.

He turned to them now. "So, how do we make this the best birthday party your mom has ever had?"

"Balloons," Katie suggested, clapping with delight. "And lots and lots of presents. We should go shopping."

Cal looked at Ty and Kyle. "You guys need to do any shopping?"

"I've got my present for Mom," Ty said. "I got a copy of that picture the paper ran of me throwing the final strike in the championship game. I had it framed for her."

"And I made her a book on the computer," Kyle said. "It's all my best jokes. I've got illustrations and everything."

"She'll love that," Cal said, then looked at Katie. "What about you? Did you make something for your mother?"

"I painted her a picture at school, but it's not very good," she said worriedly. "Maybe I should buy something, but I already spent my allowance."

"I imagine your mom will love the picture more than anything you buy," Cal said. "So it sounds as if the presents are under control. Do your grandmother, Dana Sue and Helen usually come to this party?"

Ty nodded. "Dana Sue and Helen do, but we haven't called 'em yet because we weren't sure it was a good idea to have a party this year."

"Okay, then, you call them and tell them it's on for tomorrow night," Cal said. "Call your grandmother, too. She should be here for this one. I'll order a cake."

"No way," Kyle protested. "Dana Sue always bakes the cake."

"But *I* wanna do it this time," Katie argued. "I'm big enough this year." She cast an imploring look at Cal. "Can I, please?"

Since Cal had decided that hiding an engagement ring in the cake might be just the right touch, helping Katie to bake one made a lot of sense. "How about you and I give it a shot? You tell me what kind and I'll buy the ingredients."

Kyle regarded them with a worried expression. "I think I'll tell Dana Sue to go ahead and bake one just in case."

Cal ruffled his hair. "Hey, what's with the lack of confidence? I think Katie and I will make a great baking team. Dana Sue will probably want to hire us as pastry chefs."

Ty rolled his eyes. "If you ask me, love's made you kinda goofy."

Cal laughed. "You just wait, young man. It's the best kind of goofy there is."

"Do we really need to have this meeting right now?" Maddie asked Helen. "I'm anxious to get home."

"I know," Helen said. "I'm coming to the birthday party, too, remember? I thought you'd rather I give you this here, rather than in front of the kids."

She pulled an envelope from her purse and handed it to Maddie.

"The divorce decree?" Maddie whispered, clutching the thick, official-looking envelope in a hand that had suddenly turned ice-cold.

Helen nodded. "You okay?"

"I just wasn't expecting..." Maddie began, then shook her head. "Of course I was, but not today. When it didn't come a couple of weeks ago, I guess I kind of shoved the whole idea out of my mind."

"It was bound to catch you off guard whenever the decree came through," Helen said. "I understand that. Seeing it on paper makes it final." She studied Maddie worriedly. "You weren't hoping for some kind of last-minute reprieve, were you?"

Had she been? Maddie didn't think so. She was more than ready to move on. Eager, in fact. Maybe Dana Sue's conviction that Bill's relationship with Noreen was rocky had shaken her a little, but not enough to make her question the final outcome. Her marriage was over. She'd known it for the better part of a year now.

"No," she told Helen. She stared at the envelope, not really wanting to open it and see the words in black and white. "I guess I just never figured I'd be one of those statistics. I thought Bill and I were stronger than that, more devoted to each other and our family."

"You've known for months now that it was a lie, at least on his part," Helen reminded her.

"Doesn't make it any easier," Maddie said. "I feel like a failure."

"You didn't fail," Helen said heatedly. "If anyone did, it was Bill." Her expression mellowed. "But the truth is, Maddie, sometimes these things just happen and it's nobody's fault. I've handled a lot of divorces over the last fifteen years, and at the core of most of them is the same thing. People change. It's the universe's one constant. Nothing stays static."

"Then why on earth does anyone ever get married?" Maddie asked in frustration. "With all those odds stacked against you, why bother?"

"Are you asking in general, or are you talking about you and Cal?"

Maddie frowned. "Both, I guess."

"Some people are just optimists," Helen told her. "Or maybe there's something about love that can make you forget all the odds and statistics and pain. It's that same kind of amnesia that allows women to have more than one baby after they discover that childbirth's no picnic. Love is powerful enough to convince you that this time will be different."

Her gaze met Maddie's. "For what it's worth, I think you and Cal can make it. Ever since the school board meeting when he said what he did right out there in front of God and everyone, whenever I'm around the two of you, I believe in the power of love." She grinned. "And coming from a cynic like me, that's saying something."

Maddie shoved the unopened envelope into a desk drawer. "I imagine Bill has his copy by now, too."

Helen nodded. "I imagine so."

"Then I guess he and Noreen will be setting their wedding date."

Helen gave her an odd look. "Does that bother you?"

Maddie thought about it. A few weeks ago it would

have shaken her to her core, but now? Surprisingly, she felt nothing.

"No," she said, relieved to be able to say it with conviction.

Helen seemed strangely relieved. "Good for you. Now, get out of here and head home to your party."

"You're not coming with me?"

Helen glanced at her watch. "It's not supposed to start for another hour. I'll be along in plenty of time. I have to make a couple of stops first."

Maddie grinned. "You haven't bought my present yet, have you?"

"Of course I have," Helen insisted, then chuckled. "Okay, I admit it. I know what I'm getting you, but I haven't had a chance to go by the store. And as long as you know my shameful secret, you might as well help me out."

"Help you out how?"

"Do you think Cal would prefer to see you in black lace or red?" she inquired innocently.

Maddie moaned. "Please do not give me sexy lingerie in front of my adolescent boys," she pleaded. "Or in front of Cal, for that matter."

"Just trying to help," Helen told her. "I thought it might give him ideas."

"I think Cal has plenty of ideas on his own, thank you very much. We've been out on half a dozen actual dates now and it's getting harder and harder to send him home."

"If you say so. I'll try to tame it down for the young folks," Helen promised. "I'm thinking flannel now. Maybe with a high neckline. The covered-up look can be a turn-on."

Maddie waved her away. "Just go."

"See you in an hour. Don't cut the cake without me."

"Cal and Katie would never allow it. They baked it themselves. They wouldn't even allow me in the kitchen. I just pray it'll be edible."

"Don't worry about it," Helen advised. "Enough frosting can make almost anything edible."

Maddie was counting on that.

Despite the divorce decree she'd left in her desk, Maddie was surprisingly lighthearted as she walked home. She'd wanted to ignore her birthday this year. She hadn't wanted to be reminded that she would officially be eleven years older than Cal, at least for a couple of months. Ten years was bad enough.

But ever since her conversation with her mother, she'd decided to forget about the whole age thing and focus on the man who'd made her happier than she'd dreamed possible. In fact, she had a surprise for him after the party that she predicted would pretty much make this birthday unforgettable for both of them. Despite her earlier protest to Helen, a little black lace might have come in handy.

When she arrived at the house, she could hear laughter from the kitchen. Hearing Cal's deep laugh blending with Ty's, Kyle's and Katie's made her smile. There were party hats and streamers on the dining-room table along with brightly colored paper plates and matching napkins. There was a pile of presents at the end of the table. Looking at the display, she decided it might be an even better party than the previous year's when Bill had called at the last minute to say he couldn't make it home. It had been the first of his lies.

One of the family traditions was to play music from the year—or at least the decade—the person was born, so Maddie went to find her stash of CDs with music from the late sixties. She'd just put a mix into the CD player when the doorbell rang. Opening it, she was shocked to find her ex-husband standing there.

"Bill, what are you doing here?"

He looked past her into the dining room and spotted the decorations. "Oh, hell, I'm sorry. It's your birthday, isn't it? I forgot."

"It doesn't matter. Come on in. You look upset." She studied him intently and realized she'd never seen him quite like this before. His shirt was wrinkled, his tie askew. Even more surprising was the day's growth of stubble on his cheeks.

"Is this about the divorce?" she asked him. "The papers took me by surprise, even though I'd been expecting them."

He regarded her with bewilderment. "The divorce?"

"You didn't know? It's final," she said. "Helen brought me the papers a little while ago."

"I see," he said as if they were of little or no importance. "I hadn't seen them yet, but I haven't been in the office. I imagine my attorney sent them there." He headed straight for his favorite chair and sat down, then hung his head as if he couldn't bear to look at her.

She studied him with dismay. "If it's not the divorce, did something go wrong at the hospital? Is that why you look as if you haven't slept in days?"

"I haven't slept, I haven't even been at the office in a couple of weeks," he told her. "I took some time off. I needed to think."

Maddie sat on the edge of the sofa across from him. "Think about what? What's wrong, Bill?"

He finally met her gaze. "Noreen and I have split up," he said, then added with a touch of belligerence, "Go ahead. You can say it."

"Say what?"

"I told you so."

Maddie shrugged, unwilling to play that game with him. "It hardly matters now."

"You were right," he said bitterly. "I was an idiot. It was a mistake from the beginning. Noreen figured that out before I did."

"Then breaking up was her idea?" Maddie asked, trying to keep the amazement out of her voice. Maybe she hadn't given Noreen as much credit as she deserved. Even more amazing was that no one in town had found out about the split. She hadn't heard a word, though she couldn't help wondering if that was why Helen had regarded her so warily earlier. Had she known?

"Actually Noreen left a couple of weeks ago. She moved home to be with her folks in Tennessee."

"I'm sorry," Maddie said, not knowing what else to say. Did he want her sympathy? Was he here expecting her to gloat? What? "So why are you here?"

Bill's exhausted gaze caught hers and held it. "I want to come home, Maddie," he announced with a perfectly straight face, even as Maddie's mouth fell open. "I want us to try again. And before you say no or toss me out the door, I want you to think about our family and what's best for all of us."

The audacity of the suggestion astounded her. "The way you did?" she scoffed.

He winced at her tone. "No. You're smarter than I am. You don't walk away from things this important without a fight."

His attempt to twist this around and make it seem as if she were the only roadblock to their recapturing their marital bliss made her want to smack him. "How dare you come here today and throw this in my lap? We're divorced, dammit! Your choice, not mine, but I've made the best of it. I'm not interested in looking back."

He looked shaken by her declaration, but he pressed on. "It's a piece of paper, Maddie," he said. "That's all it is. We can get married again. In fact, maybe it's for the best that the divorce came through. With a new ceremony and our kids standing up for us, it'll be a real second chance. A fresh start." He was clearly warming to the theme he'd chosen to win her over. "I'll do this however you want, whenever you want. You make the rules. You set the date. I've spent the past two weeks thinking this through and it's the right thing to do. I know it is."

Maybe if there'd been even a touch of humility in his tone, she would have given his plea more thought, but he was still the same Bill, the cocky, assured man with all the answers, never mind that they'd come months too late. It was all just words, and not very convincing ones at that. He hadn't even uttered a real apology for all he'd put them through.

As she sat there listening to him, Maddie clutched one of the birthday napkins that the kids had picked out for her party. She prayed they remained in the kitchen and heard none of this. She didn't want them to be as shaken and confused as she was.

"I can't do this now," she said at last, her voice tight with tension. "You need to go."

"Let me stay for the party," he countered. "Let it be a real family celebration."

"You walked out on this family," she reminded him. "So, no, you can't stay, not today."

His expression faltered at that. "Cal's coming?"

"He's already here."

"I see," he said, his voice turning cold.

"No, Bill, I don't think you do. He and the kids planned this party for me. I will not have it spoiled because you've suddenly had a change of heart now that your girlfriend's abandoned you. You can't waltz in here and assume that things can go back to the way they used to be."

"I'm not assuming anything, but they can be that way again," he insisted. "I believe that, I believe in us."

Before she realized what he intended, he pulled her to her feet and kissed her, taking his time about it. She detected a hint of desperation in the kiss.

"Marry me again, Maddie," he said. "We can get back everything we lost. I swear it."

Maddie wanted to scream that she didn't trust his promises, not anymore.

But before she could utter a sound, she heard Katie's gasp from the dining room and then the kitchen door banged open and closed again.

She cast a furious gaze at Bill. "See what you've done! How could you?"

"What?" he asked blankly.

"You've just turned your children's lives upside down yet again," she said wearily. "And you did it every bit as thoughtlessly and impulsively as you did the last time."

She left him standing there as she went to see just how much damage he'd done this time with his lack of consideration for anyone's feelings but his own.

CHAPTER TWENTY-THREE

Cal and Katie were coming out of the kitchen to put the somewhat lopsided, pink-frosted birthday cake on the table when he overheard Bill Townsend's proposal and guessed the rest. He felt his stomach drop. Beside him Katie gasped, then whirled around and raced back into the kitchen. Cal met Maddie's dismayed gaze for barely a heartbeat, then turned and went after Katie.

He barely had time to hunker down in front of the little girl and take her hands in his, before Maddie and Bill followed them into the kitchen.

"Hey, Katie-bug," Bill said, a weary smile on his face. He held out his arms, but Katie continued to cling to Cal's hands.

"Did you come for Mommy's birthday party?" she asked her father, regarding him with distrust. "Is that what you meant?"

Ty stood there, scowling, his body tense. "What's going on?" he demanded. "Why are you here? We didn't invite you. We have everything planned and now you're going to ruin it all." He looked at Cal. "It's ruined, isn't it?"

"It's okay, Ty," Cal reassured him. "Nothing's ruined."

"I don't need you interfering in a conversation between me and my son," Bill snapped.

"He has more right to be here than you do," Ty retorted. "You left us!"

Bill heaved a sigh. "I know, son, and it was a terrible mistake. I can't tell you how sorry I am that I put all of you through that. I've already told your mother that I want to come home for good," he said, aiming a hard, pointed look at Cal.

Though Cal's every instinct screamed at him to stay right here and claim this family as his own, he knew what he had to do. He faced Maddie. "I should get out of here and let you guys talk," he said quietly. "This is a family matter."

"No," she said, her expression pleading.

He bent down and gave her a hard kiss. "Talk," he said. "I'll call you later."

"But the party," she protested. "You and the kids worked so hard."

"We'll have it tomorrow night. No big deal."

She stood up. "I'll walk you to the door, then."

When they reached the front door, she said, "I had no idea he was coming over here, much less that he was thinking along these lines."

"I know."

"He said he and Noreen are over."

"I figured as much, if he wants to move back in here." He searched her expression. "What do *you* want?" As soon as the words were out of his mouth, he shook his head. "Sorry. That's not a fair question. He's just hit you with this. We'll talk later."

"But Cal—"

"Later," he said firmly and closed the front door behind him. He was afraid if he lingered for even a moment, he'd do or say something to try to convince her she belonged with him. She didn't need the pressure. The decision was hers and hers alone.

As much as he might hate it, those two had a history. They had kids. And they were the same age, same generation. Cal knew exactly what she was going to decide. And when she told him it was over, he didn't want her smug, unworthy ex-husband sitting there listening as she tried to let him down gently.

He hadn't even made it to his car when Dana Sue and Helen pulled in behind him, blocking his way.

"Where are you going?" Dana Sue asked. "Did you guys forget something? I can run out for it."

Helen studied him with an assessing look. "This isn't about party favors or ice cream, is it?"

Cal shook his head. "Bill's inside."

"Damn him," Helen muttered. "I *thought* that was his car on the street. What does he want or do I even need to ask? I know Noreen left him."

"He wants Maddie," Cal said tightly.

Dana Sue stared at him with a shocked expression. "But their marriage has been over for months."

"Apparently Bill doesn't see it that way," Cal said. "I really need to get out of here."

"You're leaving?" Dana Sue demanded indignantly. "What's wrong with you? Get back inside and protect Maddie."

He managed a half smile. "Maddie can take care of herself."

"Well, I know that," Dana Sue said with a wave of her hand. "But she's vulnerable to him, especially today."

"Why today?" he asked.

"The divorce is final," Helen explained.

He sighed at the irony. "Tell that to Bill. He seems to want to come back and take up where he left off."

"He actually said that?" Helen asked, looking as dismayed as he felt. "In front of the kids?"

"In so many words," Cal confirmed. "Katie and I only caught the tail end of the conversation he had with Maddie, but he generously repeated some of it for Ty and Kyle's benefit."

"Damn him!" Helen repeated, this time with even more feeling. "I'm with Dana Sue. You need to go back in there and fight for what you want—I'm assuming that's Maddie and the kids." She scowled. "Or don't you want them enough to fight for them?"

"I love them enough to give them a chance to figure out what's best for them," he said.

"If that isn't a bunch of noble hogwash!" Dana Sue said with scorn. "Maddie needs to know you care enough to fight for her."

"Maddie knows how much I care," he said.

"How?" Dane Sue demanded. "Have you made a commitment to her? Have you told her you love her? Proposed? Done anything she can hold on to? Or is she going to have to weigh Bill's concrete offer against your ambivalence?"

Cal thought of the ring he'd buried in her birthday cake. The kids knew just which slice to give to their mom. It was the only slice that had a lopsided, malformed rose on top. The ring was between the layers.

"You'll have to trust me," he told them. "Maddie knows how I feel, or she will before the evening's over if they go ahead with the party."

If some twist of fate put that slice on Bill Townsend's plate, Cal hoped he'd break a tooth on that diamond.

"You're making a mistake," Dana Sue said, her tone

dire. "Bill might be a jerk, but he can be very persuasive when he wants to be. How else do you suppose he got a beautiful young woman like Noreen, even if it all fell apart in the end?"

"Maddie's not a naive twenty-four-year-old," Cal reminded her.

"You think she's going to stay with Bill, no matter what you do, don't you?" Helen said. "That's why you're leaving."

"I'm leaving because her ex-husband and the father of her children just announced he wanted a second chance. She needs to be able to consider that without me in her face."

"Men and their stupid pride," Dana Sue said with disgust. "Go home. Lick your wounds. That's what you're really doing. You don't want a bunch of witnesses just in case she chooses Bill over you."

Cal could hardly deny that. He had faith in what he and Maddie had. He just couldn't be sure it would hold up against her sense of duty to her kids and the history she had with Bill.

"You're right. I'd rather not force Maddie to make a choice with everyone she loves hanging on her every word. Come on, you know this is what I have to do. She needs time to think. She doesn't need Bill and me in there haggling over her like she's the last piece of prime rib in the butcher shop."

"Well, it's a good thing we don't feel that way," Dana Sue snapped. "I intend to go in there and stop her from making the second-worst mistake of her life."

"What was the worst one?" Cal asked.

"Marrying Bill the first time," Dana Sue said.

"Amen to that," Helen said. She met Cal's gaze. "And while I think you're making a mistake to walk away right now, I understand and admire you for doing it. You and

Maddie have me believing in love again. I hope to hell you don't ruin that for me by carrying this damn nobility thing too far."

Cal laughed at the annoyance in her voice. "To be perfectly honest, I hope so, too." He glanced at Dana Sue, who was still seething. "You going to move your car out of my way?"

"No!" she snapped.

"Fair enough." He considered trying to maneuver around it as Maddie's mother had done a few weeks ago, but the rosebush was just now starting to recover. "I'll walk."

Dana Sue nodded. "Maybe that will get your blood circulating back to your brain."

"Don't mind her," Helen said, giving him a commiserating look. "Come on, Dana Sue. Instead of berating Cal, let's get inside and save the day before this whole mess spins out of control."

"I can't wait till Maddie's mom gets here," Dana Sue said. "I bet she'll have plenty to say about this reconciliation."

Cal didn't envy any of them. From the look in Maddie's eyes when he'd left, he had a hunch the chaos was already way past anybody's attempts to save the day.

Bill was surrounded by a sea of hostile faces. He'd expected an uphill battle with Maddie, but he hadn't counted on the arrival of Dana Sue, Helen and his former mother-in-law to make matters worse. Obviously his timing sucked. Even the kids had been very wary about, if not hostile to, his stated desire to come home, and indignant at being sent from the room when it became clear that a discussion about his relationship with their mother—and not a birthday celebration—was on the agenda.

"Maybe I should go," he said eventually. "We can talk about this later, Maddie, after you've had time to consider what's sensible."

"Now, *there's* a romantic thought." Helen shook her head. "By all means, Maddie, do what's sensible. Don't listen to your heart." She seared her best friend with a look. "And if you do, I promise you'll regret it for the rest of your life."

Bill tried to counter Helen's remarks. "Look, sweetheart," he said, "I've put all my cards on the table. I thought long and hard before doing it because I wanted to be sure it was the right thing. Now I'm trusting you to do the right thing, as well. You always have. Whenever you're ready, we'll talk."

"She has nothing left to say to you," Dana Sue declared. "You're divorced, remember?"

Maddie cast a warning look at her best friend. "I can speak for myself."

"I know," Dana Sue said. "I'm just putting in my two cents'. Sue me."

"If we're all going to say what we think, I have a few things I'd like to get off my chest, too," Paula said.

Bill knew there'd be nothing pleasant coming out of her mouth. "I think I can guess where you stand."

"Really?" Paula said. "Maybe I just wanted to say that Maddie needs to remember that you're the father of her children."

Bill didn't think for a second that she was going to let it go at that. "And?"

Paula gave him an approving look. "You're smarter than I remembered. I was also going to say that that is not a good enough reason for her to take you back. The way you treated her was deplorable. That's the bottom line. And while I will live with and support whatever decision Maddie makes, there's only one I will truly respect."

"You can't even consider the possibility that I've learned from my mistakes?" Bill asked, stung by her comment, even though he'd been expecting something very much along those lines. He knew he deserved her wrath, but it cut just the same. Until he'd gotten involved with Noreen, he thought he'd been a good husband and father. Paula seemed to have forgotten about all those years when he'd been devoted to her daughter and their family.

"No, I can't consider that possibility," Paula said, her expression unrelenting. "It's been my observation that men who treat their marriage and their family in such a cavalier manner don't learn from their mistakes. They repeat them."

"I won't," he said.

"And Maddie should believe that because?" Dana Sue demanded.

"Okay, enough," Maddie said. "As much as I appreciate all the advice and moral support, ultimately this is my decision."

"Agreed," her mother said.

"And you need time to think about it, consider all the ramifications of what you decide," Bill said.

"No," she said, her gaze lifting to his. "I don't."

Bill swallowed hard at the certainty in her voice. This wasn't going the way he'd hoped. He could see it in the pitying look in her eyes.

He forced himself to say it before she could. "It's Cal, isn't it?"

Maddie nodded. Her gaze went from her mother to Dana Sue and Helen before coming back to him. "I know all of you thought I didn't know my own mind, that I'd put the kids ahead of what I want and need, and in some ways you were justified in thinking that. My kids are the most important things in my life and I would do just about anything for them."

"But—" her mother began.

Maddie didn't allow her to finish. She held up her hand. "I would do anything *except* make myself miserable. I won't turn myself into a martyr for the sake of my children." When she met Bill's gaze, her expression was sad. "I couldn't marry you again, Bill. You're not the man I married and I'm not the woman I was when I was married to you. It would never work."

"How can you be sure if you won't even give us a chance?" he asked, hating the pleading note in his voice. He realized how much he'd counted on being able to win her over. From the minute Noreen had walked out the door of their apartment, he'd been obsessed with winning Maddie back. He'd considered every angle, debated all the right arguments to make it happen. But it hadn't been enough.

"I'm sure," Maddie replied, "because I love someone else, someone who values who I am now, not someone who values the way I was. Because my heart races when I see him, because he makes me and my children happy." She glanced at her mother and smiled. "Because Cal is my soul mate, Bill. It's taken me a long time to realize it, but you never were."

He saw the conviction in her eyes and knew he'd lost. Maybe their marriage would have ended someday anyway, but it had happened now because of his stupidity and recklessness. He had no choice but to concede defeat graciously.

Ignoring the other women in the room, he leaned down and pressed a kiss to Maddie's brow. "Be happy, then. Cal's a lucky man."

She smiled at him in a totally confident way. He recognized that self-confidence because for a while, because of him, she'd lost it. His heart ached.

"Yeah," she said happily. "He really is."

It was after midnight when Maddie let herself into Cal's apartment, shed her clothes and slipped into bed beside him. As if he'd been waiting for her, he sighed and folded her close so she could hear the steady beating of his heart.

"Who's with the kids?" he murmured.

"My mother. She said since it was for a good cause she'd break all her rules and babysit for the whole night."

"A good cause?"

"You and me."

"I wasn't sure there would be a you and me after this afternoon," he admitted, then drew his head back to look deep into her eyes. "I guess since you're here in my bed, I was wrong."

"You were," she agreed. "There was never a doubt in my mind. I would have told you that, if you'd stuck around." She tweaked a hair on his chest. "Finding the engagement ring in the birthday cake pretty much clinched it. It was just what I needed to risk coming over here and climbing into bed with you."

She could feel his smile against her cheek. "You found it, huh? How come you cut the cake?"

"Actually the kids insisted," she told him. "They seemed to have an idea that Bill showing up would give you cold feet, so they decided to do the asking for you."

"Did you give them an answer?"

"Nope. I saved that for you."

"And? Should I assume that your presence here in my bed is the answer?"

"Nope. This is the birthday present I'm giving myself,"

she teased. “By the way, are you certain you weren’t sure of the outcome from the beginning?”

“Absolutely not, why?”

“You left the door unlocked.”

“This is Serenity,” he reminded her.

“And we have thieves, the same as anyplace else.”

“I don’t want to believe that. I like thinking this town is perfect, just the way I know you’re perfect.”

Maddie laughed. “Definitely delusional,” she assessed. “Maybe I should reconsider my decision.”

“Which decision would that be? Not going back to Bill or coming over here?”

“Marrying you. I was all set to say yes…”

For an instant he looked genuinely stunned. “You mean it?”

Maddie laughed. “Don’t look so shocked. I’m not letting you take it back now.”

He held her tighter. “Never.”

She reached for her blouse and pulled the simple diamond ring out of a pocket and held it out to him. “I rinsed the icing off,” she told him.

“Then you won’t object if I slip it on your finger?”

She frowned. “That’s it? That’s your idea of a proposal?”

Cal grinned. “I’m naked. Do you really want me out of this bed and down on one knee?”

Maddie laughed. “I think I do.”

“Okay, then,” he said, throwing back the sheets and climbing out of the bed.

Maddie sucked in a deep breath at the sight of all those muscles—and an impressive arousal. “Maybe the proposal can wait,” she said, beckoning him back to bed and settling into the comfortable intimacy that was so much better than anything she’d ever imagined.

"You know what this feels like?" Cal asked eventually, holding up her hand and sliding the diamond ring onto her finger, then pressing a kiss on top of it.

"What?"

"Stealing home."

Maddie rested her head on his chest and noticed that his heart was still beating rapidly. "Thanks to my son, I know exactly what you mean. Bottom of the ninth, with the game on the line and a win just ninety feet away."

"Exactly," he confirmed.

"I figure I owe Ty for a whole lot more than teaching me baseball terminology," she told Cal.

"Oh?"

"If it weren't for him getting into so much trouble a few months ago, I might never have known just what an incredible man his coach is."

Cal smiled. "Just a word to the wise," he cautioned. "Don't tell him that."

"Why not?"

"If he thinks he gets the credit for bringing us together, he's liable to use it against us."

"How?"

"He's a teenager. He'll find a way."

"I'm not worried," Maddie said. "I happen to be in love with a man who knows just about everything there is to know about teenage boys."

Cal laughed. "Boys, yes, but when Katie hits her teens, you're on your own, darlin'. If it were up to me, she'd never leave the house."

"I guess we'll just have to do the best we can to get them all grown up and on their own."

Cal tucked a finger under her chin. "How would you feel about adding one more to the mix before we call it quits?"

Maddie sat straight up in bed, stunned by the question and the hint of longing she'd heard in his voice. "Excuse me? I'm forty-one years old."

"A very sexy, healthy forty-one. We could do this."

"You're crazy," she said. "I'm—"

"Don't you dare say you're too old," he told her. "I've read all the literature. A pregnancy wouldn't be without some potential risks and complications, but it's possible. Will you at least think about it? Talk to your doctor?"

Maddie studied him, nervously fingering the ring that already felt as if it belonged on her hand. "Is this a deal breaker for you?"

He regarded her incredulously. "Absolutely not. I don't have to see a kid with my genes running around to be happy. If it turns out that you hate the idea or the doctor says it's unwise, that's that. We can always consider adoption. I love kids, Maddie. Yours, ours, a kid who needs a home. And no matter what, we'll make this decision together."

She studied him with wonder. "More kids? I never even considered such a thing, but you know what? It feels right. We have a lot to offer, don't we?"

His expression turned serious. "And just in case it crossed your mind, you'll have all the help you need so you can work and raise our family at the same time, okay? This isn't some sort of either/or situation. I know how important The Corner Spa's success is to you."

"You're amazing. Where were you twenty years ago?" she asked, then held up a hand. "Wait! Please don't answer that."

A grin spread across Cal's face. "Okay, but just so you know, I was already imagining that one day I'd meet a woman just like you."

"Oh, you were not. You were ten," she protested.

"A very precocious ten," he replied. "Want me to demonstrate a few of the moves I was already considering?"

She smiled. "Why, yes," she said, already filled with anticipation. "I believe a demonstration would be the perfect way for this evening to end."

Cal grinned. "If I do it right, this evening isn't going to end. It's going to be just the beginning."

And so it was.

CHAPTER TWENTY-FOUR

When word of the engagement leaked out, along with news that it would be a very short one, the town of Serenity embraced Maddie's marriage to Cal as if everyone had been for the relationship all along. If Maddie had had her way, they would have had a quiet ceremony at the end of summer with just family and friends present, but Helen and Dana Sue arranged one of their margarita nights in early July specifically to press her to make it big and splashy, something for folks to remember.

"You don't want one single person to think you're still questioning whether you and Cal are right for each other, do you?" Dana Sue demanded, then grinned as she urged some more of her guacamole on Maddie, then put a second margarita into her hand. "Besides, you need to stake your claim in the most public way possible, so those women who were fantasizing about Cal don't get any ideas about stealing him from you."

"Cal and I don't need to prove anything to anyone," Maddie protested.

"Okay, if you won't do it to make every female in town

envious, do it for us?" Dana Sue pleaded. "Helen and I need a chance to catch a bouquet."

"I could toss two of them, even at a small reception," Maddie suggested, wondering if her head was spinning because of the change in plans, the stifling summer heat or the margaritas.

"It doesn't count if it's a setup. We have to grab those bouquets fair and square against real competition," Dana Sue argued.

Maddie exchanged a bewildered look with Helen. "Do you remember that being a rule?"

Helen shrugged. "Don't ask me. Besides, I think all this nonsense about catching a bouquet is just a smoke screen. Dana Sue wants to throw you a big party. She's had the menu all planned for weeks now, ever since she found out about the ring in the birthday cake."

Maddie stared at her. "You have?"

"Well, yes," Dana Sue admitted, embarrassed. "I just wanted to make a contribution to your big day."

"You can be a part of it without cooking," Maddie told her.

"But cooking is what I do best." Dana Sue's expression turned wistful. "And I really, really want to try my hand at a fancy wedding cake with at least six tiers and a cute little bride and groom on the top. Erik said he'd help me, since wedding cakes are his specialty. You can't do that for a dozen people. It would be crazy."

Maddie turned to Helen. "What about you? Why do you want me to have a big wedding?"

Helen, the most confident woman in Serenity, blushed like a girl. "Do I really have to answer that?"

"You do if I'm going to subject Cal to some fancy blowout instead of the quiet ceremony he's been expecting," Maddie told her.

Helen took a bracing sip of margarita before replying. "Okay, I'm living vicariously," she admitted. "Who knows if I'll ever have a wedding of my own, so I want to be part of one with all the bells and whistles."

Maddie regarded her with bemusement. "You were my maid of honor when I married Bill, and that wedding had all the bells and whistles."

"True, but I was too young to appreciate it. And I was also struggling with the fact that I hated Bill even then and thought you were making a terrible mistake. This time I'm genuinely happy for you."

Stunned, Maddie sat back on her chaise longue and took a long swallow of her margarita, then gazed from one woman to the other. The hopeful, eager expressions on their faces were too much for her. The wedding might be for her and Cal, but her best friends had earned a right to have a say in it, too. They'd stood by her for months now, given her a new purpose and taken a risk on her business capabilities when few others would have.

"Okay, then," she said at last. "Let's have ourselves a wedding!"

"Really?" they asked in unison.

"Cal won't freak out, will he?" Dana Sue asked worriedly.

Maddie smiled. "Not as long as he doesn't have to do anything but show up at the church."

"He won't have to do a thing," Helen promised. "You won't have to lift a finger, either. Dana Sue and I will take care of everything."

"Can I at least pick out my own dress?" Maddie asked, wondering if she hadn't just signed away too much control over her own wedding.

"As long as we get to come along," Dana Sue said.

"And get final approval," Helen added.

Maddie lifted her glass in a toast. "A negotiator to the end," she told Helen. "Deal."

Cal squirmed as Hamilton Reynolds tried to tighten the knot on his tie. "You're strangling me."

"Oh, hush up, son. You don't want to walk into church looking as if you've never worn a tuxedo before, do you?"

"I'd rather walk in there not wearing a tuxedo at all," Cal grumbled. "This was supposed to be a quiet little ceremony way back in September. Now it's almost Thanksgiving." He frowned. "How many people do you suppose are in the church?"

Ham gave him a pitying look. "Three hundred or so, from the looks of it. Those gals sure know how to throw a party."

Cal shuddered. Even when Maddie had told him that she'd turned the reins for their wedding over to Dana Sue and Helen and that they couldn't pull it off by the end of summer, he'd had no idea what they were in for. When he'd questioned them about why it had gotten so out of hand, he was simply told they were "making a statement."

He still hadn't figured that one out, but he'd seen Maddie's eyes shining with anticipation and clamped his mouth shut. He'd concluded he could endure a few hours of expensive commotion if it made her happy.

He was still telling himself that three hours after the ceremony when the lavish reception with its surprisingly good garage band showed no signs of slowing down. Beside him at the head table, even Maddie was beginning to wilt a little.

"Can we get out of here yet?" he whispered in her ear. "I'd actually hoped to spend my first honeymoon night with my bride and not with three hundred of her nearest and dearest friends."

She grinned at him. "Patience, Cal. We have a whole lifetime ahead of us. Just look at Helen and Dana Sue out on the dance floor. They're having a ball. We can't cut this short."

"So this is for them," he said, finally getting it. "I thought so."

"It made them happy to do it for us," Maddie admitted. "I couldn't say no." Her expression brightened. "Oh, look, Ty's finally dancing with Annie. She looks as if she's died and gone to heaven. I hope he realizes that she has a huge crush on him and treats her kindly."

Cal studied Ty—his new stepson—with the eye of a man who could still remember how careless teenage boys could be when it came to fragile emotions. "Maybe I should have a talk with him," Cal said. "Boys Ty's age can be idiots when it comes to girls. They can miss a lot of signs and wind up trampling all over a young girl's heart."

Before Maddie could respond, Annie suddenly sagged in Ty's arms.

"Oh my gosh, did you see that?" she asked, already on her feet and running.

Cal reached the couple before Maddie, who'd been hampered by her wedding gown and high heels. Ty was clinging to Annie, trying to carefully lower her to the floor, his expression bewildered.

"I don't know what happened," he told Cal. "One minute she was fine. The next she passed out or something. Is she okay?"

Cal knelt beside her and felt for a pulse. It was weak and rapid. "Get Dana Sue," he told Maddie.

"Is she okay?"

Cal gave her a curt nod. "She just fainted. Bring some water when you come back."

"I'll get it," Ty said, sounding relieved to have something to do.

Cal brushed a hand over Annie's pale cheek. "Come on, sweetie, wake up for me, okay? Come on, Annie."

She blinked at last and opened her eyes. "Coach?"

Cal forced a reassuring smile. "Hey, there, Sleeping Beauty."

"What happened?"

"You fainted."

Color bloomed in her cheeks. "While I was dancing with Ty?"

Cal nodded.

"Oh, God," she said, misery in her eyes. "He'll never speak to me again."

"Sure he will," Cal said just as Ty returned with the water.

Ty knelt and held out the glass. "You're awake," he said, obviously relieved. "You scared me."

Annie accepted the water but wouldn't look at him. "I feel like such an idiot," she whispered. "I'm sorry, Ty."

"Hey, it's not your fault," Ty said just as Dana Sue rushed up, her expression frantic.

"She's okay," Cal told her.

Dana Sue insisted on kneeling down and checking Annie for herself. "Have you eaten today?" she demanded.

"Mom!"

"Dammit, I want to know. Have you eaten?"

"She had some cake," Ty said.

Dana Sue kept her gaze on Annie. "Anything else?"

Tears welled up in Annie's eyes. "Mom, don't make a scene. I'm fine."

"You are not fine," Dana Sue said. "You passed out."

Maddie hunkered down and hugged Dana Sue. "She's

okay now. We'll go with you to take her home. Or to the emergency room if you think that's best."

"I don't know what's best," Dana Sue whispered, looking stricken.

"Mom, I'm fine," Annie protested, struggling to sit up. "See? No hospital, please. Just take me home. I'll eat some soup or something. I promise."

Maddie's gaze remained on Dana Sue's face. "Up to you, sweetie."

Her gaze still pinned on her daughter, Dana Sue finally sighed. "I guess we'll go home, but you guys don't need to come with us. Helen will come. You need to go on your honeymoon and forget about everything back here." She clutched Annie's hand tightly and gazed up at Maddie, then at Cal. "We're going to be okay."

Cal awaited Maddie's decision. He knew she was torn between leaving with him and sticking by her friend.

Maddie studied Dana Sue intently, then nodded at last. "We'll call you in the morning to check on how Annie's feeling."

Dana Sue nodded.

Cal bent down and scooped Annie up in his arms. The girl weighed next to nothing. "I'll take you out to the car."

Dana Sue gave Maddie a kiss, then followed Cal, along with Ty.

When Annie was settled in the back seat, Ty gave Cal a questioning look. "Is it okay if I go with them?"

Cal nodded. "Sure. Run inside and let your grandmother know that you'll be home later, so she doesn't worry."

Cal studied Dana Sue and noted that her eyes were still shadowed with concern. "You sure you don't want Maddie and me to stick around and help you? We can get a flight out of here tomorrow."

"Absolutely not," Dana Sue said. "I closed the restaurant for the day today and my staff can cover for me tomorrow, so I can keep an eye on her. Annie will be at Doc Marshall's Monday morning if I have to drag her there by her hair."

"See that she is, okay?" he said. He held her gaze, trying to impress on her the urgency of the situation without scaring her and Annie.

Dana Sue's eyes watered at his somber tone. "I will. I promise. Now go back in there and get Maddie. Make her happy, you hear?"

"I'll do my best," Cal promised.

But when he walked back inside, he found Maddie sitting on a chair, her head being held between her knees by her mother. Her cheeks were as pale as Annie's had been a few minutes earlier.

"What the hell happened?" he demanded.

Paula gave him a wry look. "She fainted."

Cal felt as if he'd plunged into the Mad Hatter's Tea Party by accident. "Is there something in the water? Is everyone in the place going to faint?" he asked, hunkering down beside his wife and taking her ice-cold hand in his.

Paula chuckled. "I don't think so. I'll leave you with your bride. She can explain."

Cal stared at Maddie, whose face was still ashen. "Well?"

"You know that dream of yours?"

He stared at her blankly. "Dream? Marrying you, you mean?"

She smiled. "No, the other one."

Cal still didn't get it. "This was the big one, Maddie."

"You told me you wanted to add to our family," she reminded him.

When the implication of her words sank in, Cal sat down hard, right on the floor at her feet. He felt a little faint himself.

"A baby?" he whispered.

Maddie nodded. "I guess we got a little ahead of ourselves."

"A baby," he repeated, awestruck.

"Looks that way. I'd hoped to wait to tell you on our honeymoon, but the way things are going, we might never get to our hotel."

"Do the kids know?"

She shook her head. "Only my mom, and she only knows because she guessed."

Panic spread through him. He'd wanted this more than anything, but now? When they were still at their wedding reception? Before they'd even had a chance to talk it through some more? He studied Maddie's face to see if she was as freaked out as he was. Aside from being a bit pale, though, she looked happy. Really happy.

"Is it okay?" he asked. "Should we stay here and see the doctor?"

"I've already seen the doctor and everything's fine," she assured him. "And we are going on this honeymoon, Cal Maddox. You promised me an incredible trip and I'm holding you to it."

For the second time in less than thirty minutes, Cal scooped a woman into his arms. This one had a nice healthy heft to her, the kind of curves that made a man's blood heat. He looked into Maddie's shining eyes. "It's going to be a helluva ride, isn't it, Mrs. Maddox?"

"Apparently so. You ready for it?"

"I've been waiting all my life."

* * * * *

Keep reading for a sneak peek at
A Slice of Heaven
the second Sweet Magnolias novel
by #1 New York Times *bestselling author*
Sherryl Woods.

Now a Netflix Original Series!

CHAPTER ONE

The smell of burning toast caught Dana Sue's attention just before the smoke detector went off. Snatching the charred bread from the toaster, she tossed it into the sink, then grabbed a towel and waved it at the shrieking alarm to disperse the smoke. At last the overly sensitive thing fell silent.

"Mom, what on earth is going on in here?" Annie demanded, standing in the kitchen doorway, her nose wrinkling at the aroma of burned toast. She was dressed for school in jeans that hung on her too-thin frame and a scoop-neck T-shirt that revealed pale skin stretched taut over protruding collarbones.

Restraining the desire to comment on the evidence that Annie had lost more weight, Dana Sue regarded her teenager with a chagrined expression. "Take a guess."

"You burned the toast again," Annie said, a grin spreading across her face, relieving the gauntness ever so slightly. "Some chef you are. If I ratted you out about this, no one would ever come to Sullivan's to eat again."

"Which is why we don't serve breakfast and why you're sworn to secrecy, unless you expect to be grounded, phoneless and disconnected from your email till you hit thirty,"

Dana Sue told her, not entirely in jest. Sullivan's had been a huge success from the moment she'd opened the restaurant's doors. Word-of-mouth raves had spread through the entire region. Even Charleston's top restaurant-and-food critic had hailed it for its innovative Southern dishes. Dana Sue didn't need her sassy kid ruining that with word of her culinary disasters at home.

"Why were you making toast, anyway? You don't eat it," Annie said, filling a glass with water and taking a tiny sip before dumping the rest down the drain.

"I was fixing you breakfast," Dana Sue said, pulling a plate with a fluffy omelet from the oven, where she'd kept it warm. She'd added low-fat cheese and finely shredded red and green sweet peppers, just the way Annie had always liked it. The omelet was perfect, a vision suitable for the cover of any gourmet magazine.

Annie looked at the food with a repugnant expression most people reserved for roadkill. "I don't think so."

"Sit," Dana Sue ordered, losing patience with the too-familiar reaction. "You have to eat. Breakfast is the most important meal, especially on a school day. Think of the protein as brainpower. Besides, I dragged myself out of bed to fix it for you, so you're going to eat it."

Annie, her beautiful sixteen-year-old, regarded her with one of those "Mother! Not again" looks, but at least she sat down at the table. Dana Sue sat across from her, holding her mug of black coffee as if it were liquid gold. After a late night at the restaurant, she needed all the caffeine she could get first thing in the morning to be alert enough to deal with Annie's quick-thinking evasiveness.

"How was your first day back at school?" Dana Sue asked.

Annie shrugged.

"Do you have any classes with Ty this year?" For as long as Dana Sue could remember, Annie had harbored a crush on Tyler Townsend, whose mom was one of Dana Sue's best friends and most recently a business partner at The Corner Spa, Serenity's new fitness club for women.

"Mom, he's a senior. I'm a junior," Annie explained with exaggerated patience. "We don't have any of the same classes."

"Too bad," Dana Sue said, meaning it. Ty had gone through some issues of his own since his dad had walked out on Maddie, but he'd always been a good sounding board for Annie, the way a big brother or best friend would be. Not that Annie appreciated the value of that. She wanted Ty to notice her as a girl, as someone he'd be interested in dating. So far, though, Ty was oblivious.

Dana Sue studied Annie's sullen expression and tried again, determined to find some way to connect with the child who was slipping away too fast. "Do you like your teachers?"

"They talk. I listen. What's to like?"

Dana Sue bit back a sigh. A few short years ago, Annie had been a little chatterbox. There hadn't been a detail of her day she hadn't wanted to share with her mom and dad. Of course, ever since Ronnie had cheated on Dana Sue and she'd thrown him out two years ago, everything had changed. Annie's adoration for her father had been destroyed, just as Dana Sue's heart had been broken. For a long time after the divorce, silence had fallen in the Sullivan household, with neither of them wanting to talk about the one thing that really mattered.

"Mom, I have to go or I'll be late." A glance at the clock had Annie bouncing up eagerly.

Dana Sue looked at the untouched plate of food. "You haven't eaten a bite of that."

"Sorry. It looks fantastic, but I'm not hungry. See you

tonight." She brushed a kiss across Dana Sue's cheek and took off, leaving behind the no longer perfect omelet and a whiff of perfume that Dana Sue recognized as the expensive scent she'd bought for herself last Christmas and wore only on very special occasions. Since such occasions had been few and far between since the divorce, it probably didn't matter that her daughter was wasting it on high school boys.

Only after she was alone again and her coffee had turned cold did Dana Sue notice the brown sack with Annie's lunch still sitting on the counter. It could have been an oversight, but she knew better. Annie had deliberately left it behind, just as she'd ignored the breakfast her mother had fixed.

The memory of Annie's collapse during Maddie's wedding reception last year at Thanksgiving came flooding back, and with it a tide of fresh panic.

"Oh, sweetie," Dana Sue murmured. "Not again."

"I'm thinking for tonight's dessert I'll make an old-fashioned bread pudding with maybe some Granny Smith apples to add a little tartness and texture," Erik Whitney said before Dana Sue had a chance to tie on her apron. "What do you think?"

Even as her mouth watered, her brain was calculating the carbohydrates. Off the chart, she concluded, and sighed. Her customers could indulge, but she'd have to avoid the dessert like the plague.

Erik regarded her worriedly. "Too much sugar?"

"For me, yes. For the rest of the universe, it sounds perfect."

"I could do a fresh fruit cobbler instead, maybe use a sugar substitute," he suggested.

Dana Sue shook her head. She'd built Sullivan's reputation by putting a new spin on old Southern favorites. Most of the time, her selections were healthier than some of the traditional butter-soaked dishes, but when it came to desserts, she knew her clientele preferred decadent. She'd hired Erik straight out of the Atlanta Culinary Institute because the school's placement officer had ranked him the best pastry chef candidate they'd seen in years.

Older than most graduates, Erik was already in his thirties. Eager to experiment and show what he could do, Erik hadn't disappointed her or her customers. He was such a huge improvement over her last sous-chef, a temperamental man who was difficult to work with, that Dana Sue counted her blessings every single day that Erik could double as a sous-chef and pastry chef. He'd quickly become more than an employee. He'd become a friend.

Moreover, there was already a high demand in South Carolina for Erik's wedding cakes. He'd raised the traditional cake to an art form that rivaled anything seen at fancy celebrity weddings. Dana Sue knew she'd be lucky to keep him for another year or two at most before some big-city restaurant or catering company lured him away, but for the moment he seemed content in Serenity, happy with the latitude she gave him.

"We did plenty of fruit cobblers over the summer," she told him. "The bread pudding sounds great for tonight. You're cooking for the customers, not me."

When was the last time she'd allowed herself so much as a teaspoonful of any of Erik's rich desserts? Not since Doc Marshall had given her yet another stern lecture on losing the fifteen pounds she'd gained in the past two years, and warned her—again—that she was putting herself at risk for diabetes, the disease that had killed her mother. That should have been warning enough for Dana Sue without the doctor reminding her constantly.

She'd thought that working with her two best friends to

open The Corner Spa would keep her so busy she'd stay on her diet. She'd also convinced herself that the spectacular surroundings they'd created would give her an incentive to exercise. So far, though, she'd gained five more pounds testing all the healthy drinks and low-fat muffins they'd put on the spa menu. There was a peach-pear smoothie that might be worth dying for.

Putting on weight might be an occupational hazard for a chef, but Dana Sue laid some of the blame on the collapse of her marriage two years ago. When she'd kicked Ronnie Sullivan out of her house for cheating on her, she'd consoled herself with food—unlike her daughter, who'd chosen to avoid it.

"You're not the only person in Serenity worrying about sugar," Erik reminded her. "I can adapt."

"So can I. It's not as if I'll starve, sweetie. Tonight's menu will have plenty of vegetables and three healthy main courses. Now, go work your magic. Our regulars expect something amazing from you every time they come in."

"Okay," he said finally, then gave her a penetrating look. "You want to tell me what else is on your mind?"

She frowned at him. "What makes you think there's something else on my mind?"

"Experience," he said succinctly. "And if you won't talk to me, then go call Maddie or Helen and get it off your chest. If you're as distracted during the dinner rush as you were during lunch, I'll have to spend the whole evening bailing you out."

"Excuse me?" she said tightly, not one bit happy about the accuracy of his comment.

"Sweetie, half a dozen meals came back in here because you'd left off some part of the order. It's one thing to forget to send out french fries. It's another to leave off the meat."

Dana Sue moaned. "Oh, God, I was hoping you hadn't noticed that."

Erik winked at her. "I notice most everything that goes on in here. That's what makes me a good backup for you. Now, go make that call, you hear?"

Dana Sue held in a sigh as Erik went to gather his ingredients from their well-stocked storeroom, and her own thoughts returned to her daughter. It was impossible for her to go on denying that Annie was getting skinnier by the day. She claimed she was no thinner than the models she saw in magazines and on TV, and that she was perfectly healthy, but Dana Sue thought otherwise. Her clothes hung loosely on her bony frame, Annie's ineffective attempt to disguise just how thin she really was. Dana Sue was convinced she was starving herself so she wouldn't turn out like her mom—overweight and alone.

Despite a frantic pace with the lunch crowd, which usually energized her and kept her focused, today Dana Sue hadn't been able to shake the image of that abandoned brown sack. Usually Annie made a pretense of eating something just to keep her mother off her case. Now Dana Sue wondered if that left-behind paper bag, with its turkey sandwich on whole-grain bread, celery and carrot sticks and a banana, was a cry for help.

Satisfied that Erik could watch over the dinner preparations in the state-of-the-art, stainless-steel kitchen, Dana Sue slipped into her small, cluttered office to follow his advice and call Maddie at the gym. Whenever her world seemed to be crumbling, she turned to her two best friends—Maddie Maddox, who was managing The Corner Spa, and attorney Helen Decatur—for sensible advice or a shoulder to cry on. Over the years, they'd grown adept at providing both. Nobody in Serenity messed with one of the Sweet Magnolias without tangling with the other two, as well.

They'd bolstered each other through schoolgirl crushes, failed marriages and health scares. They'd shared joys and sorrows. Most recently they'd gone into business together, which had brought them closer than ever, their various skills complementing each other nicely.

"How are things in the world of fitness?" Dana Sue asked, forcing a cheery note into her voice.

"What's wrong?" Maddie asked at once.

Dana Sue bristled at being so easily read for the second time that afternoon. She obviously wasn't as good at covering her emotions as she'd like to be. "Why do you automatically assume something's wrong?"

"Because it's less than an hour till your dinner rush starts," Maddie said. "You're usually up to your eyeballs in preparation. You don't make casual, just-to-chat calls until after nine when things start to settle down again."

"I am way too predictable," Dana Sue muttered, making a vow to change that. Once, she'd been the most reckless and daring of all the Sweet Magnolias. But since the divorce, knowing she had a daughter to raise and send to college—her ex-husband made the court-ordered child support payments, but that was all—she'd turned cautious.

"So, what is it? What's wrong?" Maddie repeated. "Did somebody complain about their quiche at lunch? Were the salad greens from the produce vendor not crisp enough?"

"Very funny," Dana Sue said, not the least bit amused by Maddie's reference to her perfectionism. "Actually, it's Annie. I really think she's in trouble again, Maddie. I know you and Helen have been worried all along about her eating habits and weight loss. The collapse at your wedding freaked all of us out, but that was almost a year ago and she's been getting better since then. I made sure of it." Suddenly overwhelmed by a wave of unfamiliar helplessness, Dana Sue added, "Now I just don't know. I think I've been deluding myself."

"Tell me what happened," Maddie commanded.

Dana Sue related the morning's incident. "Am I making too much of her ignoring the breakfast I'd fixed and leaving behind her lunch?" she asked hopefully.

"If that was all you had to go on, I'd say yes," Maddie replied. "But, sweetie, you know there are other signs that Annie has an eating disorder. We've all seen them. When she passed out at my wedding, it was a warning. If she's anorexic, that kind of thing doesn't miraculously go away. She's probably just gotten better at hiding it from you. She needs counseling."

Dana Sue still clung to the hope they'd gotten it all wrong. "Maybe it's just back-to-school jitters, or maybe she's eating the cafeteria food at school," she suggested. She wondered if Maddie's son might have noticed something. "Could you talk to Ty? He might have some idea. They don't have any classes together, I know. Annie told me that much today, but maybe they have the same lunch hour."

"I'll ask him," Maddie promised. "But I'm not sure teenage boys pay the slightest bit of attention to what girls are eating. They're too busy scarfing down everything in sight."

"Try," Dana Sue pleaded. "Obviously I'm not getting anywhere talking to her. She just gets defensive."

"I'll do my best," Maddie promised. "I'll ask Cal, too. You can't imagine the kind of gossip my husband overhears in the locker room. Who would have guessed that a baseball coach would know so much? He may be the school's best resource for staying on top of what the kids are up to.

Sometimes I think he knows when students are in trouble before their own parents do. He certainly did in Ty's case."

"I remember," Dana Sue said, recalling how concern for Ty had drawn Maddie and Cal together. "Thanks for checking into this, Maddie. Let me know what you find out, okay?"

"Of course. I'll give you a call later tonight," her friend promised. "Try not to worry too much. Annie's a smart girl."

"But maybe not smart enough," Dana Sue said wearily. "I know this kind of thing can happen because of peer pressure and all the role models these girls see on TV and in the movies, but Annie also has a lot of issues thanks to her dad running around on me."

"You think this has something to do with Ronnie?" Maddie sounded skeptical.

"I do," Dana Sue told her. "I think she convinced herself it wouldn't have happened if I'd weighed a hundred and five. Of course, I haven't weighed that since seventh grade."

"You're also five-ten. You'd look ridiculous," Maddie said.

"Probably, but it might be kind of fun to test the willowy look on the men in Serenity," Dana Sue said with a wistful note. Then she added realistically, "But it's never going to happen. No matter how hard I try these days, I can't seem to lose more than a pound, and that never stays off long. I'm destined to be tall but frumpy."

"Sounds as if Annie isn't the only one who could use a body image lecture," Maddie said. "I'll get Helen over here first thing in the morning. When you come by to drop off the salads for the café, we'll fix that thinking of yours right up. You're gorgeous, Dana Sue Sullivan, and don't you forget that for a single second."

"Let's just focus on Annie for the time being," Dana Sue replied, dismissing her own food issues as well as Maddie's loyal attempt to bolster her spirits. "She's the one who could be in real trouble, not me."

"Then Helen and I will help you deal with it," Maddie assured her. "Have the Sweet Magnolias ever let each other down?"

"Not once," Dana Sue admitted, then hesitated as a distant memory came back to her and made her smile, temporarily wiping out her anxiety over Annie. "Wait. I take that back. There was that time you two left me twisting in the wind to deal with a cop after we played a prank on our gym teacher."

"That prank was your idea, and we didn't intentionally leave you behind," Maddie corrected. "We thought you could run faster. We came back for you, didn't we?"

"Sure, right after the cop called my folks and threatened to haul me off to jail if he caught me doing anything that stupid again. I was so scared I was throwing up by the time you came back."

"Yes, well, there's no need to dwell on ancient history," Maddie said briskly. "We will be there to help with Annie, whatever she needs. You, too."

"Thanks. I'll talk to you later, then."

When Dana Sue placed the portable phone back in its charger, she felt the first faint stirring of relief. She'd faced a lot of turmoil and had triumphed with Maddie and Helen by her side. They'd gotten her through her divorce and helped her open her restaurant when she hadn't been convinced she could do it. Surely this crisis—if there even was a crisis—could be tackled just as easily if they all put their heads together.

Annie hated her physical education class. She was a complete and total klutz. Worse, Ms. Franklin—who weighed about a hundred pounds soaking wet and had boundless enthusiasm for anything athletic—was always scowling at her, as if there was something wrong with her. Usually Annie scowled right back at her, but today she couldn't seem to summon up the energy.

"Annie, I'd like to see you after class," Ms. Franklin said, once she'd tortured them all by making them jog around the track. Twice.

"What do you suppose she wants?"

"I doubt she's going to ask me to go out for the track team," Annie joked, still trying to catch her breath. She'd never been athletic, but lately even the slightest bit of activity left her winded, unlike Sarah, who looked as if the run had been no more than a stroll between classes.

Sarah, who'd been Annie's best friend since fifth grade and knew most of her deepest, darkest secrets, studied her worriedly. "You don't think she's going to say something about you being out of shape, do you? Grown-ups get all freaked out if they think we're not ready to compete in some marathon or something. I mean, who'd want to do that?"

"Not me," Annie agreed, relieved that the odd racing sensation in her chest had finally eased a little and she was able to breathe more normally.

"Maybe she found out about you passing out and ending up in the hospital."

"Oh, come on, Sarah. That was last year," Annie griped. "Everyone's forgotten all about it."

"I'm just saying, if Ms. Franklin thinks you're going to crash in her class, maybe she'll let you out of it."

"As if," Annie scoffed. "Nobody gets out of PE without some kind of doctor's note, and Doc Marshall will never give me one. Not that I'd ask. If I did, my mom would have a cow. She still gets all weird about me not eating the way she thinks I should." She rolled her eyes. "Like the way she eats is so healthy. She's packed on so much weight since my dad left, no man will ever look at her twice. I'm never letting that happen to me."

"How much do you weigh now?" Sarah asked.

Annie shrugged. "I'm not sure."

Her friend regarded her with disbelief. "Oh, you are, too, Annie Sullivan. I know perfectly well you weigh yourself at least three or four times a day."

Annie frowned. Okay, maybe she was a little obsessive about making sure that she never picked up an ounce, but she couldn't trust the scale at home to be accurate. So she weighed herself again on the one in the locker room. And sometimes again if she stopped by The Corner Spa to see Maddie. Even if she knew her weight to the last ounce, it didn't mean she wanted her best friend to know. Besides, it wasn't the number on the scale that mattered. It was the way she looked in the mirror. She looked fat and that was all that mattered. Sometimes when she saw herself in all those mirrors at the spa, she wanted to cry. She couldn't figure out how her mom could even bear to walk into that room.

"Annie?" Sarah said, her expression worried. "Are you below a hundred? You look to me like you weigh less than ninety pounds."

"What if I do?" Annie said defensively. "I still need to lose a couple more pounds to look really great."

"But you promised you'd stop obsessing about your weight," Sarah said, an edge of panic in her voice. "You said passing out when you were dancing with Ty was the most embarrassing moment of your life, and you'd never be in a position for that to happen again. You told everyone you'd keep your weight at least at a hundred pounds, and even that's pretty skinny for your height. You promised,"

Sarah emphasized. "How can you have forgotten all that? And you know it happened because you weren't eating."

"I hadn't eaten that day," Annie countered stubbornly. "I eat."

"What have you had today?" Sarah persisted.

"My mom fixed me a huge omelet for breakfast," she said.

Sarah gave her a knowing look. "But did you eat it?"

Annie sighed. Sarah evidently wasn't going to let this go. "I don't know why you're getting so worked up over this. What have you eaten today?"

"I had cereal and half a banana for breakfast and a salad for lunch," Sarah replied.

Annie felt like throwing up just thinking about eating that much food. "Well, good for you. Don't come to me when you're too fat to fit into your clothes."

"I'm not gaining weight," Sarah said. "In fact, I've even lost a couple of pounds by eating sensibly." She gave Annie a chagrined look. "I'd give anything for a burger and fries, though. To hear my mom and dad talk, that's all kids ever did back in the day. They went to Wharton's after football games and pigged out. They went there after school and had milkshakes. Can you imagine?"

"No way," Annie said.

The last time she'd eaten a burger and fries, she'd been having lunch with her dad. That was the day he'd told her he was leaving, that he and her mom were getting a divorce. Of course, after she'd witnessed her mom tossing all his stuff on the front lawn, it hadn't come as a huge shock, but it had made her sick just the same. She'd left the table at Wharton's, run into the restroom and lost her lunch right there.

Since that awful day, nothing had appealed to her. Not the burgers and fries she'd once loved, not pizza or ice cream, not even the stuff her mom had on the menu at the restaurant. It was like her dad had yanked her appetite right out of her, along with her heart. Finding out that he'd cheated on her mom, then watching that huge, embarrassing scene on the front lawn, had pretty much killed any desire to ever eat again. Annie knew her mom had been right to do that, but it had left her feeling all alone and empty inside. Her dad had been the one guy who'd always thought she was the most beautiful, special girl in the world. She supposed he still did think that, but he wasn't around to tell her. Hearing it on the phone wasn't the same. No matter how many times he said it, she dismissed it because there was no way he knew how she really looked these days. It was just so much blah-blah-blah.

"It would be kinda nice to hang out at Wharton's, though, wouldn't it?" Sarah said wistfully. "A lot of the kids still go after school."

"Go ahead and do it," Annie said. "Don't let me stop you."

"It wouldn't be any fun without you," she protested. "Couldn't we go just once? We don't have to order what everyone else is having."

Annie was already shaking her head. "Last time I went with my mom and Maddie and Ty, they all stared at me when I ordered water with a slice of lemon. You'd have thought I'd asked for a beer or something. And you know Grace Wharton gossips about everything. My mom would know in an hour that I was in there and didn't have anything to eat or drink."

Sarah looked disappointed. "I guess you're right."

Annie felt a momentary twinge of guilt. It wasn't right that her hang-ups were keeping her best friend from having fun. "You know," she said at last, "maybe it would be okay.

I could order a soda or something. I don't have to drink it." Her mood brightened. "And maybe Ty will be there."

Sarah grinned. "You know he will be. All the cool guys go there after school. So, when do you want to go?"

"Might as well be today," Annie said. "I have to go see Ms. Franklin now. I'll meet you out front after I'm finished and we can walk over."

Wasting money on a drink she wouldn't even sip was a small price to pay to spend an hour or so around Ty. Not that she was fooling herself by thinking he would pay the slightest bit of attention to her. Not only was Ty a senior, he was a star on the baseball team. He was so beyond her reach. He was always surrounded by the most gorgeous girls in his class. He seemed to like the tall, thin ones with long, silky blond hair and big boobs. Annie, at only five foot three, with chestnut curls and no chest to speak of, couldn't compete with them.

But she had one thing none of those girls had. She and Ty were almost family. She got to spend holidays and lots of other special occasions with him. And one of these days, when she was thin enough, when her body was absolutely perfect, he was going to wake up and notice her.

Don't miss A Slice of Heaven
A Sweet Magnolias novel
Available wherever MIRA Books are sold!